Necrosis

A Reapers Oath Series: Book Two

Peg N. Gremlin

To the ones who have walked through the shadows,

To those who have heard the whispers of doubt, of fear, of the unknown calling their name...

To the lost, the weary, the ones who have faced the dark and wondered if they'd ever find the light again...

This is for you.

For every battle you fought in silence.

For every scar—seen or unseen—that tells the story of your survival.

For every time you stood on the edge of despair and chose, against all odds, to keep going.

The darkness may beckon, but it does not own you.

You are more than the ghosts that haunt you.

You are more than the pain you have endured.

You are still here. And that means you are unstoppable.

With all my heart,

~Peggy

Acknowledgements

Thank you to all 47 people who have read and purchased book one. You made me believe this story was worth finishing... and above all— worth telling. The amount of love I have received from everyone who has read "Thanatophobia" is amazing and my only regret is naming it after a mental illness which suppresses it on all social media platforms.

A big thank you to my indie author best friend, S.B Ellie, for pushing me every day and helping me decompress with silly tiktok lives— chasing after the masked men. You made writing not feel as lonely and I am ever so thankful to call you my friend. You are my "Sadie" to my "Layla"— and I can't wait for the day I can post your published work on my social media platforms to hype you up the same way you hype me up. Love you so much!

Dear Reader,

Your mental health matters.

Here are the chapters that you can skip over and not miss any part of the story:

Chapter 29

– <u>Ashton POV</u> – *Child loss, rape insinuation, death of a pregnant woman*

Chapter 30

– <u>Luca POV</u> – *Rape*

Chapter 31

– <u>Vassago POV</u> – *gruesome death*

Chapter 32

– <u>Saygin POV</u> – *Rape insinuation, gruesome death*

Please remember to read the Trigger Warnings!

Trigger Warnings

Please remember that your mental health matters! I am very detailed with the Trigger Warning list for whatever I wrote in the past and will write in the future. Please make sure that the trigger warnings are not your triggers so you can thoroughly enjoy the story I am trying to present you with.

Violence & Abuse
Physical assault

Graphic Violence (detailed fights, war, battles)

Weapon Use (Sentient Weapons)

Kidnapping

Emotional & Psychological Themes
PTSD & Trauma

Emotional abuse

Parental neglect

Suicide Ideation

Supernatural & Religious Themes
Supernatural violence

Death & Afterlife

Forced bonding

Mythological entities

<u>Sexual & Relationship Themes</u>

Unwanted advances

Implied sexual assault/coercion (past tense)

Chapters surrounding characters back stories with either brushing topics on rape or going into detail.

Sexual Themes

Sounding

Toxic Relationships (past tense)

Sex with Sand

<u>Mental Health</u>

Grief & Loss

Depression & Anxiety

Self harm

Child Loss (past tense, reoccurring memory)

Miscarriage (past tense, reoccurring memory)

Abortion (past tense)

<u>Other Potential Triggers</u>

Obsession

Body horror (severe injuries, detailed description of beings from the Underworld that are uncanny or hard to cope with)

Parental manipulation

Gaslighting

Narcissism

Betrayal

CHAPTER ONE

Azrael

TEARS DON'T FALL - BULLET FOR MY VALENTINE

"Layla!" I scream down our bond thread. "Layla!"

Fucking answer me, Tiny Mouse.

I can feel her—barely. The thread between us is faint, but it still holds. She's alive. Just barely, but alive. The bond wavers, stretched thin like a fraying rope, and I grit my teeth against the sickening churn in my gut.

I dig my fingers into the dirt, clawing at the broken ground as if I can physically reach her, as if she's just beneath the surface waiting for me to pull her free. Blood smears over my knuckles, mixing with the dust, and my breath comes in ragged gasps. She was just here. And now she's gone. Stolen from me.

"We need to regroup with Ashton and Lydia."

Vassago's voice is distant, a whisper against the deafening roar of my own frantic thoughts. The weight of his hand clamps down on my shoulder, firm but grounding. When he pulls me back, I resist. My body is a live wire of tension. It's fighting against the force trying to take me away from where she was last standing. I won't leave her. I can't.

"Azrael!" Vassago barks, shaking me hard enough to snap my head back. "She's gone! We have to move!"

I don't want to go. I don't want to breathe without her. But I let him haul me up anyway. My body is heavy against his as I lean into him for support. My legs refuse to work, but I force them to move, dragging myself forward like a male bound by chains. My grip tightens around Orcus' handle, the scythe's blade scraping against the stone, carving a jagged line in our wake.

"She can't be dead," I say hoarsely, my voice barely more than a breath.

"Drepane is with her." Orcus' voice slithers through, strained, almost pained. "Give him time to heal her. We will reach out to him."

Time? We don't have time. Not with Memetim. Not with the possibility of being in the Empty.

My jaw clenches so hard my teeth might crack. Rage coils in my stomach, sharp and acidic, eating through the panic threatening to consume me. Why am I such a goddamn failure? Why do I keep failing her? Why can't I be everything she *needs* me to be?

"Ashton!" Vassago calls ahead.

Footsteps pound against the stone, fast and urgent. Ashton skids to a stop in front of us, eyes wild as they dart between us, searching... counting.

"Where is Layla?"

Silence drags between us like a blade.

"I think Memetim took her to the Empty," Vassago answers when I don't.

Because I can't. Because I'm still screaming down the bond, clawing at the fragile thread between us, desperate to hold on to what little is left. I can feel her slipping, fading, and it feels like someone is peeling the skin from my bones.

I'm coming for you, Tiny Mouse. Don't you dare give up on me. I'm coming.

Ashton swears under his breath, but his panic is nothing compared to Lydia's. She lets out a broken sound—a mother's wail, raw and guttural. It rips through the air, slamming into my ribs and shattering what little breath I have left.

"She's gone," Lydia sobs, fighting Ashton's grip as she tries to push past him. "She's gone! We have to—"

"She's *not* gone," I snarl, cutting her off.

I push away from Vassago, shoving past them all as I force my battered body forward. My knees nearly buckle, but I don't stop. I can't stop.

"She's *not* dead," I say hoarsely, my voice barely more than a breath.

It's not a plea. It's not a hope. It's a vow. I'll find her. Even if I have to tear through every layer of existence to do it.

I know exactly where I'm going.

"Azrael!" Ashton calls after me, his voice sharp with urgency. "Where the *fuck* are you going?"

I don't answer. I don't need to.

The castle looms ahead, a monolith of darkness against the storm-laden sky. Its jagged spires pierce the heavens like obsidian knives, a fortress built not to protect but to *contain*. The cold stone has *never* been a home—only a fucking prison, a cage forged to hold a goddamn monster.

But this time, I step toward it willingly. Because I *know* who's responsible.

And I'm going to make him fucking pay.

Footsteps echo behind me—three distinct rhythms, three unwavering shadows. Some of my *most* loyal comrades. My only fucking friends. Just about the only ones I trust in this gods-forsaken realm. They don't question. They don't falter. They follow, because they know as well as I do: The war isn't over... the war starts *here*. Right fucking *now*.

With a flick of my wrist, the castle doors explode inward before I even reach them, the heavy iron slamming against the walls with a deafening crash. The torches along the corridor gutter and roar to life as I pass, my fury feeding their flames. Shadows dance wildly, stretching long and jagged against the cold stone, mimicking the destruction they know is coming.

I don't stop. I don't hesitate. I am hunting.

The moment I slip into my true form, the castle shudders in recognition. My power bleeds into the air, thick and suffocating. Blue fire erupts along my body, licking up my arms, scorching through my joints like liquid vengeance. It doesn't hurt. It's like this fire was *made* for me—*born from me.*

The walls crackle, the stone groaning under the heat. Banners curl inward, their fabric blackening before igniting, disintegrating into nothing. The very foundation trembles beneath my steps, as if the castle itself fears what's coming.

Good. It should.

Because I will burn this place to the fucking ground.

I will turn these halls into a tomb, trap every single *bastard* inside and drown them in their own screams. I will make them beg. Make them feel the fear I felt as a child, cowering under my father's whip, waiting for a mercy that never came.

Not one of them spoke up for me *then*. Not one of them spoke up for Layla *now*.

They let this happen. And I will make them suffer for it.

I raise my bone-carved hand and flick my wrist. The doors to the throne room explode off their hinges, crashing inward with a deafening boom.

A goblin shrieks, his voice cut short as the heavy doors flatten him against the marble. His silver tray clatters across the floor, food splattering in grotesque streaks of red and gold. Across the room, my father startles, frozen mid-bite, his goblet trembling in his grip.

Pathetic.

This is the so-called Lord of the Underworld? A god who feasts while the realm rots, while his own son claws through hell and back just to keep the worlds from crumbling.

I will burn this castle to its foundation. I will rebuild it—brick by fucking brick—shaped not by greed or vanity, but by Layla's will. However, she wants it. However, she dreams it. Because she is the future. And my father? He is nothing but a relic of failure, a corpse still clinging to its decayed throne.

I take a step forward, the ground splitting beneath me as heat ripples through the air. The blue flames wreathing my body lick higher, charring the once-immaculate walls, turning gold filigree into dripping slag.

"What is the meaning of this?" Hades growls, rising from his seat. His voice is sharp, commanding—he thinks it still holds power over me.

It doesn't.

"Azrael, calm down!" Ashton shouts behind me, his voice strained with desperation. He lunges for my arm, but the second his fingers graze my robe, he jerks back with a sharp cry. *"Fuck!"*

Burned.

If I weren't drowning in my frenzy, I might have cared. Might have pulled back. But right now? Right now, I am consumed by the weight of every goddamn failure.

Vassago—kidnapped. Tortured.

Luca—ripped from his life. Losing his home. Losing his fucking coffee shop.

Song—dead. A young angel with so much more left to do, her light snuffed out before it had the chance to shine.

And Layla—my mate. My *everything*. Taken from me. Trapped in the Empty, where I can't reach her. Can't hold her. Can't whisper to her that I will fix this... that everything will be okay.

Because it's not okay. Nothing is fucking okay. And I am done pretending it is.

My hand lifts, fingers curling into a claw. The shadows obey. The air tightens.

Across the throne room, my father stiffens, and for the first time in my existence, I see it.

Fear. A slow, creeping terror slipping into his eyes as he realizes— I am not his son anymore.

I am his *executioner*.

"Fucking. Die." The words tear from my throat like a growl from the abyss, thick with venom and finality. My voice reverberates through the chamber, shaking every wall.

"You did this." My grip tightens. Hades chokes. His eyes bulge, hands clawing at his throat like he could rip away my power. Like he could stop the inevitable.

"You insufferable piece of shit." The walls tremble, cracks splintering outward like veins through marble. "You're the reason my mate is gone. You let Memetim take her. You let this happen!"

Chunks of the ceiling break loose, crashing onto the floor with earth-shaking force. The throne room groans under the weight of my fury, the very foundation buckling. Torches flare wildly before snuffing out, plunging the room into flickering, erratic chaos.

But I don't need light to see him. I can feel the fear bleeding from his body, the way it coils around him like a serpent tightening its grip.

Yet even as his breath hitches, as his body spasms in my fucking hold, there is still a shadow of defiance in his gaze. Arrogant to the last fucking breath. It only feeds the inferno burning inside me.

I squeeze harder. Hard enough to feel his feeble heartbeat stutter. Hard enough to watch his body convulse, his legs kicking uselessly against the stone.

Let him suffer. Let him know what it means to be so goddamn powerless. Like the way I was when he let this world *break me*. When he let Layla be *taken*.

A sudden warmth wraps around my waist—soft, trembling. A stark contrast to the cold fury radiating off me.

"Azrael." Lydia's voice is fragile, almost lost beneath my storm of fury. But she holds on, pressing her face against my side, her arms tightening. "Layla wouldn't want this," she murmurs, voice thick with grief. "Layla would want you to use this anger to *find* her." A small sniffle. "We can deal with Hades later."

Her words carve through the rage, through the all-consuming, festering need to end him here and now.

My jaw clenches. My fingers twitch. And then, with a slow, deliberate breath, I let go. Hades collapses to the ground with a sickening thud, gasping, coughing, dragging in desperate, ragged breaths. He's still alive.

For now.

But when I bring Layla home? When I tear through the Empty to bring back what he let be taken- There will be no mercy.

No one will be there to stop me.

"This isn't done." My voice is low, razor-sharp, laced with a promise of carnage. "Come near me or *anyone* I care about, and I will *fucking* kill you."

I don't wait for a reply. I don't need to.

I turn my back on him, uninterested in the words of the very being who should have guided me, who should have pushed me to be better, instead of breaking me until I feared for my own existence.

He doesn't call out. He doesn't fucking dare to.

For the first time in my entire existence, I feel it—a sliver of power over him, the weight of centuries of his dominion cracking beneath my heel. He is nothing to me now. A withering god gasping for air on the floor of his crumbling kingdom.

Good. Let him stay there. Let him feel what it's like to be powerless.

I stride out of the castle, my steps unyielding. Lydia, Ashton, and Vassago trail behind me, their silence heavy with unspoken grief, with the weight of what's just transpired.

My body aches. My soul screams.

But the bond pulses faintly in my mind—like a distant heartbeat, fragile, flickering. *Layla*.

She's still there.

Still *fighting*.

And as long as that pulse remains, I *will* tear through the fabric of life itself to bring her home.

CHAPTER TWO

Ashton

POISON & WINE - THE CIVIL WARS

I have to stop running from Sadie. Stop ignoring the echo of her voice in the back of my head, the way she lingers in my thoughts like a stubborn melody I can't seem to shake.

But how the fuck do I tell her she's lost someone else? *Again*?

How do I break her already fractured heart with the truth—that another being she loved, another person she fought so hard to protect, is *gone*?

And how the hell do I do that while we're still learning how to handle this bond. The emotions—overwhelming and tangled—that neither of us were prepared for?

Why did I do this?

Am I attracted to Sadie? Yeah. Absolutely. Would I risk my life just so she could take one more breath than me? Without a second thought. Even though I know damn well she'd use that breath to make some sarcastic remark, probably at my expense, just to piss off whatever poor bastard tried to take her out.

That's just Sadie. And fuck, if I don't admire it.

So why did I fucking do this? Why did I propose something so *permanent*, so binding, to a mortal—a being so fucking *fragile*?

Maybe because I knew. Deep down, I knew that if something ever happened to her, it wouldn't just break me—it would break Layla.

Proposing the bond made Sadie immortal. It protected her from disease, from aging, from the inevitable decay that claims all mortals in the end. But it doesn't protect her from everything. It doesn't shield her from murder, from pain, from the horrors that lurk in the dark, waiting to tear her apart.

It doesn't stop the nightmares.

It doesn't stop the overwhelming dread that if she dies, I will *feel* it. I will feel every second of her fading, and it will rip me apart, piece by fucking piece, until there's nothing left of me.

Maybe that's what this was. My way of keeping Layla happy, keeping her safe, keeping her world intact in whatever way that I could. My duty as her friend, her protector, her ever-loyal companion.

Or maybe... maybe I was just *fucking selfish*.

Maybe I couldn't bear the thought of Sadie slipping away from this world, leaving a void in me I would never hope to fill.

I rake a hand through my hair, exhaling sharply, but it does nothing to steady me.

Fuck. Layla.

Where are you?

The moment Azrael's bond sealed with Layla, something shifted.

Not just in him. Not just in her. In the *Underworld itself.*

It was like an unseen force snapped perfectly into place, and now, this undeniable pull tethers us all to her. It's not just instinct. It's not loyalty. It's something deeper—something primal. It feels as though the very gravity of this realm has changed, and she's become the center of it all.

The new ruler.

Not by force. Not by fear. But by something infinitely more powerful.

We belong to her.

Every ounce of my being screams at me to keep her safe. To fight for her. To *stand beside her*—not because I have to, but because there is no other choice. Because the moment that bond was forged, something ancient and irreversible took root in all of us.

And Sadie...

Sadie is tied to me now. Whether I meant for it to be this way or not, she is *mine* to protect. Mine to fight for. And when I tell her what's happened—when I watch grief darken those sharp, defiant eyes, when I feel her pain slam into me through our bond—will she ever forgive me?

For waiting?

For hesitating?

For being a coward when she needed me to be strong?

I exhale sharply, raking a hand through my hair again.

Is this what Hades was afraid of all along?

Did he know? Did he feel the shift coming long before we did? Did he sense that the moment Azrael and Layla's bond locked into place, he would become nothing more than dust?

Because that's what he is now. A relic of a world that no longer needs him.

A king without a throne.

A ruler without a kingdom.

And his safety? It's nonexistent.

If Layla doesn't kill him, Azrael will.

And if Azrael doesn't...

I might just do it myself.

Word is spreading—*fast.* The Underworld is in chaos, and Hades is at the heart of it. They call him the reason war is coming. They say he's to blame for the unrest, for the fractures forming in a realm that once knew some semblance of peace—if you weren't fucking tangled in the Underworld government's corruption, that is.

And somehow, *somehow*, I've been dragged right into the storm with him.

Azrael. You beautiful, reckless dumbass.

Centuries apart—no contact, no letters, no visits—and now, the moment we're finally in the same room again, we're rubbing two brain cells together, charging headfirst into destruction like we never stopped.

A reckless, impulsive, destructive wavelength that we share.

Fucking idiot.

I roll my eyes as I watch him reach for my front door knob.

He hasn't spoken since Lydia talked him down from killing Hades.

No outbursts. No snarled threats. Not even a sarcastic quip from Orcus.

Just silence.

And that's what unsettles me most.

Because Azrael isn't silent.

Not unless something inside him is *breaking*.

And I can't even begin to imagine the storm raging inside his head right now.

Layla is everything to him. That's the essence of this—this whole fucking nightmare. Losing her, knowing she's out there suffering in the Empty and that he wasn't strong enough to stop it—By the gods, it must be tearing him apart. And there's nothing I can do to fix that. Not a damn thing.

Hell, it's not like I'm in any position to fix my own mess either.

I keep telling myself I did it for Layla—forming this bond with Sadie to protect her, to keep her close to Layla. To make sure Layla would always have her best friend by her side, even when things went to shit. But the more time drags on, the more that excuse starts to feel like a fragile fucking lie, falling apart with every passing second.

Because the truth?

The truth is, the second I walked away to track down Lydia, something inside me snapped. The distance from Sadie was unbearable, like my ribs were caving in, like my heart had developed this hollow, aching spot that only she could fill. I felt like I was being stretched thin, like I was a wire ready to snap. Every second away from her made me want to fucking scream. Hell, it made me want to rip through anyone who got in my way just to get back to her.

Lydia? She saw it immediately. She saw the bond taking hold, curling its greedy fingers around my chest, suffocating me with every heartbeat. And now? Now I don't know if I made the *biggest mistake* of my existence or if I've just sealed my own fate, like a fucking idiot.

Then, just when I think I might implode from all this confusion, Sadie bursts through the door like a goddamn hurricane. Her wild black curls bouncing with every step, her eyes blazing with something raw and untamed. Before I can even process what's happening, she's slamming into me, her arms wrapping around my waist like she's afraid I'm going to vanish if she lets go.

And then she kisses me.

Hard. Desperate. As if she's been waiting for this moment as badly as I have. Like she needed this just as much as I did, and fuck—*so did I.*

I kiss her back, a reflex, but it's more than that. It's a need. A hunger. I pull her closer, letting her take the weight of all my regrets and swallow them whole before I can drag them into the light. The bond between us? It's not just serious—it's *suffocating. Overpowering.* But it's real, and it's *consuming.*

Maybe I should've thought this through more before doing something this... extreme. Maybe I should've given myself more time, more space to breathe, but that's not who I am. I'm an idiot, and now I'm here, tangled up in something I can't get out of.

Or maybe...

I let my gaze wander over Sadie's thick figure, taking in the curves that make my pulse race, the soft swell of her breasts pressed against me, the way her scent, that intoxicating mix of strawberries, fear, and arousal, fills the air. For fuck's sake!

I've been with plenty of women. Mortals, immortals, warriors, aristocrats—name a category, and I've probably ticked it off. None of it ever meant anything. Because, apparently, I'm an arrogant asshole. I was fine with that. Hell, I've got the reputation to prove it.

But then there's her.

And now I'm not sure I want to be that guy anymore.

This woman who devours me every chance she gets. Who looks at me like I hung the fucking moon. Who worships the ground I walk on without me ever asking.

Is this why so many supernatural males prefer mortal women? Is this why they abandon the hardened warriors of our kind for something softer?

Because to mortals—we are *gods*?

Fuck.

If nothing else, at least Sadie makes a damn good pet. But if I don't figure out how to rein in these emotions fast, I'm going to be in a hell of a lot of trouble.

"Where is Layla?" Sadie's voice rips me out of my thoughts, sharp and cutting. Her gaze flickers between the three of us—four, if you count Orcus, who's been uncharacteristically quiet.

The air shifts. It thickens. It's fucking suffocating.

Azrael's rage radiates through the room like an electric storm, his body vibrating with barely restrained fury. It's a ticking time bomb ready to go off. But then Lydia places a firm hand on his shoulder, the only tether holding him to any semblance of sanity.

"We don't know," Azrael mutters finally, his voice gravelly like broken glass scraping against the floor.

Sadie takes a step back, confusion knitting her brows. "What do you mean, you don't know?" Her voice cracks, trembling, but not from fear—pure disbelief. She scans the room frantically. "Where's Vassago?"

Azrael doesn't answer. He just storms past us, heading down the hall toward his room with a fury that could level mountains. And I don't stop him. I can't.

How the hell is he supposed to deal with this?

He *wanted* the mating bond. He thought he could handle it. And now? Barely twenty-four hours into it, he's already lost his mate.

Gone.

"Vassago went to find out what he can," I say dryly, watching as Sadie's breathing picks up, erratic. "He's trying to learn whatever he can so we can hopefully find Layla."

Sadie's lips part, but nothing comes out for what feels like forever. Then, in a voice barely louder than a breath—"What do you mean? Where is Layla?"

Tears well up in her eyes, but it's not just the sight of them that wrecks me—it's the fucking flood of emotions crashing through the bond.

It's too much.

A goddamn tsunami of pain, grief, and panic. It slams into me like I'm standing in the middle of the ocean during a storm. I try to push it back, but it's like trying to hold up an umbrella in a fucking hurricane. It doesn't stand a chance.

I grit my teeth, digging my nails into my palm, bracing for the emotional explosion.

And then, suddenly—

I want to kill Azrael.

For not doing enough.

For breaking his fucking promise.

For failing to *protect* Layla.

I shake the thoughts away, swallowing the rage and grief before it consumes me whole. But it's getting harder. And the worst part is—there's nothing I can do. Nothing I can fix.

"Memetim set a trap, we believe." My voice is tight, every word scraping the inside of my throat like sandpaper. "She attacked Layla, and before Azrael could get to her... Layla's body just—disappeared."

Sadie flinches like I slapped her, her eyes going wide with disbelief. "What do you mean, *disappeared*?"

I exhale sharply through my nose, trying to steady myself, to keep my voice from breaking. "We don't know, Sadie. But we'll figure it out. And we will find her."

I brace myself for the breakdown. For the tears. For Sadie to crumble like she did the last time she lost someone she loved.

But instead, she does something I didn't expect.

She locks her gaze onto mine, and in that moment, everything fucking changes.

The grief is still there, but it's morphing into something darker. Something colder. Her expression hardens, and the shift in her energy makes the air around us feel like it's been thickened with steel. Her anger simmers, seething beneath the surface, and I can feel it—sharp and dangerous, a blade ready to cut.

And just like that—her rage isn't aimed at Azrael anymore.

Now it's aimed at me.

And I don't fucking get it.

What did I do now?

Chapter Three

Azrael

How Villains Are Made - Madalen Duke

"I think Drepane moved her," Orcus says, his voice unexpectedly calm.

I freeze. The words slowly filter through the fog in my mind, but they feel like distant echoes, too far to grasp. A bitter flicker of hope tries to ignite in my chest, but I stomp it out before it has a chance to spread. Hope is a dangerous thing—too fragile, too easily crushed.

"But why the fuck wouldn't he tell us?" I snap, my voice sharp, more accusing than I intended it to be. "Why would he move her and not communicate with us?"

It doesn't make sense. It doesn't sit right. If Drepane had any part in this—if he'd been able to move her—why the silence?

"He could have used up a good portion of his energy," Orcus reasons, his tone annoyingly measured, as if he's been expecting this question. "And it's not like anyone is there to replenish him. He might be resting. All we can do is give him some time."

Time.

Time is a luxury I don't have. Not when Layla is gone. Not when I don't know where she is or what's being done to her.

I grind my teeth so hard I think they might shatter, clenching my fists at my sides until my nails dig into my boney palms.

"But what if it wasn't Drepane?" The words scrape from my throat like glass. "What if Memetim had her moved? What if she's being tortured right now?"

The thought burns through me, searing my insides. I punch the wall in frustration. The stone cracks beneath my knuckles, and the pain—sharp and brief—barely registers. It's nothing. Nothing compared to what I feel inside. It's like my ribs are being ripped open, something clawing, trying to tear its fucking way out of me.

Orcus hums, a slow, deliberate sound. "Feel the bond, Azrael. She's alive. For now, she's okay."

"Alive doesn't mean she's *okay!*" I growl, spinning toward him propped against the bed, my voice dripping with fury. "She's not okay until I can see her with my own eyes. Until I can *hold* her and know that she's safe. This bond—this fucking thread between us—it's not *enough.*"

I start pacing, my boots slamming against the cold stone floor like war drums, the sound echoing in the empty room. Each step is a reminder of how powerless I feel. The bond tugs at me, a faint pulse of warmth in the cold darkness. It reassures me that she's alive—but it doesn't tell me *how* she's alive, or *where* she is, or if she's suffering.

And the worst part? The worst part is that *I* could have done something. I could have been faster. Stronger. More prepared.

The thought of Layla—alone, scared, in pain—makes my stomach churn. The fury inside me is a live wire, my body vibrating with it, like a crackling storm ready to tear apart everything in its path.

Memetim's sickening grin flashes in my mind. The way she enjoys toying with her prey. The way she takes pleasure in their fear.

I will fucking kill her.

The need to move, to act, is so overpowering that I can feel it in every muscle, every nerve, like a beast pacing in a cage. My entire being is coiled tight, ready to break.

But what do I do with this? What can I do with this rage when it's all directed at a fucking shadow? A threat I can't touch. A pain I can't reach.

I stop pacing, closing my eyes for a moment. I can feel the pull of the bond again, weak but there—faint reassurance, like the softest whisper against the chaos in my head.

But it's not enough. Not enough until I know she's safe.

I need her back. And no matter the cost, I'll bring her back. I start to pace again. Back and forth. Back and forth.

"Your temper isn't going to fix anything," Orcus chimes, his voice dripping with mockery. "Unless, of course, you plan to intimidate the realms into giving her back."

I don't hesitate. "I'm planning to rip apart anything—or anyone—that stands in my way," I snap, the words a deadly promise. "Starting with Memetim."

"Bold talk. But you're not *thinking* straight."

I stop pacing, my body brimming with tension, my fists clenched tight. "Then enlighten me," I growl. "What's the plan, oh wise one?"

"For starters?" Orcus raises an imaginary eyebrow. "Don't go rushing head-first into a trap."

I glare at the scythe propped casually against the bed. His sentience is like a thorn in my side, unyielding and relentless.

"Do you have anything useful to say?" I seethe. My voice is low and dangerous. "Or are you just here to lecture me?"

"Both," Orcus replies with casual indifference. "You're the Prince of Death. Act like it. *Think*. Strategize. Drepane is loyal to Layla; he wouldn't abandon her. If he moved her, there's a reason. If Memetim's involved, charging in blindly is suicide."

The words hit me like a punch to the gut. I know he's right. I fucking know it, but the knowledge doesn't make it any easier to swallow.

I pace again, the need to do *something* eating at me from the inside out, but Orcus' words keep rattling around in my head like an unforgiving drumbeat. I try to ignore them, but they won't let me.

"And if she's in pain?" I ask, my voice softer now, cracked with something dangerously close to desperation.

"She's strong," Orcus responds without hesitation, his voice steady. "Stronger than you give her credit for."

That hits me harder than I care to admit.

Stronger than I give her credit for.

The words rattle through me, like a stone sinking deep into a lake. They should have been comforting—meant to reassure me—but instead, they dig at something raw inside. Something I can't put into words.

Layla... she's been through hell. I know she has. I've seen it in her eyes, in the way she holds herself. She's fought through so much—fear, pain, betrayal—and she's still standing. Still fighting.

But still—

"She shouldn't have to be," I mutter, the words nearly lost in the sea of my thoughts. My voice cracks, just a little. I swallow hard, trying to hold it together, but it's a losing battle.

"She doesn't have a choice," Orcus says, quieter now, his tone almost sympathetic. "Neither do you."

His words hit me like a fucking tidal wave, crashing over me with brutal force.

Orcus is right again. Layla's been through more than anyone should ever have to endure. More than I can imagine. She's survived, but she's not *living*. She's barely hanging on, fighting to stay in one piece.

And I—*I* should've been there for her.

I should've protected her.

The guilt gnaws at me, deep and hungry, like an animal clawing at my chest. Every time I think of her, every bruise and cut she's endured, the ache inside me grows. It's not just guilt; it's a suffocating weight pressing down on me. I should've been faster. Stronger. *Better.*

She doesn't deserve this.

She never should've had to face any of this alone.

I slam my fist into the wall again, harder this time, the stone shattering beneath the force. But it doesn't make the pain go away. It never does.

Orcus sighs, his tone uncharacteristically soft. "You'll find her, Azrael. But only if you focus on what needs to be done. Not on what's already happened."

But I don't want to hear that right now. I don't want to focus on the fucking plan. I just want to *fix* it. I just want Layla back, safe and whole, in my arms where she belongs.

But that's not how this works, is it?

I let out a shaky breath, trying to pull myself together. It's not enough. It never feels like enough. But it has to be.

For her. For Layla.

I pick Orcus up, placing him in the straddle on my back. I can feel the cold metal of Orcus pressed against me, his presence a grounding force I can't ignore. Even he seems to sense the storm raging inside me, the tension winding through me like a taut string ready to snap. Every movement I make feels sharper, tighter, as if the very air around me is too thick to breathe. His usual mocking tone is gone, replaced by a heavy silence that lingers in the space between us. Even Orcus knows what's at stake now. I'm not just fighting for the Underworld. I'm fighting for her.

The door creaks open, the sound cutting through the suffocating quiet. Ashton leans against the frame, his posture relaxed, unaffected by the gravity of the situation. "Are we having a heartfelt moment, or is Azrael planning to try to destroy other half of the Underworld?"

His voice, so annoyingly calm, hits me like ice water. It's as if nothing ever shakes the man. I want to snap at him, demand that he takes this seriously, but I don't. It's just Ashton. I know he's not trying to piss me off; it's his way of breaking the tension, even if it never works the way he intends.

"Depends," I mutter, running a hand across my face, grounding me just enough to keep from losing my mind. "Do you have news?"

"Not exactly," he replies, his voice still as even as ever. It's that calm before the storm, like the world's holding its breath. "But Vassago's working on tracking her. He's confident he'll find something soon."

"Soon isn't good enough," I bite out, the words sharper than I intended. My voice cracks as I swallow down the frustration clawing at my throat. It's not enough. None of this is enough if I can't get to her in time.

"I'm aware," Ashton says, completely unfazed, his gaze never wavering. "But unless you've developed omniscience overnight, we're at a standstill until we get more information."

I clench my fists, my nails biting into the bone of my palms, using the pain to ground myself. I take a deep breath, the scent of death and decay heavy in the air around us, grounding me, but it does little to ease the pressure in my chest. Ashton's right, damn him. I can't control this. I can't control *any* of this. And it fucking kills me.

"So what do we do in the meantime?" I ask, my voice low, barely containing the simmering anger. "Sit around and wait?"

"No," Ashton replies, his tone suddenly serious in a way I'm not used to hearing from him. "We prepare. Memetim's always three steps ahead. If she's involved, we'll need every advantage we can get. And that includes a clear head."

I force myself to relax, to let the anger dissipate, but the weight of exhaustion presses down on me like a boulder. A clear head. If I had one, maybe I wouldn't feel like I'm losing myself in this fight. But right now, it feels like my mind is a storm, and I'm trying to navigate it with nothing but a flicker of light.

"Fine," I mutter, though the word tastes bitter, like ash on my tongue.

Ashton's gaze hardens, and for a brief moment, I see the seriousness in his eyes, the mask of indifference slipping just enough to reveal something far more somber beneath. He nods once, a silent agreement, and then steps back, vanishing into the hall without another word.

I glance at Orcus, the scythe still resting against my back like an unspoken promise. The bond hums again, faint but steady. For now, it's all I have. A fragile thread that connects me to Layla, the one thing that keeps me from losing myself completely. But "for now" won't last forever. The bond is too weak. Too distant.

Ashton straightens slightly, his usual laid-back posture shifting. "By the way, Luca made food. He said to let you know it's ready whenever you are."

I let out a breath, jaw still clenched, my joints aching from the tension I've been holding. Ashton's words—those damn words—cut through the fog just enough to make me stop. Luca's food. The only thing that's ever had any chance of grounding me, even if just for a moment... if maybe, I wasn't so far gone.

"Does he think a meal will fix everything?" I mutter, half to myself, bitterness seeping into my tone.

"Well," Ashton says, a smirk tugging at his lips, but there's a flicker of something more in his eyes—something that almost feels like understanding. "You've got a wall full of cracks that says it couldn't hurt. Besides, he's right. You need to keep your strength up. Layla would murder me if I let you fall apart before we find her."

The mention of her name is like a knife, stabbing deep into the raw wound in my chest. It flares up, sharp and cruel, a pain I can't escape. Layla's absence is a constant ache, lingering in the back of my mind, and it's only getting worse with every second that ticks by. The need to find her, to fix what's been broken, is all-consuming. It gnaws at me, relentless and unforgiving.

I push away from the wall, the weight of her absence pressing harder with every step I take. It feels suffocating, like I'm drowning in it. She's out there, somewhere, and I'm helpless to reach her.

"Fine," I snap, my voice low and colder than I intend. "I'll eat. But if Vassago doesn't have answers soon, I'm done waiting."

Ashton's expression softens just a fraction, but there's no pity in his gaze. Ashton's not the type for pity. No, he's the kind of friend who would rather drag me back into the fight, force me to stand again, than let me wallow in this hopeless mess. He knows me too well.

"Yeah, I get it," he says, his tone shifting, more serious now. "But remember, you're not alone in this. Not by a long shot." His hand rests on my shoulder, the touch heavy with a silent promise. "We'll find her, Azrael. *You* will find her."

CHAPTER FOUR

Ashton

THE OTHER SIDE - RUELLE

The dining room in my home is a strange sight—elegance twisted by the tension crackling between its occupants. The polished obsidian table gleams under the dim light, but it's nothing more than a reflection of the coldness in the air. It's always been my sanctuary, a place where even the darkest thoughts seemed smaller over a good meal. Tonight, though, Luca's cooking seems to fight against the weight that presses down on all of us.

Sadie's perched at the end of the table, looking every bit like a storm in this quiet chaos. Her usual bubbly energy is nearly suffocated by the somber mood, but she's always had a knack for breaking the silence, even when it's unwelcome. Not tonight, though. Tonight, the silence feels heavier, thicker than it has in a while. The air hums with unspoken words, regrets, and frustrations.

"So, is this what it's like eating with Death today?" Sadie's voice cuts through the tension like a lightning bolt, full of irreverence. She leans back in her chair, her eyes flickering over the room with that mischievous glint that never truly fades from her gaze. "Gotta say, it's a little more..." She pauses, raising a hand like she's searching for the right word, her lips twisting into a playful grin. "Gloomier than I imagined."

A few chuckles echo softly, but it's not the same. The room feels like it's holding its breath, unwilling to truly exhale. I shoot her a look, one of those "what the hell are you doing?" glances. She meets my eyes with that stubborn little smirk, the one she knows irritates the hell out of me, but I don't try to stop her. Sadie isn't someone who can be stifled, even by the weight of the world.

"It's only gloomy because you haven't stopped talking since you sat down," Orcus quips from his perch against the wall, his voice dripping with mockery. His tone cuts through the silence like the blade he is, sharp and biting, and a little too eager to pierce the tension. "If you'd just stuff your face, we might all enjoy the silence."

Sadie gasps, clutching at her chest with exaggerated theatrics. "Excuse me? Are you body-shaming me, Mr. Sentient Scythe?" She puts on a show, pretending to be appalled, but the mischievous sparkle in her eyes say otherwise. "Because let me tell you, I've been *very* self-conscious about my snacking habits lately. It's a touchy subject." She pouts dramatically, but it's all for show. The woman's nothing if not a diva.

"I'm shaming your talking habits," Orcus shoots back, his voice thick with disdain. "Though if your snacking keeps you too busy to speak, I'll gladly encourage it."

The back-and-forth is like clockwork now. It's an odd comfort, a reminder that, even when the world's falling apart, Sadie and Orcus can still bicker like an old married couple. But the lightheartedness doesn't stick around long. Not when the reason we're here lingers in the corners of the room, silent and suffocating.

Luca lets out a quiet chuckle from his spot near the kitchen doorway, his arms crossed casually as he leans against the frame, watching the scene unfold like it's a favorite movie. His eyes flicker over the room, taking in the chaos of it all with a look of puzzled intrigue. "Don't let him get to you, Sadie," he says, his voice dripping lazily. "Orcus is just mad he doesn't have a mouth to eat with."

Sadie doesn't miss a beat, her grin widening at the opportunity to get another jab in. "And no hands, right?" She adds, glancing over at Orcus with a playful tilt of her head. "Must suck to be stuck as a weapon. No hands, no snacks, no cuddles."

She raises her eyebrows, her tone light and teasing, and somehow it manages to cut through the tension in the air, just a little. Even with everything weighing down on us, Sadie's got this knack for making people laugh when they don't want to. It's a dangerous skill.

I can't help myself. "Don't pretend like you'd want to cuddle with him," I say, a smirk tugging at my lips. "The guy can barely hold a conversation, let alone a spoon."

Sadie's eyes twinkle, her grin never faltering. "Cuddles? I'd settle for a decent conversation, but hey... beggars can't be choosers." She shoots Orcus a wink, her voice syrupy sweet as she leans back in her chair, stretching like a cat that is just uncoiling from sleep.

Orcus' red aura narrows, but there's no real anger behind it. More amusement, if anything. His pride still bristles, but it's like watching a lion shrug off a stray flea. "I don't need hands to be effective," he snaps, his tone sharp, the challenge clear in his words. "Unlike some of you, I actually serve a purpose."

He then releases his aura as if that alone should settle the argument, though none of us are actually scared of him. Not really.

Lydia raises an eyebrow, swirling her wine in her glass, the deep crimson liquid catching the dim light of the room, reflecting like blood spilled in a forgotten corner. She takes a long, leisurely sip, a small smile curving her lips. "No hands, no snacks, no cuddles," she repeats, her voice low and honeyed, mocking sympathy, her eyes never leaving Orcus. "Must be hard, Orcus. Struggling with the little things, huh?"

I bite back a chuckle, but Orcus' pride is already taking a hit. He doesn't know how to take Lydia's brand of biting humor. Her calm, collected demeanor only makes it worse.

"You're all insufferable," Orcus grumbles, though it's obvious he's trying—and failing—to keep the smile from breaking through. "Honestly, if you were any more insufferable, I'd need a new job."

Lydia arches an eyebrow. "Oh, please. If you could ever get a job that didn't involve being used as a weapon, I'd be shocked."

I lean back in my chair, watching the back-and-forth unfold. It's moments like this that remind me of how messed up all this really is. The world could be ending outside and here we are—laughing, arguing, acting like it's just another Tuesday. But there's a strange comfort in it, too. Even in moments like these, I can't help but feel a little lighter. The absurdity of it all temporarily distracts me from the darker thoughts that always seem to be lurking, ready to swallow us whole.

Sadie grins, her mischievous energy undiminished despite the heaviness in the room. "Being a glorified death stick really makes you indispensable."

"Glorified death stick?" Orcus' tone darkens, the playful edge gone. His red aura narrows in that way he does when he's genuinely offended, his pride pricked enough to warrant a serious response. "Watch it, mortal, or I'll—"

Before he can finish the threat, Vassago interrupts. His calm voice cuts through the noise razor blades in snow. He doesn't raise it, doesn't shout, but the weight of it lands heavily on everyone in the room. All the playful banter dies immediately as if his presence alone is enough to shift the atmosphere. "*Enough*," Vassago says, his gaze sweeping over us, first lingering on Orcus, then Sadie, and then the rest of the group, taking us all in like a general surveying the battlefield. "If we're going to sit here bickering all night, we might as well be productive about it."

The room stills. It's strange how quickly the mood shifts when Vassago speaks. No one dares challenge him, even though we all know the guy doesn't need to raise his voice to command respect. There's an undeniable power in his silence, something that demands focus.

Orcus scowls but doesn't argue, his pride shrinking back into the corners of his mind. Sadie, too, seems to deflate, her grin faltering as she takes a deep breath and leans forward, elbows on the table.

I catch her eye for a brief moment. She's always been the one to fight through the darkness, but even she can't pretend like the weight of what's coming is something we can laugh off. We all know what's at stake now. We're no longer just playing at this. This is the real deal, and it's coming for us whether we're ready or not.

Luca pushes off the doorframe, his casual smile replaced with something a little more serious as he picks up a knife and starts absentmindedly carving into the bread on the counter.

Sadie groans, slumping dramatically in her chair, her posture that of someone who's been deprived of the satisfaction of a proper tantrum. "You're no fun, Vassago," she mutters, the words laced with playful defiance, even if the edge of frustration tugs at her voice.

Vassago doesn't flinch. He never does. His response comes smoothly, his voice almost a purr with quiet confidence. "I'm not here to be fun," he replies, a steady calmness to his words, like he's already resigned to the weight of what's ahead. "I'm here to figure out how to get Layla back."

The moment he says her name, the room shifts. It's like the very air around us tightens, the atmosphere heavy with the weight of those words. Layla. Her absence is a gaping wound that we're all trying to ignore, but it's there, lingering in the corners of the room.

Azrael, who's been eerily silent up until now, reacts before anyone else. His fingers tighten around the edge of the table, the knuckles popping loudly in the stillness of the room. His broad shoulders stiffen, his posture tense, as though he's struggling to hold back a storm. His head stays bowed, his features hidden in the shadow of his robe, and for a moment, I see something raw—a vulnerability, a desperation that he rarely allows anyone to witness. It's unsettling, even to me.

Luca, clearly uncomfortable with the sudden shift in the mood, clears his throat. His voice falters slightly, as if trying to find the right words to break the tension. "So, uh, how's the food? Good? It's good, right?" His awkward attempt at normalcy falls flat, the words hanging in the air like an afterthought, but there's something endearing about the effort, even if it doesn't quite land.

"Fantastic as usual," Lydia responds, her voice steady, betraying none of the tension that seems to suffocate the rest of us. She offers a polite smile, her usual poise intact despite the heavy atmosphere. "It's a shame you don't have a café here, Luca. You'd have us all as loyal regulars."

Luca forces a tight smile, the strain of the situation visible in the set of his jaw. "I'll take that as a compliment," he replies, his tone carefully neutral, though there's an edge to his words—like he's trying to force calm over an oncoming storm. "Even if I'm stuck cooking for mortals and immortals alike here."

"Don't forget sentient scythes," Sadie adds with a mischievous wink, her playful tone attempting to lighten the moment, but even her jests can't cut through the thick fog of tension that's settled over us. Orcus grumbles under his breath, clearly not appreciating the humor at his expense.

But the light-hearted banter doesn't last. Not in a room where grief and fear sit just beneath the surface, threatening to crack wide open at any moment.

Azrael stands abruptly, the scraping of his chair against the floor cutting through the room like a jagged knife. It's loud. Too loud. The sound alone makes everyone freeze, even Orcus. The tension multiplies as the room becomes suffocating in the silence that follows. His broad shoulders are rigid, his frame stiff and coiled, like he's holding back something darker, something heavier than any of us can understand. The air feels thicker, pressing down on all of us, but especially on Azrael, whose anger and frustration seem to manifest with every taut muscle in his body.

For a moment, no one speaks. No one moves. It's like the world has paused, hanging on the edge of something fragile. It's the kind of silence that speaks volumes, each breath echoing with unspoken words. We're all aware of the cracks, of the breaking, but none of us know how to fix it.

I exchange a glance with Vassago, who is sitting so still, so calmly, that he might as well be carved from stone. His gaze softens, just the tiniest bit—an expression I don't often see, one that holds understanding, even empathy. He knows Azrael's pain, has witnessed it for longer than I have. And yet, the calm in his eyes can't erase the knowledge of how fragile Azrael is right now.

"He'll come around," Vassago murmurs low enough for only a few of us to hear, his voice steady and sure, though there's a quiet sadness beneath the surface. "But we just need to give him time."

I nod, acknowledging the truth in his words. I know Azrael, I know how he works. How he carries the weight of everything on his shoulders, but I also know that this is different. This is a breaking point. Time won't fix it, but it's all we have left to give him.

"Time isn't on our side," I reply quietly, my voice almost a whisper. My gaze shifts back to Azrael, still standing by the window, his silhouette sharp against the darkening sky. He seems so distant, so unreachable, every inch of him a fortress built from years of solitude and responsibility. The tightness in his posture speaks volumes—he's holding everything back, but the cracks are there, threatening to splinter open. The storm inside him is brewing, and I can feel it from here, in the space between us.

I hesitate, my words catching in my throat, but then I add softly, almost as if speaking aloud will somehow shift the weight of the situation, "Not this time."

The words hang in the air, a quiet confession of the truth we all fear—that time, for all its promise, might not be enough to save us. Not this time.

Sadie shifts uncomfortably in her seat, the usual fire in her eyes dimming as she feels the full weight of my words. For once, her confidence fades, leaving a quiet tension in its place. She looks at me, lips pressing into a thin line, then her gaze moves toward Azrael. She's trying to read him, I can see it in the way she tilts her head, but it's futile. There's nothing to read—just that same wall of silence, as if he's made of stone.

"We'll get her back," Sadie says, her voice quieter now, but steady. The words are firm, unshakable. It's a promise, one laced with a quiet, burning resolve. "We have to."

The room falls into another heavy silence, but this time it feels different. It's not just the weight of uncertainty—it's the kind of silence that presses in on us, like the world is holding its breath. Even Orcus, whose sharp tongue is usually a constant presence, seems to sense it. For once, he doesn't have a snide remark to offer. The usual banter is gone, replaced by something heavier.

The bond that ties us all together—fragile and frayed as it may be—feels like the only thing we can cling to right now. It's not enough, not nearly enough, but it's all we've got.

I exhale slowly, trying to ease the tightness in my chest, but it doesn't help. The knot remains, a solid weight I can't seem to shake.

"Luca," I say, breaking the stillness, my voice rough and raw. It feels foreign to me, a little too sharp, like it's struggling to break free from the weight of everything else. "Bring out the dessert. Maybe it'll sweeten the mood."

Luca doesn't answer right away, but I see the slight nod of acknowledgment as he stands and heads to the fridge. His footsteps are quiet, careful, like he's trying not to disturb the fragile moment we're all holding on to. The others shuffle in their seats, returning to their places, but there's no laughter this time. No playful jabs. Just a collective resignation. The tension lingers in the air, a constant hum of unspoken fears.

When Luca returns with the dessert—a simple creation, but one of his specialties—the moment almost feels like a return to normalcy. The clink of plates, the soft rustling of forks, the gentle sigh of relief from Luca as he sets things down—it's all an attempt at bringing us back, to give us something to hold on to, if only for a moment.

But even with the food in front of us, the air still feels thick, almost suffocating. It's a false sense of comfort, a temporary reprieve from the storm we know is coming. We're far from okay, but that's the thing about moments like this. They're fleeting, fragile, and yet, they carry their own kind of weight.

For now, we're here. All of us, in the same room, with the same quiet understanding that the road ahead is uncertain and dangerous.

And sometimes, that's all we can ask for.

Chapter Five

Ashton

Hurricane - Thirty Seconds To Mars

Azrael stood by the window, his back to the room, his bony fingers tapping rhythmically against the sill—an unconscious rhythm, a telltale sign of the storm raging inside him. Every tap seemed to echo with his frustration, each click a resounding pulse of anger and helplessness. The rest of us were still seated, but the banter we'd shared earlier had long dissipated, swallowed by the gravity of the situation. Silence filled the space, heavy and oppressive, hanging over us like a dark cloud ready to burst. It was the kind of silence that made you feel like you were sinking, suffocating under an invisible weight.

None of us dared speak, not yet. There was too much hanging in the air, too much at stake. I could feel the tension in the room, a tightness in my chest, as if the very air was thick with unspoken words. Everyone was waiting—waiting for Azrael to break, waiting for someone to say something, anything, to ease the pressure. But no one did. Instead, we sat in our own private turmoil, lost in our thoughts, as the storm inside Azrael continued to brew.

Then, the door creaked open.

Exu stepped in, his presence filling the room immediately. He was a towering figure, dark caramel skin absorbing the dim light of the room as if he belonged to the shadows. His locs framed his face, giving him a timeless, otherworldly aura. As always, his expression was unreadable—stoic, deliberate. But today, there was something else in his eyes. A heaviness. A furrowed brow, a tightness in his jaw. It wasn't the calm demeanor I'd grown used to. No, this time, there was a storm brewing behind his gaze, too.

A murmur passed through the room before silence took hold again. Exu didn't need to say anything else. His presence spoke volumes. But when he did, his voice was steady—yet it carried an edge that made my skin prickle. "I've found her."

The words hung in the air for a moment, but they hit me like a sucker punch to the gut. I could feel the collective shift in the room—every breath held; every heartbeat stilled. We were all waiting for more. Waiting for something that would tell us this nightmare could be over, that maybe, just maybe, there was a way out of this mess.

Azrael's head snapped around, his posture suddenly rigid, like a predator homing in on its prey. His gaze locked onto Exu with such intensity that it felt like it could cut through stone. "Where?" His voice was barely a whisper, but the force behind it was undeniable, like every fiber of his being was hanging on that single word.

Exu didn't flinch. Instead, he held Azrael's gaze for a beat longer than necessary, and when he finally spoke, his words dragged the air down, crushing any hope we might've had left. "She's been *confirmed* to be in the Empty."

A collective shudder seemed to ripple through the room. The air grew even heavier, thick with dread and disbelief. The Empty. The afterlife for supernaturals, a place of endless nothingness, devoid of hope.

I could see it in Lydia's eyes first—the way her usual calm composure tightened, the tremor in her fingers as she set her glass down on the table. She was already calculating the impossible: How do we bring someone back from the Empty? How do we fight the impossible?

Sadie, ever the source of light and levity, glanced between the rest of us, her brow furrowed, confusion etching her features. For once, her usual sass was absent, replaced with uncertainty. I could hear the wheels turning in her head, trying to make sense of the words Exu had just spoken, but the answers weren't easy.

Luca's calm, ever-reserved nature faltered as his brows furrowed, his lips pressed into a tight line. I could tell he was calculating, too, running through possibilities in his mind—none of them good. His gaze flicked from Exu to Azrael, and I could almost feel the unspoken question between them. *What now?*

The room had descended into chaos, not in sound, but in the way we each struggled to cope with the impossible news. The silence was no longer just oppressive—it was suffocating, a weight too great for any of us to bear.

But Azrael? He didn't move. He didn't flinch. His gaze never wavered from Exu, and for a long moment, it was as if the world had stopped moving altogether. I could feel the rage simmering beneath his resolve, a storm waiting to break. His knuckles were clenched around the edge of the window as if he were holding onto whatever sliver of control he had left. It was the first time I'd seen him like this—this raw, this vulnerable—and it made my stomach turn.

"The Empty," Azrael muttered, as if testing the words, as if saying them out loud would make them real in a way that hadn't been before. "She's for sure in the Empty?"

Exu's gaze softened for just a fraction of a second, his eyes understanding, but it was fleeting, quickly masked by his usual stoic demeanor. "We'll get her back. But it won't be easy."

"I don't care how hard it is." Azrael's voice was low, a growl in his throat. "We're not leaving her there."

Lydia leaned forward, her gaze narrowing. "We need a plan. There's no way to go into the Empty without one."

"You're right," Exu agreed, his voice measured. "I'll need time to gather information. But we don't have the luxury of time. The longer she's there, the more…" He let the sentence hang, and I knew what he meant. The longer she was trapped in the Empty, the more she could slip away, lost forever.

"The Empty?" Sadie finally asked, her voice uncertain, a little too soft. "What is that?"

Vassago sighed, a low, rumbling sound, like the distant warning of thunder. He leaned back in his chair, his gaze distant as if the very mention of the place pulled him somewhere far away, somewhere dark. For the first time in a long while, I saw something that looked like dread in his eyes. The kind of dread that lingers long after the threat is gone. The kind you don't get over easily.

Vassago says grimly, his voice heavy with the weight of a truth none of us wanted to face. "The Empty is unstable, unpredictable. Its very existence is corrosive. To enter it is to risk losing yourself entirely—your mind, your soul, your very essence."

There was a pause. The air seemed to thicken, suffocating us all with the weight of those words. I could feel the tension in the room, like a taut wire stretched too thin, ready to snap at any moment.

Azrael's eyes were fixed on Vassago, but there was no fear in his gaze, only determination, a fierce hunger for action that had become all too familiar. He took a step forward, his body rigid, his voice a sharp blade cutting through Vassago's explanation. "But it's not *impossible* to enter?"

Exu, who had been silent until now, held up a hand, his expression firm but with a flicker of hesitation in his eyes. It was subtle, but it was there. He was always the calm one, the mediator, but even he seemed unsettled by the idea. "Technically, no. But practically? Yes. Even if you could find a way in, navigating the Empty without being consumed by it is—"

"I'll do it." Azrael's voice was low, but the finality in it left no room for argument. His words slammed into the air like a declaration of war.

The room fell into an eerie silence, broken only by the faint creak of the chair beneath Vassago as he sat back, the weight of Azrael's words settling into the space between us like a cold shadow.

"You don't understand what you're saying." Vassago's voice rose slightly, frustration leaking through the cracks of his usually calm demeanor. "The Empty doesn't just take. It'll tear you apart. Piece by piece, it'll unravel everything that makes you who you are."

Azrael's eyes locked onto Vassago's, burning with the intensity of a thousand storms. "Do you think I care about that?" he shot back, the words almost snarled, like a challenge. His fists clenched at his sides, his knuckles popping, but it didn't matter. His resolve was unwavering. "She is there. *Alone*. Probably terrified. I'm not going to sit here and do nothing while she's—"

"*Azrael*," Exu interrupted, his tone cutting through the rising tension like a sharp blade. He stepped closer, his presence a grounding force in the chaos. "Listen to me. If you charge into the Empty without a plan, you won't be saving her. You'll be condemning yourself."

The words hit Azrael like a physical blow. His jaw tightened, his gaze flickering with anger, but he didn't back down. He never did. "Then we make a plan," he said, his voice thick with determination, the edge softening only slightly. "There has to be a way. I'm not leaving her there."

I could see the way the room had shifted, the mood darkening. We weren't just talking about saving someone anymore—we were talking about the very real possibility of losing Azrael, losing *all* of us. But I couldn't argue with him. The thought of Layla—lost, trapped in the Empty—was unbearable. And Azrael, for all his stoic distance and sharp edges, wasn't going to let her go. Not now. Not ever.

The silence that followed was oppressive, thick with the gravity of what we were facing. Vassago rubbed his temples, his frustration palpable, but beneath it all, there was something deeper—something unspoken, a pain in his eyes that I wasn't sure I could bear to confront. He muttered under his breath, his voice low but heavy with the weight of his own emotions, "You're not the only one who wants to save her."

His words hung in the air, unspoken regret threading through them. The truth was, Vassago didn't just want to save Layla—he was *willing* to sacrifice more than he let on. He cared for her, and though he hid it behind layers of duty and practicality, the ache in his voice was unmistakable.

"Oh, cut the Guardian Angel bullshit role." Azrael growls.

Vassago doesn't say anything, he just growls under his breath in response.

The room was tense, every person in it caught between their own fear and the pull of their loyalty to Azrael, to each other. I could feel the storm gathering in all of us, the uncertainty and the fear mixing with the resolve. But we had no choice. We couldn't let Layla stay there. The Empty was a place for the lost. And we couldn't afford to lose anyone else.

"I'll find a way," Exu said quietly, the weight of the promise heavy in his words. "But it won't be easy. There's no guarantee that—"

"I don't care about guarantees," Azrael cut him off, his voice a steel blade in the silence. "*I care about her.*"

We all looked at Azrael, knowing full well that his self-esteem was unshakable. The rest of us? We had our doubts, our fears. But in this moment, we were bound by something stronger than hesitation. We were bound by the simple truth that Layla needed us.

And if there was even a sliver of hope that we could save her, then we would fight for it. Even if it meant fighting the Empty itself.

Sadie's hands were wringing in her lap, the usual fire in her eyes replaced with a quiet, almost helpless sorrow. She blinked rapidly; her breath shallow as she fought to keep the tears at bay. She wasn't the type to break, not in front of all of us, but the sight of Azrael's pain was a weight none of us could ignore. "We will get her back," she whispered, her voice trembling, but even as she spoke, I could hear the uncertainty in her words. She was trying to convince herself just as much as she was trying to reassure the rest of us.

The room felt smaller, suffocating under the gravity of what we were about to undertake. Luca's mouth opened as if to speak, but then he hesitated, caught in the midst of his own thoughts. I saw the struggle in his eyes, the confusion, the fear. He hadn't been with us long, but he was already tied to this. To *her*. His gaze flickered between Azrael and the rest of us, the weight of the decision heavy on his shoulders. "What's the plan, then?" he finally asked, his voice unsure but laced with quiet resolve.

Exu's gaze flickered from Azrael to the rest of us, the old man's silence settling like a fog in the room. "A plan doesn't mean we throw ourselves into the Empty blind," he said, his voice firm, though tinged with something that sounded close to regret. "We need to think about every risk, every consequence. Because if we don't—" He trailed off, his words unfinished. Whatever came after that sentence was something none of us wanted to hear.

Azrael's fingers drummed against the table, the rhythmic tapping a clear indication of his growing agitation. The tension in the room thickened, his frustration nearly palpable. "I'm not waiting. Not any longer." His voice was low, but there was no mistaking the steel in it. He finally turned toward the window; his silhouette bathed in the eerie red moonlight. His posture was rigid, almost unnerving in its stillness. "She's in there. And I'm going to get her."

The silence that followed was suffocating, thick with the weight of his words. But it wasn't just Azrael's grit that hung heavy in the room—it was the dread of what we were truly facing. The Empty was beyond any of us. We couldn't even begin to imagine its depths, its cruelty.

It was Lydia who finally broke the silence, her voice a soft but steady thread weaving through the tense atmosphere. "If there's a way," she said quietly, her gaze unwavering as it locked onto Azrael, "we'll find it. But we need to be smart about this. The Empty isn't something we can fight with brute force. We'll need knowledge, strategy, and..."

"And what?" Azrael's voice came like a whip, razor-sharp and full of impatience. His tone was brittle, fraying by the second, his patience already worn thin.

Lydia paused for a moment, her eyes fixed on Azrael, the weight of her next words hanging in the air. "And hope," she finished softly, her voice barely above a whisper. "Because without that, we're already lost."

Her words landed like a stone dropped into the still waters of the room, sending ripples through all of us. For a moment, the air seemed to still, each of us caught in the gravity of what she'd said. Azrael, ever the stoic, turned his head away, his eyes narrowing in irritation, his jaw clenching as he fought against the storm of frustration building inside him.

The stillness stretched, suffocating, unbearable. His muscles were taut, coiled with so much pent-up energy that the slightest provocation could snap him. His hands curled into fists, his fingernails digging into his palms as if he were trying to hold back everything he felt. But there was nothing gentle in his silence. It was pure, unadulterated *rage*.

"I don't care about *hope*," Azrael's voice broke through the quiet, raw and cutting. The words hung in the air, jagged and jagged. "I care about getting her back. I care about *now*."

Sadie's breath hitched in the corner of the room, and I could see the way her body stiffened. She had been trying to remain calm, trying to stay the anchor for everyone else, but the rawness in Azrael's voice made her flinch. I saw her eyes dart to Vassago, then to Exu, as if searching for some kind of answer, something to make sense of all of this.

Lydia's voice was unwavering, steady like the ocean in a storm. "I know you do," she said softly. "But charging in without a plan will get us nowhere. The Empty is unpredictable, dangerous. We can't just... rush in. We need time. We need to understand what we're facing."

Azrael's honey lips curled into a bitter sneer, the very expression of someone who had heard enough. "*Time*? We don't have *time*. Every second we waste, she's farther away from us."

The words hit harder than any of us expected. Time was the one thing we didn't have, and Azrael's impatience had always been his Achilles' heel. He could barely sit still when the stakes weren't life and death. But now? Now it was different. Layla was in the Empty. And we were running out of time to save her.

I could feel the weight of Azrael's words, the fire burning in his chest. But I also knew Lydia was right. If we didn't approach this carefully, we might end up losing more than just Layla.

Azrael didn't care about *that* though. The only thing that mattered to him was her. And nothing—*nothing*—was going to stop him from getting her back.

CHAPTER SIX

Azrael

TIME IS RUNNING OUT - MUSE

Orcus' voice broke through my thoughts, tinged with curiosity and something resembling hope. *I can sense Drepane's presence*, he said, his tone growing more certain. *He's waking up.*

I closed my eyes, pushing everything else away, letting my consciousness stretch outward, reaching for Drepane's bond. It flickered to life—raw and tenuous, like a flame battling against the wind. The connection between us hummed with the weight of everything unsaid, the unspoken fear, the desperate hope, and a glimmer of something more. The bond felt weak, strained, as though Drepane had been battered by forces far greater than anything I'd ever encountered.

Drepane, I called, my mental voice sharp and demanding. *I need you to explain. How did you end up in the Empty?*

There was a long, oppressive silence that stretched out between us. My mind strained, desperate for any response, but all I could feel was the pulse of the connection, fragile and distant. And then, finally, his voice broke through. *I... I had no choice. I acted to protect her.*

My stomach twisted at the words. The exhaustion in his voice was palpable, and the thought of Layla... *my* Layla, somewhere out there, trapped in that forsaken place...

By sending her to the Empty? Orcus' voice interjected, dripping with disbelief.

Drepane's voice grew sharper, the strain of exhaustion thick in every word. *Do you think I wanted this, you insolent clone?* His frustration bled through. *I didn't have time. She was already weakened from Memetim's attack. If I hadn't acted, she would've died.*

A wave of guilt and anguish swept over me, the burden of everything that had led us here crashing down. My hands clenched into fists, and for a brief, savage moment, I wanted to shatter everything around me. *And now she's trapped in a realm where Death would have been kinder.*

How is she? I could barely keep my voice steady as the rage and despair clawed at me.

Resting. Healing. Drepane's tone softened, as though he could sense the storm brewing inside me. *I've done what I can to stabilize her, but the Empty's influence... it's taking everything I have to shield her. That's why I couldn't contact you until now.*

The Empty. A realm where souls eroded, where time twisted into a cruel, endless spiral. It wasn't a place meant for the living. Layla was mortal—no matter how much fate had twisted her existence; she wasn't built to withstand its horrors. Every second she remained there was a second too long.

I exhaled sharply, trying to rein in the seething fury beneath my skin. *We need to get her out.* My voice came out more like a growl than a statement.

Orcus hummed; amusement laced beneath his usual arrogance. *No shit.*

Drepane's energy wavered, the connection flickering as though he were struggling to hold onto it. *Azrael... I don't know if I can keep her safe much longer.* There was something almost pleading in his voice.

My mind raced, spinning with questions, each one worse than the last. *What about Memetim?* I asked, pushing my thoughts toward Drepane with urgency. *Did she have a hand in this?*

There was a hesitation—long enough to stoke my anger, to turn it into something darker, something more violent.

She didn't put Layla in the Empty directly, Drepane admitted at last, his words slow, careful. *But her attack forced my hand. Memetim knew what she was doing, though. She's playing a long game, Azrael. This was her way of crippling you—of testing how far you'll go to get Layla back.*

Memetim. That name felt like acid in my throat. It burned, stung with every mention. The bitch had orchestrated this entire nightmare from the beginning, twisting fate to her liking, all to see how far I'd go for Layla.

She wanted to make me choose. She wanted to see if I would break.

But I wasn't going to fucking break.

I'll make her pay for this, I growled, the words dripping with venom, with a fucking promise.

Drepane's voice carried something heavy, something close to regret. *I know. And I'll help you. But you need to be careful. The Empty... it's not like anything you've ever faced. It's not just a realm.*

I could hear it then—the plea in his voice, subtle but there. He wasn't afraid for himself. He was afraid for Layla.

And that thought twisted something deep inside me, fanning the flames higher. *Don't worry about me,* I snapped. *Just tell me how to get to her.*

The bond between us trembled, flickering like a dying ember. I felt a sharp pang of something. Maybe guilt. Maybe something else.

You have to understand, Azrael, Drepane said softly, *this won't be easy. Even for you. The Empty will feed on your weaknesses, your doubts. And you'll have to face things in there... things you've buried deep inside yourself.*

I clenched my jaw, the rage burning too hot to be doused by caution. My vision sharpened, every nerve in my body humming with the singular, undeniable purpose that had taken root inside me. *I'm not afraid of the Empty, Drepane. And I'm not afraid of whatever I have to face in there to get Layla back.*

A beat of silence. Then—

Good. But you need to know... she's not alone in here.

Something inside me went still. The air around me felt heavier, pressing down like a weight I wasn't sure I could shake off.

What do you mean?

Drepane's presence wavered, exhaustion bleeding into the bond. *Memetim has already planted the seeds. She'll have... things in the Empty with her. They'll feed off her fear, her pain. And they'll try to destroy her.*

The weight of his words struck like a blade to the gut. Layla—trapped in that forsaken void, surrounded by horrors that fed off suffering. I imagined her alone, fighting against the dark, against things she couldn't even see, bleeding and breaking in a place where death would have been a mercy.

I couldn't allow it. I *wouldn't* allow it.

The storm inside me rose to something unstoppable, a force beyond reason, beyond restraint. *Then I'll destroy them all,* I said, my voice low, dangerous. *I will burn the Empty to the ground if I have to. Layla is coming home. And nothing—not even Memetim—will stop me.*

A long silence followed. When Drepane finally spoke, his voice was heavy with something close to resignation.

He hesitated, *But remember, there's no going back from this. The Empty will change you.*

I exhaled, letting the weight of the moment settle deep into my bones. *Let it change me.*

The storm raged inside me, unrelenting. And I had no desire to stop it.

I'll go to the ends of this damned realm to bring her back. And if it kills me... then so be it. I'll die for her.

Drepane's presence flickered, his voice quiet but firm. *I know you will.*

But I knew one thing for certain: no matter what happened next, I was not going to lose Layla. Not now. Not ever.

My jaw tightened, a growl slipping from between my teeth. The shift in my demeanor was immediate, and the others in the room fell silent. I felt their eyes on me, a heavy, unspoken awareness settling over the space, but I couldn't afford to care. Every second, every breath felt like an eternity, and the only thing that mattered was Layla. Her absence was a constant ache, a wound no amount of time could heal.

How long until she recovers? I demanded, my voice low, cold, and unyielding. I wasn't asking. I was demanding an answer.

Drepane's voice was soft, but there was a weight to it, like he knew the wrong words could shatter what little restraint I had left. *That depends,* he said carefully. *She's strong—stronger than even I anticipated. But the Empty takes a toll on everyone. She needs time to rebuild her strength—time I have to give her while keeping the realm's influence at bay.*

His exhaustion was a tangible thing, pressing against me through the bond like an iron chain. He was holding the line, but it was costing him.

And you? Orcus asked, his tone uncharacteristically gentle, almost... concerned. *You sound like hell, Drepane. How much longer can you keep this up?*

Long enough, Drepane answered, though the faint waver in his voice betrayed him. *Just focus on finding a way to get us out of here. Until then, I'll keep her safe.*

A sharp, biting laugh escaped me before I could stop it. *Keep her safe?* The words were quiet, but they carried a deadly edge. *How long can you really keep her safe in that place, Drepane?*

Silence. He didn't answer. He didn't have to. I could feel the truth like a blade pressed against my throat—he was running out of time. And so was she.

I opened my eyes, scanning the room. Sadie was watching me with open concern, her brows drawn tight, her lips parted as if she wanted to say something but thought better of it. Lydia's expression was unreadable, but her grip on her glass was ironclad, the veins in her fingers standing out like they might snap. The tension was suffocating, an invisible noose tightening around all of us.

I'm not waiting anymore, I said, the words slipping out before I could stop them. They were a promise, a vow to myself as much as to them. *I'm going after her. I don't care what it takes.*

The atmosphere shifted, an unspoken ripple of unease moving through the room. I could feel it, but I couldn't read them—not now. Not when the only thing I could focus on was the burning rage in my chest, the hollow ache where Layla should be.

"Drepane's awake," I said aloud, forcing myself to keep my voice steady. Each word was a struggle for control, a tightrope walk between sanity and the inferno threatening to consume me. "He's healing Layla, but it's taking everything he has. Memetim forced his hand."

Sadie's eyes locked onto mine, wide and searching. "And Layla?" Her voice barely rose above a whisper, as though speaking her name too loudly might shatter whatever fragile hope we had left.

"She's alive." I swallowed hard, the weight of those words settling in my chest like an anchor. Alive wasn't enough. Not yet. Not when the Empty still had its claws in her.

Vassago leaned forward, his elbows resting on the table. There was fire in his gaze, sharp and unyielding, like he was waiting for the order to strike. "So, what do you want us to do?" His voice was steady, but there was an edge to it—the same quiet resolve I saw in myself.

"Research," I said, the command leaving no room for argument. "We find a way to fucking save Layla."

No hesitation. No doubt. I wasn't leaving without her.

I turned on my heel, striding toward the exit of the dining room. Each step felt heavier than the last, the weight of rage, grief, and desperation pressing down on me with every breath.

"Where are you going?" Ashton's voice stopped me in my tracks. It wasn't an accusation, but more of a concern. He knew me too well—knew what I was capable of when my restraint started to crack.

I didn't look back. "I need to rest." The lie tasted bitter on my tongue. I couldn't exactly tell him I needed a form of anger management they would frown upon.

Because this fury, this helpless rage clawing at my insides, wasn't something I could just let sit. It needed an outlet. And I already knew where to find one.

Memetim had taken Layla from me. The thought twisted my stomach, the fury bubbling beneath my skin like molten fire. She had *touched* Layla. Had tried to claim her. Had tried to *take* her from me.

And I wasn't done.

Not by a long shot.

Dash Madden.

The name burned in my mind like an unholy brand, a reminder of the past Layla had barely escaped. He was still breathing. Still walking. And I was going to change that.

I would take him. Use him. Break him apart piece by piece until there was nothing left but blood and regret. Until the air reeked of his suffering. Until I felt *something* other than this unbearable emptiness where Layla should be.

Ashton stepped forward; his brow furrowed in concern. *"Azrael."* My name was a warning, edged with something softer beneath it. "Don't let this consume you."

I laughed, dark and humorless. "It *already* has."

And I walked away.

Chapter Seven

Azrael

Death of a Bachelor - Panic! At The Disco

Sneaking out of Ashton's home was harder than I had anticipated. It's difficult to avoid someone who sees everything, and even harder when your own weapon has the mouth of a damn talk-show host.

"This is a bad idea," Orcus muttered for the third time, his voice slithering through like an unwanted whisper. "You're not exactly subtle when you're pissed, young reaper. Maybe rethink the whole 'murdering a guy in cold blood' thing?"

"It's not in cold blood," I corrected. "It's very much premeditated."

"Oh, well, that makes it better."

Despite his grumbling, I managed to slip out. Orcus, for all his bitching, wasn't *trying* to stop me—just providing his usual color commentary.

Finding Dash's home wasn't difficult, either. If anything, it was disappointingly easy. Almost insulting. A man who had played a hand in Layla's suffering, a man who had aligned himself with Memetim, should have been harder to track. Instead, his location was practically gift-wrapped for me.

I shouldn't have been surprised. Dash Madden was a coward. He wasn't smart—just desperate, just weak. And weak men never hid well.

His house sat nestled deep in the countryside, surrounded by nothing but trees and silence. The kind of place where privilege meets paranoia—a home bought with blood money, tucked away in isolation. No neighbors. No security. No one to hear him scream.

Perfect.

I stepped forward, allowing the darkness to unfurl from within me, tendrils of shadow curling around my limbs, my form shifting into something more than mortal. More than a male of the Underworld.

I wanted him to see me.

To know, with every fiber of his being, that he had run out of time.

I push his front door open and step inside. The air is stale, thick with the scent of cheap beer and the lingering remnants of a long, unkempt day. I stalk my way through the house, moving with purpose as I pass the dining room, then the kitchen. The faint glow of the TV flickers in the living room ahead, where he's sprawled out on the couch like the arrogant, entitled prick he truly is.

Dash Madden.

I watch him for a moment—shouting at the screen like a brainless idiot. He's coaching from his couch, screaming at athletes on TV as though they can hear him. His words are unintelligible, lost in the chaos of his mind, his own little world of delusion. He has no idea I'm here. No idea that the very thing he's been waiting for is standing just behind him.

I stand there, silent, watching him. His stupidity makes my blood boil, but it's more than that. He's an abomination in my eyes. He's the reason Layla's been torn apart.

The thought of it—the betrayal, the hurt he caused her—makes the hunger rise up inside me again. It claws, gnawing at my insides, urging me to take him, rip him apart, make him pay for every moment of pain he's caused.

Orcus hums in my palm, vibrating with a hunger of his own. I feel the cold edge of the scythe, urging me toward violence, toward destruction. It's like a silent plea for me to stop, but I know he is just as hungry for the chaos as I am. And still, I do nothing.

I need this. I deserve this.

This man hurt *our* mate.

This man *destroyed* our mate.

I will *hurt* and *destroy* him.

I lean in closer, my breath warm against the back of his neck. I can feel the hair on his skin standing on end, a shiver running down his spine as my presence finally sinks into his awareness. His muscles tense, but his back stays turned to me, his mind still trapped in the game he's so obsessed with.

"Hello, Dash," I say, my voice low, smooth. I force myself to sound calm, to bite back the overwhelming urge to tear his ear off with my teeth.

His head jerks up at my voice, and the stupid grin he's wearing falters for a second, then he stands, slowly, turning to face me. His eyes flick to my form, scanning me with a strange lack of fear. Instead of the terror I'm used to seeing, there's something more calculating in his gaze. Something smug.

I watch him—his pulse, the way his breath hitches, the shift in the color in his life expiration above his head. It starts out green, the usual hue, but as I watch him, I make him feel it. I make him feel the power I have over him. Slowly, his expiration starts to seep through, and the green in his date bleeds into yellow the color of someone whose end is drawing near.

I let the numbers roll slowly. I let the minutes and seconds stretch out, making him suffer just a little longer. Then it stops at red.

"I've been waiting for you to finally show your ugly face," Dash says, smirking as if this is some twisted game. He doesn't get it; doesn't realize how far beyond the point of no return he is. But he'll understand soon enough. "How's Layla?" He adds.

His smirk only makes me want to rip it off his face.

I can feel the heat of the moment pulsing under my bones, the adrenaline coursing through my joints as the rage settles deeper into my fucking bones. Dash Madden has no idea who he's dealing with.

"I'm not here for games," I say, my voice rough now, a growl breaking through the calm. "I'm here for you."

I walk around the couch slowly, circling him, letting the tension build between us. Dash stumbles back a step or two, his eyes darting nervously between me and the door. I can tell he's calculating his options, but there's nowhere for him to go. No way out.

He shifts to the side, clearly realizing I've made up my mind. He gives me just enough room so I can squeeze through and sit on the middle cushion, sprawling out like I own the place.

"How did you get tied into the Memetim chaos?" I ask casually, watching him squirm.

His eyes flick to the crow tattoo on his forearm and his lips curl into a sneer. "She bargained a deal. I took it."

Orcus hums in the back of my mind, a low, rumbling sound that matches my own growing anger. "What was the bargain?" He asks aloud.

Dash looks at me with arrogance, still not fully grasping the gravity of his situation. "Wouldn't you like to know?"

I lift a finger, releasing my newfound energy. It surges through the room, the air vibrating with power, and before Dash can even blink, he's lifted off the ground.

I see the panic in his eyes now.

"Orcus asked you a question," I say, my voice hard, "It would be in your best interest to answer."

He thrashes in the air, his feet kicking out, but I hold him with an iron grip. "Memetim promised me a seat at the throne in the Underworld."

I can't help but bark a laugh. It's almost pathetic. "Excuse me?"

"You heard me!" Dash yells, defiant, though it's clear his confidence is slipping.

I tilt my head, considering his words. The sheer delusion is almost amusing. "And what? You thought you'd rule alongside Hades?"

"She said I had potential!"

Orcus vibrates with laughter in my grip. *That's the funniest thing I've heard in centuries.*

I stand, stepping closer, and watch as Dash struggles against the invisible hold I have on him. His breath comes out in short, panicked bursts now, the reality of his situation finally setting in.

I wave my finger to the side, the force behind the motion sending him crashing into the wall with a sickening thud. His body slumps, a ragdoll in my grasp, groaning in pain. The sound is oddly satisfying, like a relief I didn't know I needed.

"Why?" I ask, my voice low, dangerous. "What did she want in return?"

Dash struggles to catch his breath, his face contorted in pain. He pushes himself up with trembling arms, but I wave my hand again, sending him back down, pinning him to the floor with a flick of my wrist. The floorboards groan under the pressure, his body convulsing as the weight of my power presses against his ribcage.

"Someone named Vassago," he gasps out, his voice shaking. "She needed him gone so she could get closer to Layla. I had to attack Layla to weaken him, she said."

The words cut through me like a blade, sharper than anything I've ever felt. My grip on reality teeters as the truth settles in my bones. She used him to hurt my mate. She used him to hurt her. To break her. To draw her into some sick game she had no choice but to play.

I feel the vibration in my palm before I realize I'm gripping Orcus so tightly my knuckle bones were numb and popping. The scythe hums, eager, hungry.

"Where is Memetim?" I ask, my voice void of anything but death itself.

Dash gasps, his body writhing beneath my hold, but he can't escape. "She comes every few nights," he chokes out. "That's all I know. I swear."

A pathetic noise slips from his throat, something between a sob and a whimper, and I can feel it now—the moment the reality sinks in for him. He knows he's not leaving this room alive.

"I swear to god, I promise," he pleads, his voice wet, his face pale.

I lean down, my breath fanning over his ear. "I. Am. Your. God."

His pupils blow wide with terror just as I release my hold on him. For a second, just a second, he thinks I'm giving him mercy. He sucks in a breath, his shoulders trembling, his fingers twitching as though debating whether to move or not. His body is frozen in indecision.

And that's when I strike.

I move fast—too fast. My hand wraps around his throat, and I lift him from the ground effortlessly, pressing him against the wall. He kicks, claws at my wrist, his nails digging into my bone, but it's useless. His strength is nothing compared to mine.

I squeeze, watching as his lips part in a strangled gasp, his airways constricting. The veins in his forehead bulge, his eyes bloodshot and darting wildly.

I release just enough for him to suck in one desperate breath, then slam him back against the wall. His head cracks against it, a dull, meaty thud.

"You put your hands on my mate," I murmur, tilting my head, studying the way his lips tremble. "You cut into her. You left her to bleed out."

His lips part, but no words come out. Just wheezing, gasping, desperate little noises that make my skin crawl with disgust.

I drop him. He collapses in a heap at my feet, clutching his throat, coughing violently. I let him sit with it for a moment. Let him think I might spare him. Let him think I have an ounce of humanity left... but I don't.

Then I wave my hand, and his body is yanked into the air, arms and legs spread wide. I twist my wrist, and he jerks, his limbs snapping to unnatural angles. A choked scream tears from his lips.

I walk toward him slowly, watching his face, drinking in every ounce of agony. "I should drag this out longer," I muse, tapping my chin. "You deserve it, don't you?"

He nods frantically, tears streaking down his face. "Yes," he sobs. "Please. Please just—"

I don't let him finish.

I flex my fingers, and his body convulses as I send raw energy through him. His screams are ear-shattering. His now pale skin is splitting in jagged, gory lines as the power eats through him—peeling muscle from bone. He writhes, twitches, his eyes rolling back, and for a moment, I almost feel pity.

Almost.

Then, with a final twist of my wrist, he bursts apart—blood, bone, and sinew raining down in thick, wet splatters. The walls are painted crimson, the floor slick with the remains of his pathetic existence.

I exhale, rolling my shoulders, letting the silence settle over me.

Orcus hums, satisfied.

The hunger that gnawed at my insides, the rage that fueled me... it's finally *almost* quiet.

CHAPTER EIGHT

Ashton

DO I WANNA KNOW? - ARCTIC MONY

I feel like I'm channeling my parents, those moments when they knew I was sneaking out but never said a word. They just waited—silent, patient in the dark hallways—ready to butcher my ass once I slipped up. But Azrael is a grown male. I can't exactly discipline him, but curiosity? That I can't ignore. I want to know where he went, why he felt the need to hide it from me.

I sit in the darkness, absentmindedly playing with the specks of cosmic sand between my fingers. It's my trademark, my gift: this sand that mimics the night sky of the mortal realm, a subtle mark that lets me know I've touched it. I can feel Azrael's presence before he even turns the knob, the scent of iron on the air, sharp and familiar. I smile to myself, amused. It's like he never changed. A predator trying to sneak back into its lair. Too bad I'm better at it than him.

The door creaks open slowly, and I catch the faintest outline of his skeletal frame, attempting to slip past me unnoticed. It's like watching him all over again during our training days—no matter how hard he tried; he could never tell when I was nearby. No scent. No sound. I was always there, waiting in the shadows, a constant presence. And now, I'm still here, watching him make the same mistakes.

"Hello, Azrael," I whisper, keeping my voice low as if we're both trying to be sneaky. Because we are, aren't we?

He jumps, the sound of his boots scraping against the floor betraying his shock. "What the fuck, Ashton?"

I flick my fingers upward, the lights flickering on, my curiosity growing with every passing second. Azrael's usually so composed, so perfectly controlled, but tonight? Tonight, he's drenched in blood—head to toe, like a horror show gone wrong. And beside him, Orcus is just as covered, like some twisted pair of executioners.

I rub my jawline, my mind struggling to process the sight.

"Want to share the details about your little secretive adventure that I apparently wasn't invited to?" I ask, my voice light, teasing—part of me just wants to get a rise out of him.

Azrael shoots me a sharp glare, toeing off his blood-slicked boots by the door. "You weren't invited for a reason."

I lean against the doorframe, crossing my arms. "I thought we did everything together, Az. Here I go, thinking I'm your best friend after you got me tangled in all this drama. But, hey, I'm clearly not your first choice when it comes to who you bring along for the messiest jobs."

Azrael doesn't say anything, just grunts, shoulders stiffening as he walks past me down the hallway. His steps are quick, his back straight, like he's trying to leave me behind. But I can't help but smirk. He's never been good at outrunning me. In fact, no one has. I take my time, enjoy the chase. "I had to take care of something." He finally grumbles.

"Take care of what?" I ask, matching his pace without even breaking a sweat. My steps are almost silent, like I've become one with the shadows, and that's exactly the way I want it.

Azrael doesn't answer immediately. He's always the master of silence when he doesn't want to give something away. But I can feel the tension in the air—the blood on him, the heaviness in the atmosphere. Something is off, and I'm not going to let him get away with brushing me off this time.

"You know," I continue, voice lowering just enough to make it clear I'm not backing off, "this whole 'I needed to take care of something' excuse doesn't work on me. I'm your best friend, remember? So, what the hell is going on, Azrael?"

His jaw tightens, his body stiffening even more, like he's weighing whether to lash out at me or just keep walking. The silence stretches between us, thick with unspoken words.

And then, finally, he cracks. He exhales sharply, letting the words spill out. "I did what I had to do, alright?" His tone is defensive, like he's trying to convince himself as much as me. But there's something in his eyes—a flicker of guilt, or maybe exhaustion. Something that makes my suspicion grow.

I stand my ground, raising an eyebrow. "What's that supposed to mean? You just walked in here, covered in blood, and you think '*I had to*' is enough to explain all of it?"

He moves toward the door to his room, hand reaching for the handle. But before he can open it, I casually flick my fingers, locking it with a soft click.

"Orcus," I say, looking at the scythe gripped in Azrael's hand. "You're his sidekick. You've been hanging around long enough to know what's up. Spill it. What happened?"

Orcus hums in that infuriatingly casual way of his, completely unaffected by the scene unfolding in front of him. "Oh, it's simple," he says, voice dripping with sarcasm. "He killed Memetim's pet."

I stare at him. Then I glance at Azrael. The silence between us speaks volumes. I push further. "And?"

"And," Orcus continues, rolling his glowing eyes, "he didn't even break a sweat. Like he's done it a thousand times before."

Azrael sighs, the sound carrying an edge of frustration. He leans against the doorframe, clearly exhausted by the conversation. "I needed stress release," he mutters, as if that's an excuse for everything.

I look at him for a long moment, assessing the situation, the blood still clinging to his clothes like a second skin.

"Stress release?" I repeat, a dry laugh slipping from my lips. "You know, I'm not sure that's the kind of thing you just 'release' on your own. You've got a lot to explain, Az. This isn't the Azrael I know. Something else is going on here, and I'm damn sure you're not telling me the whole truth."

Azrael doesn't meet my eyes. His gaze falls to the floor as his fingers twitch. "I don't have time for this right now," he snaps, though it's weak.

He knows I'm right.

I step closer, dropping the cosmic sand in a cascade of shimmering light, watching it drift around us like stars falling from the sky. I let it linger, the magic crackling around me.

"I'm not letting this go, Az," I say quietly. "Not until you tell me what the hell is really going on."

He doesn't answer. He doesn't need to. Because in the end, I already know. And it's only a matter of time before Azrael cracks, and the truth comes spilling out.

Before I can even get another word in, the air shifts. It's subtle, but I feel it. Sadie's presence.

She's quicker than I expected—faster than I gave her credit for. And before I can even tell her to go back to our room and wait, she's already standing next to me, eyes wide in surprise. The moment she takes in the sight of Azrael, covered head to toe in blood, her breath catches.

I hear her soft whimper before I see her lips move.

"What the fuck did you do?" she demands, her voice sharp, but there's a distinct edge of worry underlying it, like she knows this is bad—*really bad.*

"For fuck's sake!" Azrael snaps, spinning around to face us. His hollow eye sockets blaze with blue fire, an inferno of rage swirling deep in the blackness. His fury's rising fast. "*I killed Dash Madden!*"

A deafening silence falls. Not even Orcus makes a sound, and that's saying something. The air grows thick, heavy with the weight of Azrael's words, as if they're too much for any of us to process right away.

But then... Sadie giggles? "Oh. My. Fucking. God. Grim Boy!" She's practically bouncing on her heels, excitement practically radiating off her. "Tell me! Did he beg for mercy? Was he scared? Did he try to run? I need the deets... now!"

I blink, caught completely off guard.

That's my mate, the one who shares my soul, the same person who can turn the world upside down with a few words. And here she is, giggling over someone's *brutal* death.

There's no denying it: Sadie is just as fucked up as Azrael.

Azrael lets out an exasperated sigh, running a blood-soaked hand through his hair like it's no big deal. "You're both insane," he mutters, but I catch the slight smile tugging at the corner of his mouth. It's small, almost imperceptible, but it's there. He's not as unaffected as he wants us to think.

Sadie's grin only widens, her energy infectious even amidst the chaos.

She leans in, practically pressing herself against Azrael, not giving him an inch of space. "Come on, Death Boy, I want to know! I mean, was it satisfying? You had to have enjoyed it a little." She laughs, and the sound of it—loud and carefree—hits me like a punch to the gut. It's both unsettling and oddly comforting, like her madness makes everything else seem a little more bearable.

Azrael glares at her for a second, clearly debating whether to give in or snap back. But the truth's already spilling from him. "Yeah. Yeah, I guess I did. I enjoyed it."

And there it is. That's the problem with Azrael. He never hides who he is, not really. His darkness, his violence—they're always right there, at the surface, like it's nothing to be ashamed of. It's armor, a shield, a part of him that has never left. But knowing this—knowing how far he's gone for Layla, for this fucked-up world—we can't blame him.

Dash Madden deserved it, no question. The bastard was poison, a rot in the heart of everything. But it doesn't mean we can just let it slide without asking questions.

I cross my arms, leaning against the doorframe, watching them both like some twisted, dysfunctional family. "You're both a damn mess," I mutter, shaking my head. "But I get it. Just... next time, don't leave me in the dark, Azrael. We've been through too much for that."

Azrael's gaze flickers for a moment—regret? Maybe. Or maybe just a quiet recognition of the bond we've shared for centuries. Something passes between us, unspoken, as if the years are closing in on us. I don't push it further, not this time. I can feel he's not ready to fully open up about what he really felt during the whole thing—and honestly?

That's fine. For now.

But Sadie? She's not letting this go. Not a chance.

She's still grinning like a madwoman, bouncing on her feet, absolutely refusing to back down. "Come on, Grim Boy, I know there's more. You have to tell me about the blood. The screaming. The *fun* parts. Details. Now."

Azrael meets her gaze, his grin twitching like he's about to give in. "Sadie," he starts, his voice lower, teasing even. "You're all kinds of *fucked up*, you know that?"

She shrugs, not even a little bit ashamed. "You're just mad 'cause I'm more excited about this than you are."

I can't help but chuckle despite myself. It's a weird fucking dynamic we've got going on here. But it works. Somehow, it works. And as much as I want to roll my eyes at their insanity, there's something comforting about it.

This chaos—it's *ours*. And nothing will change that.

Still, as I look between Azrael and Sadie, something in me can't shake the feeling that this is just the beginning. That darker paths are calling to Azrael.

That maybe, just maybe, the blood he's spilled tonight isn't the end, but the beginning of something much more dangerous.

But hell, I'm not going to stop him. None of us will.

CHAPTER NINE

Azrael

PANORAMIC VIEW - AWOLNATION

Talking to Sadie helped ease the edge of my pain, but it doesn't compare to having Layla here with me. It's like holding onto a piece of her—just a fraction of the warmth, the connection. I told Sadie everything she wanted to know about Dash, even though she wasn't thrilled about how quick I made his death. She was satisfied with the fact that Dash is gone, though, and most importantly, that he can't enter the Underworld. That alone gives me some comfort, knowing Layla will never have to worry about him haunting her in either of her worlds.

I lay in the bed we shared, but it's so cold, so empty without her beside me. There's no soft breaths against my chest, no quiet sighs or little whimpers filling the silence. I've never felt this hollow, this robbed, before.

I close my eyes, trying to let the bond between us reach out, stretching toward her. *Layla...* My breath leaves me in a sigh as I caress the delicate thread of her life in my mind, a whisper of hope, a thread of desperate longing. I ache for her—her presence, her touch. The warmth of her skin, the sweetness of her lips, the love in her eyes. I need to feel her. I need her back in my arms. *Layla, please, let me know you're okay.*

The plea echoes through the bond without any fear, without any care for who might hear it. Orcus might roll his eyes, or Drepane might growl in annoyance, but in this moment, I don't care. I can't.

I feel a subtle vibration against the thread—the gentle hum of Drepane's presence. He's still with her. Still protecting her. It's something I've failed at time and time again, a constant failure that weighs on me like a thousand pounds. *If only...*

If only your father hadn't abused you so much, making you afraid of who you were truly meant to be, Young Reaper.

The words hang in my mind, like the gravelly growl of a beast gnawing at my soul. Drepane's voice isn't like Orcus' smooth, almost silky rasp. No, Drepane's voice is raw—guttural. It digs deep, gnawing on my nerves.

Drepane... The thought makes a shiver run down my spine. He scares the hell out of me.

But the truth is, he belongs to my mate, just as Orcus does. And he belongs to me. The weight of that responsibility presses down on me like a stone on my chest. The thought of failing her again—of losing her—suffocates me.

I grip the sheets beneath me, my fingers curling into them, as if holding onto the fabric will somehow anchor me to something real. The bed feels too big, too empty. I'm still holding onto that thin thread of hope, that promise I made to her. No matter how far away she is, I'll get her back.

I can't entertain the thought of losing her forever. The way she looked at me, her trust, her love—it's the only thing I have left to keep me tethered to this world, to the reason I'm still breathing.

And if there's one thing I'm certain of, it's that nothing, *nothing*, is going to stop me from bringing her back into my arms.

How is Layla? My voice cracks through the bond, the weight of the separation pressing into every word. It's rough, desperate, like the ocean crashing against a cliffside.

She's still stirring. Drepane's voice hums, calm but firm, as though the simple act of telling me was a sacred trust. *I can show you.*

Show me? The disbelief slips out before I can stop it. I never realized that was even possible. The bond I share with her, with Orcus, with Drepane—there's so much more to it than I ever imagined.

Please... I beg him, my voice raw with the weight of everything. There's no pride left in me, no arrogance—just the crushing, heart-wrenching need to know she's okay.

Without warning, the world around me blurs, my body jerking forward as the air thickens, thickens until I feel as though I'm falling without a solid ground beneath me. The pull is intense, ripping through my body, but I trust Drepane. I let him guide me, twisting through the void of realms. I don't know where we're going, but I let go, letting him pull me deeper into the nothingness.

And then, with a sudden jolt, everything stills.

I stumble forward, trying to catch my breath as my vision clears. My eyes lock onto the sight before me—*Layla.*

She lies in a blanket of ash, her small body almost swallowed by the chaos around her. She's beautiful, even in the midst of her suffering. The softness of her, the strength of her, it's all there—wrapped up in a fragile, broken package. Her breath is shallow, but steady, a soft vapor forming in the air with each exhale. Her once-pristine armor is now torn and battered, deep cracks running through the surface. Blood stains it as it once dripped to the earth below her. Her hair—once so neatly pulled into a tight bun for war—is now a tangled mess, falling in loose strands around her face, plagued with light crimson streaks the soft skin.

My chest aches. I want to rush to her, pull her close, but I know I can't. Not yet. She's alive, thank the gods, but there's something darker looming over her. Something *wrong*.

My eyes never leave her, though. Not even as I take in the presence of Drepane, who lies draped over her, like a protective shield. His violet energy pulses around them both, creating a glowing cocoon that keeps the darkness at bay. He's healing her, keeping her warmth alive, but I know it's not enough. Not yet. Not when I'm still so far away.

But I *will* get to her. I will bring her back.

And no matter what, I won't fail her again.

How do I get to you both? The words spill out of me, a near whisper, but the desperation in them is unmistakable. The ache in my chest only grows stronger, gnawing at me with every passing moment.

There's a powerful hybrid named Saygin. She's Hecate's granddaughter. Find her, and her mate Quinn Veyrik. Drepane's voice hums in my mind, low and steady, as though he's carefully choosing each word. *Quinn was once a mortal who meddled in a forbidden ritual and found himself thrown into the Empty. The Empty devoured him, twisted him... turned him into a shadowkind.*

Void-born, I mutter under my breath, the weight of the term sinking into my bones. I've heard the stories—whispers about beings who are born of nothing, caught between realms, capable of shaping the void around them. I understand the meaning all too well.

Correct. Drepane's voice doesn't waver. *He is the only one recorded to have escaped the Empty. He used shadow navigation to open pathways through the Empty, tearing a fabric long enough for him to escape.*

The words hang heavy in the air, each one carrying more weight than the last. Quinn Veyrik isn't just any being—he's a force. A force capable of bending reality itself, warping the very fabric of existence. If anyone can get me to Layla, it's going to be him. But I can't help but to let my mind wander to the nightmare bedtime stories about him we were told about when we were kids.

I glance at Drepane's glowing purple aura, the only source of light in this suffocating void. The soft violet light casts an eerie glow on the jagged contours of the cavern, enough to make out the edges of the nothingness around us. But it doesn't bring comfort. It only highlights the darkness closing in on us.

How do I find them? The question leaves me quietly, the urgency burning behind it. I don't have time to waste. Every second is another moment I'm not with Layla. Every moment she's exposed to whatever horrors are lurking in the Empty—*I can't afford it.*

Ask Ashton, Drepane's voice strains, vibrating with effort. *I can't hold this much longer, Azrael. My apologies. I have to protect the young one.*

The words strike me like a blow. My chest tightens, a heavy pressure bearing down on me. I don't want to leave Layla, not when she's so fragile, so vulnerable. But Drepane's voice is unwavering, firm. *I can't protect her from here much longer.* The reminder is like ice to my veins.

I nod, the motion sharp and slow, acknowledging what I must do. I hate it—*hate it*—but there's no other choice. The anger builds within me, hot and savage. Anger at the powers that keep pulling us apart. Anger at the endless obstacles between her and me. But I push it down. I don't have the luxury of letting it consume me.

Without warning, the pull comes.

It rips me away from Layla, from the Empty, with a violent tug. It's unlike traveling through realms—there's no sense of balance, no ease. It feels as if my very soul is being wrenched from its place, my body cracking and splintering under the strain. My bones ache in protest, my joints scream, but I can't fight it. I can't hold on. My breath is ripped from me, and every instinct in my body tells me that this is wrong—that I shouldn't leave her.

But I can't stop it.

Then, with a sudden jolt, the world solidifies around me. The disorienting, violent pull releases its grip, and the familiar sight of my room comes into sharp focus. The walls are the same. The bed, the shadows—*but it doesn't feel like home without her here.*

I stagger, disoriented by the shift, my body aching from the strain. My chest feels hollow—tight with the absence of Layla. The familiar surroundings do nothing to ease the suffocating pressure building within me. The room is too quiet. Too empty. I almost can't breathe without her beside me.

I grip the edge of the bed, steadying myself, my mind racing with thoughts of where to go, how to find Saygin and Quinn, how to get back to Layla. But no matter how fast I move, I know it won't be fast enough. *Time is against me.*

CHAPTER TEN

Ashton

KILLER QUEEN - QUEEN

"That's a name I haven't heard in a while," I mumble, mostly to myself.

"So, you know her?" Azrael asks, his voice laced with curiosity.

I let out a hollow laugh, the sound carrying more weight than I intend. Part of me wants to keep my experiences with Saygin buried deep. But there's no hiding from Azrael—he's seen too much of me for that. It's Sadie, though. It's the way her eyes are fixed on me like a hawk, that makes my stomach tighten. I shuffle a pile of books from my desk, pretending to focus on something else.

"I know her very well," I finally admit, the words escaping like air from a balloon with a slow hiss. As I slide the books back on the shelf, I do it a bit too roughly, the thud echoing in the silence.

"How? Do you think she will help me? Where can I find her?" Azrael presses, leaning forward with that intensity I've come to expect.

I pause, my mind racing, wondering how much to say. He's not ready for this. No one is. And honestly? I'm not ready for the conversation with Sadie that's about to follow. I shift uncomfortably, hoping I can delay the inevitable. "Is there anyone else we can look for?" I ask, trying to steer us away from Saygin's name.

Azrael's jaw tightens, and his desperation seeps into his tone. "Drepane specifically asked for Saygin and her mate, Quinn Veyrik."

The weight of his plea presses on me like a stone in my chest. Shit. I can't avoid this any longer. "Orcus, you familiar with her?" I ask, looking for a quick escape, praying my old friend will take the conversation in a different direction.

"No," Orcus replies flatly, the word hanging in the air like a challenge. "I'm not familiar with Saygin."

Well, damn.

I rub my temples, a dull headache already forming. "Saygin is a fae-god hybrid. She's Hecate's pet project—her pride and joy, but, uh, let's just say she's not exactly a *normal* being. Not that anyone really is around here." I pause, eyeing Sadie out of the corner of my eye, hoping she won't say anything. "She's much older than us, Azrael, but she has... *quirks.*"

Sadie's eyes narrow, her curiosity now visibly piqued, but she doesn't interrupt.

I exhale slowly, trying to brace myself. "Saygin doesn't do favors. She doesn't help people out of the goodness of her heart. Oh no. She has... barters. And they're not exactly *simple* ones."

Sadie's expression shifts from interest to full-on skepticism. "Barters? What does that even mean?"

I glance at Sadie, the words choking in my throat. "She doesn't do anything for free. She asks for something in return—usually something very... strange."

Azrael's facial expression changes, the tension creeping into his voice. "What do you mean by 'strange'?"

I sigh, closing my eyes for a moment, preparing for the inevitable fallout. "Sounding," I say, my voice low.

There's a brief, painful silence before Azrael and Sadie speak in perfect unison: "Sounding?"

Sadie's eyes widen. "What's that?"

"Oh, fuck me." I slump in my chair, my face burning. This isn't how I wanted this to go. Not even close. "It's... a sexual act." I cringe, trying to make myself invisible in the chair.

Sadie's jaw drops. "Wait, what? A *sexual act*?" Her voice cracks slightly with disbelief.

"Yeah," I mutter, bracing myself for the worst. "It involves... sticking objects into a guy's... yeah. You get it, right?"

Sadie bursts into an explosion of laughter, practically falling out of her chair. Her laugh echoes off the walls like a sugar-high hyena. "I need to know *more!*" she gasps between fits of laughter, clutching her stomach.

Azrael stares at me, his eyes wide, a mixture of disbelief and concern brewing in his expression. "How did you get tangled up with someone like that?"

"Better question," Orcus cuts in, voice as dry as ever. "How do you know what 'sounding' is?"

I swipe a random notebook from my desk, flipping through the pages with exaggerated care, pretending to be absorbed and busy. "My suggestion?" I murmur, trying to steer us back on course. "Bring Luca with you."

A pause. And then Orcus' voice, deadpan as always: "We are not sacrificing the wolf's dick to save Layla... are we?"

Azrael freezes, his expression turning from confused to horrified. "Wait." His voice cuts through the tension like a knife. "Are you seriously suggesting we *involve* Luca in this?"

"Hell yeah, we will!" Sadie's voice rings out from the hallway like a battle cry. The door slams open as she jumps up with unrestrained excitement. "Luca!" she screams down the hall, her voice full of urgency and glee.

"Poor wolfy," Orcus adds, clearly amused, as if he's watching a theater show.

Sadie's cackling laughter rings out from down the hall. "Poor Luca," she mocks, her voice shifting into exaggerated sympathy. "But hey, it's for Layla, right?"

Azrael crosses his arms, his expression hardening, but his voice is laced with disbelief. "You're not seriously suggesting that *we* use... that, to help Layla?"

"Hell yeah!" Sadie responds without hesitation, her tone dripping with mischief and enthusiasm.

"Sadie, this is insane." Azrael rubs his boney forehead, his voice edged with a level of frustration that could trigger an earthquake.

I lean back in my chair, looking at him with a crooked smile. "Look, man, sometimes desperate times call for desperate measures. And if you want to save her, *maybe* this is one of the strange methods that *might* work." I glance at Azrael. "I'm sure you'd understand better than anyone."

Azrael runs a hand across his skull, looking like he might lose his mind. "I don't know if I'm ready for this."

I smirk, leaning back in my chair. "Well, I guess we're both in the same boat then, aren't we?"

Sadie's voice echoes from the hallway once again, followed by the sound of hurried footsteps, Luca's muffled groan filtering through the door. "Luca!" she yells again, her voice filled with a disturbing mix of excitement and anticipation.

I look over at Orcus, who's clearly getting a kick out of all this. "What do you think?"

Orcus' voice is raspy but tinged with a grin. "Might as well. If nothing else, it'll make one hell of a story."

"Right," I deadpan, glancing back at him. Because that's what this is. A *fucking* story.

But underneath the sarcasm, there's a reality sinking in. This isn't funny anymore. Not one bit.

Suddenly, the door to the hallway swings open with a creak, and Luca walks in, his face a mixture of confusion and annoyance. "What the hell is going on here?" he asks, his gaze jumping from Sadie to Azrael and then to me, like he's just walked into the middle of a circus.

I step forward, nodding. "We need your help."

Luca raises an eyebrow, clearly already bracing for the weirdness that's about to unfold. "What kind of help?"

Sadie flashes a grin so wide it could light up the room. "Oh, don't worry. It's nothing you can't handle."

Luca deadpans, looking thoroughly unimpressed. "Like?"

"We're hungry, Luca. Are you hungry? We're *starving*." Sadie strikes a pose, crossing her arms over her chest, giving the full 'please, have pity on us' act.

I raise an eyebrow, watching her. The theatrics are so over-the-top, I almost expect a dramatic sigh to follow. Still, it's got *potential*—I mean, it might actually work edging Luca into the topic.

"Wait, so you're telling me…" Luca pauses, his expression flat, "You only called me in here because you want me to cook for you?"

Sadie's grin stretches wider. "Yes! That's exactly what we need right now! We're absolutely famished!"

Luca stares at her, his head tilting like she's just sprouted a second head. "You're really serious about this? This is what you called me in for?"

"Luca," Sadie says, her voice deadpan and almost accusatory. "Do we ever joke about food?"

Luca doesn't even flinch. "I don't know, Sadie, you joke about a lot of things." He glances at her, then back at Azrael and me like he's considering whether he's fallen into some strange nightmare.

Sadie doesn't miss a beat, practically bouncing on her heels. "Come on, you know you're the best cook. I mean, who else could make something that actually tastes good in this place?"

Azrael shoots me a glance from across the room, and I can see a smile threatening to break through the serious mask he's trying to keep. "She's got you there," he says, barely suppressing the grin. "I can't even remember the last time I cooked anything worth savoring."

Luca looks from Sadie to Azrael, his shoulders sagging in defeat. "Fine. Fine, I'll make something." He holds up a hand, like he's surrendering, before giving

Sadie an exaggerated sigh. "But if I end up making something that's somehow *even worse* than whatever disaster this place calls 'food' because I am now under pressure, I am blaming you."

Sadie winks, grinning like she just won a small victory. "Deal. And trust me, you'll get extra gratitude... in the form of a free pass on all future weird requests."

Luca groans and shakes his head, muttering under his breath as he starts to head back out. "I should've known better than to walk into this place. You guys are all insane."

Sadie watches him go, clearly pleased with herself. "You hear that? He's *volunteering.*"

Azrael chuckles under his breath. "At this point, I'm starting to wonder if *I* should start cooking. Maybe I'll be the one who would have the free pass from all weird requests in the future."

I lean back in my chair, smirking. "Yeah, good luck with that."

Sadie bounces again, clearly already planning her next round of chaos. "Oh, I'm definitely gonna put that to the test."

CHAPTER ELEVEN

Azrael

I SEE RED - EVERYONE LOVES AN OUTLAW

I stare at Luca, gnawing on a piece of toast like it's the most normal thing in the world. He's sitting there, content as hell, going on about how good his food tastes. And here I am, trying to drown the panic rising in my chest like it's some kind of race against time. I should be happy, right? He's enjoying the meal he made for us, for me. Yet, all I can focus on is the quiet churning in my gut. He's completely oblivious to everything—the plan we're setting into motion, the risk he's about to take. All he sees is a hearty breakfast and casual conversation.

And now, I'm going to just fucking use him.

For my mate.

The guilt claws at me from the inside, gnawing away.

Ask him, Azrael, Orcus chimes in, his voice an infuriating echo in my mind. I can almost hear the sarcasm dripping off every word.

Why can't you fucking ask him? I growl back, not caring that I'm essentially arguing with a weapon.

I'm an 'insufferable piece of metal,' Orcus reminds me, his voice smooth as glass, though the amusement in it is clear. *Merely a tool.*

Ah, now you want to state the obvious, I mutter, rolling my eyes. The conversation feels like it's going in circles—endless loops that I can't seem to escape. I've been holding on to this for a short amount of time, making it feel like a fucking eternity, and yet I can't bring myself to say the words.

I turn my attention back to Luca, who's casually spreading jam on his toast, blissfully unaware of the storm I'm weathering internally. I try to focus on him, but it's hard when all I can think about is how I'm about to drag him into this mess. He doesn't deserve this.

"Are you okay, Az?" Luca's voice is gentle but probing, like he's trying to peel back layers that I'm not ready to let anyone touch.

I meet his gaze, trying to offer some semblance of normalcy, even though I feel anything but that. I rub the back of my neck, hoping the movement will ground me somehow. "I'm fine. How are you?" The words feel forced, like I'm trying to convince myself more than him.

Luca hesitates, his gaze sharpening as he watches me. I can tell he sees right through the mask I'm wearing, and I can't help but admire the hell out of him for it. "I'm... good," he says slowly, then looks away, his thoughts clearly gathering. "Today's the first time since..." He stops himself, his voice dropping. "It's nice of you to finally join us at the table and actually... talk. It almost feels like family again."

The words hang in the air like they have weight—like they've got a gravity all of their own. The emphasis on "almost" stings in a way I wasn't prepared for. It's a reminder that I've been distant, that I've pushed everyone away while I've been consumed by my own struggle.

I never stopped to think about how everyone else might feel. How they've been dealing with Layla's absence. How they've been left to pick up the pieces I've scattered. I've been so focused on getting her back that I forgot about them—about their emotions and guilt.

Luca's right. I've been distant. Detached. So caught up in my own suffering that I failed to notice the cracks in the beings who care about me. The silence stretches between us, and it feels suffocating. Family—the word hits me like a punch to the gut. It burns. It stings. It's a reminder of everything I've taken for granted—the laughter, the connection, the fleeting moments of peace that I let slip through my fingers. All shattered the moment Layla was taken.

"I... didn't realize how much I've pulled away," I finally admit, the words tasting foreign as they leave my mouth. A part of me wants to pull them back in, but I can't. I have to own it.

Luca gives me a small nod, his eyes soft with understanding. But I can see it—the glint of suspicion in his gaze. He's waiting. Waiting for the real reason I've been acting so weird at the dinner table, waiting for the truth to spill. He knows I'm hiding something, and damn it, I can't lie to him. Not now.

Poor sweet Luca. Orcus' voice vibrates in my mind, a constant reminder of the weight of my decisions. *Fucking ask him!*

I swallow hard, trying to brace myself for what comes next. "I have a lead to find Layla," I murmur, barely above a whisper, like saying it out loud will somehow make the truth worse.

Luca's eyes widen, a flicker of hope sparking in them. "Yeah?" His voice is soft, like he's afraid to let himself believe it.

"Yeah..." My voice falters as I try to push through the wave of guilt. "I have to find a fae goddess named Saygin."

Luca, ever the optimist, takes a sip of his coffee, nodding like he's taking everything in stride. "Saygin?" He pauses for a second, then continues, his voice light and almost playful. "That's actually a really *pretty* name."

I can't help but chuckle at his attempt to find the silver lining in all of this. "Yeah, pretty name. Pretty much *nothing* like a pleasant conversation, though."

Luca raises an eyebrow but doesn't press further. Instead, he takes another bite of toast, his tone casual, like we're just two guys talking over breakfast.

"Fae goddess, huh? Sounds... interesting. I'm guessing it's not as simple as asking for directions?" He grins, and for a second, it almost feels like everything's okay again. *Almost.*

"Yeah, something like that." I can't help but smirk back, even though the weight of everything still hangs over us.

Luca leans back in his chair, giving me a wry smile. "You're always full of surprises, Az. But hey, if anyone can make a fae goddess give you what you need, it's probably you."

I chuckle dryly, but the laugh doesn't quite reach my hollow eyes. "If only it were that easy."

I can't stop myself from letting out a short, exasperated sigh. "Would you like to come along?" I finally ask, the question hanging in the air like a heavy weight.

Luca's eyes widen, and he chokes on his bite of eggs, his face contorting in disbelief. "You didn't trust me to fight in the war but trust me enough to accompany you to find a fae goddess that will help us get Layla back?" His voice cracks with frustration, the words dripping with every ounce of disbelief he feels.

"It wasn't about trust, and you know that, Luca!" My frustration builds, but I try to keep it in check, though the words are barely controlled. "Look around us. Do you see any other werewolves?"

Luca's jaw clenches, his eyes narrowing as anger rises in him. "But you wouldn't give me a chance! You took the choice from me!" His voice grows louder, the raw emotion spilling over. I hear the hurt in his words, and it stings—more than I want to admit. It wasn't just about the war. It was about me leaving him behind, making decisions for him without considering his own will.

Before I can respond, the dining room door slams open, and Vassago strides in like he owns the place. His presence fills the room—heavy, undeniable. He doesn't look like he's just returned; his hair is a mess, disheveled as if he'd just woken up from a nap.

Don't do it, Azrael, Orcus warns, his voice low and cautious, but I can't ignore the timing. I just can't.

"Vassago." I smirk, trying to mask the tension, the unease building in my chest. "Wanna go on an adventure?"

Vassago's footsteps echo as he moves across the room, the sound clashing with the clinking of plates and silverware. He doesn't immediately look at me, but I can feel the weight of his gaze sharpening. "Depends. What do you have in mind?"

I say calmly. "I need to find a being named Saygin." His body pauses mid-motion.

His movement falters for a second, and then he slowly turns to face me, his expression unreadable, like a mask hiding something beneath. "Hecate's granddaughter?"

"Yeah..." I say, my voice tight, not sure what to expect next.

"If you knew what most of us knew," Vassago begins, his voice a low murmur, "you might reconsider."

I meet his gaze head-on, refusing to back down. "If you won't go..." I pause, my voice tightening, "I'll have to bring Luca with me."

Vassago chokes on his coffee, clearly caught off guard by my bluntness. "Don't you know her *bartering* system?" he asks, wiping coffee from his lips with the back of his hand, all nonchalance.

Luca, who's been watching the exchange unfold with growing confusion, turns to Vassago. "What do you mean?" he asks, unaware of the dangerous territory we're venturing into.

Vassago, quick to recover, leans in toward Luca as if he's about to share a deep, dark secret. "Saygin is—"

"A wonderful fae female of the Underworld," I interrupt sharply, cutting him off before he can get too far into his explanation.

The tension in the room thickens, becoming almost suffocating. I wasn't expecting Vassago to know Saygin—hell, I wasn't expecting *anyone* to know her. And now I'm left wondering: How does he know her? How does Ashton know her? And why does it feel like everyone, but Luca and I, are aware of the minefield we're about to walk into?

Luca looks between the two of us, his expression shifting from confusion to suspicion. "You're all acting like I'm missing something," he says, his voice quiet but edged with growing concern. "What's really going on here? What's so dangerous about this Saygin?"

"Saygin is a powerful necromancer," Vassago explains casually, cutting his eggs with precision, "surpassing even her grandmother. But..." He pauses, taking a bite as though it's just another normal conversation. "Saygin loves to feel like she has control over powerful males who ask her for help."

Luca, clearly hooked now, doesn't miss a beat. "What kind of help?" he asks, not pausing to chew as his eyes flick between Vassago and me, genuinely intrigued.

Vassago picks up his fork again, taking a leisurely bite, looking at Luca like he's about to drop some juicy gossip. "Let's just say..." He lowers his voice, leaning in closer. "Saygin's mate doesn't ask her for *anything*. Not even to wash a dish. It's something she calls sounding."

Luca blinks, his confusion morphing into something deeper. "What does she do? What is sounding?" His voice drops, a mix of curiosity and hesitation.

Vassago leans in slightly, lowering his voice even further, making sure no one else hears the next part. "You've lived in the mortal realm your whole life, right?" he asks, his gaze sharp as he sizes Luca up. "What is it they say all the time? Ask *Google*." Vassago grins like he's about to deliver the punchline of a joke.

Luca freezes, his eyes going wide. "I don't have phone reception, and Google doesn't exist here! The closest thing we have to Google is *Orcus*." He turns to my scythe, which is resting on the table, dark and silent, not even glowing. "Hey, Orcus, care to give us a lesson?"

Orcus doesn't respond. As usual, he's completely uninterested in offering any help or humor, leaving the air heavy with awkwardness. I swear, sometimes

I think he's just biding his time, waiting for us to get ourselves into these ridiculous situations.

Vassago chuckles, clearly amused by Luca's frustration. "Good luck with that, kid. Orcus doesn't exactly do 'helpful,' does he?" he says with a smirk.

I feel my face flush with embarrassment, and for once, I'm oddly grateful that Orcus stays silent. The last thing I need is him making a snide comment about the situation.

"So, what's the deal with this... mate of Saygin's?" Luca asks, still clearly trying to piece together the bizarre conversation. "Is he like kidnapped or something?"

Vassago's smile turns predatory as he leans in closer. "Let's just say the things Saygin likes to do with her mate aren't exactly... traditional. Not to mention Quinn is more terrifying than he looks." He lowers his voice, his tone dropping to something almost conspiratorial. "I think the less you know about her bartering system, the better."

Luca looks utterly taken aback, his face filled with confusion and a growing sense of wariness. "And I'm supposed to help with all of this? What do you guys need me to do?"

At this point, Ashton, who has been sitting in the corner, completely silent up until now, can't help himself. "Wait, wait, wait." He leans forward, raising a hand like he's about to make an important announcement. "Did we just skip over the fact that you're all talking about Saygin *like she's some casual acquaintance*?" He glances around the table, incredulous. "Are we seriously just *casually* talking about a fae goddess who probably has the most dangerous 'bartering system' you could imagine? I don't know about you, but that sounds like a one-way ticket to a very *messed-up* place."

Sadie, who's been quietly watching the entire scene unfold, suddenly pipes up with a grin, leaning in toward Luca. "Don't worry, Lu. The only thing more messed up than this conversation is what Saygin does for fun. Trust me, we'll figure it out. We're professionals, right?" She winks at Vassago, who rolls his eyes, clearly unimpressed with her sarcasm.

Luca looks between all of us, his face growing more skeptical by the second. "Professionals? If this is what being a 'professional' looks like, I might just retire early." He leans back in his chair, arms crossed, eyes narrowed. "So, we're just gonna waltz into this fae's home and hope this all works out?"

"Pretty much," Vassago says, shrugging like it's the simplest thing in the world. "But, hey, if you're not up for it, I can always just let Az take the fall. He's good at falling on his face."

I smirk, trying to ease the tension, but inside, I'm already bracing for what comes next. We're about towalking into Saygin's home and unconventional ways.

Chapter Twelve

Azrael

Seven Nation Army - White Stripes

The banter flows easily between the three of us, a welcome distraction from the ever-present ache of Layla's absence. I try not to let my focus slip from the task at hand, but every now and then, I can't help but catch myself thinking about her—her laughter, her smile, the way she always had something snarky to say, even when she was scared. It all feels like a distant dream now.

Luca, kicking stones with the exaggerated dramatic flair that's somehow become his trademark, groans again. "I don't know how you got me into this mess. What if she kills me?"

"Hey, what did I promise you?" I say, trying to ease the tension, my voice light. "Ashton's with us. You're not alone in this. You've got moral support."

Ashton rubs his eyes with the dramatic flair of someone who's been awake for far too long. "Yeah, and Sadie thinks this whole thing is hilarious, by the way."

Luca gives him a deadpan look. "And that's supposed to comfort me?"

"I'm here for moral support," Ashton chimes in, his voice so dry it could probably crack a window. "If Saygin decides to rip you to shreds, at least you'll get a killer workout."

Luca narrows his eyes at him. "What if she decides to *sound* me? Do I get a discount on the service?"

Ashton doesn't even miss a beat, grinning wickedly. "Discount? No, no, my friend. That's a premium service. You're looking at a whole other price range."

I snicker, throwing an arm around Luca's shoulders like we're best friends in some kind of twisted buddy cop movie. "Hey, at least it's a once-in-a-lifetime experience, right?"

Luca glares at me, eyes narrowing with that 'I'm plotting your death' look I've come to know well. "Yeah, I'm really not sure I want to experience that once-in-a-lifetime thing. Ever."

"Oh, don't worry," Ashton quips. "I heard the whole 'sounding' thing doesn't come with a satisfaction guarantee."

"Great," Luca mutters. "So, I might just leave with PTSD instead of a full refund."

I laugh, shaking my head.

"If she decides to sound the Sandman, would Sadie feel it?" Luca asks suddenly, his voice laced with genuine concern.

I stop mid-step, the question hitting me like a truck. Ashton and I both pause as if we've been hit with the same realization.

"How annoying has Sadie been lately?" I joke, glancing sideways at Ashton to gauge his reaction.

Ashton's deadpan look says everything. "I'm not doing that shit again with Saygin," he mutters, shaking his head.

I throw my hands up, pretending to be shocked. "I knew she did that to you! How could you not tell me?"

"Yeah, well, it wasn't exactly something I was going to bring up over lunch," Ashton sighs, his face darkening as if remembering something unpleasant. "My first mission after you got your permanent Grim role was in Africa. Some mortals decided to dabble with dark magic, and they brought back the dead. My father sent me to ask Saygin for help." He gives a low, humorless laugh. "She wasn't exactly a pleasure to deal with. Not a nice female."

Luca, ever the optimist, laughs nervously. "But Africa is good now, right?" He snickers harder. "We should have gotten Exu to handle this for us. He would probably know how to make Saygin behave."

Ashton raises an eyebrow. "Exu? He dated Saygin."

Luca's eyes widen in shock. "Oh. Well, that explains so much. No wonder he always looks like he's got a stick up his ass."

I can't help but laugh. "There's more to Exu than meets the eye."

Luca gives a playful smile.

Orcus' voice rings out, humming with amusement and a note of warning. "Well, I'm telling Exu when we get back. I'm sure Exu will appreciate that heavy reminder, Luca. You said you wanted to start training, didn't you?"

Luca shoots Orcus a skeptical look. "Bro. Don't."

Ashton glances at Luca with a wry grin. "Yeah, maybe that's not the best idea."

Luca, growing increasingly frustrated, runs a hand through his hair. "I think I'm about to lose my appetite," he mutters.

"Speaking of which," Ashton continues, his grin turning wicked. "How's the chef situation, Luca? Think you'll be able to cook something up for us after we survive this Saygin experience?"

Luca shoots him a sideways glance, clearly unamused. "I think after this, my cooking career's on *indefinite* hiatus."

The banter continues as we walk, our words an easy distraction from the weight of the journey ahead. But even amidst the jokes and laughter, I can feel it—the deep emptiness left by Layla's absence. She should be here with us, teasing me, her laugh a sharp contrast to the silence around me. But she's not, and it's up to me to bring her back.

Luca's expression shifts, suddenly serious. "By the way," he says, his voice quieter, "I didn't know Exu dated Saygin. How did that happen?"

Ashton snorts, clearly amused. "Complicated, my friend. Exu and Saygin's relationship? Complicated. They've got a history. Trust me. But Exu's the only one who could handle her special brand of crazy."

"I wouldn't call it crazy," I interject, trying to keep things light. "Maybe 'eccentric' is a better word. Or 'dangerous.'"

Luca's grin returns, a playful gleam in his eye. "Dangerous? Please. How bad could she be? Worst case, she turns me into a toad or something. Could be worse, right?"

"Oh, it could be worse," I agree, nodding. "Like getting turned into a bug, then eaten by a bird. That'd be a fun way to go."

Luca shudders. "Okay, okay. I'll take the toad. They're spicier."

"Good choice," I say, rolling my eyes, though I can't help but smirk. "Just hope she doesn't slap you around with a couple of thousand-year-old curses. You might be stuck with a bad hair day for a century."

Ashton chuckles. "A bad hair day sounds like a fate worse than death."

"I wouldn't be so sure," Luca replies, his tone dripping with mock seriousness. "There's something humiliating about being a toad. Even a bug could look better than some of the choices we're making here."

We all burst into laughter, the sound of it filling the air.

For a moment, I let myself forget the weight on my shoulders and just enjoy the camaraderie. The ache from Layla's absence is still there, but it's easier to bear with these guys around.

I won't let it drag me down. Not now, not when we're so close to finding her.

I push forward, my heart pounding with the weight of the journey, but a fire is starting to burn in my chest. One step closer to Layla.

One step closer to proving to her that I've changed—that I'm the male she deserves, the male who will never fail her again.

The thought drives me, though the path ahead is still shrouded in uncertainty. I've walked through darkness before, but this time, it feels different. This time, the stakes are higher. This time, I won't let her slip away.

Luca's silence breaks, his voice a little more serious than usual. "So... this Saygin. She's the real deal, right? There has to be more to her than just being a really fucking scary lady, right?"

Ashton glances over at him, letting the weight of the situation settle in. "Yeah. She's one of the most powerful beings in the Underworld. But she's not just *some* fae goddess. If we want her help, we're gonna have to play by her rules."

I tap my chin thoughtfully, my usual nonchalance replaced with a rare seriousness.

Luca whispers "And her rules are a bit... unconventional."

A bitter chuckle escapes me. "Unconventional doesn't even begin to cover it." The thought of her makes my skin crawl. Saygin isn't someone you deal with lightly, apparently. But we have no choice. If she's the key to finding Layla, then I'll do whatever it takes.

Luca glances between Ashton and me, his eyebrows raised in disbelief. "So, what's the plan here? We just walk in, say 'hi,' and hope she'll give us some help? Or is this more of a 'come prepared to beg for mercy' kind of deal?"

I stop walking, pivoting to face him, my tone more serious now. "More like 'bring your best bargaining chip and pray it's enough.' But if you prefer to beg for mercy, go for it."

Luca mutters something under his breath, his face shifting between apprehension and amusement. But the grin he can't suppress says it all. "This is either going to be the worst decision of my life or the *weirdest* adventure I've ever been on. Layla better be thankful she's like my best friend and I fucking love her."

I shrug with a knowing look, but the weight of the truth settles on my shoulders. "You're not wrong." It's a weird kind of adventure, but we don't have a choice. We're walking into the unknown, each step bringing us closer to the heart of the Underworld—and to Layla. And no matter what happens, I won't let her down again.

CHAPTER THIRTEEN

Ashton

LOVE IS MADNESS - THIRTY SECONDS TO MARS FT HALSEY

The guys have been joking the entire walk, keeping the mood light despite the heavy air around us. It's clear that Azrael's trying to push the weight of the situation aside with humor, but let's be honest—I'm pretty sure he's avoiding the inevitable. He's fooling no one, especially not me. He's walking into Saygin's realm in his true form, as if that's going to somehow make this less... *dangerous.*

Dickless asshole.

Sadie's voice rings through my head, a snarky whisper that feels like she's right beside me, even though I know she's back at home. *If I didn't know any better, I'd think you were in love with Azrael.*

I chuckle to myself, shaking my head as I shoot a glance at the two of them. *He's my brother. He's the only being I can trust with my life.*

Oh, saying a lot, since your best friend trusted him with hers and now she's dead, she retorts, her words sharp and biting. It's her usual sarcasm, but it still stings more than I'd like to admit.

For a moment, I freeze, her words landing a little harder than they should. *She's not dead,* I say, my voice tight as I force the emotion down.

Sadie doesn't let up. *She also is not here for me to have our normal girl talk with... is she?* she adds, clearly enjoying the chance to get under my skin.

I roll my eyes and shake my head. *I'll be home as soon as I can, and I promise, if you don't behave, you'll* regret *it.*

I can almost feel her playful smirk through the bond, like she's teasing me from across a room. *Sandy sir, is that a threat for a good time? Or are you going to let me down?*

Her words make the heat creep up to my face, and I can't help but grin despite myself. *You won't be able to walk for days,* I growl, trying to stay serious, but failing miserably.

She purrs back, her voice dripping with amusement. *Make it weeks, and I will be a pro brat.* I can practically hear her laughing on the other side of the connection, knowing she's pushing my buttons as usual.

I roll my eyes, but it's hard to suppress a smile. *You're impossible.*

The connection with Sadie lingers in the back of my mind, a constant, playful reminder of her presence. She's always there, even when I'm trying to focus on something else. Right now, it's the task at hand—getting through this with Saygin and keeping things together. I can't afford to be distracted by her teasing.

But then she hits me with another one. *Also, Sandman, lowkey hope you get volunteered as tribute for the sounding. Truly think I might take a page out of Saygin's book.*

I almost trip over my own feet at the thought. The very idea of it is enough to make my stomach turn, but I fight back the laugh that wants to escape. *You do realize you'll feel it too, right?* I respond, trying to keep my composure.

Her response is instantaneous, full of mischief. *What's immortality if I don't try everything at least once?*

I roll my eyes again, my lips twitching in a grin I can't hide. *I'm not volunteering for anything. You can forget about it.*

But even as I say it, I can feel the discomfort creeping in—the kind that comes from her being so persistent. Her boldness is like a fire I can't quite escape from, no matter how hard I try. I try to focus on the group, on the task ahead, but she's always there, just a thought away.

And right now, I really need to focus. Because getting through Saygin's bargain—and keeping everyone in one piece—is no laughing matter.

But for fuck's sake, why does Sadie have this effect on me?

Never in my life have I experienced something like this. A boner around a group of guys? Really? The thought alone is enough to make me shift uncomfortably. I silently reposition my pants, trying to make room for the ridiculous reaction she's causing. Fucking hell.

Fuck you, I shoot back through the bond, trying to keep my cool.

Her response is instant, smug as hell. *Empty promises. My ass better be red when you come home, and my pussy better be in so much pain I need an ice pack. If you can't promise that, keep the bond silent, bro.*

Goddamn it. The shit she says—it's like she's intentionally poking at every nerve I've spent a lifetime building around myself. She doesn't stop. She pushes and she challenges me. And that? That's something I've never allowed a female to do. Not once. I've always been the one in control, always held onto that dominance like it was part of my soul. My jealousy, my need to be the one in charge—it's always been a part of me. But Sadie? She's rewritten every damn rule I have had for myself.

And now, I can't help but let my mind wander. I remember the first night she arrived in the Underworld. Hell, I even remember before that, when I dragged both her and Layla here with the damn wolf. The image of Sadie in those ridiculous pink fluffy slippers, that tiny crop top barely containing her large, swollen tits—those things were practically suffocating in that shirt, by the way. I could feel my blood pressure rising the entire time.

Layla, being Layla, had to get her to change into one of her oversized t-shirts. Sadie wasn't thrilled, but she did it without a fuss. No questions asked. She even ditched the blue jean shorts that were barely long enough to cover her ass cheeks. I still remember the whine she let out when she had to do it.

She'd been ready to go to a party, and when I smelled her—sweet strawberries and cream—it was like a fantasy scent, one that knocked me out cold. It was so innocent, so fucking sweet, but the second I caught it, I knew there was no turning back. That scent is fucking etched in my brain.

Now? She smells like me. Like leather, musky and *bold*. But when she's aroused, it's like a damn switch flips, and that scent of strawberries hits me first. Every time she's near me, I get lost in it. My mind, my body—it all goes *hazy*.

When she locked eyes with me for the first time—those brown eyes full of fiery lust—I felt it, deep in my gut. Sparks. A fucking jolt to my core. I tried to mask it, tried to keep my calm, laid-back demeanor, but there's only so much you can hide. That moment, when she touched me after Layla threw something at me—I couldn't hold back anymore.

Her fingers brushed over my arm, so casual, but it felt like she was claiming me. And by the gods, that touch had been electric. I hadn't been able to suppress the urge to pull her closer, to feel more of her. She does this to me—makes me go crazy, even feral at times. Makes me forget about the walls I've spent so long building around myself. Crumbles them with just a look, a touch, a *fucking breath*.

Goddamn it, Sadie!

She's making me question everything—my control, my nature, my fucking self. The walls? Every time she speaks, they crumble just a little more. And I'm letting her. She's trying to tear me down, piece by piece, and I'm willingly letting her do it.

How the fuck did this happen?

When I got her to my room, I couldn't help myself—I devoured her. My body responded to hers like a fucking beast, and we didn't even take a water break before diving back in for round five. Then round six. Seven. Shit, it kept going—eight, nine, ten... what the fuck was wrong with us?

Eleven rounds.

Fuck.

We were like animals—no rest, no pause. Just pure need, hunger, maybe a little bit of madness. Every touch, every kiss, every movement felt like it wasn't enough, like I needed more. It was chaos, and I was losing myself in it.

But when it was all over, when I finally watched her sleep peacefully beside me, something inside me tightened. I let myself indulge in the rare sight of her, the vulnerability on her face—something she didn't often show. For a moment, I let myself feel it, feel *her*, as if the world outside this room didn't exist.

Then reality hit like a freight train, crashing through my mind.

Sadie was *mine*.

It wasn't just the physical attraction. It wasn't just the way my body had responded to hers in every single way. No, it went deeper. It ran *deeper*. Learning the bond she shared with Layla—seeing how she was woven into the fabric of my Queen's life—pushed me even further into solidifying whatever the hell this was between us. But it wasn't just that. It wasn't *solely* about *her*.

I was going to protect Sadie because her existence mattered. It mattered to Layla. She was a part of *her* world.

And by the gods, I fucking hated it.

I am regretfully an Underworld soldier, a weapon trained to protect the fucking Hierarchy. That is my life— it is my fucking duty. It ran through my veins, painfully, like a chain that tightened with every heartbeat. But when it came down to it, Sadie had slipped through the cracks of my control and found her place in my life, whether I was ready for it or not.

She wasn't just Layla's best friend; she was mine, too, even if I hadn't admitted it aloud. Even if the bond between *us* wasn't something I could fully make sense of just yet.

And for fucks sake, by the gods, I wanted her. I wanted her in a way that terrified me. Not because I feared losing control—no, I feared losing *her*. Because no matter how many walls I built, Sadie was starting to tear them down without even trying.

I'd sworn an oath to the Underworld, a life of duty and honor, but when it came to her, I felt like I might be willing to break it all...

For her.

And then, of course, dumbass's voice broke my train of thought:

"You knock," Azrael points to Luca, a smirk tugging at the corner of his mouth.

"Why do I have to knock when it is me you two are sacrificing to her for her sick pleasures?" Luca huffs, hands on his hips. "Ashton! You knock!"

I roll my eyes, but reality slaps me hard in the face. Without thinking, my hand instinctively rises and knocks on Saygin's door. Guilt and regret flood me, overtaking any shred of control I had left. My face heats up, and I quickly try to mask the embarrassment with a quick spell, but it's pointless. I'm pretty sure both Azrael and Luca see it anyway.

Luca snickers. "Look at you, Sandman, turning red like you just got caught with your hand in the cookie jar!"

"Shut up," I mutter, fighting the urge to smack him upside his head.

A few moments pass, the air thick with tension, before the only sound that follows is someone calling for help—panicked, like they've just realized they've been dragged into something they shouldn't have agreed to. The shuffling of feet comes closer. Then, with an exaggerated swing, the door creaks open, revealing *her*.

Standing in the doorway is a tall, scrawny woman with icy white hair, her fae ears pointed delicately at the tips. Her emerald eyes sparkle with something much darker than just curiosity—desire, maybe?

She grins widely, baring sharp fangs in a way that would make most mortal men break out in a cold sweat. "Ashton?" Her voice is sweet but tinged with something dangerously inviting. "Back so *soon*? Come in, come in! Quinn will be delighted to see you!"

I blink, caught off guard by the way she said that. Not exactly the warmest greeting, but it was certainly memorable.

Luca looks around like he's trying to figure out if he has any other options. "You sure we can't just throw a rock through the window and call it a day?"

I shake my head, even though the thought sounds appealing for about a second. "If we did that, I'd be the one stuck cleaning up the mess," I mutter, looking back at the doorway where Saygin stands, the smile never fading from her lips.

"Oh, don't be such a buzzkill," Luca continues, his eyes darting back and forth between the door and us. "I'll make it quick. Just a quick rock, maybe a scream, and then boom. Our problem is solved."

Azrael rolls his eyes. "You're an idiot, Luca. Now, get in there before Saygin gets bored and does something *way* worse."

With a deep sigh, Luca reluctantly takes a step forward. "Yeah, sure. But if I come back in pieces, I'm blaming you both."

"You're the one who signed up for this," I point out, offering him a smirk, even though I'm dreading what the hell we're about to walk into.

Saygin watches us with amused eyes, still smiling like she has all the power in the world. And maybe she does now. "Come in, come in, *boys*."

Luca looks over his shoulder at us, his face twisted with hesitation. "Right."

I just shake my head, muttering under my breath. "You're going to need a drink after this."

Sadie's voice suddenly rings through my mind like a sharp, teasing whisper: *I hope you survive the adventure, Sandman. But not too unscathed.*

My lips curl into a smirk despite myself. *Oh, I'm sure I'll be fine, Sadie,* I reply silently. *I've dealt with worse.*

A dark laugh echoes in my head as we finally step inside. Saygin's attention snaps back to us, and I can't shake the feeling that this is just the beginning of something much worse.

CHAPTER FOURTEEN

Azrael

PANIC ROOM - AU/RA

"How soon are we talking? I'm still trying to understand your lingo down here," Luca asked, scratching his chin like the phrase might physically materialize into something he could comprehend.

Saygin grinned, slow and sinister, the kind of grin that sent a cold shiver down my spine. "I'd say within the past forty years, maybe?"

Luca frowned. "That's... not recent at all."

I chuckled under my breath, looking at Luca. "That's probably because the Underworld doesn't run on your mortal timeline, Luca. Try '*lifetime*' instead of '*lately*.'" I turn away from Luca, facing Saygin. "He definitely hinted it's been around four hundred years since he's last seen you," I said, side-eyeing Ashton, who—despite being caught in a blatant lie—maintained his usual stone-cold, unbothered demeanor. Like he didn't just attempt to Jedi mind-trick the entire room.

"Oh, did he?" Saygin's smile widened, taking on a feline quality, like she'd caught a particularly entertaining mouse in her claws. "Goodness, no. I think

Ashton is just being bashful and embarrassed. He used to swing by regularly after he lost—"

"Okay," Ashton cut her off, his voice flat, but I caught the warning laced beneath it. "Azrael needs your help."

I arched a brow, not bothering to hide my suspicion. There was no way in the nine circles of hell this so-called friend of mine just enjoyed being around Saygin. He had to be bribed, blackmailed, or masochistic.

I glanced over at Luca, who was sweating bullets, using one hand to awkwardly groom his beard as if that might make him look less like someone rethinking every life choice that had led him here.

"Come in," Saygin said smoothly, stepping back to allow us entry. "Let's discuss."

We followed her inside, and the moment we crossed the threshold, I knew this was a mistake.

Males—some of them barely more than skin and bone—were chained to the walls, suspended from the ceiling, or strapped into horrifying contraptions that made Orcus hum in eerie recognition. Some of them begged us to run. Others screamed for help; voices raw, desperate.

Luca made a sound that was probably a whimper, though he tried to disguise it with a throat-clearing cough.

"Oh," Orcus mused loudly. "A lovely little house of horrors. Shall we stay for dinner? I imagine the appetizers scream."

Not helping, I thought, trying to mask the shudder crawling down my spine.

I kept my expression neutral, but my jaw clenched. "Cozy place you got here."

"Thank you," Saygin said, completely unfazed by my sarcasm. "I like to keep things... lively."

Luca leaned closer to me, voice barely above a whisper. "Is this a sex dungeon or a murder dungeon?"

Saygin turned her head slightly, as if she'd heard him, then winked. "Why not both?"

Luca went rigid. I could practically hear the gears turning in his mind, trying to process what exactly he'd just heard.

Ashton, entirely unaffected, moved forward into what could only be described as a grand living room—a stark contrast to the horror show of an entryway. A red velvet sectional dominated the space, rich and luxurious. The lighting here was dim but warm, as if Saygin had tried to make the torture den feel *homier...*

And there, sitting comfortably on the couch, watching television like he didn't have front-row seats to a symphony of suffering, was a male.

His black hair was thick and streaked with pink, combed back neatly. His skin was... peeling. Flesh curling away to expose his jawbone beneath. And his eyes—pitch black, abyssal voids—locked onto us with amusement.

Then, he grinned. A wide, delighted grin, like we were old friends dropping by for tea.

"Ah," Orcus said in my mind, his tone dry. "A rotting corpse that smiles. My favorite."

I said nothing.

The male, still grinning, gestured to the empty seats. "Make yourselves comfortable."

Luca visibly recoiled. "I'm good standing."

Orcus snickered. "Smart boy. Less chance of *ass-possessing* spirits that way."

I shot Luca a glance, trying to stifle a grin. "Yeah, don't take a seat. You might end up with more than just an uncomfortable conversation."

Luca's eyes flicked to the male on the couch, and he swallowed hard. "I'll stand with you, Azrael. If that's cool."

I wasn't sure whether to laugh or pity him. "You know, I've got to say—being a mortal being in the Underworld is the *best* way to keep you on your toes."

"Yeah, well, I think I'd prefer to be a *living* mortal being in the mortal world right about now." Luca's voice was tight, the humor long gone.

"Oh, don't be such a baby," I said, nudging him with my elbow. "I mean, look at him—he's just a big pile of skeleton at this point."

Saygin, clearly amused by our little back-and-forth, tapped her nails lightly on the armrest of her chair. "Enough with the pleasantries. You've come here for something, haven't you?"

Luca's eyes darted to her, then back to the male on the couch, then to me. "Yeah, but I'm starting to think *maybe* it's not worth it."

"Ah, Luca, always the pussy," Orcus says dryly. "Come on, get your head in the game. We're not here for a tea party."

He grimaced. "If this is what you consider a 'business meeting,' I don't want to know what you do for fun."

I raised an eyebrow. "You'd be surprised."

Ashton sighed, rubbing his temples. "Azrael, stop being dramatic and sit."

I crossed my arms. "I think I'll stand, too."

The corpse-male let out a chuckle, dark and guttural. "Suit yourselves. I imagine we have much to discuss."

Luca muttered under his breath, "Yeah, like how to not get murdered in a dungeon."

Orcus hummed. "Oh, I think it's far too late for that, pup."

Luca made a strangled noise of distress. I sighed. This was going to be a long conversation.

"You must be Quinn." I reached out, offering my hand.

Quinn took it, his grip deceptively firm. His fingers curled around my palm, nails dragging along my bones in a way that sent a subtle warning through my nerves.

It wasn't a greeting—it was a message.

"Hello, Azrael," he murmured, tilting his head slightly, those pitch-black eyes studying me like I was an amusing puzzle. "Would have never imagined having *royalty* in our home."

Then, as if we weren't surrounded by chains and screams, he stood with an easy grace and clapped his hands together. "Come! Come. Make yourself at home!" He patted the couch, like we were guests at a friendly dinner gathering instead of a living room of horrors. "How can we help you?"

Be careful, Azrael. He is fae-bonded. He knows their tricks. Make sure you properly word your requests. Orcus' voice slithered into my mind, his tone more serious than usual.

I'm aware, I muttered back.

I settled Orcus onto the couch beside me, resting him within reach. "We need help."

"With?" Quinn asked, settling back into his seat like this was a casual conversation.

"My mate is in the Empty. I would like to bring her back home."

Saygin scoffed, leaning forward with an unimpressed sneer. "Just get a new mate." Her dark gaze raked over me from head to toe, like I was something easily replaced. "Not worth the hassle."

A slow, familiar burn of anger ignited beneath my skin, curling in my joints like embers ready to blaze.

"She's my Fated Mate." My voice came out low, guttural, edged with a growl.

Saygin stilled. Her entire demeanor shifted, as if the weight of my words carried something she hadn't expected.

"I knew I felt a shift in the Hierarchy not long ago," she murmured, tapping her nails against the damn armrest. "A fairly new bond." Her sharp eyes flickered back to me, assessing. "So, Your *Majesty*, how exactly did you lose her?"

Bite your tongue, young Reaper. Orcus warned.

I inhaled sharply, forcing down my irritation. "Memetim planned a trap, and we fell for it," I admitted. "Drepane moved Layla to the Empty after Memetim attacked her. He was trying to protect her but ended up being trapped there, too."

Saygin let out a long, exaggerated sigh and dramatically dropped her face into her hands. "You lack critical thinking. Oh my! The Underworld is *doomed.*"

Orcus cackled. "Oh, I like her. Can we keep her?"

I resisted the urge to hurl him across the room.

"Drepane sent me," I pressed.

Saygin didn't lift her head. "An old friend," she muttered, fingers rubbing at her temples.

I gritted my teeth. "Are you going to help us or not?"

Quinn moved faster than I anticipated. Before I could react, cold steel pressed against my skull—a dagger, sharp enough that a single twitch would split the bone.

"Don't you *dare* throw attitude and shade to my mate," Quinn murmured, his voice devoid of warmth.

Luca let out a very undignified *squeak* behind me.

I barely moved, keeping my expression neutral. My fingers twitched toward Orcus. Not that I needed a weapon. But I could feel the scythe thrumming with anticipation, eager for a fight.

For a moment, the air in the room thickened, charged with tension. Luca fidgeted nervously beside me, but even his usual bravado faltered in the face of Quinn's lethal calm.

I could feel Quinn's eyes on me, cold as the blade at my neck.

"Do not mistake my hospitality for weakness, Azrael," he said, his voice like ice. "You'll show respect here, or you'll leave with far less than you came."

"Respect?" I scoffed, but I made sure my tone was carefully measured. "You're threatening me with a knife in the safety of your own home, and you expect respect?"

Quinn's grin widened, as if he'd anticipated my retort. "Respect isn't a gift, Reaper. It's *earned.*"

I met his eyes, my own gaze unyielding. "And you think I owe you that?"

"No," he replied, voice smooth as silk. "But you owe my mate."

Saygin's eyes glinted with mischief, but she remained silent, letting Quinn do the talking.

The air hung heavy between us, thick with unsaid words.

I leaned forward slightly, just enough to show that I wasn't backing down. "I didn't come here to argue. I came for help."

Quinn's hand relaxed, and the dagger lowered slightly, though the threat still lingered in the space between us. "Fine," he said with a drawl. "I'll help. But don't think this makes us friends. You get what you came for, and then you leave us be."

I nodded, feeling the tension begin to loosen, but my fingers remained close to Orcus, ready for anything. "Understood."

Luca exhaled loudly, stepping away from me as if he'd been holding his breath the entire time. "Well, that was fun. Can we get on with it now?"

Orcus snickered in my mind. "He has a way with words, doesn't he?"

"You're not helping either," I muttered.

Luca shot a glance at Saygin. "Is it too late to throw a rock through the window and call it a day?"

Saygin's lips curled into a smile. "You can try. I'd like to see you succeed."

Ashton, ever the peacekeeper, stepped forward with a sigh. "Apologies for my friends, Quinn." His tone was calm, as if this entire situation was normal.

Quinn hesitated for a second longer before lowering the blade some, turning around to view Ashton.

"Oh!" His expression brightened instantly, like a switch had flipped. "Ashton! You've returned!"

He turned toward Saygin with an excited grin, gesturing wildly. "Look, honey! It's Ashton!"

Saygin tilted her head shooting him an annoyed glare. "I can *see* him, Quinn."

Luca leaned toward me, whispering under his breath, "What the *fuck* is happening?"

Orcus chuckled darkly. "A very dangerous dinner party, pup. And we're the main course."

I exhaled sharply, my patience wearing very thin. "Can we get back to the part where you help us?"

Quinn released his deadly grip on me, his lips curling into an amused smirk as he sauntered toward Ashton. Without hesitation, he pulled him into an embrace, wrapping him up like they were long-lost brothers.

Ashton barely moved, his entire body going rigid.

"Can we ask," Luca spoke up, his voice teetering on the edge of hysteria, "why Ashton is treated like royalty here? And why he isn't a stranger?"

He looked like he was about two seconds away from a complete mental breakdown.

Quinn pulled back, resting an arm on Ashton's shoulder like he was some prized possession. "Ashton is very *dear* to our hearts." His voice took on a wistful lilt. "After his mission in Africa, he just... never left."

"Well, he did leave once," Saygin interjected, her tone sharp. She shot a pointed look at Ashton.

"He mated with a high-cheekboned hybrid fae female." She puffed, folding her arms across her chest. "Then forgot we existed."

"Can we not talk about this?" Ashton pleaded, his voice uncharacteristically small.

I stared at him, my mind whirling. Ashton had a mate? He never told me. Not once.

Saygin, of course, ignored his plea entirely. "What was her name, sweetheart?"

Ashton's jaw clenched.

Quinn grinned, the kind of grin that suggested he was enjoying this far too much. "Isolde. That was her name."

"Was?" Luca echoed, eyes darting between them. "What happened to her?"

Quinn made a sound of mock sympathy. "Oh, poor Izzy. Were you two living under a rock?" He gestured between me and Luca like we were clueless children. "Ashton murdered his own father for what happened to her."

Luca's face drained of color.

Saygin circled Ashton like a predator, her long fingers trailing across his chest, then moving lower to grip the edge of his robe. With a slow, deliberate motion, she peeled it off his shoulders. "Friends don't keep secrets from each other, Ash," she purred. "Why don't you tell them what your father did?"

Ashton's hands curled into fists at his sides.

"Because he thought Isolde wasn't worth your time?" Saygin pressed, tilting her head.

"Or do you prefer to ignore she ever existed?" Quinn's smirk deepened, his voice turning into something colder. "And the unborn son you lost with her?"

The room turned frigid.

Ashton flinched.

His breath hitched, and I saw it—the way his chest rose and fell a little too fast, the way his eyes turned glassy, swollen with something he refused to let spill over.

Quinn and Saygin were relishing in his suffering.

"*Enough!*" My voice boomed through the space, sharp and commanding. The walls seemed to vibrate with it, the tension snapping like a frayed wire. "Ashton has his reasons. No need to bring it up."

But the damage was already done.

I looked at him, really looked at him, and what I saw sent a crack through my ribs.

Ashton—the ever-calm, ever-unshaken Sandman—stood there, raw and exposed. He wasn't just upset.

He was *broken*.

And I had never imagined anything in this world could break him.

"She was passed around between his father and his comrades," Saygin continues, her voice a cruel melody. "Before being thrown into the prison for the males to finish her off."

A tear falls from Ashton's eye.

A single, fucking tear.

It glistens like a dying star, a fragile, fleeting thing, before disappearing against his pale skin.

"Ashton spent weeks searching for her," Saygin says, circling him like a vulture. "Feeling her pain. Hearing her screams. But he failed her, too." She smiles, slow and venomous. "The difference? When he finally found her, *he* had to be the *one* to give her a merciful death. I sure hope that won't be the case for *your* mate, Azrael."

Ashton's whole body tightens. His hands tremble at his sides.

"She was weeks away from birthing their first son," Saygin purrs, running her finger along his jawline. "But she was too far gone to be healed. She begged you, didn't she, darling Ash? To end her suffering?"

Ashton doesn't answer. He doesn't breathe.

Quinn tilts his head, watching Ashton with predatory amusement. "What was your son's name again?"

"Caelum." Saygin doesn't even hesitate, looking at her mate as if this is all a lovely conversation over tea. "Ashton was so distraught... he ran to us to keep his mind from remembering. Quinn and I showed him *so many* new tricks." She leans in, nipping at Ashton's ear.

"Enough!" I shoot to my feet, knocking into Saygin just hard enough to put space between her and Ashton. His head stays down, his face shadowed, his hands still shaking. "We don't need your help," I snap.

Saygin laughs, the sound full of honey and poison. "Oh, *sweetheart*," she croons. "You haven't been around many fae, *have you*?"

I grind my teeth.

"We're more twisted than the Grimm Court," she continues. "You're stuck here now until you give me what I *want*."

"I said we don't need your help. I'll find Layla on my own."

"Die trying, right?" Quinn muses, twirling a dagger between his fingers. "That's the thing about immortality. We aren't invincible. We can still be wounded. We still get sick. We can still be *murdered*." His smirk sharpens.

A cold weight settles in my stomach.

"Very thoughtful of you to bring me a wolf, by the way," Saygin muses, looking Luca up and down like he's a particularly appetizing meal. Luca stiffens. "But for something this extreme?" She clicks her tongue. "I need more than one male for payment."

I move before I can think, placing myself between her and Ashton, who hasn't spoken since Caelum's name was uttered. "Ashton is off-limits."

Saygin cackles. "Oh, honey. I've had his *dick* in my mouth so many times, the thought of him *undressed* bores me."

Quinn pouts, running a slow tongue over his bottom lip, the peeling skin quivering. "I can still taste him, though."

What.

The.

Fuck.

I feel Luca go rigid beside me. His sharp inhale is muffled, but not enough.

No judgment. I *won't* judge Ashton.

I refuse to.

"I don't have a dick, Saygin," I say, voice steady despite the chaos clawing in my skull. "I'm useless to you."

Saygin grins.

"Oh?" Quinn chuckles. "*Them eye holes work, boy.*"

Luca makes a strangled sound.

And for the first time since stepping foot in this gods-forsaken place, I feel the distant, *pulsing beat of fear.*

"How much do you love Layla?" Saygin purrs, her grin razor-sharp. "What would you do to bring her back home—so you can *kill* daddy and let your *whore* sit on the throne he wanted *Vassago* to have?"

Something inside me snaps.

Heat burns through my veins, searing from the inside out. The secluded channel of power I now keep buried, leaks—spilling through the cracks of my control.

Blue fire trickles down my right arm, consuming Orcus' red aura in a violent flash.

I move.

Before Saygin can react, I slam her against the wall, Orcus' handle pressed hard against her throat.

Quinn lunges toward me—

I don't even look at him before flicking a finger in his direction. He slams against the opposite wall with a strangled gasp.

"Don't you *dare* talk about your Queen like that, you *trashy bitch fae*." My voice is low, lethal. I lean in, inhaling the scent of burning flesh as my fire sizzles against her skin. "You will help me get Layla out of the Empty. And you will *not* touch *any* of us males."

Saygin laughs, but there's fear in her eyes now.

"Hades was hiding a gem this entire time."

I don't dignify her with a response. Instead, I shove away from her, turning sharply—knocking over a curtain in the process. The fabric ignites instantly, flames licking up the length of it.

Saygin watches, eyes glinting with something unreadable.

"You're coming back to Ashton's manor with us." My tone leaves no room for argument.

I release them both and stalk toward the door.

Quinn gasps, still struggling for breath. "Who do you think you are, *boy*?"

Behind me, Ashton chuckles darkly. "He's your *fucking* king."

And then… he follows me.

Luca lingers just long enough to grab a handful of pretzels from the coffee table before slipping out behind us, completely silent.

Saygin sighs dramatically. "Do I at least get to taste-test the wolf?"

I don't turn around.

The next curtain erupts into flames.

CHAPTER FIFTEEN

Ashton

*W*e *will have company.* I let Sadie know through our bond. *Make sure the maids get everything in order.*

There's a pause before her response, hesitation laced in her tone. *Will they even listen to me?*

You're Mrs. Somner now, I remind her. *They have to listen to you. My maids and help are yours to command.*

Another pause. This one quieter, softer. And then I feel her presence thread gently through my essence—warm, grounding, unwavering. She doesn't respond with words, but she doesn't have to. She lingers in the background, a quiet anchor against the storm brewing inside me. I exhale slowly, letting her silent support settle around me.

Then Saygin ruins it.

"Have you told the mortal woman about Izzy?"

The words hit harder than they should. A blunt force against ribs already seemingly fractured.

"No," I say, keeping my voice flat, emotionless.

Wishful thinking that this trip would be uneventful. That I wouldn't have to talk about it. That I wouldn't have to remember.

But Saygin never lets wounds heal.

Every second here is *torture*.

I keep my gaze fixed ahead, but my mind betrays me. It drags me back—back to *her*, back to *them*.

Isolde's face, soft and mischievous, floats in my mind. Her laughter, always teasing, always warm. *We'd make a great team, you know,* she once told me. *Sandman and Sandwoman. Could you imagine the power we'd hold?*

I used to. I used to imagine it all.

I try not to think of Caelum. Try not to remember the quiet moments where I'd dreamed of his first breath, his first cry, his tiny fingers curling around mine. A life that never came to be. A future that was stolen before it even had a chance to exist.

Seventy-four males.

That's how many I cut down before reaching the prison.

Seventy-four.

Seventy-four who had torn Isolde apart from the inside out. Who had laughed as they kept her blindfolded, kept her drugged—making sure I could hear her screams but never find her.

I was too late.

I couldn't save her.

I couldn't save either of them.

My jaw clenches, muscles locking as I force the memories back into their cage.

Across from me, Luca shoots me a small, hesitant smile. He mouths, *Just breathe.*

I almost laugh.

He has no idea what kind of pain he's offering comfort for. No idea what kind of horror lurks beyond the veil he's still too naïve to see. He's got it easy. And I'd be lying if I said I wasn't a little jealous of his blissful ignorance.

And Saygin? She's not just dangerous. She's *unapologetically* dangerous.

My gaze shifts to Azrael. Something is wrong with him.

There's an energy inside him now—something ancient, something that's consuming him. It's awakening, feeding on him, twisting into something bigger than he realizes.

And if he can't rein it in, it's going to devour him.

Babe, are you okay?

Sadie's voice is soft, hesitant. I can feel the worry rushing through our bond, curling around me like a thread she refuses to let snap.

I hesitate. *I'm just fine, little nightmare. Can't wait to make it home to you.*

A lie.

Not because I don't want to go home to her—I do. More than anything. But because I'm not fine.

And maybe... maybe I never will be. Maybe I can't fully give myself to Sadie—can't love her the way she deserves—because I never came to peace with what happened to Isolde and my son.

Caelum.

The name feels like an open wound, never quite healing, never quite closing.

Orcus hums, his voice slithering like he's been waiting for the perfect moment to pounce. "You should tell Sadie."

I shift uncomfortably. Sadie is not the kind to ignore withheld secrets.

"I know," I mutter, jaw tightening. Because he's right.

Sadie isn't the kind to let things go. And I've already granted her immortality, which means an eternity of her hating me if she ever finds out I've been keeping this from her.

It's not just a secret. It's *the* secret.

The one thing blocking me from getting too close to her. The ghost between us.

I swallow the lump forming in my throat.

But there's one thing I do know—I've made sure Sadie is protected.

Something I failed to do for Isolde.

The maids, the help, the guards... the spells woven into the very foundation of the house. I refuse to be ignorant again.

I will *not* let anything happen to Sadie.

I inhale slowly, forcing the words out like they physically pain me. "I just need to find the right time to tell her."

If there *is* a right time. If I tell her now, she'll explode.

Orcus scoffs. *"Sadie can handle it. She's more understanding than you think."*

I don't answer. Because I'm not sure she can. Or maybe, deep down, I just don't want to say it out loud.

There's a long pause before Orcus speaks again. *"You should have told us."*

I open my mouth, but another voice cuts in.

Azrael's. "If I had known, I wouldn't have let you come." His tone is grim, heavy. "But what's done is done, and I apologize."

I blink at him, startled. "For what?"

Azrael exhales, his usually unreadable expression cracking, just for a second.

"Because I couldn't protect you."

His words hang between us, unspoken history pressing in.

Azrael studies me for a moment, his gaze sharp, assessing. Maybe waiting for me to back out. Maybe wondering if I actually will tell Sadie the truth.

I shrug it off and look up at the sky, its deep red stretching endlessly above us. Our moon, permanent and unwavering, bathes the world in its haunting glow.

No sun here. No true morning. Just endless nights.

It fits.

"When we get home, I will tell her," I say.

CHAPTER SIXTEEN

Layla

GRAVITY - SARA BAREILLES

*P*ain.

It's the first thing I register—deep, gnawing, all-consuming. It drags me from unconsciousness like a cruel, unrelenting tide, pulling me under, and forcing me back into my body.

A *mistake.*

Because my body is *wrecked.*

Every nerve screams, my bones feel like they've been shattered and hastily glued back together, my muscles barely holding me upright. It's like I've been chewed up and spit out, my insides rearranged just enough to keep me breathing.

Something wet clings to my skin beneath my armor, making the fabric feel heavier, suffocating. Blood—too much of it—mixes with sweat, grime, and something worse. The putrid stench of iron, dirt, and piss coils around me.

Piss.

The realization twists my stomach, disgust curling up my throat. Whatever happened before I blacked out, it had been bad enough that my body gave up its last shred of dignity.

I inhale sharply, forcing my eyes open, but all I see is *nothing*.

Not darkness. Not shadows. Just nothing.

It's an abyss stretching in every direction, infinite and hungry, pressing in around me like I've been swallowed whole.

No sky. No landmarks. No sense of up or down.

Only the faint, pulsing glow of Drepane's purple shield keeps me from believing I've woken up in my own grave.

"Young reaper. You're awake."

Drepane's voice hums through the stagnant air, gentle yet laced with something unreadable. Relief? Concern? Hesitation?

I swallow past the dryness in my throat, but it feels like I've inhaled dust and razor blades. "What... happened?" My voice cracks, barely above a whisper. "Where are we?"

"An accident happened."

That's not an answer.

Drepane glows brighter, its violet aura shifting, casting eerie, wraith-like shadows in the nothingness around me.

"We are somewhere... between."

Between *what*? Life and death? The mortal world and the Underworld?

Between *fucked* and *even more fucked*?

I turn my head to assess the damage, but the moment I move, a sharp, nauseating jolt of pain stabs through my side. The air punches out of my lungs, and I clamp my teeth down on a groan.

When I finally look down, my stomach knots.

Blood. So much blood.

It's dried, crusted, and smeared across my abdomen, just below where my armor ends. A new scar, angry and jagged, cuts across my skin.

That wasn't there before.

The gravel beneath me—if I can even call it that—is soaked in more blood. *My* blood. The sight of it makes my head spin.

I brace my palm against the ground, ignoring the way my fingers tremble as I push myself upright. The air here is different. *Wrong.*

It's heavier than even the Underworld's oppressive atmosphere. It presses against my chest like a weight I can't throw off, thick with something unseen, something lurking just beyond Drepane's protective glow.

My fingers tighten around his handle, the familiar presence of my sentient weapon grounding me.

"Okay," I whisper, mostly to myself. "No need to panic. I've been through worse."

Have I? No. I fucking haven't.

A sick feeling twists in my gut.

Because this time... I'm not sure I truly have been through worse.

Panic rises like bile in my throat, cold and fast, coiling around my ribs, sinking its claws in. My pulse pounds against my ears, too loud, too fast.

I can't die here.

I can't.

I force a slow breath through my nose.

Calm down. Think.

Drepane wouldn't have protected me if there wasn't a reason. Which means I have a way out. I just have to—

A sound.

A whisper.

No... not a whisper.

A scratching.

Like claws dragging across stone.

Slow. Deliberate.

And *close.*

I freeze, every muscle locking up.

Drepane's glow flickers like a heartbeat.

We are not alone.

"Where is everyone?" My voice cracks as I whip my head around, my eyes frantically searching the suffocating blackness beyond Drepane's soft glow.

Nothing.

No landmarks. No familiar figures. No Azrael.

No one.

A cold rush of panic surges through my veins. My breath quickens, uneven and ragged, as my fingers tremble, brushing over the inked rose marked on my wrist—my mating bond.

The mark that should be *bold* and *vibrant* is... fading.

I watch in horror as the edges blur like ink dissolving in water, seeping away into my skin as if it was never there to begin with.

Something inside me shatters.

"Drepane, where are we?" My voice wavers, but I force it steady, my grip tightening around my weapon's hilt like it's the only thing anchoring me to reality.

For a long moment, Drepane says nothing. Then, finally— "The Empty."

His voice is devoid of its usual smugness, stripped bare, eerily quiet.

The Empty.

The word sends a violent shudder through me.

I swallow hard, my throat dry, my thoughts scrambling to piece together what that means. I know the Empty... It's the place where supernatural souls go when they are unclaimed—when they have no afterlife, no tether, no second chance. Azrael has told me about this place...

My stomach twists. "Where is everyone?"

My voice rises, shaking with barely contained hysteria. I don't mean to yell, but the words tear out of me, jagged and raw.

"Home." Drepane sighs, his glow pulsing—regretful, almost sorrowful. "Azrael is looking for a way to get us out of here."

A sharp, unsteady breath rushes from my lungs. *Home.*

They're home.

But I'm *here.*

Alone.

Trapped.

"Am I dead?"

The words leave my lips before I can stop them, foreign and unfamiliar, like speaking them aloud will make them real.

"No, child." Drepane's response is calm, but the weight of it settles in my chest like a stone, pressing down, down, down—until it feels like I might suffocate under it.

I exhale shakily, forcing myself to think. "Then how the hell did we end up here?"

"I already had the Empty open," he admits, his glow flickering.

I blink. *"What?"*

"I didn't mean to move us inside it, but all of my energy was already placed there. So now, here we are." His words hang heavy between us, settling in the silence like a death sentence.

A sickening realization slithers over me, cold fingers up my spine.

"You can't pull us out." Not a question. A statement. A truth I don't want to hear.

Drepane hesitates. Then— "No."

The admission stings, and I can tell it pains him to say it. *But it doesn't change the reality of our situation.*

"It doesn't work like that," he continues. "On the outside, the Empty can be opened. On the inside, it can't be. Think of it as a bottle. You can open the bottle from the outside, but if you were somehow, unfortunately, inside the bottle... you wouldn't be able to open it from within."

The analogy settles in my gut like a lead weight.

Trapped.

No way out.

I push against the ground, trying to stand, but the moment I lift myself, a dizzying wave crashes over me. My vision tilts, the void around me spinning, and a sharp, biting pain lances through my side.

My knees buckle.

I hit the ground with a choked gasp.

Drepane hums disapprovingly.

I clench my jaw, squeezing my eyes shut for a moment before forcing them open again. My body feels *wrong*—weighed down, sluggish, like the Empty itself is clawing at me, trying to pull me deeper into its grasp.

"Can Azrael hear me from here?"

The question comes quieter this time, slipping through clenched teeth.

Drepane hesitates. "Yes."

A flicker of something—*hope*—ignites in my chest. It's dim, weak, but it's there, flickering like a candle in a storm.

I close my eyes, inhaling slowly, and reach out.

The bond is still there, *faint*, but there. A thread of life woven between us, delicate but unbreakable. I let my mind stretch toward it—

—and the moment I touch it, an explosion of raw emotion crashes into me.

A tidal wave of *pain*.

Of *fury*.

Of *guilt*.

Azrael's emotions flood into me, searing-hot and overwhelming. It's too much, too intense—I can barely breathe under the weight of it. His anger at himself, his devastation, his fear for me—it all *burns* through my chest, constricting my heart until it aches.

I grit my teeth, holding onto the bond, refusing to let go.

Azrael.

No answer. But I feel him.

I feel the way his power coils, untamed and *dangerous*, how it *writhes* like something alive, barely contained.

He's unraveling.

Because of me.

And if I don't find a way out of here soon...

He might lose himself completely.

Azrael...

I reach deeper, grasping for him through the bond, clinging to the one thing that feels real in this suffocating abyss. The darkness here is too thick, too consuming, pressing into me like it's trying to unravel my existence thread by thread. I feel *hollow*, drained, like the Empty is feeding on something deeper than just my body.

Azrael, I'm scared! The admission is raw, slipping through the tether between us like a confession I can't take back. *I don't know how much longer I can do this.*

For a terrifying moment, there's silence.

Then—

Layla?

His voice *shatters* through my mind, clear as if he were standing right beside me, pulling me back from the edges of the abyss.

A breath stumbles out of me, my chest tightening. He's there. *He's there.*

I grip the bond tighter, my thoughts spilling into him in a desperate rush. *I'm in the dark. I'm wasting away. Fuck I am so fucking scared, Azrael!*

His emotions crash against mine—a wave of guilt, rage, *love*.

I know, Tiny Mouse. I'm coming. I promise you that. But beneath it all, beneath the pain and frustration and desperation, his promise *anchors* me.

The weight in my chest lifts—just slightly, just enough. *He's coming.* He will get me out of here. He won't let me stay lost.

I got Saygin, Drepane. Azrael says.

Did she give you any problems? Drepane's voice cuts through the silence, as calm and composed as ever. His question sends a ripple through the bond, shifting the atmosphere.

Orcus' response is tinged with humor despite the circumstances. *Azrael almost cooked her, but not really.* Orcus offered a rough chuckle. *Did you know Ashton was almost gay for the staying?*

I blink. *What?*

I wonder if that's why he fancies Azrael so much. Orcus laughs again, clearly enjoying himself.

I frown, my mind still trying to catch up. Who the hell is Saygin? And *what* does Orcus mean by *almost cooked her*?

Drepane? I ask slowly, my mental voice hoarse from exhaustion.

He hums in acknowledgment, his glow pulsing softly around me.

Who is Saygin? I press.

A Fae god hybrid, Drepane explains smoothly, as if this is just another casual conversation. *She's incredibly powerful, and she uses her wisdom to her advantage. Nothing is free to Saygin. Especially if it is a male requesting services.*

His words settle uneasily in my chest.

Saygin sounds *dangerous*—too dangerous to be trusted easily.

But I can't afford to dwell on that. Not when I'm *still here*, still sinking into the weight of this place.

Azrael's voice cuts through again, steady, resolute. *We are almost home with Saygin and Quinn. I will keep you updated.*

"*Home.*"

The word tugs at something inside me.

Home. I want to be *home*. I want to be at home... *with him*. I want to feel his arms around me, solid and real, instead of this lifeless void swallowing me whole.

There's so much I want to say to him. *I love you.* It sits on the tip of my mental tongue.

But I *can't* say it.

I don't know *why.*

The words are too heavy, too final. They feel like a promise I don't know if I can keep.

What if I never get out of here?

What if this darkness takes me away from him forever?

What if I *can't* get back to him?

The fear coils around me, tight, suffocating.

Then, his voice—soft, certain, unwavering—slips through the bond like a prayer.

Layla, I love you. Please stay safe.

My chest *aches.*

I open my mouth, but the words refuse to come.

I feel it—I feel it in my bones, in my soul, in the way my entire being craves him—but I can't force the words out.

Instead, I let my fingers drift across the bond, caressing the thread between us. I pour everything into it—my love, my fear, my pain, my longing.

It's the only thing I can offer.

CHAPTER SEVENTEEN

Azrael

DON'T LET ME DOWN - THE CHAINSMOKERS

"I just spoke to Layla. She's awake."

The words felt heavier than they should have. Relief and dread warred inside me, twisting together like a slow, strangling noose. Layla waking up should have been a good thing. Should have meant she was still fighting. But in the Empty? Awake just meant she was *conscious* enough to *suffer*.

Drepane had shielded her while she slept, kept her unaware of what festered around her in that forsaken place. Now that she was awake, there was no veil, no mercy. She'd see it all. Feel it all. And knowing Layla, she wouldn't just endure it—she'd *carry* it.

The Layla I knew might not make it out of this the same.

Ashton, perceptive as ever, paused with his hand on the door handle. "Is she okay?"

His voice was steady, but I caught the undercurrent of concern. He wouldn't push, but he needed to know.

"For now." I rubbed the back of my neck, trying to shake the exhaustion weighing on me. "Orcus is sending energy to Drepane to replenish him... but Orcus isn't enough. He doesn't have ancient energy."

I sighed, long and tired. This time, frustration edged into it.

Orcus, naturally, took that as his cue to vibrate with barely contained amusement. He radiated the same energy as someone who knew exactly how to piss you off and *lived* for it.

Then there was *them*—Saygin and Quinn, perched in their little corner of the group like chaos incarnate, looking too fucking pleased with themselves. Their expressions were smug, self-satisfied, the kind of look that made my fingers twitch with the urge to break something. Preferably something belonging to them.

Saygin, in particular, had the aura of someone who had just upended a high-stakes poker game and was waiting for the explosion. Quinn, her equally insufferable counterpart, walked beside her with an expression that practically screamed, *Don't hate me because I'm "beautiful"; hate me because I'm better at this than you.*

I clenched my jaw.

I still hadn't had time to deal with the fact that they'd *outed Ashton* like that. That wasn't their fucking story to tell. It wasn't a game to be played, not when it came to Ashton. I hadn't seen the fallout of it yet, but I would. And I wasn't going to forget.

"I'd give anything to wipe those smirks off their faces," I muttered under my breath.

Ashton twisted the doorknob. Before I could so much as inhale, *Sadie* came flying through the entrance like a human-sized meteor, *slamming* into Ashton with the force of an emotional wrecking ball.

The house *shook.*

Literally.

I had to take a step back, shaking my head. There would be *no* peace tonight.

When those two reunited, the house didn't get *rest*—it *vibrated* with their chaotic energy, like the prelude to a natural disaster. You could almost *feel* the pressure in the air, like the split second before lightning cracked the sky wide open.

And fuck me, I wasn't in the mood for it.

I left them to their emotional fireworks and made my way toward the kitchen, Luca trailing behind me like a tortured man heading toward the gallows.

Saygin, of course, was right on his heels—moving with that eerie, weightless grace of hers, her presence disturbingly silent. It would have been comical if it wasn't so goddamn unsettling.

Luca didn't acknowledge her. Whether it was intentional or sheer *terror-induced ignorance*, I had no idea. But the dude was *sweating bullets*.

I muttered under my breath, mostly to myself. "Luca's kitchen magic."

Luca *needed* the distraction. The moment he stepped into the kitchen, his hands were moving, grabbing ingredients, shifting into his natural flow. It was mechanical, efficient, *desperate*. Like if he could just *focus* hard enough, he could pretend the nightmare trailing him wasn't real.

The scent of brewing coffee filled the space—a small comfort in the shitstorm that was called my fucking life.

Every few seconds, Luca's gaze flicked to me, wide-eyed and desperate. A silent plea.

Help. Me.

I didn't.

Meanwhile, Saygin perched herself on the counter, her feet swaying idly as she observed Luca like some kind of predatory fae *gremlin* waiting for her moment to pounce.

And Quinn? That smug bastard was lounging beneath her, staring at Luca like he was the lead character in a very *entertaining* horror movie.

I narrowed my eyes. "Quinn, you're staring. You know that, right?"

Quinn blinked, then flashed me a lazy, shit-eating grin. "What? Just admiring Luca's *culinary* skills."

Luca *visibly* tensed.

Quinn continued, unfazed. "I didn't know you guys had a secret chef on your team."

Luca muttered something in under his breath that *definitely* wasn't complimentary.

I smirked but didn't let it distract me. Saygin's energy was still *off*—all over the place, shifting between *amused* and something *I didn't trust.*

I exhaled slowly. "Luca, just focus on the food. You're doing great."

It was my version of throwing the guy a life vest.

He gave me a look that screamed, *Fuck you, help me.*

Quinn, sensing weakness, leaned forward on his elbows. "So, Luca... what exactly *are* you?"

Luca nearly dropped the knife he was holding.

His entire body tensed, like he was physically bracing for impact.

His eyes flicked to Saygin, who was still grinning like she knew something he didn't.

I sighed. "Quinn, can you not?"

"What?" Quinn's expression was the definition of fake innocence. "I'm just making conversation."

"No, you're stirring shit," I deadpanned.

"I thrive in chaos."

"I hope you choke on it."

Quinn grinned. "Ooh, sweet talk me *more, Azrael.*"

Before I could reply, Saygin finally spoke. Her voice was smooth, laced with something dangerous. "I think I already know what Luca is."

Luca stilled.

Saygin leaned forward, gaze locked onto him like she was peeling him apart layer by layer. "You reek of mortality. But there's something else, too."

Luca's grip tightened on the counter.

Saygin smirked. "You've forgotten yourself, haven't you?"

Silence stretched.

Something *cold* slithered down my spine.

Luca didn't answer.

He didn't even fucking *breathe.*

Saygin's grin widened, fangs flashing. "I can fix that."

I stepped between them before this *shitshow* could escalate. "Saygin, if you want to live through the night, I'd suggest you shut the fuck up."

Her gaze flicked to me, considering. Then, with an exaggerated sigh, she hopped off the counter, brushing past Luca. "Fine, fine. I'll behave. *For now.*"

I didn't trust that for a goddamn second.

Luca finally exhaled.

I clapped him on the back. "Still breathing?"

He nodded, barely.

Quinn smirked. "For now."

I rolled my eye embers. "Someone's getting stabbed before the night is over."

Orcus, from his corner, called out: "I volunteer Quinn as tribute!"

Quinn cackled. "You'll have to try harder than that, big guy."

I fucking hate my life.

Saygin, however, wasn't done. "Is there a reason you're so... uptight?" she asked, her voice dripping with amusement as she continued to watch Luca, her eyes never leaving him.

"I'm not uptight," I replied flatly. "I'm just... tired. And dealing with too many things right now."

"Too many things, huh?" Orcus' voice cut through the air. I gave him a deadpan look, not in the mood for his antics.

"You know, if I didn't know any better, I'd say you're overcompensating." Orcus chuckled. "You're so much fun when you're tense. Come on, let it go. What's one more thing in this clusterfuck?"

I glared at my scythe, but he just laughed louder, his amusement only adding to the chaos in the room.

I took a deep breath, forcing myself to calm down. "I need a drink," I muttered, reaching for the cabinet where the liquor was kept. The night was only just beginning, and I could already feel the weight of everything bearing down on me. It wasn't going to get easier, but at least there was some comfort in the madness. At least for now.

"Never seen a wolf before?" Orcus's voice cut through the thick tension in the air, the sarcastic edge in his tone giving me just a moment of distraction. He always knew how to poke at the right moment.

Saygin's eyes snapped to Orcus, and I felt a slight vibration pulse through the bond. The damn blade was restless, as if it knew this conversation could spiral into something dangerous. Or maybe that was fear shivering through. But it hummed with energy, ready to strike if needed. One thing was certain: we would protect Luca. No matter what.

"I've never seen one up close before. He moves so fluently. Dancing in the kitchen." Saygin's voice was smooth, almost reverent, as her eyes stayed fixed on Luca. "Is he always this perfect and beautiful?"

Luca paused, his movements slowing, then stopped completely. The shift in his posture was almost imperceptible, but it was there. He knew the look in her eyes was more than just admiration. I could feel it too—the way he tensed, his muscles coiled, ready to spring if the situation demanded it. But it was clear: he was *scared. We both were.*

We both knew Saygin wouldn't kill us, but her games? They were deadly in a different way. She couldn't be trusted with something so... *fragile* as Luca. Not when she was capable of twisting any situation into a bargain.

Luca glanced toward me, his eyes wide, a mix of confusion and fear in them. I could almost hear his thoughts—he didn't want to be caught up in this.

"Luca's coffee shop was destroyed by Memetim in the mortal realm. Ashton brought him here to keep him safe." I said the words with an almost deadpan like expression, trying to steer the conversation back under control. No way in hell was I letting Saygin get her claws into Luca, not after everything he'd been through.

"How sweet." Quinn's voice was dripping with sarcasm, clearly finding amusement in the exchange.

"I've never had wolf before. Luca... is it?" Saygin's voice took on a teasing note, as though this was some kind of game she'd been dying to play. "I will offer a bargain for you—"

"Hell no!" I stood, the words leaving my mouth before I could stop them. There was a sharp edge to my voice, one that came with the promise of protection, the same protection I would offer anyone in my inner circle. "You will do what I require you to do and *leave* Luca out of this."

Saygin raised an eyebrow, an almost childlike smile tugging at the corner of her lips. "So protective. You'd do anything to keep your little wolf safe, wouldn't you?"

"I said no." My voice was firm, unwavering. There was no room for negotiation, not with this.

Her smirk only widened, an unsettlingly sharp gleam in her eyes. "I will rebuild the shop of your dreams in the mortal realm." Saygin's voice dripped with triumph as she leaned back, clearly thinking she'd won some kind of victory.

Luca stared at her, and for a brief moment, I thought I saw the conflict in his eyes. Was he actually contemplating this? The thought sent a sting of worry through me. I couldn't let him fall for her manipulations.

"Don't take her offer, Luca. I'll have a shop built for you here in the Underworld if you want, or I can build one in the mortal realm." My glare was ice-cold, a silent warning, but Luca didn't seem to care. His focus was entirely on the food in front of him, like my words didn't even register.

Luca scratched his beard absentmindedly, continuing to chop vegetables with deliberate slowness. "Let me think about it."

A vertebrate twitched in my neck, and I could feel the annoyance rising. This was ridiculous. He knew how dangerous she was. He *had* to know.

"There's nothing to think about! Are you seriously considering her bargain?" I snapped, my voice sharp, but Luca didn't even flinch.

"No. I'm not. Maybe." He shrugged, not even bothering to turn around and look me in the eye. "I want my coffee shop back, but I love being able to cook for my friends. It's peaceful here. But I miss being a getaway for the mortal supernaturals. After all, Azrael, you keep saying I don't belong here."

I stared at the back of his head, frustration boiling over. *Is this idiot seriously weighing his options like it's just some casual decision?* Of course, you don't belong here, Luca. I'm trying to keep you safe, and you're considering giving that all up for a shop? A goddamn coffee shop?

Orcus's voice came from the back of my mind, smooth and knowing. *Luca wouldn't last a minute when she pulls the object close to his little wolfy dick. You and I both know that, Azrael.*

I snorted, exasperated, and rubbed my temples. He was right. Luca didn't understand the power Saygin wielded. This whole situation was a trap, and he was about to walk straight into it.

I lean back in my chair, fingers drumming against the table, my mind racing. This is a game, and Saygin's playing it like she always does—manipulating every little thing. The thought of her using Luca like that makes my blood boil. I can't let that happen.

This bitch better be worth it. She better not be yanking my leg and better fucking bring back my mate.

I tense up as Saygin's cackle echoes through the kitchen, making the hairs on the back of my neck stand on end. It's hollow, mocking, like she knows exactly how this is going to play out, and I'm just a pawn in her game.

I turn to Luca again, and my voice comes out sharper than I intended. "You really want to deal with her? Are you that desperate for your shop?"

Luca doesn't answer at first, and for a moment, I wonder if he's reconsidering. But he turns his head finally, meeting my eyes with an expression I can't read. "No," he says quietly. "But I'm not going to jump into this blind, Azrael. I need time to think. I can't just make this decision based on what *you* want."

My anger flares again, but I hold it back. He's right, in a way. I can't control his choices, no matter how much I want to. But that doesn't mean I'm going to stand by while Saygin plays with his life.

"Fine," I mutter, my tone darker. "But don't say I didn't warn you when things go south. You don't know what you're dealing with."

I turn away, back to the table, the tension in the room suffocating. Orcus' presence in my mind is like a low hum of amusement, but I'm not in the mood for it. The situation is too dire. Luca's indecision is only making everything harder, and I have a sick feeling that this is only the beginning.

Saygin's laughter still echoes, and I can't shake the feeling that the game she's playing is much bigger than I could ever fucking anticipate.

CHAPTER EIGHTEEN

Ashton

I Was Made For Lovin' You - YUNGBLUD

"What do you mean?"

Sadie's voice trembled, her wide eyes shimmering with unshed tears. She looked like she was standing on the edge of a cliff, barely holding herself together. And I was the sole reason she was fucking standing there.

I let out a long, frustrated sigh, dragging a hand through my hair. This wasn't how I wanted this conversation to start. Hell, this wasn't a conversation I wanted to have at all. But Saygin was in the kitchen, and I knew if I didn't tell Sadie first, the fae goddess would. And she'd probably find a way to make it sound a thousand times worse.

"Saygin's here," I muttered, stepping closer to her.

Sadie blinked, her lips parting slightly before pressing into a thin line. She crossed her arms, her fingers gripping her elbows like she was physically holding herself together.

"I just—I needed to tell you before she did," I continued. "I *value* you, Sadie. I don't think I can handle you being upset with me."

I reached for her hand, needing that connection, that grounding touch, but she yanked it back like I'd shocked her.

Her jaw clenched.

"You had boyfriends before me, Sadie. I'm not mad at you for that," I said, my tone clipped. But then, with a sharp huff, I added, "And I'm *definitely* not holding a grudge against you for aborting Dash Madden's Satan spawn."

I stared at her.

I shouldn't have said that.

I took a slow breath, steadying myself. "Sadie," I said carefully, "you are my mate. There's no 'breaking up' and 'finding someone else.' My body is literally *wired* to *serve* and *protect* you. You are *it* for me."

I wasn't sure if she heard the desperation in my voice, but I knew she felt the conviction.

Sadie's brows furrowed, her face twisting in confusion. "You were going to be a *father*, Ashton." Her voice cracked slightly, but she quickly masked it with frustration. "How the *hell* am I supposed to compete with someone who was willing to give you a baby?" She flung her hands up. "We never even *talked* about this! What do we want out of this? Do we want kids? *Can* I even carry your baby?" Then, as if she couldn't help herself, she narrowed her eyes suspiciously and muttered, "I read the fucking *ACOTAR* series, Ashton—how would that even work? Feyre barely made it out alive!"

I blinked.

She's fucking serious.

She just compared our bond to something out of a goddamned mortal book series.

"This is *reality*, Sadie," I said, my voice softening but still edged with frustration. "Not some book you found at a thrift store or library. Isolde is *dead*. You're *alive*. My bond with Isolde is *gone*—that's how we were *able* to bond. You're not *competing* with her."

Sadie studied me for a long moment, and I could feel the weight of her emotions pressing against the thread between us, tangled and knotted with uncertainty, fear, and something else she wasn't ready to name.

Then she hit me with the question I'd been dreading.

"You miss her?"

The question I just somehow *knew* would pop up in this conversation... *Shit.*

It's a trick question if I'd ever heard one.

I could feel the air around us tighten, stretching like a tripwire, just waiting for me to step wrong. Say the wrong thing, and I'd be in emotional purgatory.

Nope. *Not* going there.

She needs an *orgasm*.

The thought hit me so fast that it almost made me laugh. Not the *most* appropriate solution, but damn if it wasn't an effective one when it comes to her.

Before she could press further, I grabbed her face gently and kissed her hard.

Sadie stiffened for half a second, caught off guard, but then she melted against me. Her hands fisted my shirt, pulling me closer, and for a moment, the storm between us dissipated.

I deepened the kiss, pouring every ounce of emotion I couldn't say into it. I knew she felt it. The way her body relaxed, the way the tension in our bond unwound like a taut rope finally giving way.

When we finally broke apart, she let out a shaky breath, her forehead resting against my chin. Then, with a smirk, she muttered, "Your dick game isn't *that* magical, Ashton."

I huffed out a laugh. "We'll see."

She rolled her eyes but grinned. "We'll revisit *this* conversation later."

Her hands, however, were already working on my belt buckle.

I arched a brow, amused. "Later, huh?"

She shot me a look that sent heat straight through me. "But first," she said, her voice dropping to a low, sultry whisper, "I need you inside me... *now.*"

I barely had time to react before she yanked my robe off my shoulders—giving up on the belt buckle—tossing it aside like it offended her.

I grinned. "Well, *someone's* impatient."

"*I said now,*" she growled, backing me toward the nearest wall.

I chuckled, but the sound turned into a groan when her fingers skimmed down my stomach, expertly unfastening the rest of my clothes.

"Sadie," I murmured, reaching for her.

I ran my hands down her sides, tracing the curves of her body, my fingers slipping under the waistband of her shorts.

"I'm serious, Ashton," she whispered, her breath hot against my neck.

I didn't need any more encouragement.

"Oh, I know," I said, my voice husky as I flipped us, pressing her against the wall. "I know *exactly* what you need."

Her laughter melted into a gasp as I gripped the fabric of her shirt and tore it in half, the sharp rip echoing through the room.

Her bra followed, discarded like an afterthought, the last piece of her mortal world slipping away.

I cup each breast in my palms, bringing her hardened nipples to my mouth. She pauses, her hands still fumbling with my pants, letting out a soft purr. My tongue circles her areola before gently sucking, moving to the other breast. Her hands find the back of my head, pulling me closer, smashing my head into her breasts. A movement I don't need the bond to interpret for me. It speaks for itself with her reaction.

I smile, knowing her all too well.

The argument we had moments ago will fade, erased by the fire building between us. She'll forget it all, consumed by the pleasure I'll give her.

I pull away, guiding her into a kneeling position. I unfasten my pants, my cock already aching, and I gently stroke it slowly, keeping eye contact with her. "Open your mouth," I command, my voice low.

She listens without hesitation.

Grabbing her curls, I twist her hair into a firm ponytail, holding it in place with just enough pressure to remind her who's in control. I push into her mouth, thrusting in and out with deliberate force, maintaining my grip on her fucking beautiful wild, curly black hair to steady her.

"Suck," I demand.

And like the willing mortal she truly can be, she does. A groan escapes my lips as I lean back, the sensation overwhelming, the warmth of her mouth feels so fucking perfect around me.

Sand swirls from my pouch, surrounding us, and takes shape, forming gentle hands that caress and massage her breasts. Her moans vibrate against me, her pleasure echoing through her body. A strand of sand curls around her throat, a subtle squeeze, matching the frantic pace of her movements. Her tongue runs along the head of my cock.

I thrust harder before stopping suddenly. I *can't* cum yet. I lift her chin, wiping the remnants of me and excess saliva from her lips. She opens her mouth, and I slip my finger inside, guiding her to suck it clean, her eyes locked on mine.

"Lay down," I say, my voice steady, gruff and deep, but laced with a quiet command, pointing toward our bed.

She listens without hesitation, the tension between us palpable as she moves to obey.

The sand shifts with her, wrapping around her thighs as she slips out of her booty shorts. She never wears panties, always teasing me with her boldness. She's my *personal god damn nightmare*, testing my every instinct, pushing me to the edge. I can't help but respond, no matter how hard I try to control it. I can feel the air thick with her arousal, the way she's drawn to me, even as I try to stay calm. Her large tits bounce as she positions herself on *our* bed.

"Get on all fours." My voice is low, edged with a darker intention today. I want her to feel the change in me, to see the shift. I want her to meet Saygin and Quinn and see that I'm not the same Ashton they once knew, the sweet, gentle version they once played with.

The sand swirls around her, knocking her arms out from beneath her and pulling them behind her back. It lifts each leg, causing her to tumble onto the bed, bound in a way that leaves her vulnerable yet still fierce. My *precious* mate, hogtied, a picture of fucking restrained desire.

I run my finger down her slit, feeling the wetness that greets me, perfectly warm and eager. She whimpers softly at the contact, her body responding even as I barely graze her.

I shift her position on the bed, kneeling behind her, giving me space to steady myself. My hands grip her tied limbs, holding her in place as I tease her entrance with the tip of my cock.

Slowly, I press forward, the heat of her pussy surrounding me. She tightens around me before loosening again, a slow rhythm that builds with each thrust. The bed rocks against the wall as I pick up speed, the sound of her moans and whimpers filling the air.

I lean into her ear to whisper, "I *love* how you act all mouthy, but the second I get my hands on you, you turn *soft for me.*"

Her breaths quicken, and the room grows darker, the sensation of her nearing climax making me lose control. I increase the pace, her release coming in a scream that echoes through the house, using her tied limbs as an anchor to keep her body from rocking away.

I pull out, lowering myself to press my mouth to her, tasting the remnants of her pleasure. I lap my precum and her arousal from her body, sucking and running my tongue through her pussy, pushing it into her entrance to taste her deeply. I pull back, and my fingers trace through her folds, moving with a purpose, before I reach for her lips.

"You really think you're that good, huh?" Sadie mumbles, trying to pretend like she has control of her breathing.

"Oh, little nightmare. I don't think. *I know.* Now, taste how sweet you are today," I murmur, and when she hesitates, I forcefully press my fingers into her mouth, dragging my hand across her face, feeling the moisture of her tears as they stain her skin. I run my cock through her folds, circling her clit- teasing her before I push the head through her entrance… feeling the warmth and tightness I love so damn much.

"You are so full of yourself." She murmurs, barely audible. But I could fucking hear her. I could hear her sass which earned an extra tough thrust, rewarded with a squeak escaping from her lips.

With my other hand, I position myself again, thrusting quickly and harder, pushing us both to the edge once more. The room darkens, stars swirling as we both lose ourselves in the moment.

The house trembles with my release, the walls are quivering in response as a deep growl rumbles from my chest. Pleasure crashes through me, raw and consuming, and before I can stop myself, I spill inside her.

The golden sand surrounding us dissipates, swirling like a dying storm before retreating back into my pouch, leaving behind only the warmth of her body pressed against mine while she is still wrapped around my cock.

My muscles go slack as I collapse beside her, breathless, and my heartbeat still hammering in my ears.

Sadie lets out a breathless chuckle, turning her head to look at me with a lazy, satisfied grin. She turns herself around in the bed to lie on her back. Sweat glistens on her skin, her curls are a tangled mess against the pillows.

"Sandman stamina is a *real* thing," she gasps, amusement laced in her voice.

I let out a breathy laugh, still coming down from the high. "Told you," I murmur, turning onto my side to face her. "But you didn't believe me."

She smirks, stretching out like a satisfied cat. "I believe it now. Though for the sake of *research*, we might need to test it a few more times."

I grin, reaching out to brush my fingers along the curve of her waist. "Careful, Little Nightmare. You might just get addicted."

Her lips twitch, and she lets out a dramatic sigh. "*Too late.*"

Sadie hums in satisfaction, her fingers tracing lazy circles on my chest. "So, what happens if you get *too* worked up? Does the house just… disintegrate?"

I chuckle, tucking a stray curl behind her ear. "Nah. Worst-case scenario? You wake up in an entirely different dream realm." I smirk, full sarcasm. "Or I accidentally summon a sandstorm in the living room."

Her eyes widen. "You mean to tell me I could've been *yeeted* into another plane of existence because you got a little *too* into it?"

I shrug, amusement tugging at my lips. "Only if you push me past my limit."

Sadie props herself up on one elbow, her grin turning wicked. "Sounds like a challenge."

I groan, throwing an arm over my face. "I *really* shouldn't have said that."

She giggles, snuggling closer, her fingers dancing along my abdomen. "No take-backs. Now I *have* to know what happens if I push you too far."

I peek at her from under my arm. "If you do, don't complain when you wake up in some dreamscape where the sky rains moonlight and the ground is made of soft marshmallows."

Sadie gasps, eyes lighting up. "That sounds *amazing.*"

I shake my head with a laugh. "You say that now, but wait until you try running through a marshmallow field. I imagine it fucking *sucks.*"

She bursts into laughter, the sound warming something deep in my chest. I wrap an arm around her, pulling her against me, our bodies molding together effortlessly.

For a moment, it's just us, the afterglow settling into something soft, something *real*. The weight of everything—Saygin, the Empty, whatever bullshit we'll have to face next—lingers in the back of my mind, but right now? It doesn't matter.

Right now, all that matters is *her*.

CHAPTER NINETEEN

Azrael

TOXIC - BRITNEY SPEARS

"Y ou called it," Orcus hums, a sly grin tugging at his lips.

"Called what?" Saygin asks, her emerald eyes narrowing in curiosity.

"The house vibrating like that," Luca mumbles, stabbing his food with a distinct lack of enthusiasm. "Ashton having an orgasm." His voice is flat, dripping with sarcasm.

Vassago, entirely unbothered, grabs a plate and sits next to Luca, casually sipping his drink. "Damn. That's some supernatural stamina."

"That's new," Quinn quips, flashing a dark smile that could rival the devil's himself.

"Is it?" Luca groans, rolling his eyes so hard I'm surprised they don't fall out. "Because that's all we've experienced under this roof since they sealed their bond—nonstop moaning, creaking walls, and the occasional fucking *thump*." He waves his fork toward the ceiling. "Honestly, I think Ashton's got a permanent boner now."

Vassago barely suppresses his laughter, while Saygin cocks her head, as if trying to decipher a particularly complex puzzle. "Do werewolves not have mates?" she asks, inching closer to Luca, who leans away like she just offered him a poisoned apple.

"We do," he says warily, crossing his arms. "But it's different for mortal supernaturals. More or less like a marriage, ya know? Pretty straightforward, no magical fireworks or soul-binding nonsense. No one's house randomly starts shaking because we're banging our partner into next week." He takes a bite of his food. "Less *'magical.'*"

I lean back in my chair, letting the conversation play out, but something about Saygin's presence still needles at me. She's gotten *far* too comfortable in our dynamic. Her smug energy is suffocating. She can feel my stare burning into her, and of course, she doesn't ignore it.

Instead, she smirks. "Are you upset I'm talking to your *pet*, Azrael?" she asks, voice dripping with faux innocence, though the sharp edge beneath it is unmistakable.

"He's not my *pet*. He's my *friend*." My voice is cold, clipped.

"Imagine being this protective over a *lesser supernatural*." She tilts her head, feigning sympathy. "Too bad your mate didn't get the same decency."

The room goes still.

My vision tunnels, my anger ignites like a match thrown onto gasoline. The next thing I know, I've lunged across the table, my fingers wrapped around her delicate throat. I lift her off the ground with terrifying ease, the sound of her breath hitching sharp against the silence.

But she doesn't struggle.

She doesn't panic...

Instead, she fucking *smiles?*

"Tighter, *daddy*."

For a brief moment, my mind goes completely fucking blank.

Vassago chokes on his drink, spluttering before bursting into laughter. "Oh, *fuck,* this is priceless. Azrael, my dear baby brother, I think you just walked into a trap."

Luca groans and shoves his plate away. "Great. Now we're all part of Saygin's BDSM fantasy."

Orcus says with mock contemplation, "Honestly, I'm just surprised she didn't call him 'Master.'"

Saygin's grin widens, tilting her head as best she can with my grip still firm on her throat. "Would that do it for you, love?" Her voice is a sultry purr. "Should I get on my knees, too? Be a good little submissive trashy bitch fae for you and suck your little Grim Reaper cock."

My knuckles go numb. "Keep testing me, Saygin. See where that gets you."

She gasps theatrically, as if I've just proposed a marriage. "You *promise?*"

Vassago wipes a tear from his eye, shaking his head. "Azrael, *I swear,* if you don't let go of her, she's going to have an orgasm right here on the damn table."

I *shove* her back, and she stumbles, laughing like I just whispered the best joke in the universe. My anger is a drum in my ears, the irritation crawling under my joints like an infestation.

She rubs her neck, clearly enjoying herself. "Mmm, rough hands. I wonder how they'd feel curving into something else—"

"*Saygin,*" Luca cuts in, rubbing his temples. "For *fuck's sake.* Can you go five minutes without making this a sex thing?"

Saygin taps a finger against her lips, pretending to think. "*No.*"

I exhale sharply, pinching the bridge of my nose. "You are *insufferable!*"

"And yet," she purrs, stepping closer, voice like silk laced with poison, "you *can't* keep your hands off me." A wicked gleam shines in her emerald eyes. "If I didn't know better, I'd say you *enjoyed* that little moment of aggression."

"What did we just walk into?" Sadie's voice slices through the room, thick with confusion and that trademark sass of hers. Her wild black curls are an absolute disaster. Makeup smudged like she'd just had a run-in with an alley cat, and a scent hanging around her like she's spent hours tangled in sheets.

I can practically smell Ashton's presence on her—sex, arousal, and something I can't quite place but definitely isn't innocent. She stumbles into the room like she's waltzing into a normal dinner party, but the thick tension clinging to the air? Yeah, that wasn't on the invite.

Her eyes dart between me, Saygin, and the others. "Is it... going to always be like this? I thought we were just having dinner, not a wrestling match."

I give her a half-smirk, taking a slow breath as I slide back into my chair. The last thing I want is to make this mess any worse for her, but this whole circus? Yeah, it's about to go off the fucking rails.

"Yeah, well," Luca chimes in, swallowing his bite like he's immune to the madness. "Sometimes dinner comes with a side of drama. It's better than a reality TV show around here."

"More like *Underworld's Kitchen*," Quinn mutters under his breath. His tone is low, but there's the unmistakable glint of amusement in his eyes, like he's one wrong word away from throwing popcorn at the chaos.

I exhale sharply, leaning back further in my chair, running a hand across my skull, eyes flicking to Sadie. I try to keep my composure, but the tight knot in my chest makes me feel like I've swallowed a stone. I'm not sure if it's the stress or the absurdity of the situation, but I mutter under my breath, "We're all *so fucked*."

And that's when it all goes from bad to fucking worse.

I snap my eyes back to Saygin who is getting back into her chair with a force that makes her slightly gasp, but it's not out of fear. No, she coughs, a damn laugh escaping her lips as she looks at me through half-lidded eyes. "I will do *anything* for you to do that again in your *mortal form*, Az."

My glare could melt glass, but she's still smirking like she just won the damn lottery. "In your dreams," I growl, sitting back down, the leather of the chair creaking under the weight of my frustration.

"If you promise, I swear... *I'll* be *gentle*." She purrs the words like they're coated in honey, her lips curling into something dark. She's fucking chaos in a too-tight dress, and I'm just waiting for her to take a bite.

"Fuck off, Saygin!" I snap, my patience thinner than it's ever been.

Luca, clearly in self-preservation mode, scoots his chair away from Saygin like she's about to sprout talons. I can practically hear the wheels turning in his head: *Better safe than sorry.*

Saygin leans back, clearly entertained by the dynamic, and her gaze sharpens as she speaks, "It amuses me how scared you males are of a powerful supernatural female. Makes you all feel *lesser*, doesn't it?"

I raise an eyebrow at her, but there's no use in arguing. She does have us all on edge.

"Oh. I like her." Sadie's voice rings out, and I can practically hear the mischief in her tone before I even turn to look at her. She points a finger at Saygin like she's some sort of mythical creature—maybe because she is to Sadie, but it doesn't make this any less annoying. "Are you the one Ashton was telling me about?"

Sadie doesn't even wait for an answer before she yanks Luca out of his seat, not even bothering to apologize or ask if he's cool with it. She moves his plate down the table, her movements smooth like she owns the damn place, before flopping into his chair like it's the most natural thing in the world.

Saygin eyes the whole scene, her lips curling into a smirk that I can't help but admire, even though I really, really shouldn't. "You must be the mortal woman Ashton bonded with," she says, voice sickly sweet, her gaze sharpening with curiosity. She reaches her hand out, her long nails clicking against each other, the sound echoing through the room. "I'm Saygin."

"Nice to meet you," Sadie says, leaning forward eagerly, her excitement practically spilling out of her. "It's so nice to finally meet a supernatural woman! I mean... female," she stammers, catching herself like she just realized how much she's fan-girling.

It's a bit sickening how quickly Sadie is lapping up every word that leaves Saygin's lips. But I can't help it. This is who Sadie is—always hungry for *adventure* and *chaos*.

Ashton strolls in just then, like he's not the least bit fazed by any of this. He takes the seat next to me, completely unfazed by the storm brewing around him. He leans in close, his breath warm against my ear, and whispers, "What did I miss?"

I look at him, my frustration bubbling up to the surface, and I lean in just enough so only he can hear me. "Oh, nothing much. Just another round of *Saygin being Saygin* and Sadie... well, being Sadie. Nothing to see here." I flash him a dry smile, my sarcasm thick. "This is just dinner, right?"

Ashton grins, his eyes twinkling with mischief, his tone utterly deadpan. "Yeah, sure. *Dinner*. I think this one's going to be a five-course meal of stress."

I take another sip of my coffee, letting the warm liquid settle in my chest. "Luca's thinking about accepting a bargain with Saygin, and Sadie's practically falling at her feet like Saygin's the fucking queen of BDSM. Not sure if you're into *sounding*, but I'm giving you a heads up. Sadie might be in the mood to experiment soon, and I sure hope you don't have residual PTSD from Saygin in the past."

Ashton just nods, not even looking up from his plate. "I'll keep that in mind," he mutters, the same deadpan expression still on his face. "I'll let you know if I get the call for a threesome."

I choke on my coffee, coughing as it burns the back of my throat. "Fucking *hell*, Ashton."

He flashes me a grin, clearly enjoying my reaction, and leans back like he's too damn comfortable in his own skin. No nerves, no tension. Just... the usual Ashton. "What? You don't think I'm qualified for the job?" He raises an eyebrow at me, clearly amused.

I roll my eyes, wiping my mouth with the back of my hand. "Jesus Christ." Fuck.

Not me picking up mortal lingo from Sadie.

I'm about to say something else when I hear Sadie's voice pull me out of my train of thoughts. "Azrael?"

I glance over, and the worry in her eyes catches me off guard. "Have you heard from Layla?"

The air in the room shifts instantly, and I let out a heavy breath, rubbing the back of my neck. The weight of the situation is back, and it hits me harder every time I have to talk about it. "She woke up not too long ago. She's scared, but Drepane's doing what he can to protect her. Saygin is supposed to help us get her out of there."

Sadie looks at Saygin, her brow furrowing with a mix of concern and suspicion. Saygin, of course, doesn't even bother to acknowledge the question. Instead, she leans back in her chair with the same disinterest she's had since we arrived back home, exuding a calm that's almost predatory.

"We'll discuss details in the morning," she drawls, stretching like a lazy cat who just rolled out of bed. "I'm tired. *Ashton.* Do you mind tucking me in?" She adds a teasing smirk, practically purring the request, leaning forward just enough to make the whole thing sound too intimate.

"As if," Ashton deadpans without missing a beat, his eyes never leaving his plate as he casually shovels food into his mouth. He's not even phased by Saygin's... *advances.*

Saygin lets out a theatrical sigh, pretending to be disappointed, but there's a glint of amusement dancing behind her eyes. "Luca?" She leans over the table with exaggerated grace, her gaze sweeping across Sadie's shoulder to catch Luca's attention.

Luca, bless his heart, is doing his absolute best to pretend none of this is happening. His fork moves in precise circles over his plate like it's the most important thing in the world right now. "No, thank you," he mutters, not even bothering to glance up. He pushes the food around like he's trying to will it into something less *awkward.*

I snort at the scene, shaking my head. *Luca is the only one who's playing this cool.* The rest of us? We're deep in the circus, and we've all lost track of where the clowns are hiding.

CHAPTER TWENTY

Layla

RUN FOR YOUR LIFE - K. FLAY

It presses against my skin, clinging to me like something alive, damp, suffocating—like the despair has a will to live on its own. I hate it. I hate the way the shadows curl around my ankles, the way they murmur against my ears in voices I can't quite make out. I run my fingers along the walls as I move, desperate for something solid, something real, but even the stone feels wrong—too rough, too cold, too much like bone.

"I wouldn't explore the Empty if I were you, Layla," Drepane hums, his voice thick with warning.

I bite the inside of my cheek. "I just don't like the dark." The words are quiet, nearly swallowed whole by the oppressive silence.

"You are announcing your presence," he continues, unbothered. "Monsters from your deepest nightmares live here, and they are most certainly unforgiving." His tone drips with amusement, as if the idea of me being torn apart could be entertaining.

I know he's right. I can feel it in my bones—the weight of the air pressing down on me, the way every breath tastes stale, rotten, like the remnants of something long dead. The dark is suffocating, thick like ink, and I can't shake the feeling that something is watching me. For fucks sake, I feel so god damned vulnerable.

"You will feel even more vulnerable under a troll's foot. Being crushed," Drepane adds, voice flat, casual. Like he's commenting on the weather.

I swallow hard and squeeze my eyes shut, forcing myself to stay still. Panic won't help me. Panic will get me killed.

"Stay out of my thoughts, Drepane."

"Aren't you lovely?" he mocks. "I save your life, and this is how you treat me? Pathetic."

I grind my teeth, fighting the urge to snap back. I'm not in the mood to argue with a sentient sickle that enjoys running its mouth more than it should. Right now, I have bigger problems—like the fact that I'm alone in a place where things lurk. Where things hunt!

"I just want to go home!" The words burst out before I can stop them, sharp and raw, a plea I hate myself for making.

But there is no home here. No safety. Only endless black and the sound of my own breathing.

"The smart thing to do is find another dark corner to crawl into and wait," Drepane advises coldly. "They're coming. You just have to be patient."

I wrap my arms around myself, fingers digging into my sleeves. I'm hungry. Exhausted. I can feel the emptiness gnawing at me, not just in my stomach, but deeper—something hollow spreading inside me like a sickness.

"Drepane," I whisper, swallowing past the tightness in my throat. "I'm hungry."

Silence.

Then, he sighs. "Oh, how tragic."

I shake my head, pressing my knuckles against my mouth to keep from screaming. "I hate you," I mutter, though my words lack bite.

"No, you don't," he muses. "You hate the Empty. You hate feeling *powerless.*"

I don't respond. Because he's right.

A shiver rakes down my spine. The silence is stretching too long, too heavy. The air feels thick, it feels charged—almost like the moment before a storm breaks. I listen harder. There's something... something just beyond the edge of hearing. A distant vibration, a noise so low it almost blends into the quiet. A low growl.

I freeze.

"Please tell me that was your stomach," Drepane murmurs, voice barely above a whisper now.

I swallow, pressing a hand to my stomach, willing it to stay silent. "I think so," I whisper back.

A beat of silence.

Then—another sound. Deep. Wet. Something shifting. Breathing.

My blood turns to ice.

"Drepane?" My voice wavers despite myself.

"Yes, Layla?" His usual arrogance is gone.

"That's not my stomach."

The growl slithers through the darkness, deep and hungry. The floor beneath me seems to tremble, ever so slightly.

And then, somewhere in the black, something moves.

"I know, dear. *Stay still.*"

Drepane's voice is softer now, but the warning in his words weighs heavy, like a hand pressing against my chest. I barely hear him over the pounding of my heart and the rush of blood in my ears. My breath comes quicker, shallow and desperate, as though the darkness itself is sucking the air from my lungs.

"I'm scared," I whisper, the admission clawing its way out of my throat before I can stop it.

I hate this. The helplessness. The way the shadows seem to move with purpose, creeping closer, curling around me. I press my back against the cold, rough stone, fingers digging into the wall as if I could anchor myself to something solid, something real. But the Empty doesn't feel real. It feels like a nightmare, one that keeps stretching longer and darker, threatening to swallow me whole.

"I know," Drepane murmurs, quieter this time, almost mournful. Like he understands. Like he's seen this before.

Another growl slithers through the air, low and wet, vibrating through the walls. Moving closer...

I squeeze my fists so tightly that my nails bite into my palms. Every muscle in my body screams to run, *to move*, to do anything but stand here frozen. But I can't. The moment I move, it will know. It *already* knows.

The air shifts.

Hot. Foul.

A breath—not mine—brushes the back of my neck, thick with the stench of rotting meat and something sickly sweet, something so wrong.

A single strand of hair, loosened from my makeshift bun, tickles my cheek, and my body reacts before my mind does.

I flinch.

The growl stops.

For a moment, there's nothing but silence.

A silence so absolute it feels like the Empty itself is holding its breath.

Don't move. Don't breathe. Don't think. Drepane hums in my mind, his voice slicing through my panic, calm but unyielding. *Don't make a sound.*

Azrael's voice cuts through the suffocating terror—low and steady, wrapping around me like something warm, something safe. *Is everything okay?*

His words settle into my mind, grounding me, tethering me to something outside this hell. I cling to them, to him, as if holding on hard enough will make the darkness less fucking real.

Drepane answers before I can. *Talk to her, Azrael. Keep her calm. Her very existence currently relies on her being calm.*

I suck in a shaky breath, barely daring to move my lips. *Azrael, I can't—*

The growl comes again, so much closer now. This time, I *feel* it more than I hear it. The ground vibrates beneath my feet, my bones rattling with the sheer weight of the sound. My body locks up, every instinct screaming at me to *run*—but I can't. I can't fucking move!

The air is too thick. The stench too strong.

I can feel it *smelling me.*

Azrael's voice slides into my mind again, softer this time, a lifeline against the dark. *Tiny Mouse, I can't wait for you to come home. Our home, not Ashton's home—our home.*

A sharp ache blooms in my chest. He's trying to keep me calm. Trying to distract me. But it only makes the fear worse, because what if I never make it back? What if this thing—whatever it is—gets to me first?

I press my lips together, fighting back the wave of hysteria rising in my throat.

I have to stay calm. I have to be strong. I have to—

But I can't.

The heat against my skin intensifies. The growl deepens, guttural, hungry. My body trembles, my breath coming in shallow, rapid bursts. Tears sting my eyes. My hands shake.

I clutch at the thin thread of connection between Azrael and me, my last tether to sanity, and I let my fear pour into it—raw and unfiltered.

Azrael, I am so fucking scared! The words barely form before they shatter, breaking under the weight of my terror. I can't think, can't move, can't *breathe.*

Azrael's response is immediate, his voice sharp, urgent, desperate in a way that makes my chest tighten. *I know, I know. I am fucking coming for you. I promise.*

A beat of silence.

Then, softer—almost gentle—*What color do you want our room to be?*

The question catches me off guard. The absurdity of it, the casual normalcy in the middle of all this horror.

I want to answer. I want to focus on something—*anything*—other than the monster breathing down my neck.

But I can't think of colors.

I can't think of anything except the heat of its breath curling against my skin, the oppressive darkness pressing in, the feeling of being *hunted*.

Azrael, I whisper, my mind barely forming the words. *It's right next to me.*

The growl rises to a snarl, deep and reverberating through my bones.

And then the darkness moves.

What is it, Drepane? Azrael's voice is softer now, a steady pulse through our thread, caressing the edges of my unraveling mind. It should soothe me. But nothing can soften the way the darkness *breathes* around me.

I squeeze my eyes shut, trying to ground myself, but there's no escaping the truth pressing in on all sides. The air is thick, sticky with something unseen, something waiting. My pulse pounds at the base of my throat, every beat a painful reminder that I am *alive*—and something in this abyss knows it.

I can't tell, Drepane finally answers, but there's a weight in his hesitation, a heaviness that settles into my bones like lead. *But I'm pretty certain it's an undercat.*

The moment the word registers, terror *spikes* through me, sharp and electric.

An undercat?

What is that?

Azrael goes silent.

For the first time, I *feel* his silence, the weight of it like a hand pressing down on my chest. When he speaks again, his voice is quiet, more to himself than anyone else.

She can't even fight that.

The words settle in the pit of my stomach like stones.

I don't need him to say what comes next. I already know.

If I can't fight, I *can't* survive.

But before the panic can sink its claws deeper, Orcus' voice slips into my mind, light and playful—completely out of place. *Layla, are you a good singer?*

I blink, momentarily thrown. *What?*

Orcus' voice carries the kind of casual amusement that feels *almost* cruel in a moment like this.

Not really. I manage, my voice barely above a whisper, my throat so tight it hurts.

Like... fat lady breaking glass bad or tone-deaf walrus bad?

A laugh—small and shaky—bubbles up before I can stop it.

A fucking laugh.

I can't with you, Orcus! I shove at him through the bond, but the distraction clings to me, an anchor against the terror gnawing at my ribs.

Wait! His voice sharpens, turning suddenly serious. *Listen. They're used for Grim Beasts. One hasn't been bonded in centuries, but it's possible. Out of all the things you could've run into, this is the best-case scenario.*

Best-case scenario?

That's like saying drowning is the best way to die.

It doesn't make sense. It doesn't ease the panic clawing at my throat. But *something* in his tone—something firm, something sure—makes the fear shift, just slightly. And right now, I need any edge I can get.

Drepane's voice enters the bond thread again, softer than I've ever heard it. *Layla, you need to open your eyes and slowly turn so Orcus can see.*

I freeze. No.

I can't! The raw emotion in my voice rips free before I can stop it. I can't move. I can't look. I can't face it.

Azrael's voice is absolute. *Yes. Yes, you can!*

His words settle over me like an unshakable truth, his certainty wrapping around me like armor.

Babe, you are stronger than you think. I have faith in you. You are so brave. His voice dips lower, softer, like he's right here beside me. *But we need to see what you're up against.*

A tremor runs through me.

Azrael is calm. Steady. Completely opposite of what I feel.

But his belief in me is real. Unwavering. And I latch onto it, clinging to his presence like a lifeline.

I can still feel the hot air on me... My voice is barely audible, but I know he hears it.

The air is thick. Too thick. Like a living thing pressing down, pushing into my lungs, suffocating me in the heat and something maybe ancient.

I squeeze my fists so tight that my nails dig into my palms.

I need to breathe.

I need to move.

I need to look.

My body protests every tiny movement, every inch that I force myself to shift. But I listen to Azrael's voice in my head, repeating over and over—*You are strong. You are brave.*

And then, with a deep, shuddering breath, I slowly open my eyes.

At first, it's nothing but darkness.

And then—

Two massive, glowing orange eyes.

Larger than my fists. Staring. Unblinking. Just watching.

My breath catches, the world narrowing to that gaze—deep and consuming. My heart lurches painfully, and I swear I can *feel* it staring into me, peeling back every layer, every weakness, every fear.

A sharp hum rumbles through the air, low and inquisitive. The growl from before is gone, replaced by something else.

Something *curious.*

An undercat, Orcus breathes, voice tinged with something that almost sounds like *awe.*

I can't look away.

It's waiting.

Waiting for something.

And for the first time, I wonder—

Is it hunting me?

Or is it listening?

What do I do now?

The words rush through, mentally. It sounds so small and fragile, trembling against the weight of the creature in front of me. My voice feels insignificant, like a damn whisper in a storm.

Orcus answers without hesitation, his tone so casual it makes my head spin.

Sing it a song.

I blink. *Sing it a—*

The thought dies before I can finish it, my mind tripping over the absurdity of the suggestion.

Sing it a song? The words feel alien, ridiculous, like my brain is rejecting them outright. *Orcus, I don't even know what to sing!*

Then hum, he replies, and I can hear the shrug in his voice, like this is the simplest thing in the world. *Figure it out.*

My stomach knots. The undercat's glowing orange eyes remain fixed on me, unblinking, assessing. I don't know if it sees prey or something else, but I *can't* just stand here frozen.

So I do the only thing I can.

I hum.

My breath trembles once more as I close my eyes, forcing my hands to stop shaking as I pull a tune from the depths of my panic-stricken mind.

Amazing Grace.

It's not a choice. I don't even think about it. It's just there, surfacing through the chaos like muscle memory, something my mother used to sing under her breath while cooking, while cleaning—while worrying... which seems so silly now after all I have learned about *life*.

The first note is shaky, fragile. But I keep going, my voice barely carrying past my lips.

The moment the melody forms, two voices cut through the thread in unison.

Are you fucking kidding me? Orcus growls, his exasperation practically tangible.

Azrael is only a fraction softer, but no less incredulous. *Mouse. Really? Amazing Grace?*

I don't answer. I can't.

Because something shifts.

The undercat's massive pupils contract slightly, the glow of its eyes narrowing into thin, focused slits. But it doesn't feel like a threat. If anything, the air around me grows lighter and softer.

Then—

A sound.

Not a growl. Not a snarl.

A low, steady purr.

It vibrates through the cavern, a deep, resonant hum that I feel in my chest. Like it's... responding.

I keep humming, my pulse erratic, but I don't stop. I can't. The tunnel around us begins to glow—soft purples and blues, flickering like fireflies in the dark. It takes me a second to realize that it's Drepane, his light pulsing in sync with the song, like he's guiding me, anchoring me to the moment.

And for the first time since stepping into this abyss, I feel something other than fear.

I feel *hope*.

My breath steadies as I take in the undercat's huge frame.

Its body is massive, a deep navy blue that looks almost black in the dim light, speckled with bright yellow spots that *move*, shifting as if they're alive. It reminds me of a starry sky, wild and infinite. Its head is impossibly large—four times bigger than mine, at least—with powerful, predatory features. Its mouth slightly open to reveal gleaming, razor-sharp teeth. But it doesn't strike.

It just watches.

Now touch her nose. Orcus' voice is quieter this time, but insistent. It sounds so fucking "sure". Like he knows something I don't.

My breath catches. *What?*

Touch it, he repeats, as if this is obvious.

Panic flutters in my chest again. *Are you insane?*

Yes, but that's not the point. If she lets you touch her, you bond. If she doesn't... well. A pause. *Let's just hope she does.*

I want to argue. I want to demand an actual plan, something that doesn't involve me sticking my hand near a mouth full of knives.

But I don't.

Because the undercat is waiting.

It hasn't moved. It hasn't backed away. And for some reason, I can't shake the feeling that this is one of the only ways I might make it out of here *alive*.

I swallow hard. My hands are shaking again, but I force them to still.

Then—slowly, cautiously—I take a step forward.

The creature doesn't flinch.

I raise my hand, palm up, my fingers barely inches from the smooth surface of its nose.

For a second, nothing happens. The undercat is so still I wonder if I imagined everything—the hum, the purr, the shift in the air.

Then—

It moves.

Just the smallest tilt of its head, just the faintest lean forward.

My fingertips brush against warmth.

A shudder runs through me, through it. Like something clicks into place.

And for one impossibly still moment, I swear the entire Underworld is holding its breath.

CHAPTER TWENTY-ONE

Azrael

LAST RESORT - FALLING IN REVERSE

I can *feel* it.

The bond thread snaps into existence, a sharp jolt of electricity lancing through my chest, burning through me like a live wire. My bones and joints crawl, the sensation foreign and *wrong,* twisting through my very bones. It doesn't settle like it should. It writhes, pressing into me, threading through my being like a force that doesn't belong.

It's pushing me out.

Pushing *Orcus* out.

Like we're not even worthy to *help* her.

A growl catches in my throat, my body locking up as the force pulls. It's not just magic—it's something deeper, something raw and primal, coiling around Layla's thread like a viper sinking its fangs into her, claiming her.

I brace against the table, my fingers digging into the wood hard enough to splinter it.

The pain—*fuck, the pain.*

A scream rips out of me, a sound torn from deep within, part agony, part rage. It echoes through the room, cutting the tense silence like a god damn blade.

I feel eyes on me.

Sadie.

I don't even have to look at her to know she's watching, her gaze heavy and worried, like she can feel the weight of this pressing down on me, like she knows something is *wrong.*

The room is too small, too *tight,* the walls closing in.

And Saygin—she stops mid-step, turning toward me with something almost like concern flashing across her features.

Is it my scream? The bond? The pain? The shift of something *dark?*

I push against it, force my will into the bond, trying to reach Layla, to anchor myself to her thread.

But the beast's thread—that *thing's* thread—

It's braiding into hers, twisting around it like it fucking owns her.

Layla's scream *shatters* through my mind, raw, broken—

And I *feel* it.

Like claws raking through my insides, like my very soul is being torn open.

"Goddamn it." The words are barely a growl, more breath than sound. My vision wavers as I push harder, but it's like trying to hold back the ocean. The storm of fear, of *pain,* hits me like a sledgehammer, knocking me back a step. Orcus is with me, both of us *fighting,* but it's not enough.

Layla is too far.

Too deep in this mess.

Every time I reach for her, I'm struck with a lightning bolt of agony.

And then—

It stops.

The pain vanishes. The screams cut off.

I stagger, the sudden emptiness a gut punch. The silence is unnatural, coiling in my ears like a trap.

I don't trust it. Not for a second.

Layla? I reach out, my voice sharp, urgent—panic creeping in despite myself.

For a moment, nothing.

Then—

I'm here.

Soft. Strained. Breathless.

She's alive.

That's all that matters.

That's all that *should* matter.

But I can still feel her pain, like an echo of something deep in my bones, it's like a ghost of the suffering that's not entirely gone.

I'm fucking coming, Mouse. The words come low and rough, more a promise than a statement. *We are coming in the morning. I promise you. I'm coming to fucking get you.*

She doesn't respond.

The silence stretches between us, thick, suffocating.

My stomach churns, the restless need to move—to fucking act—is burning through my limbs.

But there's nothing I can do.

Not now.

Not yet.

So I hold onto the bond, onto that fragile, fraying thread, even though it feels like I'm trying to stand against a thousand storms.

I exhale sharply, forcing my breath to steady, forcing my hands to still.

I know, Orcus rumbles at my side, his voice a careful blend of amusement and concern. *I'll admit, Mouse's bond is... impressive. But you? You're looking a little worn out, Azrael. Think you can handle it? Maybe we should ask Ashton to borrow some of his supernatural male stamina.*

I growl, sharp and immediate, barely holding back the impulse to snap.

Don't fuck with me right now, Orcus. My voice is razor-edged, shaking with the barely leashed *need* to *move*. To do something. *This is not the time for jokes.*

My hands tremble.

I ignore it.

Because right now, the only thing that matters is getting to her.

"Is everything okay?" Sadie's voice was soft with concern, but I could hear the underlying *panic* threading beneath it.

I exhaled sharply, trying to focus on anything other than the tight knot in my chest, the lingering weight of what had just happened.

"Layla," I managed to say, my voice dry as sandpaper, cracking under the force of it.

Sadie stood up so fast her chair scraped against the floor, her eyes flashing. "Is she okay?" Her gaze locked onto mine, demanding an answer.

"Yes." Orcus answered for me before I could even open my mouth, his tone far too casual given the circumstances. "She just bonded with an undercat."

The room froze.

Vassago and Ashton both stopped chewing at the same time. A synchronized choke followed as they nearly inhaled their food.

The shock in the air was thick, hanging between us like the aftermath of a bomb.

"What's an undercat?" Luca asked, genuinely confused as he wiped his mouth with a napkin, utterly unaware of the magnitude of what he'd just heard.

"A very *huge* cat," Vassago said after sipping his coffee, his tone so deadpan that the absurdity of it hit even harder.

Luca stared at him for a long, long beat before shaking his head. "That... doesn't exactly answer my question."

"There hasn't been a new Grim Beast keeper in centuries," Ashton cut in, now leaning back in his chair, his expression shifting into something thoughtful. "I think the last one Exu tried with was *Nyxian,* but he turned out to be a shadow forger."

I smirked despite the tension still coiled in my chest, rubbing the back of my neck. "Do you expect anything less from your Queen?"

Ashton didn't miss a beat. "Honestly? She surprises me every chance she gets, so... no."

That made me exhale, if only a little. The tightness in my chest refused to fully ease. Layla was still out there...

But I couldn't lose her.

Not like this.

"Where's Lydia?" I asked, my voice less sharp now but still edged with frustration. Her absence was like a thorn, an irritant I couldn't shake.

"She returned home so her mortal husband wouldn't be worried she was gone for too long," Vassago answered, carrying the dirty dishes to the sink. "Told me to send her a messenger dove when we find Layla."

My jaw tightened.

Lydia had her own priorities.

I got it. I did.

But it didn't help the gnawing feeling that she was always a step ahead of me, always slipping through my fingers before I could *really* figure her out.

I turned to Saygin, who had been standing in the doorway, silently observing the whole exchange.

"We leave in the morning," I said firmly, my tone final.

"Not possible. Quinn needs time to gather everything to open the portal."

My jaw clenched, fists tightening as frustration coiled like a vice in my chest. "I said... we leave in the morning. Ashton will send for whatever the fuck you need. We are leaving. Layla is in danger, and I *will* go get her."

The silence that followed was thick, nearly suffocating. Saygin tilted her head, watching me with an unreadable expression before finally speaking, her voice eerily steady. "I just have a question, Azrael."

I turned to her, eyes narrowing. "What?"

"Is she worth losing more than you enter the Empty with?"

The question landed like a punch to the gut, forcing the air from my lungs.

"I will risk anyone's life for my mate." My voice was steel, unwavering. I turned to Ashton, knowing he understood what I meant better than anyone. "Anyone with a bond this strong would do the same. Ashton killed his own father over Isolde. Would you not risk everything for Quinn?"

Ashton nodded, his voice rough. "No hesitation."

I shifted my gaze to Quinn, expecting an agreement or something, but there was nothing. Instead, Saygin's response was quick, almost dismissive. "Honestly? No. Males are replaceable." She shrugged. "Mates can be replaced. I'm not risking my life, or his, or anyone else's just because I feel like I'm not *whole without* them. I was fine *before*. I'll be fine *after*."

Her words didn't sit right with me. The cold detachment, the complete lack of anything real—it was the opposite of what I felt for Layla. I could barely breathe without her, and Saygin just... didn't get it.

"Not everyone has that mindset," I muttered, frustration leaking into my voice.

Saygin smirked, tilting her head. "*Womp. Womp.* Life goes on. I will have Quinn send the list of supplies to Ashton for him to get it *all*. We'll get your mate back, Azrael."

Her words did nothing to ease the burning in my chest. The urgency. The need.

And then, with a sharp inhale, she added, "Even if, originally, you were going to sacrifice the *wolf* for my bargain."

Sadie, who had been unusually quiet, suddenly choked on her drink. "Wait. Poor Luca. Why would you *do* that, Azrael?"

Her eyes flicked to me, the devil's own shit-eating grin spreading across her lips.

"Oh, mister 'I will do anything to get Layla back,' but when it comes to sounding, you're quick to run away."

I glared at her, irritation and amusement warring inside me. "Sadie, if you weren't Layla's friend, I'd have to seriously reconsider your life choices. It was *your* idea!"

"Oh, I'm sure," she purred. "But, I mean, it's kind of true, isn't it?" She lifted a finger, mimicking a cat's paw and meowing. "Mister 'I will do anything to get my mate back,' but when the heat of the moment comes, you're all talk." She completely ignored my statement.

I narrowed my eyes, fighting the smirk threatening to break through my scowl. "Careful, Sadie. Keep it up, and I'll send you to the Empty for a vacation, courtesy of Orcus."

Her eyes widened for half a second before she burst into laughter, shaking her head. "You're fucking impossible, Azrael."

"Sadie, not *now*." Ashton's voice was low, barely above a growl.

Sadie raised an eyebrow, unfazed. "Ah. You want to say something now?" Her smirk didn't waver. "You skipped over the part where you allegedly killed your *father* over your last mate."

"Not alleged," Orcus chimed in from the back, mischief hinting in his tone. "He did."

Saygin's lips parted slightly, curiosity flashing across her face. "Interesting," she murmured, glancing between Ashton and Sadie. "He told you about Isolde, but *not* the full story?"

Ashton stiffened.

His gaze fell to the table, shoulders drawing in slightly. He looked small. Like a man standing at the edge of a storm that had long since passed—but never truly left.

The weight of the room shifted. Uncomfortable. Heavy.

I stood, walking over to Ashton with deliberate steps, placing a firm hand on his shoulder. Beneath my grip, I felt the slight tremor in his frame.

"His father didn't approve of his bond," I said, my voice steady, but sharp. "And the price was sexual torture. Isolde was weeks away from giving birth when

Ashton finally found her." I inhaled sharply, forcing the words out. "But she was too far gone. He had to be the one to give her mercy."

Silence.

I turned to Sadie, my voice dropping to something lethal. "If you hold it over his head, if you can't be *compassionate* about what happened to him—you have *no place* in the Underworld. I don't give a *fuck* if you're my mate's best friend."

I shoved past Saygin, my frustration boiling over, a sharp need to shield Ashton from the weight of this.

"We *leave* in the morning," I snapped, not sparing anyone another glance. "And that's final."

The room didn't move.

The cracks in the conversation were sealed, but the tension lingered—thick, stifling, unspoken.

CHAPTER TWENTY-TWO

Ashton

CARRY YOU - RUELLE

"Why didn't you tell me the whole story, Ashton?" Sadie's voice broke through the silence, sharp and demanding. She sat at the foot of the bed, her eyes watching me carefully as I hung my robe for the night, avoiding her gaze.

I paused, running a hand over my face. I couldn't look at her, not right now. The words felt heavy, like they would collapse in on themselves the moment I said them. "Because, if I'm being honest..." I let out a shaky breath, taking a moment to steady myself. "I have healed from losing Isolde like I did... but not from losing my son."

Sadie was silent for a long moment. I could feel her eyes on me, piercing through the walls I had built around this part of myself.

I looked up, staring at the ceiling as though I could find answers in the cracks. "I think, in a way, I'd rather have lost her than him. At least with Isolde, I could bury the hurt with the blood, the war, the chaos. But with him... it's *different*." My voice broke, and I wiped a hand across my face. Tears began to fall freely now, like they'd been waiting for this moment to break through. "I was supposed to send my son to Exu to train. I was supposed to hold him, hear his first cries, smell his scent, everything a new father would do. I didn't get to do any of that, Sadie."

Her breath caught, and I could see the guilt wash over her face. She opened her mouth to say something, but the words didn't come right away. "I... I feel like a bitch now," she finally murmured. "You should've told me the whole story."

I shook my head, the weight of my emotions threatening to crush me. "How the fuck do you talk about a child you lost along with someone you were supposed to spend your entire *existence* with?" I let out a broken laugh, bitter and self-deprecating. "How do you even start to explain that to someone who hasn't lived it? It's a pain that doesn't go away, Sadie. It *haunts* you."

I looked down at the floor, trying to blink back the overwhelming grief that surged through me. The tears kept falling, and I couldn't stop them. "It's a huge burden to lose a mate. But it's a whole other thing to lose a child, one that you wanted, one that you would dream about." My chest tightened as the words cut deeper than I expected. "I don't expect you to understand."

Sadie's eyes flashed with hurt, and she stood up abruptly, her hands trembling. "*Excuse me?*" Her voice was low, dangerous, and she stepped closer. "What the hell do you mean by *that*?"

I flinched, but I didn't back away. "Nothing, Sadie," I muttered, trying to regain control of the situation. "Let's just go to sleep. I have to leave in the morning. We'll talk later."

But as I turned to walk past her, Sadie's hand shot out, grabbing my arm with surprising strength. She pushed me back, forcing me to face her. "Don't you *dare* shut me out right *now*," she snapped, her voice trembling with frustration and something darker—*hurt*, maybe?

"Sadie—" I started, but she cut me off.

"*No.* You don't get to do that. You don't get to say something like that and then walk away from it like it's nothing." Her eyes were wild, and I could feel her anger building. "You think you're the only one with fucking baggage? You think you're the only one who's lost something? Because news flash, Ashton, I've suffered a lost too! And I won't just stand here while you throw it in my face like it's a goddamn competition!" She sat on the foot of the bed.

I swallowed hard, the walls I'd built were cracking under the weight of her words. "Sadie, it's not a competition. It's just..." I trailed off, too tired to finish. She was right. I'd been so wrapped up in my own pain that I forgot how it felt to be on the other side of this, to feel helpless in the face of someone else's suffering.

"I was forced to have my abortion," Sadie whispered, her voice trembling with rage and heartbreak. "No one even *fucking asked* me what happened. Everyone just assumed I was the party girl who didn't want the party to stop. You all assumed that I *chose* that." Her voice cracked, her brown eyes flooding with tears as they began to spill, emotions rushing down the bonding thread like a monsoon.

She stood up, her body trembling with the weight of it all. "Dash beat me when I told him I was pregnant," she continued, each word falling from her lips like a raw wound. "I tried to tell Layla, but I fucking couldn't get the courage. I couldn't get her alone. You *don't* understand, Ashton. I couldn't say it. I couldn't tell her, not like that."

I felt the weight of her emotions—her pain, her guilt, the fear she carried deep inside. It wasn't just a burden for her; it felt like it was crushing me too. I opened my mouth to say something, but no words came. Instead, I just stood there, frozen by the heaviness of her confession.

She reached out to me, her hand trembling in the space between us. "Fucking see for yourself, Ashton." Her words were sharp, laced with desperation. "If you want a baby, let's have a fucking baby. If you want it to just be you and me for all eternity, then so be it! *I love you*, Ashton. From the second I saw you in Layla's room, I wanted *you*. *I needed you*. Don't sit here and think of me as some kind of monster before you know my full story."

I nodded, the silence thick between us. Without another word, I reached for her hand, my fingers trembling slightly as I touched her skin. The instant our hands met, her memories flooded into me, an overwhelming tide of images and feelings.

The first one hit me like a punch to the gut—loud music blaring, the kind of noise that made everything feel distant and unimportant. I saw myself, standing in front of her, as she looked down at a pregnancy test, a single word appearing on the screen: *positive*. Her emotions in that moment were a whirlwind—fear, happiness, hope—and I could feel her mind spinning with names for the baby, a quiet image of rocking a tiny baby to sleep.

But then, everything shifted. The memory twisted, and I saw Dash—his dark eyes, his cruel smirk—as he pulled out a chair for Sadie at a café. Her voice, small and trembling, explained that she was pregnant, and the tension in the air was thick. Dash's words cut through her like a knife, dismissing the life growing inside her as if it was nothing. He called her a *whore*.

And I felt her heart shatter in that instant, the rage building inside her, the decision to leave, to stand her ground. But he grabbed her arm, his grip tight and suffocating, and told her she would have an abortion, that there was no other choice. And when she refused, his anger flared. He humiliated her in front of everyone, yelling to the top of his lungs that she was a *whore*.

Her memory spun faster, the scene shifting again to a different time. I saw Sadie standing, struggling with her keys, tears clouding her vision as she tried to unlock the door to her apartment after another long day. Dash appeared from behind her, a shadow in the dark, grabbing her hair and slamming her head against the door.

I felt her pain—sharp, brutal—and it tore through me, sending an ache deep into my chest. I wanted to reach out, to stop it, but I couldn't. I could only feel what she felt. He kicked her repeatedly, each blow making her body tremble in pain.

And then, in a flash, she agreed. Not because she wanted to, but because it was the only way to make him stop.

The memory fast-forwarded again, taking me to a later moment when Layla introduced Dash to Sadie. The emotions coursing through Sadie were chaotic—fear, shame, guilt—but she hid it, wearing the mask of normalcy. But it wasn't normal. It was a performance, and I could see through it, I could *feel* her pain.

And then came the final image—the one that is absolutely breaking me. Sadie, standing alone in her apartment, the weight of everything crashing down on her. She tried to numb it. She tried to erase the pain with a bottle of pills, her body shaking as she clutched the container in her hand, her vision blurring—

I shook my head violently, the flood of memories too much to bear. It was too much to feel—her raw emotions, her pain, her loss. It was suffocating, and I pulled my hand away from hers, stumbling back as my heart pounded in my chest.

"I can't... I can't see anymore," I gasped, my voice thick with emotion. "Sadie... I—"

She stood there, her hand still reaching out to me, her expression a mixture of fear and hope. "I didn't want this, Ashton. I didn't want to hurt anyone. But you don't know what it's like to be a woman forced into a corner, to have everything you love ripped away because some man has control over it. I wanted *that* baby, Ashton. I wanted it more than *anything*. I would have been a fucking *amazing* mother!"

I closed my eyes, the weight of her words settling over me like a shroud. For the first time, I understood the depth of her pain—not just the physical abuse, but the emotional torment, the loss of the one thing she could never get back. And I hated Dash for it. I hated him with everything I had.

Sadie stepped closer, her voice soft, but firm. "I just need you to *see me*, Ashton. I need you to understand that I'm not some monster. I'm not just the girl who fucked up. I'm someone who's been through hell and is still trying to find a way out of it."

I nodded slowly, my chest tight with all the emotions I hadn't known how to express. I wanted to say something, to comfort her, but the words felt hollow. Instead, I reached out and pulled her into my arms, holding her close.

"I see you, Sadie. *I see you.*"

And for the first time, I felt the weight of her brokenness—her anger, her hurt, her regret—becoming part of me. It wasn't just her pain anymore. It was *ours*.

"Sadie, I'm so sorry," I whispered, my voice thick with regret.

She looked up at me, her eyes clouded with unshed tears, but her voice was a mix of hurt and defiance. "Everyone's always so consumed with *Layla*. I'm just the side character in her story. The party girl no one gives two fucks about. No one cared to ask me how I feel, what I want…" Her voice faltered as she trailed off, the weight of her unspoken words hanging in the air between us.

Without thinking, I pulled her into a tight embrace, my arms wrapping around her like a shield. She tensed for a moment but slowly melted into me, her head resting on my chest as she let out a shaky breath.

"You and Luca are the only two beings under this roof that care about me. Everyone else hates me, Ashton," she whispered, her voice breaking.

"No one hates you, Sadie." I pulled back just enough to hold her face in my hands, gently wiping away the tears that had fallen down her cheeks. I looked down at her, the weight of everything we had just shared weighing heavy in my chest. I kissed her softly, a kiss that held everything I had been too afraid to say before. "I love you, Sadie. I was too scared to say it, too scared to *admit it*. But if something happens to you… I don't think I could live through that."

Sadie's lips quirked into a mischievous smile despite her tears, and she shook her head. "I'm like a roach, Ashton. You can't get rid of me," she teased, her eyes sparkling with that familiar fire I loved.

I couldn't help but laugh softly, the tension in my chest easing just a bit. She was right, there was no getting rid of her. Not that I'd ever want to.

"Let's not keep secrets from each other ever again, okay?" she asked, her tone earnest, her eyes locking onto mine with an intensity that made my heart skip a beat.

"I promise, little Nightmare." I pulled her close again, my arms tightening around her as if I could somehow absorb all of her negative feelings, the pain and confusion she'd been carrying for so long.

Her arms wrapped around my waist, and for a moment, everything felt right. "Do you want a baby?" I whispered, unsure of how to say the question without it feeling too much, but needing to know.

She pulled back slightly, looking up at me, her gaze soft and contemplative. I kissed her forehead gently, feeling the warmth of her skin against my lips. "If you're ready, Sand Boy, I am," she said, her voice steady but full of something else—something that made me believe she wasn't just talking about a child. She was talking about a future, about *us*.

I held her even tighter, afraid that if I let go, she might slip away again. "We'll figure this out, Sadie. Together."

Chapter Twenty-Three

Layla

Echo - Jason Walker

I use Drepane as a purple flashlight, his eerie glow casting long, jagged shadows on the tunnel walls. It's the only light I've got, and I swear it feels dimmer with each step I take. Maybe I'm imagining it, or maybe this place is just swallowing it whole like it's trying to *erase* me. My feet ache, each step a reminder that I've been walking forever. Or maybe it's only been a few hours. Time doesn't make sense down here. The hunger gnaws at me, twisting in my stomach like something alive, but at least I found some water trickling from a crack in the wall earlier. It was cold and fresh, which was nice, even if I did feel like a cave goblin lapping at a rock.

The undercat trails behind me, her heavy paws soundless on the cold stone floor. She hasn't spoken—not that I know if Grim Beasts even do that—but she hasn't looked at me either. Just follows, silent and strange, like a shadow that decided it was done being two-dimensional. I can feel her though, the weight of her presence, watching. I don't know if that's a good thing.

"Here is fine, tiny one," Drepane hums, his voice vibrating through the thick air like the hum of a cello string. It doesn't echo like it should. Instead, it settles around me, warm and full, like a lullaby without words.

I glance around at the tunnel again. Stone and dirt, dirt and stone. The walls press in on me, making the air feel thick, like it's trying to smother me. I can't even get a full breath, and every inhale tastes like dust and time. It's the kind of place where hope comes to die—or at least get really, really tired.

This isn't how it's supposed to be. I'm the heroine, right? The one who's supposed to get rescued, who gets swept off her feet by someone strong enough to fight for her, to love her through the darkness. I've read enough romance novels to know the formula. The brooding, tortured hero who doesn't believe in love but finds himself inexplicably drawn to the feisty, fragile girl who's too afraid to let anyone in. That's the story. That's how this should go.

But no one is coming. No Azrael. No dramatic last-minute rescue. Just me, lost in the dark, hoping my glowing sickle is enough to keep the void at bay.

The undercat stretches before pouncing towards a far corner tucked away, her movements eerily graceful despite her size. She circles, then settles, her large, gleaming eyes still tracking me. She yawns, flashing long, dagger-like fangs, then curls in on herself. Her soft fur glinting under Drepane's dim glow.

Something in me cracks. I cross the space and collapse beside her, too exhausted to care if she decides to use me as a chew toy. My body screams in protest, but her warmth seeps into me, a comfort I didn't realize I needed. I rest my head against her massive paw, half-expecting her to shove me off.

She doesn't.

"Is dying scary, Drepane?" The words slip out before I can stop them, a quiet, fragile whisper in the heavy dark.

Drepane hums again, thoughtful. "I've never died before, sweet girl."

That should be somewhat comforting knowing I'm not doing this alone, but it isn't. Because he didn't say I *wasn't* going to die. He didn't promise me anything.

My throat tightens, and suddenly, I can't hold it back anymore. A sob forces its way out, raw and desperate, and then another. The weight of everything presses down on me, suffocating, squeezing the breath from my lungs. My shoulders shake, and I hate it—I hate feeling weak, hate that I'm crumbling when I should be stronger.

This isn't how the story is supposed to go. There's no knight in shining armor here, no mysterious, dark figure who will fight the monsters and tell me it'll all be okay. No grand, sweeping declarations of love. Just me. Just this tunnel. Just the unbearable weight of not knowing if I'm going to make it out.

The quiet sound of my tears fill the space between us. Then, unexpectedly, I hear a voice.

A voice that isn't Drepane's.

"You won't die," the voice says softly, almost playfully.

I jolt upright, my pulse slamming against my ribs, scanning the dim tunnel for any sign of movement. My fingers tighten around Drepane's handle, my makeshift purple flashlight casting shifting shadows against the walls. My throat is dry. "Who's there?" I demand, but my voice shakes, betraying me. There's no response. Just silence. Heavy and waiting.

I whip my head toward the undercat. She's no longer curled up like a giant ball of judgmental fluff. Instead, she stands tall, her sleek body poised with an unsettling grace. She stares at me with those massive, knowing eyes, unblinking. Then, in a motion so casual it feels deliberately smug, she tilts her head.

"It's me, *silly*," she says, her voice smooth as velvet.

I blink. My mouth falls open. "What."

She doesn't repeat herself. Instead, she lifts a paw and begins licking it, completely unconcerned with my existential crisis. "My name is Flo," she says between leisurely swipes, as if this is the most normal thing in the world.

I continue to stare. Processing. Failing to process. "Flo?"

"Yes, Flo," she confirms, finishing her grooming and stretching with a deep, satisfied sigh.

"You can talk?" My voice barely gets the words out.

Flo's eyes gleam with amusement. "Obviously." She curls back into a ball—this time closer to me, as if now that the secret's out, we're best friends. "Don't act so surprised."

Drepane hums, his glow pulsing faintly. "Hello, Flo. I am Drepane." His voice reverberates in the confined space, filling the tunnel like an old song.

"I know who you are. We all do." Flo's tail flicks lazily, her voice carrying a note of something unreadable.

A chill slithers down my spine. "We?" I glance around the tunnel, my skin prickling at the idea that something else could be lurking in the shadows.

"The others," she says, nonchalant. "They're watching."

I swallow. "Others?"

Flo gives a slow blink. "Don't worry, they're just curious."

Oh yeah, that makes me feel *so much better*.

"You're Layla, the Queen of the Underworld," she continues, stretching her paws forward. "That's Drepane."

I suck in a sharp breath. *Queen.*

The word slams into me, unfamiliar and heavy, like wearing someone else's shoes that are ten sizes too big. I hadn't exactly planned on ruling anything, let alone an entire realm of the dead and supernatural beings. Hell, I'm barely in charge of myself!

"And the only thing we can't figure out," Flo muses, tail flicking, "is why you're living in the Empty."

I scoff, rubbing my arms against the tunnel's ever-present chill. "Yeah, well, that makes two of us."

I hesitate, then glance at Drepane for reassurance. His glow is steady, his warmth a silent comfort. I exhale. "I was injured. Drepane kind of... accidentally brought me here. And now we're stuck." My voice dips into something danger-ously close to defeat. "Do you know how to get out?"

Flo's ears twitch, and for a moment, she looks genuinely thoughtful. Then she stretches again, arching her back in that fluid, effortless way cats do, like she's some ancient being deciding whether I'm worth indulging.

"The tooth fairies have a portal," she finally says. "Might be able to use that."

I blink. "I'm sorry, the what?"

"The tooth fairies," she repeats casually, licking a paw like this isn't the weirdest thing she could have possibly said.

"Okay, I'm going to need a second to process that," I mutter. "Because I *know* you don't mean the tiny winged creatures who break into children's rooms and leave money under their pillows."

Flo smirks. "Do you?"

I narrow my eyes. "Do *you*?"

She just yawns.

Drepane hums beside me. "The fairies collect things. Teeth are among their more... *harmless* trades."

Flo flicks her tail, clearly unimpressed with my mortal ignorance. "They use them for portals. Something about bone magic. They never tell us the details."

I stare. I shouldn't be surprised. I really shouldn't. This entire realm is built on nightmares and things I don't understand. But still. *Tooth fairies?*

"And you think they'll help?" I ask, because hope is dangerous, but I can't help clinging to it like a lifeline.

Flo shrugs in that effortless, frustrating way only a cat can. "Maybe."

"Maybe?"

"There's a chance they will," she says, eyes gleaming. "And a chance they won't."

Oh, fantastic. Love that. So comforting.

I press my fingers against my temples. "So it's a gamble."

"Everything's a gamble," Flo purrs, completely unbothered. "But you have to ask, right?"

Right.

I glance at Drepane, who remains silent but warm, a steady presence at my side. Then I look back at Flo, who's already curling up again like she hasn't just dropped a massive, reality-warping revelation on me.

Tooth fairies. Portals. The shadows watching us.

I exhale sharply.

This might actually be the weirdest day of my life. And that's *really* saying something.

I'm about to ask her more when something tugs at me—something I can't ignore.

Why is she even talking to me? Why did she bond with *me*, of all people?

The others are watching from the dark, hidden, waiting. But *she* chose to step forward. She chose to be here.

"Why did you bond with me, Flo?" The question tumbles from my lips before I can think better of it. "Why aren't you with the others, hiding in the dark?"

Flo doesn't answer right away. She stretches out on the stone floor, shifting her weight like she's making herself at home in a place that feels anything *but* homely. Her claws flex against the dirt, then relax. When she finally speaks, her voice is low, purring, almost dreamy.

"Adventure," she murmurs. "I want to *feel* the sun touch my fur and smell flowers."

I blink. That... is not the answer I expected.

Of all the things she could have said, *that* was nowhere on my list.

"Adventure?" I echo, the word foreign in my mouth. A small, unexpected smile tugs at my lips. It's faint, barely there, but it exists.

For so long, this place has felt like a grave, like an endless stretch of *nothing*. But here is this creature, this strange, shadow-born beast, and she's *longing* for something more. Something warm. Something bright.

I guess I'm not the only one looking for a way out of the dark.

Drepane hums beside me, his glow pulsing with curiosity. "How old are you?"

Flo's ears twitch, and she narrows her luminous eyes in mock offense. "162 years old."

Drepane rumbles with clear amusement. "I thought you were a kitten."

Flo lets out a soft, melodic chuckle, the sound rich and unbothered. "Nope, just a runt." Her tail flicks lazily, brushing against the cold stone.

I watch her, thoughtful.

She may be small—by Grim Beast standards, anyway—but there's something about her. A quiet confidence. A curiosity. A desire for *more*.

And for the first time since I've been here, I feel a flicker of something I thought I'd lost.

Not hope. Not exactly.

But maybe something close.

Flo stretches one last time before curling up again, her voice softer now. "Get some rest, Layla. You'll need it."

I hesitate, my body aching, my mind still spinning. But eventually, I lower my head against the stone, letting exhaustion pull at me.

Flo's words about the tooth fairies linger in my head, but something deeper gnaws at me.

This place isn't just dark—it's full of things lurking beneath the surface, waiting. Watching.

And I can't shake the feeling that things are only going to get more complicated from here.

CHAPTER TWENTY-FOUR

Azrael

PAINT IT BLACK - HIDDEN CITIZENS

The tension in the room thickens, a suffocating weight pressing down on us as Quinn flashes his toothy grin, his eyes gleaming with that particular brand of *I'm about to be a pain in your ass* mischief.

He leans forward like a cat toying with a cornered mouse, his amusement almost palpable. "Who all will be accompanying us on this *perilous* journey?" His voice is smooth, like honey laced with arsenic, and I can practically *taste* the malice lurking underneath.

I resist the urge to snap his neck on principle. Barely.

"Vassago and Ashton," I reply, my tone clipped, final, as if that should end the conversation right there. The fewer beings involved, the better.

Quinn's lips quirk, and his gaze slides to Luca, his smirk widening with something dangerously close to glee. "No *wolf*?" The word drips from his mouth like it leaves a bad taste. Disdain curls his mouth, though a glimmer of dark humor lingers in his eyes.

"He stays here to keep him safe," I answer sharply, my patience already waning.

Luca *may* be a capable fighter, but he's still in a mortal body, and the Empty isn't the kind of place you walk into lightly. Hell, even *I'm* not certain I'll make it out in one piece. The idea of dragging him into that place—where gods and nightmares *rot*—makes my jaw tighten.

A long pause stretches between us, tension coiling tight.

Then Saygin speaks, her voice smooth and dangerously calm. "We refuse to move forward unless the wolf comes with."

A slow, cold heat unfurls in my chest.

She is *really* pushing it.

I take a breath, then another, my fists clenching so tightly my knuckles crack.

"I can kill you right here and now," I growl, my voice a quiet promise.

But Saygin just fucking *grins*—like she's *enjoying* this, like *she's* the one in control. It makes me want to snap her in half just to wipe that smug expression off her face.

"Then you'd never get your mate back," she hums, tilting her head in mock sympathy. "*Such* a predicament we're in, hmm?"

I want to rip her apart.

Slowly.

Instead, I exhale through my nose and force my voice to stay level. "What is your infatuation with Luca?"

Quinn chuckles, low and demonic, the sound curling around the edges of my nerves like smoke. "Eye candy." His gaze flickers to Luca with something dark and amused. "Helps us keep an *eye* on the prize."

The sheer audacity of this *motherf*—

I turn to Luca, half-expecting some kind of reaction—fear, annoyance, maybe even *common sense*—but he looks utterly *unfazed*. Like he's seen worse.

Which, honestly, he probably has.

He shrugs. "Weirder things have happened to me so far."

Ashton, ever the chaotic neutral, bursts out laughing. "I'll make sure he has a protection spell or two on him." He throws a lazy grin at the odd couple, his tone turning playfully mocking. "Maybe *three*."

I roll my eyes. "Not funny."

He winks. "A little funny."

I ignore him, scrubbing a hand down my face. I *hate* this.

But despite my *better judgment*, I sigh, leaning back against the cold stone wall. "Whatever. How are we getting Layla?"

Quinn leans back, stretching like a smug bastard, grinning like a *fucking* Cheshire cat. "Twist your nose, blink three times, hop on *three* legs."

Silence.

The entire room goes still.

Vassago blinks. Ashton furrows his brows. Luca tilts his head slightly, like a confused puppy.

We all exchange glances, waiting for some kind of clarification.

Quinn simply grins wider.

What.

The.

Fuck?

Saygin bursts into laughter, clutching her stomach as if Quinn just delivered the punchline of the century. "You didn't really think we'd make it that easy, did you?"

I'm teetering on the edge of my temper when Luca, of all beings, cuts in, his voice as dry as bone. "If that's how we're getting her, I'll make sure to pack some extra socks for the hopping part."

Ashton lets out a low whistle, clearly enjoying himself. "I'd *pay* to see that."

I glare at him. *Not helping.*

My attention snaps back to Quinn, my patience razor-thin. "Enough with the games. What's the real plan?"

Quinn wipes a fake tear from his eye, still grinning. "Oh, fine. No more fun for me." His smirk lingers, but something shifts—his usual amusement doesn't fully mask the glint of something sharper underneath. "There's a ritual. Simple enough. We'll need a few things—some blood, some bones, a little sacrifice. Nothing you can't handle."

I stare at him. *That's it?* A ritual? No hidden loophole? No secret catastrophe waiting to unfold?

My gut tells me not to trust this shit.

"Get to the point," I snap.

Saygin's voice slices through the tension. "Did you gather everything I asked for, Ashton?"

He nods without hesitation and tosses her a worn burlap bag. The contents shift with an eerie rustling as she catches it. Her fingers are moving with practiced ease as she rummages inside. Vials of strange, shimmering liquids. A blackened piece of chalk. A needle so sharp it gleams unnervingly under the dim light.

She pulls out a cauldron next, setting it in front of her with a dull *thud*.

Then, without looking up, she says, "Do you have anything personal from your mate?"

The question hits like a gut punch.

Layla's hoodie. The last piece of her I have.

My jaw clenches, but I force myself to answer. "It's in our room." My voice is low, the weight of her absence pressing down on every syllable.

Saygin doesn't acknowledge my hesitation, doesn't offer a word of sympathy. She just nods. "Go get it."

I don't argue.

The hall feels longer than it should, the silence stretching endlessly as I walk. Each step is heavier than the last.

When I reach the door, I stop. My hand hovers over the knob.

There's a knot in my throat, tight and painful, a reminder of how fucking *empty* everything feels without her.

I twist the knob and push the door open.

The scent of her rushes over me—vanilla and sex. It's comforting. It's agonizing. It's *everything*.

I stand there, letting it drown me. Closing my eyes, I can almost see her curled up on the bed, feel the warmth of her body against mine. I think about the way she'd murmur my name in her sleep, how she tangled her fingers in my hair when she thought I wasn't paying attention.

A rush of emotions slams into me—guilt, rage, longing, despair. It's a violent, suffocating storm, and I can't outrun it.

Before I can stop myself, tears burn hot in my eyes, spilling over. I let them fall. No one is here to see. No one to witness the way my chest heaves, how my fingers dig into the fabric of my robe as if I can somehow pull her back to me.

I miss her too, Orcus hums in my mind, his voice quieter than usual.

I swallow hard.

I don't answer.

Because there's nothing to say.

The pain of not knowing where she is—of not being able to *protect* her—is unbearable. And I don't know how much longer I can take it.

With shaking hands, I walk to the closet, shoving aside things that don't matter until my fingers brush against soft fabric—*her* hoodie.

The second I clutch it to my chest, something inside me cracks. The scent of her—vanilla, fear, something uniquely *Layla*—wraps around me like a ghost of warmth, and I squeeze my eyes shut, willing it to be enough. But it's not. It never will be.

I exhale sharply and turn back toward the others, gripping the hoodie like a lifeline.

I know what needs to be done. I know what's at stake.

But that doesn't make it easier.

I press my teeth together, forcing down the ache clawing at my ribs, but the words slip out before I can stop them.

"Fuck, Layla..."

It's not a prayer. Not a plea. Just a quiet admission to the silence pressing in around me.

And then—

Azrael?

Her voice flickers in my mind like a dying ember, soft but unmistakable. There's concern lacing the edges, the way she always sounds when she sees right through my bullshit.

For a second, I forget how to breathe.

Are you okay?

I close my eyes, inhaling slow, trying to steady the hurricane in my chest. *Yes, mouse. I am.*

It's a lie.

And we both know it.

I feel her hesitate, her presence shifting—something uncertain, fragile.

I can... She trails off, and for the first time, I sense it. The weight. The exhaustion. The fear she's trying to hide. *I can feel your sadness, Azrael.*

Her words hit harder than I expect, slipping past my defenses like a blade between the ribs. I bite down, trying to focus, but the cracks are spreading too fast, too deep.

I can't hold it back anymore. *I just miss you.*

The admission drags itself from me like a wound torn open, raw and aching. Every inch of this forsaken world, every whisper of emptiness—it all screams her name. The loneliness is a living thing, clawing at my throat, and I don't know how much longer I can keep pretending it doesn't fucking hurt.

I miss you too, she murmurs. It's so quiet, like a ghost of a touch against my mind, and it's both a comfort and a curse.

I hang onto it anyway.

Are you coming to get me?

There's hope in her voice, but underneath it, there's something else.

Fear.

A sharp chill slithers through me. The idea that she might believe—*even for a second*—that I won't find her makes me fucking sick.

Flo says I might could ask the tooth faeries to use their portal.

There's a pause. Then, her confusion bleeds into my head.

Who is Flo?

The undercat, she replies, and despite everything, she laughs—a small, familiar sound, one that should feel like home. But it only makes the ache worse.

My joints turn to ice.

Stay away from the faeries, I warn, sharper than I mean to. *They're not safe. I'm coming to get you.*

I step toward the closet where her hoodie rests, my hand hovering over it, feeling the weight of my words settle into my bones. I grip the fabric tightly, fingers pressing into it like I can somehow pull her back through sheer fucking will.

There's a beat of silence.

Too long.

Too still.

Layla?

No reply.

The sudden quiet is deafening.

My nerves slams against my ribs, my pulse roaring in my ears as I stand frozen, the hoodie clenched in my hands. The air shifts, colder than before—like a storm rolling in, like something just *changed.*

I don't know if she's gone.

I don't know if something pulled her away.

CHAPTER TWENTY-FIVE

Ashton

WHITE FLAG - BISHOP BRIGGS

I lean back against the wall, arms crossed, casually watching Saygin as she mutters something in a language I've never heard before. The sound prickles the hairs on the back of my neck, and not in the good way. I've been around long enough to hear all kinds of incantations, curses, and sweet nothings whispered in the dark—hell, I've probably said a few myself—but this? This feels... different. Unsettling.

The way she moves, the ease with which she pours vials of liquid into the cauldron, it's like she's done this a thousand times. It's smooth, practiced, the motions of someone who's been at this *exact* thing for far too long. The smoke starts curling out thick and heavy, like it has a mind of its own. It swirls in the air with a lazy elegance. Saygin inhales deeply through her nose, holds it for a second like she's savoring it, then exhales slowly. The smoke turns an iridescent pink as it leaves her lips, snaking up toward the ceiling.

"Well, that's not ominous at all," I mutter under my breath, half to myself, half because I just can't resist.

Quinn, the ever-helpful *sociopath*, finally saunters in behind Azrael, looking like he's fresh off a bad date with a power-hungry fae. Azrael's stormy scowl is a permanent fixture, and his posture screams *not in the mood*, but that doesn't stop him from clutching Layla's hoodie like it personally offended him.

The tension in the room spikes. My eyes flick from Azrael to Quinn, who, with the smug confidence of someone who knows he's about to cause trouble, snatches the hoodie from Azrael's hand and brings it straight to his face. He takes a slow, exaggerated sniff, just to make sure he's *really* enjoying the moment.

Azrael freezes. Every bone locks up tighter than a vault, and I can practically see the thoughts running through his head. The fact that Quinn hasn't already been killed means he's either a masochist or Azrael's a little too tired to deal with him today.

Quinn lowers the hoodie, still grinning like a damn Cheshire cat, meeting Azrael's glare with a sickening amount of satisfaction. "Mm. Fear. Longing. Just a hint of blood," he purrs. "She smells *delicious*."

"Put. The hoodie. Down," Azrael growls.

The room holds its breath.

"Relax, *Death Toy*," Quinn retorts, voice dripping with playful malice. "Just appreciating the essence of a queen." He sets the hoodie down beside the rest of the supplies, but the damage is already done. The air feels tenser than it did before, charged with a silent storm.

Azrael doesn't move. He's still staring at Quinn like he's already picturing the bloody mess Quinn's insides would make if Orcus got his blade on him. Probably beautiful, really.

Saygin, unfazed as ever, casually plucks a loose thread from the hoodie, then finds a single blonde hair tangled in the fabric. She drops them both into the cauldron, her fingers working with such precision it looks almost ceremonial. Each motion is deliberate, as though she's setting the pieces of a puzzle into place.

The moment the hair touches the bubbling mixture, a sharp pop splits the air, and the smoke turns a deep, swirling purple. It thickens, forming into something almost tangible. Shapes twist and writhe within it, the colors shifting as if they're alive.

And then—there she is.

Layla.

She's crouched low in a dark tunnel, her grip tight on Drepane, who's practically vibrating with tension beside her. An undercat is pressed against Layla's side, ears flattened, eyes locked on something ahead.

I don't need to see the thing they're hiding from to know it's bad news.

The smoke shifts again, pulling away to reveal what they're watching—*Memetim's crows.*

Perched on a jagged boulder, the birds stare down at Layla like they're death's personal attendants. Their beady eyes glint in the dim light, and they wait. Just watching.

And then there's *Memetim* herself.

Standing just beyond the crows, her true form fully revealed. She's unnervingly tall, a blackened skeletal frame wrapped in a deep red robe. The tips of her tattered black wings drag against the ground like they're weighted with centuries of decay. The sight of her is enough to send a shiver down my spine, a creeping sense of *wrongness* that feels almost *alive.*

She's talking to someone.

We can't see who, but we fucking need to.

"If Memetim is there, Layla is in danger," I say, my voice sharper than I intended. I barely recognize the edge in it, but it's there. It cuts through the room like a blade. "She's not just lurking. She knows Layla's there. She's reeling her in."

I glance over at Vassago, hoping I'm wrong.

The solemn nod he gives me only worsens the tension hanging in the air.

Azrael, whose focus has never wavered from the vision, finally speaks, his voice low, flat.

"I'm talking to her now."

His gaze locks on the smoke like he could burn a hole through it with just the force of his will. I don't know if that's confidence or denial, but it doesn't matter. The storm inside him is about to break.

I exhale through my nose, trying to keep my mind from racing ahead, but my thoughts keep spiraling, tangled in the web of what's coming next. Something about the way Memetim stands—her posture, the tilt of her head—there's a calculation there. She's not just waiting. She's *toying* with us.

This isn't going to be easy.

And I don't like that one bit.

"Well, this day just went from bad to *I need a drink*," I mutter, earning an almost imperceptible grunt from Vassago.

Azrael, still staring at the vision, doesn't even acknowledge me.

But I can feel it—*whatever this is*—it's not going to end the way any of us want.

Not even close.

"Who the hell is she talking to?" I ask, more to myself than anyone else, my gaze still locked on the swirling smoke. The image of Layla crouched in that tunnel with the undercat, her eyes darting around as if she's waiting for something to jump out at her—keeps gnawing at the back of my mind. The fact that Memetim is there? *Even worse*.

Vassago shifts uncomfortably beside me. His jaw tightens, and I can see the wheels turning behind his eyes, probably trying to make sense of the vision. That's not a good sign.

Luca, however, remains blissfully ignorant, his arms crossed and a grin on his face as he tilts his head toward the image. "Okay, so let me get this straight," he starts, his voice completely casual like we're discussing the weather. "The Angel of Death used to want to kill Layla. But now she's having a nice little fireside chat in a tunnel while her emotional support crows play backup?"

Ashton, meet Luca—the fucking poster child for coping through sarcasm.

"Something like that," I mutter, my gaze never leaving the vision.

"Cool, cool." Luca nods slowly. "And we're going in after her, knowing full well that this *could* be a trap."

I glance at him, a dry chuckle escaping. "Starting to regret your life choices?"

"Oh, absolutely," he deadpans.

I smirk, clapping him on the shoulder with a grin. "Good. Welcome to the club."

Be nice. Sadie's voice slithers down the thread between us, her tone edged with the kind of warning that suggests I've just stepped into dangerous territory.

What do you mean? I'm always nice. I can't help the smirk that creeps across my lips, but I fight it down, knowing she can feel it.

Luca is precious. She pauses for a second, and I can practically hear her crossing her arms. *Not to mention my bestie dude friend. Leave him alone.*

What do you mean? I'm not doing anything! If I remember correctly, it was you who wanted to sacrifice him to Saygin.

Do you not realize Luca can sense that you all don't want him around unless it benefits you guys? The group makes him and me feel so isolated. Like we don't belong here.

I roll my eyes, unable to stop myself. She completely ignored my second statement.

Roll your eyes one more time, Sand Boy, and I will practice sounding on you with a fucking dagger.

I choke on a laugh at the thought, but I know better than to let it out. Sadie does not make empty threats, especially when she's got her "I'm serious" tone going.

A sudden movement in my peripheral catches my attention. Quinn. Of course. He's staring at me again, his unsettling grin plastered on his face, eyes glinting with that usual mixture of curiosity and… who knows what else. Meanwhile, Saygin continues to pull out the black chalk with a meticulous slowness, like she's performing some dark, ancient ritual.

Quinn's always watching. It's unsettling, and I haven't been able to figure out whether he's waiting for something to amuse him or if there's a deeper reason behind it. Probably both. With him, it's hard to tell.

I meet his gaze, feeling the weight of his stare like a pressurized beam, and I can't help but wonder—what *is* he waiting for? The sick part of me wonders if it's for the exact moment when all of us will crack, when the chaos in this group finally spills over and leaves nothing behind but pieces to pick up.

"Quit staring at me, Quinn," I mutter under my breath, but he doesn't look away.

"Well, if it isn't Mr. Sandman himself," Quinn says, voice low and casual as ever. "I was just admiring how finely you wear that cape of responsibility. You know, if you ever get tired of the whole 'Reaper's sidekick' thing, there's always room for another clown in *my* circus."

I roll my eyes, resisting the urge to smack him. "If you're the ringmaster, I'll pass."

"Oh, come on," Quinn says with a chuckle, leaning in like he's sharing some cosmic secret with me. "It'd be fun! I've always wanted someone who's, you know, *less* dead inside to join the show." He winks.

That one gets me. He knows exactly how to hit a nerve.

"I'm good," I say, my tone flat, but the words are hollow. Quinn's not just annoying for no reason—there's always an agenda with him.

Saygin finishes marking the edges of the cauldron with the black chalk, her fingers moving with a meticulous grace that sends a shiver through me. She seems too calm. Too composed for what's about to happen.

I glance at the vision again. Layla's still there, the tension in her posture obvious. And Memetim? Still talking to someone unseen, pulling the strings of this twisted little play we're caught in.

I don't know who she's talking to, but I get the sinking feeling that we're all just pawns in a game much bigger than us.

"So, what's the plan?" Luca asks, his voice cutting through my thoughts as he turns to look at me.

I glance at him. "Plan? For now, we survive."

"Always the optimist," Luca mutters, rolling his eyes but with a hint of amusement.

"Someone has to be," I reply with a grin, even though inside, all I can think is how much I want this to be over.

But there's no going back now. Not when Layla's out there, somewhere. In danger.

And when it comes down to it, nothing else matters. Not Quinn's bullshit, not the looming threat of Memetim, not even the damn crows. All that matters is getting her back.

Everything else? That can wait.

CHAPTER TWENTY-SIX

Ashton

NIGHTMARE - HALSEY

Saygin kneels on the floor, her movements steady and practiced as she begins to draw on the wall. Each stroke of her chalk seems to hum with energy, the intricate sigils forming under her hands like they're alive, pulsing faintly with an otherworldly glow.

"We won't have much time," she says, her voice cool and distant, not looking up from her work. "Maybe 72 hours to get in, find her, and get back before things start getting... irreversible."

Azrael nods once, as if he's been handed a deadline, accepting it with a calmness that makes my stomach churn. Time is not on our side. But we never expected it to be.

"Quinn can walk us through the shadows, if need be. He's familiar with the territory, so he will take the lead," Saygin adds, her voice low but sure.

Quinn dips his chin in agreement, his usual unreadable expression in place, but I can't help but notice the flicker of something dangerous in his eyes. Like he's relishing the idea of plunging into the void just for the thrill of it.

Saygin doesn't pause her drawing, her fingers are moving with precision. "In the Empty, keep your guard up. There are things there that don't belong anywhere else—things older than names, things that were left behind because even the gods feared them." Her voice takes on a darker edge, a warning that cuts through the air. "Creatures far worse than anything you've encountered."

I glance at Luca. His face is carefully composed, but the scent of fear hits me like a slap in the face—sharp, pungent, thick enough to make the air feel heavier. I can practically see the wheels turning behind his eyes, the terror he's trying to suppress. It's in the way his fingers twitch, the nervous energy radiating from him like static.

Vassago notices too, and with a calm, practiced movement, he reaches out and gives Luca a firm pat on the back. "You okay, buddy?"

Luca blinks, and for a second, it looks like he might crack. Then he shakes himself off, forcing a grin that doesn't quite reach his eyes. "Yeah. Yeah. Why wouldn't I be?" he says, his voice an octave higher than usual. He exhales slowly, trying to compose himself. "Let's just get Layla and get back home so I can cook us a feast." He throws me a small, lopsided smile that doesn't fool anyone.

I mutter under my breath, weaving a protective spell into the walls of my home, my fingers flicking through the air as the runes take form. The wards shimmer briefly before vanishing, locking Sadie in a fortress no one but Exu can enter. The last thing I need is someone busting through the door.

Then, just for good measure, I cast a second protection spell—this one wrapping around Luca, a subtle layer of magic that should keep him safe, at least for now. If something happens to him, I'll never hear the end of it from Sadie. And trust me, I'd rather face a hundred demons than her wrath.

Saygin finishes her symbols, her hand hovering over the last one before she taps it three times, the sound echoing like the ticking of a clock counting down to some inevitable doom.

A pink hue radiates from the drawn door, the energy pulsing like a slow, sick heartbeat. Each pulse sending a ripple through the air. The door swings open with a creak that feels too alive, like it's pulling us in, inviting us to step closer to the darkness beyond. An unnatural chill snakes up my spine, settling into the bones of my body.

I glance at Azrael, hoping for some reassurance—anything to calm the sudden anxiety clawing at my chest. Maybe a flicker of warmth, a sign that this isn't as bad as it feels. But Azrael is as unreadable as ever, his true form offering no comfort. There's no hesitation, no flicker of doubt. Just that singular, merciless focus: *Get Layla back*.

Saygin claps her hands together, a bright, unsettling grin spreading across her face like she's about to embark on some grand journey. "Well? Our adventure awaits!"

And just like that, she's off—her body vanishing into the blackness beyond the door without a second thought, like she's done this a thousand times before. Quinn follows right behind her, swallowed by the shadows as if they've always been his natural habitat.

The rest of us linger. None of us moving forward, all of us staring at the gaping void like idiots waiting for someone else to take the plunge.

Azrael moves first, stepping into the darkness without even a moment's pause. Then Vassago follows suit, his posture stiff but resolute. That leaves Luca and me.

Luca shifts uncomfortably, casting me a look that speaks volumes—mostly about regret, self-doubt, and some really poor life choices. I exhale, my gaze lingering on the door for just a beat longer than necessary before I sigh and step forward.

Luca hesitates, then follows, dragging his feet just slightly, like he's already mentally preparing for something horrific. I can almost hear him grumbling about how his "feast" plans are probably being canceled at this point.

Orcus hums to life, the deep red glow washing over us, barely illuminating the suffocating abyss we've stepped into. The air is thick, like it's holding its breath, waiting for us to make the wrong move. The moment Luca fully crosses the threshold, the door slams shut behind us with a force that rattles my bones.

We all—except for Saygin and Quinn—jolt in place and whirl around. The door is gone. Just an empty void where it used to be.

A cold, bitter laugh bubbles up in my throat as I realize what just happened. I've heard stories, but this? This is the reality. A one-way ticket to whatever hell we've just stepped into.

"Well," I mutter under my breath, my heart racing in my chest, "this is going to be a hell of a ride."

"How do we get out of here?" Luca asks, his voice a little too tight for comfort. He's trying to play it cool, but even I can feel the edge in his tone. He's not as fearless as he lets on.

Saygin doesn't even turn around. She just keeps walking, unfazed by the heavy tension hanging in the air. "I fart three times, and the door magically appears again. *Duh.*" She waves a dismissive hand as if it's the most obvious thing in the world, striding forward into the thickening gloom.

Luca blinks, his mouth opening in disbelief. I elbow him before he can ask if she's serious, because, honestly, I'm not sure I even want to know.

Saygin lets out a small, amused snort. "I can open the door anytime I want within the 72-hour period," she clarifies, her voice light and teasing. "But I can only open it once, so, uh... try not to get lost, okay?"

Luca exhales slowly, clearly trying to process this absurdity. I can see the skepticism written all over his face, but he stays quiet.

"We're not looking for anyone other than Azrael's mate," Saygin says, her voice now steady.

Quinn smirks from the shadows ahead of us. "*Our Queen.*" He mocks.

Azrael's expression doesn't shift, but there's a subtle shift in the tension around him. His grip tightens on Orcus's handle, a silent threat to anyone who dares to say anything further. Quinn doesn't seem to notice, or maybe he's just enjoying the quiet storm building around us.

Saygin chuckles, a sound that grates on my nerves. "Not my Queen yet. Not until Hades is no longer the Lord of the Underworld," she teases, waving a hand carelessly. "Tomatoes, tomatoes."

Azrael doesn't respond. He just moves forward, and the rest of us fall in line behind him, following the flickering, crimson glow of Orcus's light as it barely cuts through the darkness ahead. The air here feels wrong, thick with an unspoken heaviness that presses down on me with each step.

We don't speak as we walk.

Because now, we're in the fucking Empty.

And *everything* is watching us.

The further we walk into the endless blackness, the more the shadows stretch, twisting like they're alive, whispering in a language none of us understand. The chill of the place gnaws at the edges of my senses, an unfamiliar energy curling in my gut like a warning.

Luca shifts uncomfortably beside me, wrinkling his nose at the scent that hangs heavy in the air. It's stale, rotting—decay thick in the atmosphere. The smell of a place forgotten, abandoned. Saygin notices, her lips curling into a smirk as she catches his discomfort.

"Sensitive nose, huh?" she purrs, her voice dripping with amusement. She trails her finger along the jagged stone wall, her nails scraping against the surface like a soft warning. "Bet you can pick up all sorts of interesting scents. Tell me, wolf, what do *I* smell like?"

Luca hesitates, and I can practically see the wheels turning in his head as he tries to figure out if it's a trick question. His face goes slightly pink as his ears tip toward a light shade of red. "Uh... like magic," he says cautiously. "And something... sharp."

Saygin grins, a knowing, almost predatory expression crossing her face. "Sharp, huh? I like that. What else?"

Luca clears his throat, looking away like he's hoping to avoid the conversation altogether. "Something sweet... but also kinda burnt?"

She lets out a low, melodic laugh, the sound carrying through the tunnel like a snake slithering into your ear. "Oh, darling, that's the scent of danger. But don't worry—I don't bite. Not unless you ask *nicely.*" Her grin widens, all teeth and temptation.

Luca stiffens beside me, and I swear I see him swallow hard. Vassago barely suppresses a chuckle, his face twisted with quiet amusement. Azrael remains utterly unfazed, his focus still locked on the path ahead. He's all business—nothing in his expression betrays even a flicker of interest in this odd little moment.

Saygin leans in slightly toward Luca, her voice lowering to something almost seductive. "No mate waiting for you back home, huh? A lone wolf running with a pack of misfits. That's a rare sight." Her words drip with sarcasm, the kind that stings just enough to make the recipient squirm.

Luca scowls, his frustration plain. "I'm fine on my own," he mutters, his voice sharper than he probably intended.

"Oh, I'm sure you are," she purrs, "but being fine and being *fulfilled* are two very different things, sweetheart."

Luca glares at her, but he doesn't have much of a response. His discomfort is palpable, practically rolling off him in waves. The tension between them is thick, and I can tell it's only a matter of time before something gives.

Vassago claps a hand on Luca's shoulder, grinning wide. "Don't let her get in your head, pup. She likes to play with her food."

Saygin hums in agreement, the sound playful yet menacing. "I do. But don't worry—I'm not planning on eating him... *yet.*"

Luca groans, clearly wishing he could vanish into the shadows. I can't help but smirk. If nothing else, this trip is going to be a hell of a lot more entertaining than I thought.

The deeper we go, the worse the air becomes. The weight of the Empty presses in around us, wrapping tight around our minds, suffocating the edges of my thoughts. And the worst part? I can feel it. Whatever is watching us—waiting for us to make a wrong move—it's hungry, and it knows we're here.

Something's coming.

And we're about to walk right into its lair.

Luca, still visibly uncomfortable, clears his throat and turns to Vassago, attempting to mask his unease with a strained casualness. "How do you even know Saygin?" His tone is light, but there's an undercurrent of wariness beneath it, like he's bracing for an answer he won't like.

Saygin grins, her smile slow and devious, as if she's savoring the moment. It makes my own amusement flare to life, knowing what's about to unfold. She chuckles under her breath before Vassago can even open his mouth, giving him a sideways glance, waiting for him to tell the truth.

Vassago sighs, rubbing the back of his neck, clearly regretting this conversation already. "A long time ago, I needed her help with something. She... gave me her terms, and I agreed."

Saygin lets out a delighted laugh at Vassago's discomfort, her eyes glinting mischievously. "Oh, tell the pup what my terms were, Vassago," she says, practically begging him to spill.

Vassago exhales sharply, avoiding Luca's expectant gaze, but Luca is not letting this go. "She... sounded me," he mutters finally, his voice low and resigned.

Luca blinks, processing the words. "She what?" The confusion on his face is almost comical, though I'm sure the reality is far from funny for him.

Saygin's grin widens, her eyes flashing with pure mischief. "You heard him. He needed my expertise, and I gave him my bargain price. A little... hands-on experience, so to speak." She shoots Luca a wink.

Luca's face contorts into a horrified expression, his mouth opening and closing like he's trying to figure out how to un-hear this. His gaze snaps to Vassago, who, to his credit, looks about as comfortable as a dog in a lion's den. "You let her shove a metal rod—?"

"Don't finish that sentence," Vassago warns sharply, his tone dark and low, but it's clear that Saygin is absolutely thriving on his discomfort.

"Hey, don't look so shocked, wolf boy," Saygin teases, her voice dripping with amusement. "Vassago here was very eager to accept my terms. I think he even *enjoyed* it."

Vassago's eyes narrow dangerously, but he says nothing more, and his silence speaks volumes. I can't help but feel a little sympathy for the guy. This is not exactly a fun story for him to tell, and it's pretty damn clear he wishes this conversation had never started.

Luca's expression is a mix of horror and confusion, and his gaze flickers from Saygin to Vassago like he just realized that the Underworld has a far darker sense of humor than he ever imagined. "I—I think I need to forget this conversation," he says with a groan, as if trying to erase the image from his mind.

"Too late," I interject, grinning widely. "Once it's out, it's out."

Luca groans again, the sound full of frustration. "I don't think I want to know what that was."

"Smart boy," Vassago mutters under his breath, still glaring at Saygin, but it's clear he's lost this round.

Saygin simply shrugs, still smirking, her amusement never wavering. "Oh, relax, pup. You should be grateful. Thanks to that deal, your buddy here got exactly what he needed to 'save the worlds'."

Luca shoots a look at Vassago, clearly still trying to wrap his mind around the whole thing. "Right," he mutters, still looking deeply unsettled. "You guys sure have a weird way of making deals around here."

Vassago doesn't respond, although his expression suggests he's too tired to keep defending himself against Saygin's relentless teasing.

Saygin winks at him playfully and keeps walking, clearly enjoying the lingering tension she's created. I can't say I blame her—this is probably the most entertainment we're going to get on this hellish trip. But something tells me we're all going to need a little more than humor to survive what's ahead.

The deeper we go into the Empty, the more I feel it—the weight of it, pressing down on my chest. The air is thick, rancid with the scent of decay and rot. I can practically taste the malice in the atmosphere, a gnawing hunger that makes my skin crawl.

Luca's posture has shifted, his muscles tense and alert. It's clear that the playful banter with Saygin has only distracted him for so long. He's on edge, just like the rest of us.

We keep moving forward, our footsteps echoing in the empty space around us. Each sound feels amplified, as if the Empty is listening to every move we make. The deeper we go, the harder it is to ignore the feeling that something is out there—something ancient, watching.

CHAPTER TWENTY-SEVEN

Layla

THE DEVIL YOU KNOW - X AMBASSADORS

The air is damp, thick with the scent of earth and decay. My fingers tighten around Drepane's handle, my pulse steady, controlled. Fear is pointless. Fear will only make me sloppy. And I am many things, but sloppy is not one of them. I think, anyways.

Beside me, Flo lets out a low, rumbling purr, her sleek, shadowy body pressing against my leg. Her glowing eyes are locked on the same figure I'm watching. There's no mistaking her—it's *fucking Memetim*.

Her skeletal form looms in the darkness, draped in that familiar red robe, her black wings casting jagged shadows that scrape across the tunnel walls. Her crows, twitchy and restless, perch around her like a living storm. I can hear their restless fluttering, a discordant melody in the otherwise still air. Memetim is talking to someone—another figure, half-drowned in shadows. I can barely make them out, but the voice is sharp, female, laced with something unnatural, maybe something ancient.

"Shatter the tether," Memetim hisses, her voice like a blade against stone. "I want to release the Empty to the mortal realm."

The other voice, raspy and hesitant, responds. "Sister, it will take time. We need a necromancer to destroy the tether."

"Why?" Memetim shrieks, the sound jagged and laced with fury. The crows around her scatter, their wings a flurry of black feathers before they reform into their chaotic swarm, a dark halo around her.

My grip on Drepane tightens.

We need to get going, Drepane murmurs in my mind, his voice faint, as though he's struggling to stay conscious.

Hold on, I snap back, trying to focus, to push through the fog that's clouding my thoughts.

Flo's tail flicks against my leg, the movement brief but sharp. *He's right, Layla. The crows know you're here. Drepane is too weak to fight right now.*

My stomach knots. I already know Drepane is running on fumes, but hearing it out loud makes me feel even more exposed. I inhale slowly, trying to steady my breathing. *How can we relay this conversation to Azrael in real time?*

I can channel it through the bond, but I won't be able to hold it for long, Drepane warns, the strain in his voice evident.

Before I can answer, Azrael's voice slices through the bond, calm but laced with concern. *Layla? Are you okay?*

Ssh. Listen. I focus, willing myself to take in every detail of their conversation. Every scrap of information could be vital.

"That Layla girl can act as a necromancer," the unknown woman says. "She's a mutt. Would she satisfy what's needed to destroy the tether?"

I swallow the bile rising in my throat. *Mutt.* It's always something, isn't it? Always a reminder that I don't fully belong anywhere. Not to the mortals or immortals. Not to the gods. Not even to myself.

Memetim lets out a cold, humorless laugh. "Think about this, Fate. If you destroy the tether, you would just be dealing with the Grimms, the Grim Court, or anyone on the council..." She pauses, and I hear the soft flutter of her crows like they're anticipating her next words. "If you refuse—I will fucking kill you. We are already in too deep for you to fake empathy."

My jaw clenches.

Fate's response is slow, deliberate, as though she's weighing her next words carefully. "It's not going to—"

"I don't care what you say!" Memetim interrupts with a shriek that vibrates the very air around me. "I can change the course to my favor!" Her wings twitch, sending a sharp, painful ripple of energy through the tunnel. I can feel her anger like a heat wave washing over me, pressing in from all sides. "How do we use the girl?"

Fate hesitates. I hear chains rattle—heavy, oppressive. "We have to bring her to the center in front of Persephone."

Shit.

I scramble back mentally, trying to distance myself from the tether. It's still open, still active, a painful pulse in my mind. *Azrael, did you get that?*

His voice cuts through the bond, cold and furious, like ice laced with fury. *Yeah, I got it. Stay put. We're coming for you. I am literally about to enter the Empty now.*

I exhale slowly, the weight of the moment pressing against my ribs. My fingers tremble slightly, but I force them still. I've been in worse situations than this—many worse situations, right? No... I haven't. But I know Azrael and the others are coming... But what if they're too late?

Flo rubs her head against my side, her purr vibrating through my bones, grounding me. *You'll be fine,* she murmurs softly in the back of my mind. *He will get you out of here. But we need to be ready.*

I nod without speaking, my eyes fixed on Memetim's skeletal figure. My body feels heavy with the weight of this place, this cursed tunnel that holds all of my fears and doubts in its depths. But there's no time to hesitate now. The stakes are higher than ever.

I push myself to my feet, silently cursing the ache in my limbs. The longer I wait here, the more dangerous this becomes.

You're right, Flo. Let's go.

I move as silently as I can, holding my breath, Drepane's cold presence in my hand. I have no choice but to keep moving forward—no matter what comes next.

Memetim wants to use me to break something she shouldn't be touching! The Empty spilling into the mortal world? That's not just destruction—that's *extinction!* And I am not about to be their pawn!

I take a silent step back. Then another. Flo mirrors my movement, eyes still locked on Memetim, her fur bristling as if she senses the growing tension in the air. The crows, restless and erratic, begin shifting again. One of them tilts its head in my direction, and I freeze.

My stomach drops.

Do they know I'm here?

A small breath escapes me, and I shift carefully, angling myself to get a better look at Fate—the one Memetim was speaking to. She's hard to see fully, shrouded in darkness, but I can make out her silhouette. Chains bind her to the wall, thick and rusted, as if they've been there longer than I've been alive. She reminds me of an old witch from some vintage TV show—ethereal yet unsettling. Her face is hauntingly beautiful, framed by long, wavy green hair that cascades over her shoulders. But her skin is too pale, too thin, and her eyes glow dimly, holding something ancient and tired.

The sight of her makes my stomach twist. She's bound. And from the way she's positioned, the chains seem enchanted, keeping her locked in place. She's helpless, but the aura around her... it's not one of weakness. It's the kind of power that makes you wonder what kind of being could be so dangerous that even chains like these were necessary.

Get out of there, Layla. Azrael's voice cuts through my head like a blade. *We are coming.*

I swallow hard, my fingers tightening around Drepane's hilt. The sickle hums softly in my mind, its presence reminding me of the danger I'm in. *When?* I can't keep the panic from my thoughts. *Azrael, I am stuck here... alone, trying to figure out how to survive!*

There's a pause, but when he responds, his voice softens. *Tiny Mouse.* The words are like a weighted sigh, filled with a softness I miss hearing from him. *I am walking through the door now. I'm coming to get you.*

I don't respond. I can't. There's nothing to say that will make this any easier. I can feel him, lingering in the bond, waiting, but I shut him out for a moment and focus on what I *can* control. There's no use in worrying about what I can't change right now. I need to stay sharp, or I'll be dead before he gets here.

I creep backward, each movement slow and deliberate. My boots barely make a sound against the cold stone beneath me, but my heartbeat rings loud in my ears, a slight hint that I'm too exposed. My breath comes in shallow bursts, but I keep it steady. Panicking will get me caught. Panicking will get me killed.

Flo's tail brushes against my leg, and I glance up at her. Her wide, glowing eyes are unwavering, focused on our next move. My stomach churns. If I wasn't sure we were already caught, her gaze confirms it. We need to hurry.

I clutch the pendant around my neck—a gift from Ashton, a piece for protection—but the comfort is fleeting. The hollow weight of it hangs in my palm like an unanswered question. I let it slip from my fingers as my grip tightens around Drepane. The sickle's presence is both a blessing and a curse. It's my only weapon here. But will it be enough?

If we don't get you out of here soon, you will die, Layla. You do not belong in a land of the dead. Drepane's voice hums softly in my mind, steady but tinged with urgency.

I nearly roll my eyes. *What do you want me to do, Drepane? You're the reason I'm here!*

There's a brief pause. Then—

We need to find Cronos' cage.

My entire body locks up. *What?* My thoughts flare with panic. *Why?* The mere thought sends a bolt of cold fear straight down my spine. I remember Cronos. My supposed fucking grandfather. But nonetheless, he is a god who devoured his own children.

Drepane doesn't hesitate. *He will help replenish me—to keep you safe.*

I can't help the dry laugh that escapes me, bitter and sharp. *Drepane, you're delusional. We're talking about a god who tried to eat his own children! Eat them, Drepane. Eat! What makes you think he'll do anything to help me?*

The answer comes immediately, unwavering, a calm force in my mind. *Because he will do anything I tell him to do.*

I stare ahead, my pulse racing. I want to scream. But I can't. Not here, not now. Not when every moment feels like it could be the last.

I won't let him hurt you, Layla.

I exhale shakily, the weight of this moment pressing against my ribs. I don't have a choice, do I?

I'm trusting you with my life, it feels like a final plea to the dark. A bargain made with a blade already half-drawn.

I won't fail you.

But what if *that's* a lie?

I shake the thought off. I don't have time to think like that. I turn away, taking one last look at Fate—the haunting figure bound to the wall—and begin to move, as quietly as I can. Every step feels heavier than the last.

I don't waste another second. I move swiftly, following the dim path Drepane illuminates for me, Flo padding close behind, her sleek form blending into the shadows. The only sound is the faint clinking of Fate's chains and the distant, restless cawing of crows.

And somewhere behind me, Memetim continues to plot my destruction.

Chapter Twenty-Eight

Azrael

I Am The Fire - Halestorm

A faint, decaying metallic scent hits me like a punch to the gut. If I were in my mortal form, I'd be on my knees, retching, but luckily for me, death doesn't have the same sensitivities. Still, it makes my stomach twist, the scent of decay hanging in the air like an unwelcome guest.

I push the unsettling feeling down, focusing on Luca instead. He's more pale than usual, his natural pink tones drained from his face, and he looks like he's barely holding it together. I can't blame him; the place we're in isn't exactly comforting. It's a wonder he's able to stand, let alone keep his composure. But that's Luca—always pushing through, even when he looks like a walking corpse. And, truthfully, he *is* a walking corpse, but that's beside the point.

"Could really use a little light," Luca mutters under his breath, his voice hoarse.

"Keep your focus, Luca," I reply, trying to keep things sharp. There's no time for complaints now. "We're getting close."

He glances over at me, raising an eyebrow. "You sure about that? Because the closer we get, the worse this place smells."

I grunt, agreeing. "I know. The decay here is... overwhelming."

"Yeah, well, at least it's not *rotting flesh*." Luca mutters, and I have to stifle a laugh. His humor, dark as it is, is something I appreciate in moments like this. Even in the face of impending doom, Luca seems to always finds a way to crack a joke.

"Don't get cocky," I warn him, but there's a smile tugging at the corner of my lips despite myself. "If you drop dead from the smell, I'm not carrying you."

Luca chuckles weakly. "Wouldn't dream of it. You'd probably leave me to rot anyway and become *one* with the smell..."

"Maybe," I say with a grin, "but I wouldn't even bother to put you down for our record books. I'd just let you go quietly."

That gets a tired laugh from him, and I feel a slight ease in the tension between us. Even if we're about to face something that could tear us apart, there's something comforting about our banter.

I keep my focus sharp, though. The tug on my bond to Layla is undeniable, pulling me closer to her with every step. It's like an anchor, and it's all I can do to keep from sprinting. That pull is the only thing I *need* to focus on.

But as we move forward, I can't help but glance back at Ashton. His usual calm, unreadable demeanor is in place, though I can see the faint tension around his jaw. His eyes are forward, his focus unwavering, but I can't help but wonder—*Isolde*—would she be here? Could we possibly find some way to bring him closure? Maybe let him see her one *last* time? I'm not sure if it's even a good idea, but I can't shake the thought.

I know the right thing to do, and I'm about to let that line of thinking go when Orcus' voice hums in my mind, cutting through the noise.

Do not overstep.

I let out a frustrated sigh, my thoughts briefly faltering. *What's that supposed to mean?*

Ashton has moved on, Orcus continues, calm and firm. *He's bonded with Sadie now. Sadie is his, and his loyalties are with her. You have no place to meddle in their bond.*

I can feel a knot forming in my stomach. *I don't want to meddle, I just... feel bad for him.*

Don't. Orcus' voice turns stern, like a father lecturing his child. *Ashton didn't ask for your pity. He's happy with Sadie. You have no place to meddle in their bond. Think about it—how would you feel if someone tried to mess with your bond with Layla?*

I chuckle darkly, adding humor tinged with bitterness. *I'd kill them.*

Exactly, Orcus says, no hint of humor in his tone. *Ashton would not appreciate you meddling. We are here to save our mate, not to play therapist. Focus.*

I know Orcus is right, damn it. I *do* know it. But there's a nagging feeling in my gut, a small voice telling me that Ashton might not have had the chance to say goodbye to Isolde before he gave her mercy.

The bond between him and Sadie—it's real, undeniable. I know that, and I will be damned if I do anything that jeopardizes it. But a small part of me wonders if Ashton got the closure he needed.

The drip of water echoes through the tunnels, steady and unnerving, like the heartbeat of the Underworld itself. A sudden scurry of movement beside us halts the group in place, freezing even me for a second. Saygin and Quinn, however, don't miss a beat. They keep walking. Their strides are so unbothered, like they're accustomed to whatever's lurking in the shadows.

"Mawkins and Corruptors," Quinn mutters, his tone casual, almost as if he's just discussing the weather. "If I were you, I'd focus on the water. Tune into that."

Luca, always the one to break the silence, leans forward a bit too eagerly. "Why?"

Quinn doesn't even glance at him. "When the Mawkins cry, you're done for. They'll send you spiraling into a loop—your worst memories, your sins, your regrets. You'll live them over and over until you lose your mind." He pauses for a second, letting the weight of his words hang in the air. "Corruptors are the guardians of the Empty. They make sure no one leaves. So, where there's a Mawkin, there's always a Corruptor."

Luca's face scrunches in confusion, a mix of curiosity and concern. "How do you know this?"

Quinn stops walking and turns, his lips curling into a smirk that practically reeks of mischief. "Ah, yes. You're not from the Underworld, are you, *Wolfy?*" His tone drips with sarcasm. "You probably never got the bedtime stories, did you?"

Luca furrows his brow. "Bedtime stories?"

Quinn steps closer, his presence looming, and as he does, Orcus' red aura catches the peeling skin of Quinn's face, making it glow faintly in the low light. "My name is Quinn Veyrik," he says, voice tinged with pride. "I'm one of the only ones alive who managed to escape the Empty." He chuckles darkly; his eyes gleaming with something far too predatory. "But I created a new kind—'shadowkin.' I'm just a scrap, a piece of shadow here, that the Empty couldn't keep."

Luca's eyes widen as the full weight of Quinn's words crashes down on him, but he's quick to recover. "So, what does that have to do with bedtime stories?"

Quinn tilts his head, that sinister grin never wavering. "Because they *love* to tell the tale of how untamed I was when I finally broke free." He leans in closer, his voice dropping to an almost gleeful whisper. "How I slaughtered an entire village."

Luca blinks, his expression shifting from disbelief to genuine horror. He speaks barely above a whisper, as if he's afraid the words might make it real. "You... slaughtered a village?"

Quinn's grin widens, and he shrugs, unfazed by the shock he's caused. "Mawkins are creeping in. Let's move."

Luca looks at me, his face a mix of disbelief and utter unease. I meet his gaze, offering a casual shrug, like this is just another day in the Underworld. Quinn's tale is *mild*, honestly. I've heard far worse stories in my time down here. But the way Luca looks at me, like he's just realized the full scope of the madness that inhabits this place, is a little amusing.

I can't help the small smile that tugs at my lips, though I quickly push it away.

But as we keep moving, my thoughts shift. The bond with Layla, once a constant, comforting pull, begins to feel... distant. It's like trying to grab smoke with my bare hands. No matter how fast I push myself, she slips further and further away. I can feel her out there—her presence—but it's fading, pulling back into a haze, unreachable.

I curse under my breath, trying to ignore the gnawing feeling in my chest. I need to get to her.

Layla!

I shout down the bond, frustration lacing my voice. My steps quicken, every stride fueled by the growing sense of urgency, the gnawing fear creeping up my spine. I need to get to her—*now*.

It takes a moment, but finally, her voice crackles through, distant and strained. *Yes?*

Stop moving. My tone is sharp, irritation slipping through the cracks. *It's hard for me to track you if you keep running! I'm trying to get to you, but you're making it impossible!* The words spill out, rough and raw, the aggravation leaking through the bond like poison.

A long pause. Too long. Then, finally, her voice returns, tinged with something that stops my heart cold. *I need to get to Cronos! Drepane is fading!*

I blink, a jolt of cold fear hitting me. *What do you mean Drepane is fading?*

The answer comes not from her, but from *him*. A faint, strained voice cuts through the bond, weak and labored, like an old friend trying to hold on. *I've exhausted all my energy protecting Layla. I... I am dying.*

The words slam into me, each syllable a cold strike. *"No."* I mutter the word under my breath, disbelief threading through my thoughts. *This isn't happening.*

Drepane's voice is barely a whisper, the fatigue palpable. *There's nothing left, Azrael. I can't... I can't keep her safe much longer.*

My heart lurches, the weight of his words settling like a stone in my chest. *This is bad,* I think to myself, my mind racing. *This is really bad.*

I grit my teeth, shoving the panic that rises in my chest down, focusing instead on the one thing that matters. *I'll meet you at Cronos' cell.*

Even if I don't know where the hell his cell is.

The words come out sharper than I intend, the desperation crawling between my joints, but I can't afford to second-guess. I can't afford to think about the consequences of failure. Layla needs me.

And I will get to her—*no matter what.*

"Oh, *fuck!*" Ashton screams, the sound of panic tearing through the air.

I whip my head around just in time to see a grotesque being, its multiple arms and glistening claws, pinning Ashton to the wall. My pulse spikes, and without thinking, I swing Orcus around. The blade cleaves through the air, meeting the creature's flesh with a sickening, wet thud.

The thing screeches, the sound vibrating through the air, but before I can strike again, it vanishes in a cloud of black smoke, leaving only the pungent stench of decay behind.

Ashton slumps to the ground, dazed, his face drained of color. The sight of him, looking so vulnerable, stabs at me with a surprising force. I turn back to the others, trying to shake off the growing fear in my chest.

Quinn steps forward, his voice eerily calm amidst the chaos. "That..." He points at the wall where the creature just was. "Was a Corruptor. More are bound to be coming, so we need to get a move on."

His words don't fully register before the air is filled with a high-pitched, ear-piercing screech that reverberates through my bones. The sound claws at my mind, sharp and relentless.

"Cover your ears!" Quinn barks, his voice cutting through the terror like a blade.

Saygin drops to her knees at Quinn's feet, her hands pressed tightly to her ears, her face contorted in discomfort. Luca and Vassago are less graceful, leaning against the wall, trying to shield themselves from the unbearable noise. Ashton locks eyes with me, panic swimming in his gaze as he fumbles, desperate, to cover his ears.

I don't flinch. In my true form, I'm apparently immune to the effects of this torture. But I can't help but glance over at Quinn. He doesn't move, though there's a flicker of concern in his eyes as he watches Saygin, still kneeling on the ground, struggling against the sonic assault.

"Azrael!" Quinn's voice cuts through the screeching, urgent and filled with a dangerous edge. "They're not going to make it if we don't find that Mawkin and destroy it!"

His words hit me like a sledgehammer. My chest tightens with the weight of what he's saying. The *Mawkin*—a creature I have never even fucking seen before, never fought, but apparently the source of all this madness. And it's up to me to take it down before it finishes off my friends.

I don't have time to hesitate.

I nod, the grim realization settling like cold iron in my gut. I've faced plenty of horrors, but this—this *thing*—is different. And I need to find it. Fast. The terror in the air is thick, but I push it down, focusing on what I can control.

I turn back to the others, my voice sharp with resolve. "We will find it, and we will end this."

The words feel like a promise, one I'm not sure I can keep, but it's all I've got.

I'll be damned if I let anything happen to them.

Chapter Twenty-Nine

Ashton

Faded - Alan Walker

I try to seal my ears, pressing my palms against them, but the screech slips through, gnawing at my mind like a parasite. My body shudders as the sound seeps deeper, reverberating in every bone, every nerve. I can feel myself slipping—reality blurs and stretches like a thin sheet of ice about to crack beneath me.

Sadie's voice echoes in my mind, her emotions flooding through the bond, frantic, desperate. I swear I can hear her heartbeat—no, wait. Is that *mine*? Everything's a fucking mess, and I can't even tell the difference anymore.

The walls of the tunnel begin to spin, twisting like a bad dream. And then, just as abruptly as it started, everything shifts. The world solidifies into a space I know all too well—an old, familiar room.

I sit up from where I've curled into a fetal position on the floor. The air is thick with the scent of nostalgia, the kind that makes my chest tighten and my stomach churn. Colorful tapestries I swore I had burned years ago now hang from the walls, their bright reds and golds mocking me with their innocence.

I walk through the room—*my home*—down halls I've long since rearranged to forget the memories. Yet, here they are again, staring me in the face.

Pictures. Of Isolde and me. Living, breathing, laughing together. There's one of her pregnant belly, my arms wrapped around it, a moment of happiness I never thought I'd relive. It's like the fucking universe is playing a cruel joke.

"Ashton?" Exu's voice breaks through the haze, calling to me. His breath catches in his chest, as if he's run miles just to find me.

I turn around, my body moving before I can think, my lips forming the words out of habit. "Yes?"

Exu looks at me, his expression dark, and for a moment, I can see his heart shattering *through* his eyes. "It's Isolde," he says, his voice tight, like it's a heavy weight on his chest. "She's *gone.*"

The words crash into me, but I don't feel the impact—not at first. "What about her?" I hear myself ask, but my throat is dry, like I've swallowed glass. It feels like I'm talking through a fog, and my mind fights to make sense of it.

Fuck. History is repeating itself. I try to move, to walk away from it—this twisted nightmare—but my feet feel like they're cemented to the floor, trapped in place. My chest tightens, my breaths shallow. I reach out, desperate to contact Sadie, to feel her presence, but the thread that once connected us is... *gone.*

But something else is there. A thread I know all too well. Isolde's.

I don't even need to listen to her emotions; they rush at me like a tidal wave. *Fear. Pain. Anger. Regret.* It slams into me, suffocating, drowning. I want to scream, but the words get caught in my throat.

This isn't real. This can't be *real.*

Before Exu can even open his mouth, I can't hold it in anymore. My voice cuts through the tension, raw and furious. "Where is she?"

The room shudders under the weight of my anger. I feel it deep in my bones, like the earth itself is trembling in fear of what I might do next.

"Your father took her."

The words hit like a punch to the gut, but they don't satisfy. They only make the blood surge in my ears, drowning out the world around me. "Took her where, Exu?" I bark, my hands shaking with the force of my rage. "Stop beating around the goddamn bush and tell me what the fuck happened to my mate!"

I try to reach out to Isolde, my mind stretching toward the bond, but all I feel is static. She's there, but barely. It's like she's been drugged, her presence too hazy, too clouded to connect with.

Shit.

I've seen this before. I've *felt* this before. The weight of it—the *helplessness,* the *fear*—grips me like a vice, choking off my air. I know how this ends. I've seen it... I've already lived it. The wreckage I'll leave in my wake, the destruction I'll unleash in my desperation to save her.

A part of me screams that I can't change this, that this is how it was always meant to be. But another part, the part I can never seem to quiet, is already fueling the fire. I'll waste all my energy if I have to. I'll burn this whole fucking place to the ground to save Isolde—and our son.

I shove Exu out of my way, my body moving on instinct, driven by the rage that's clawing at my insides. My feet find the ground beneath me, and I tear through the manor, bursting out into the cold, harsh air of the Underworld. I stand there, breathing hard, looking around—waiting for something, anything, to show me a trail.

But I know better. There's nothing. Not a fucking trace.

I materialize at my father's home, my heart pounding as I take in the surroundings. Time has moved on since I've been here—too much time. The walls feel colder, the air heavier, and the scent of decay is thick in the atmosphere.

Then I hear it.

Ashton! Her voice rips through my mind, raw and frantic.

She screams again, a sound that cuts through everything. The shriek shatters my thoughts, my vision bleeds red as pain and anger flood me in equal measure.

I turn toward my father, standing there with his smug, all-knowing grin. He doesn't even flinch as he dismisses me.

"You're better off without that *fae whore.*"

The words hit like a fucking blow. Every ounce of restraint I've ever had slips away, replaced by the fury that boils in my veins. I feel Isolde's presence fading again, the tether between us flickering as if she's slipping further away.

But it's the memories that break me. The flood of them. Isolde's voice, soft and full of love, filling the hollow spaces where there should be peace. The flashes of her face when we shared quiet moments, our plans for the future. It's all so fucking clear, but now it's tainted with images of her—drugged, helpless, her body trembling in fear.

I force the memories aside, but they still linger, heavy as a weight around my chest.

And then I see it. My father, his sick grin stretched wide, looming over Isolde. The view of him on top of her strikes like a fucking lightning bolt, and before I can even think, my body moves on its own. My hands close around his throat, squeezing as I slam him into the stone wall with a force that cracks the air.

"Who the fuck are you to tell me who I *can* and *can't* love?" I snarl, fury tearing through my words. "*Where is Izzy?*"

My father's eyes gleam with the satisfaction of knowing he's pushed me too far, but I don't give a shit. He's a dead man walking.

The world around me spins, and suddenly the room is no longer the cold, sterile home I remember. It's chaos. Blood and flames everywhere. The stench of burnt flesh is thick in my nostrils, choking me with its acrid bite.

And in the midst of it all, Isolde's screams echo through the madness. Her fear is palpable, reaching into every corner of my mind, *tearing* at me.

The air is thick with violence, and all I can think about is getting to her. But with each second that passes, my time to save her slips away.

The world stops spinning, and suddenly I'm holding Isolde in my arms.

Her blood coats my skin, warm and sticky. It's everywhere. Her mouth is open, but no sound escapes. Her eyes, once so full of life, are now dull, unfocused, flickering between this world and the next. I can feel it—the heartbeat that was once strong and steady is now a faint whisper, weakening with each passing second. Caelum's heartbeat. Our son's heartbeat. *Gone.*

I stare down at Isolde, and we both know the truth. Her blood is drying on her beaten face, caked into her hair, streaked with the pain that only someone who has been torn apart could know. The face I once adored, that I would trace with my fingers in the quiet of our nights together—it's no longer the same. It's barely recognizable, and the weight of that truth presses down on me like a ton of bricks.

Ashton... Her voice is broken, barely a whisper in my mind. But I hear it. I feel it in my bones. *Do it. Ashton, please.*

I tremble, the tears falling freely. "I can't!" The words are a scream, but they come out strangled, full of helplessness. How could I? How could I do this to her?

All our dreams are slipping away, memories turning to dust. Raising our son together, growing old—every single plan, gone in an instant. The future I thought we would have is shattered, and I'm left holding a broken, bloodied version of the woman I loved. My hands shake as I pull her closer, wishing I could somehow make it stop, make it all go away.

"I can't let you go," I whisper into her ear, my voice raw, my breath ragged. "Let me bring you to Exu and Vassago. Please, Izzy! I *need* you. We can fix this."

But we both know it's too late. Her ribs are crushed, her once-silver hair now a dark, blood-stained mess. I feel her trembling beneath me, the life leaving her with every shallow breath she takes. She reaches up, fingers trembling as she touches my hair, small strands turning silver with her delicate touch.

I will always be with you, Ash.

A few silver strands of hair fall into mine, as if she's trying to hold on for just a moment longer, but we both know she's already gone.

The pain rips through me, and against my will, my hand moves to my dagger. My fingers wrap around the hilt, the cold steel pressing against my skin. I know what needs to be done, but that doesn't make it easier.

I lower myself to her, pressing my lips to hers one last time, tasting the metallic tang of her blood. It feels like a goodbye I wasn't ready for, one that I'll never be prepared for.

And then I push the dagger through her ears, ending it.

I scream, my heart shattering as I pull her body in closer. The world spins, reality warps, and before I can process what's happening, I'm standing in my home again.

Walking down the hall.

"Ashton!" Exu calls, his voice a mix of concern and exhaustion. I hear his footsteps behind me, but I don't turn around. I can't.

Fuck.

Everything is broken.

Chapter Thirty

Luca

Breathe Me - Sia

My body trembles, a shiver running down my spine as I hear the cawing of birds in the distance. Something moves across the floor of the woods—crackling leaves, snapping branches. I whip my head to the side, eyes darting across the shadowed trees.

I should have stayed home. I should've listened. But for some reason, I refuse to go back. The pull of whatever is out here, whatever keeps drawing me deeper into the woods, is stronger than anything I've felt in a long time.

But this is madness. I should be with my pack. I shouldn't be out here in the middle of nowhere, reliving memories I wish I could forget.

Everyone thinks my father is a hero, a proud alpha with the strength to lead us all. But they don't hear the screams. They don't hear the way my mother used to beg him, her voice breaking through the walls as he raged. They don't hear the cracks, the shattering sounds of her head slamming against the floor because she burned the biscuits, as if that was a reason to destroy her.

The pack doesn't care. They never did.

The women are just breeders. The women do not matter. That's what they told me. That's what *he* told me.

"Always be my sweet boy." Her voice echoes in my head, soft and trembling, a memory of love I can never get back. *"Always show love, always be love."*

I glance around again, my eyes blurry as a rush of memories flood my mind, each one like a punch to the gut. My mother's voice, her laughter, her warmth. I hear it all like it's happening right here, right now.

She always dreamed of a cafe—bright, welcoming, filled with beautiful plants that twined around every corner, sunlight spilling through the windows. She'd talk about it for hours, imagining jazz music playing softly in the background with the smell of coffee mixed with the sweetness of fresh pastries. I remember how her caramel-tanned skin would glow in the sun, how her hair would curl around her face as she pushed me on the swing at the park, her hands warm and comforting as she held my back, making sure I didn't fall.

But no one in the pack cared about her dreams. They'd whisper behind her back, voices thick with judgment.

"She's not one of us," they'd say.

I never understood it. She looked like us. She howled at the moon with us. She loved the same way we did, fierce and unyielding.

She was my *mother*.

So why wasn't she one of us?

I stop in my tracks, the question hanging in the air like a curse I can't shake.

I continue to walk, the weight of it pressing down on me, that gnawing feeling in my gut that something is wrong. That somehow, I'm missing the answer, that it's been right in front of me all along.

And then I hear it. A rustling behind me, a flicker of movement in the shadows.

I freeze, every muscle tensing.

"Who's there?" I call out, my voice shaky, but steady.

A flicker of light catches my eye from the shadows. My body, as if acting on instinct, moves toward it. I can hear chants in the distance—familiar male voices, thick with some sick sense of power. My heart pounds in my chest, each beat louder than the last.

I hide behind a tree stump, my breath caught in my throat.

There, in the clearing, is my mother.

Tied to a tree. *Naked*. Helpless.

Her head sways back and forth, the movement slow and disoriented. She doesn't look up. She doesn't acknowledge the world around her, doesn't see me standing there, shaking, too horrified to move.

My father slaps her across the face, the sickening sound echoing in the stillness. She groans, her body jerking from the force, but there's no fight left in her. She's merely a shell.

And then I see my older brother, Marco. He's standing there, laughing. He's watching it all unfold like it's some kind of game.

How can he stand by? How can he allow this to happen to her? To *our* mother?

The men—some are strangers to me, but all too familiar in their cruelty—dance around her. They take turns, hands and mouths on her body, their actions vile and disrespectful. Marco steps forward, his grin wide, and it makes me sick to my stomach.

My mother, the woman who used to soothe my nightmares, who would smile and hold me when I was scared—she doesn't even acknowledge me. She doesn't look up. Doesn't smile. Doesn't give me that reassuring look, the one that always told me everything would be okay.

I scream.

The sound rips from my throat, sharp and guttural, but it does nothing. She doesn't hear me. She doesn't see me.

"Mommy!" I scream again, but the words feel hollow, useless. I can't reach her. I can't stop this.

I feel the pressure in my chest, my heart beating so hard it's like it's going to burst. The anger swells up inside me, hot and all-consuming. I can feel it building—like the heat of a storm before it breaks.

"Declan, get your boy out of here," one of the men say, his voice dismissive, as if I'm nothing more than an inconvenience.

My father turns to grab me, his grip tight, but I pull away. I growl, the sound raw, animalistic. It's like something inside me *snaps*.

"You're growing some balls, huh? Eight years old, and already trying to be a man? You're gonna be something *great*," he mocks, but I can hear the tension in his voice. He's trying to mask his fear.

I can feel it now. The shift. The burn in my bones as the wolf inside me claws its way to the surface. It starts with my teeth—the pain, sharp and sudden, as they begin to fall out, replaced by something much sharper. My hands tremble as my nails lengthen into claws. I can't stop it.

"Pretty early for a first shift, huh?" one of the men says, confusion seeping into his voice. But they don't understand. They don't know what they've awakened in me.

The pain is unbearable, but I can't stop. Not now. Not when she needs me.

I've got to save her. I've got to be the brave boy, the one who saves the princess and takes her far away from this. I'm supposed to be the prince in her stories, the one who takes her out of this nightmare.

But I'm not that. *Not yet.*

I'm just a boy.

Just a boy... with a wolf inside him.

But I won't stop. Not until I save her.

I feel the burn, the agonizing shift as my human skin begins to melt away. The pelt of fur grows in its place, the coarse texture of my wolf form creeping up my body, spreading like wildfire. My ears—my human ears—fade away, replaced with furred triangular tips. I reach up instinctively, my fingers trembling as I touch them, and I feel my human nails pull away, only to be replaced by long, sharp talons.

I stare at my hands, the talons now gleaming under the dim light of the woods. The shift isn't complete, but it's enough. It's enough to make them afraid.

"That boy ain't normal," I hear someone say, the voice rough and full of dread.

"I told you we should have put him down when she had him," another voice growls, fear lacing the words.

The words spiral in my mind, mixing with the sounds of the forest. The trees around me begin to twist, contorting into shapes that blur in my vision. The red haze thickens as rage consumes me. My heart is a drumbeat in my chest, thumping loud and erratic.

I look at my mother, her face a blur through the red-tinted haze. But then she looks at me. And for the first time, I see her. Not as the terrified woman tied to the tree, not as the *broken soul*, but as my *mother*. Her eyes, weak and glassy, catch mine. A small, fragile smile pulls at the corners of her lips.

It's the first smile I've seen from her in years.

I erupt. My body surges with the force of my wolf, my claws and teeth bared.

She's my mother. My kind, gentle mommy. The best mommy.

And no one is going to hurt her again.

The world shifts around me, but my vision steadies. But the color, the life, it's all gone. Everything is bathed in red, the bloodlust filling my senses.

A tap on my back startles me, and without thinking, I spin, my new talons slashing out. They strike the man behind me, his head spinning off in one swift motion. His body collapses, the head rolling across the ground in the dirt.

"He's a fucking Lycan, just like her," someone mutters, terror in their voice.

The men charge at me, clawing at my skin, sinking their teeth into my flesh. Their fists punch into my side, but I don't feel it. The anger, the rage—they fuel me. I grab whoever I can, tossing them aside like rag dolls. Their bones crack as they slam against the thick trunks of the trees, each impact echoing in the silence of the forest. It's like the time my father broke my mother's nose—hard, violent, unforgiving.

I smell the familiar scent of fear, sharp and metallic, mingling with the blood that stains the air. I take them down, one by one, throwing them like they're nothing. But there's no satisfaction in it. Just a hollow emptiness that makes the ache in my chest feel worse.

And then it's just them.

My *father*. My *brother*.

Between my *mother* and *me*.

I pause, the weight of exhaustion crashing down on me. My muscles feel torn, my body an aching heap of pain. The fight, the anger, it's all slipping away, and the exhaustion takes over. I'm too tired for this.

My father grins, a sick, twisted grin. "You took out the whole pack, son," he says, as if he's proud of me.

I growl, the sound coming from deep in my chest, raw and unfiltered. I don't care about his pride.

"Easy now, easy," he says, stepping closer. "It's me, your father." His arms open, like he expects me to welcome him with open arms.

Without thinking, I step back, my body towering over him now. I've grown. I've grown so much that I look down at him, this man who once stood above me, and now he seems so small. *So weak.*

I glance at my mother.

And that's when I see it. The dagger embedded in her chest. Blood stains her pale skin. She's not even looking at me anymore. Her eyes are closed, and the warmth I used to see in them is gone.

"Mommy..." My voice cracks, the word heavy in my mouth, the realization sinking in.

She's slipping away. The best mommy... and now she's nearly gone.

I stumble forward, my heart breaking, the weight of the world crashing down on me.

"Mommy," I growl, my voice ragged, but she doesn't respond. Her breathing is shallow, far too far apart. She's struggling to stay alive.

Marco's laughter cuts through the air, dark and bitter. "Lycan do not belong here. Your kind is an *abomination*."

The words hit me like a physical blow, but I don't let them distract me. I focus on her instead, my mother, my beautiful, kind mother. She lets out a ragged breath, her voice strained, barely a whisper. "We... are... an... abomination... because... you're... not... the... predator... with... us... *alive*..."

Her breaths are slow, painful, each one harder than the last. I can hear it, feel it. She's slipping.

In an instant, I grab my father by his hair, my talons sinking into his scalp, and with a roar, I throw him toward Marco. The two of them crash together, snarling and shifting into their monstrous forms.

It's no longer my family in front of me. They are fucking prey. They don't deserve to walk in this world. Not anymore.

Without thinking, my fury drives me. I leap at them. Their growls grow louder, but I am faster. I grab both of them by the neck, one in each hand, and slam them to the ground with such force their heads explode in a sickening splatter. Blood and bone rain around me, but I don't stop.

The moment they're gone, I shift back. The wolf inside of me retreats, leaving my eight-year-old body behind. I'm smaller now, exhausted, every part of me aching, but it doesn't matter. Not anymore.

I crawl to my mother, my small hands trembling. "Mommy..." I beg, desperate for her to breathe easier, to live. I take the dagger from her side, cutting the ropes that bind her.

Her head lolls toward me, her beautiful brown hair matted with blood.

"Mommy," I whisper, my voice breaking.

She reaches up with trembling fingers, caressing my face. "My special, special boy," she breathes, her voice weak but full of love.

Tears sting my eyes, but I force them back. "Please, stay with me..."

She shushes me gently, her voice barely audible. "Listen, baby."

I nod, my chest tight, my heart aching with every word she speaks.

"I'm so proud of you," she says, the words a fragile thread of hope. "But don't let anyone know who you are... what you are..." She coughs, her body convulsing, and a fresh splatter of blood stains the ground.

"Mommy..." My voice cracks.

She struggles, trying to lift herself up, but it's too much. Her eyes flicker, distant, rolling back in her head. "My sister will come for you. Go with her."

Her voice falters, barely a whisper now. "*I love you.*"

And just like that, she's gone. The world shifts beneath me, and I'm left kneeling in the cold dirt of the forest, clutching her lifeless body. The forest around me swirls, the trees whispering, but I can no longer hear her.

I blink, and I'm no longer holding her. I'm alone again, standing in the forest, *searching* for her.

CHAPTER THIRTY-ONE

Vassago

MAD WORLD - GARY JULES

"I'm not supposed to take a being's life, Father. I am supposed to protect life."

I scan the crowd for Exu, hoping—praying—that he will step in and put an end to this. But he isn't here. He is nowhere to be seen.

My father, imperious as ever, scowls down at me, his patience running thin. "Your role is to do whatever I *tell* you to do. This male was accused of treason, and by the laws of the Underworld, that means death." He grabs my wrist and forces the dagger into my palm, his grip bruising. "You are heir to the throne. This is your *duty* for your *throne*."

The weight of the dagger feels heavier than it should, as though it carries the weight of all the lives I was meant to protect. My wings tremble, folding inward as a deep sense of dread coils in my stomach. I want to throw the blade down, to run, to deny him—but I know the consequences of defying my father.

The accused male kneels before me, his hands bound, his body already battered from whatever torment preceded this moment. His dark eyes meet mine, pleading.

He is afraid.

Not of dying, but of being killed *unjustly*.

I am a Guardian Angel. This is not my role.

I swallow hard, my breath shaky. "He hasn't even been given a fair trial."

"There is no trial for traitors," my father snaps. "There is only punishment."

I look at the male again, focusing—diving into his mind, his memories, his essence. The truth is there, written in the raw edges of his soul.

He is *innocent*.

My stomach churns.

My father leans in, his voice dropping to a venomous whisper. "Do it, Vassago. Or you will watch me *beat* Azrael later."

I flinch.

He waits, watching my hesitation, then clicks his tongue. "Unless, of course, you'd rather take his place?"

A violent shudder wracks through me. Azrael never knew—never understood—how much I loved him.

He saw me as an extension of our father's rule, as his prison warden rather than his shield. But I was the only thing that stood between him and the full weight of our father's wrath. The only two siblings we were allowed to know of in this wretched kingdom—just us, the world against us.

And I had spent my entire life taking the blows meant for him.

"*Vassago*," my father warns, his patience snapping like brittle bone.

I look at the male again. He has stopped pleading. His shoulders have gone slack, his head bowed in quiet resignation. He mumbles something under his breath, something too soft to hear, but I feel it all the same.

He has given up.

I tighten my grip on the dagger, my nails digging into my own skin.

If I do this, I will never be the same.

If I don't, Azrael will suffer.

My father shifts beside me, sensing my hesitation, his fingers twitching as though he's prepared to rip the dagger from my hands and do the deed himself.

I exhale slowly.

Then, with shaking hands, I turn the dagger against my own palm and press the blade inward, drawing blood.

"I will not be your executioner," I whisper.

My father's eyes widen, then darken with something lethal. "What did you say?"

I meet his gaze, forcing my voice to be stronger than I feel. "I will not kill an *innocent* man."

A silence falls over the crowd, thick with shock.

And then, my father's fist crashes into my jaw.

Pain explodes through my face, but I don't fall.

I refuse to.

He grips my collar and jerks me forward, his breath hot against my skin. "You ungrateful *disgrace.*"

His voice is no longer for the crowd—it is for *me* alone, laced with a hatred I have known my *entire life.*

At this moment, I still want to protect Azrael. I *need* to. No one else will.

But I physically *cannot* kill an innocent life.

"Tch, tch, tch." Father clicks his tongue, feigning disappointment, though his amusement is evident. "It's a shame, really. Azrael will have to get extra lashings for your defiance. Would you care to explain to him *why*?"

A sharp inhale catches in my throat, and tears burn the edges of my vision.

I am caught between a rock and a corner—between my brother and this innocent man.

Between betraying everything my kind stands for and allowing Azrael to suffer for my defiance.

My grip tightens on the dagger.

The crowd stirs, eager, watching.

I raise the blade high, my chest tightening as I prepare to do the unthinkable.

Then—

A sickening squelch.

The crowd erupts in cheers, a frenzy of voices roaring in approval.

I freeze.

The dagger slips slightly in my grip, my hands going numb as I slowly look up— And lock eyes with Azrael.

His ice-blue gaze pierces through me, through everything, and my stomach sinks as I see Orcus in his hands, slick with fresh blood.

The male before me collapses forward, lifeless, a crimson pool spreading beneath him.

Azrael pulls Orcus free, the sound gutting me more than the actual act. He doesn't even hesitate when he looks up at our father and mutters, *"Done."*

Then, without another glance in my direction, he turns and walks away.

I should feel relief. The choice was taken from me.

I didn't have to make it.

I didn't have to break.

So why do I feel sick?

Why does the weight in my chest grow heavier as I watch *him* walk away with the blood of an innocent on his hands?

But our father doesn't let him get far.

The crowd is still cheering when I hear the unmistakable sound of leather *snapping* through the air.

Crack.

Azrael doesn't even have time to react before the *whip strikes him across the back.*

His body jerks forward, his footing staggering.

Then comes the *scream.*

A raw, agonized sound that rips through the air and shreds through my insides like a serrated blade.

Crack.

Another lash.

And another.

And another.

I don't move.

I don't speak.

I know better than to interfere—to *challenge* our father in public would only make this worse.

I'm still *healing* from my last punishment. I know what defiance will get me. But this? This is worse.

I force myself to stare at the male's corpse, trying—*begging*—to block out Azrael's cries.

I can't.

The sounds burrow into my skull, carving scars that *no* amount of time will ever erase.

I try to picture something else, to imagine a world beyond this horror. A waterfall, maybe. A quiet field of deer grazing in golden light.

Nothing comes.

I have no imagination.

No escape.

What does Azrael think of when he needs to escape his pain?

I glance at him—my *little brother,* now publicly humiliated, reduced to a shaking, bloodied form under our father's wrath. His skin is torn, raw and blistering, scabbing over fresh wounds that never had the chance to heal.

A deep, consuming rage coils within me.

I should have fought for you more.

I should have protected you.

I should have—

Tears blur my vision.

Then—

I blink—

And I'm standing before the male all over again.

The same dagger in my hands.

The same impossible choice suffocating me.

My brother or this innocent life?

I shudder.

And I *fail him* all over again.

CHAPTER THIRTY-TWO

Saygin

SAY SOMETHING - A GREAT BIG WORLD FT. CHRISTINA AGUILERA

I'm fighting. *Fighting* against the pull of the Mawkin's screams.

But I'm still trapped.

The loop drags me forward, my body moving on its own, forcing my feet down this familiar path—the same damn path I swore I'd never walk again.

I *know* what's at the end of this road.

Sweat pools at my forehead, dripping down from my tightly wound bun. My breath is ragged, shallow, *useless*.

Turn around.

Fight this. Now.

My pulse hammers against my skull, a drum of urgency that my body refuses to obey. I will my legs to stop. To hesitate. To do something other than carry me toward my worst nightmare.

But I haven't won.

I'm still walking toward the throne.

The throne where my *baby sister* now sits.

A throne never meant for her.

A throne built in the heart of our enemy's village—the same enemy that slaughtered our mother.

I force a breath through my teeth. Rumors are just that, rumors.

But they claw at me like truth.

The Mawkin's power drags me deeper, making the past coil around me like an iron shackle.

This isn't real.

I've lived through this before.

I bite down hard, grounding myself, forcing the pain to clear my thoughts. *Get... a... fucking... grip, Saygin!*

But my feet still move forward.

The throne looms ahead, waiting.

And there she is.

Reagan.

Her hair is still the same soft pink, strands catching in the gentle breeze like delicate silk. But the eyes that meet mine are *hard*, void of warmth—glistening with the kind of cold fury that promises a death sentence.

My death.

The Mawkin's grip tightens around my mind, warping the moment, making me live it again—forcing me to believe it again.

But Reagan...

And yet, here I stand, her gaze slicing through me like a blade.

The past is real.

It always will be.

And this time...

Maybe I don't make it out.

"Reagan."

I choke on her name. My voice is barely a whisper, but the moment it leaves my lips, she smiles.

A slow, deliberate smile.

Fangs flash beneath her parted lips, gleaming under the dim torchlight.

"Big sister," she purrs. "You're back."

I can't move.

I want to. By gods, I need to. But I am not in control of my body, no matter how desperately I want to change this moment—no matter how much I want to undo this nightmare.

I've lived this before.

I know what's coming.

And yet, I ask anyway. "What does this mean? What is all this?" My voice wavers. I already know the answer.

Reagan steps down from her throne, moving with slow, deliberate steps, her gaze never leaving mine.

"I had to get out of survival mode." She shrugs as if it's the simplest thing in the world. "I had to *overcome...* and just *live.*"

"I left so we *could* live!" My chest heaves, my fingers clenching at my sides. "What happened to the family I placed you with?"

Her smile deepens.

"I killed them."

The air is sucked from my lungs.

No.

No, no, no.

She says it so casually, like she's recounting the weather or some meaningless conversation.

"You see, sister..." She tilts her head, stepping closer, her voice sweet, venomous. "We have to do things we don't want to do so we can overcome our fears. So we can live. *Join me.*"

She waves a hand, and two guards step forward.

Dragging someone between them.

A male.

Not just *any* male.

My pulse stops.

Oliver.

His sandy blonde hair is a tangled mess, matted with sweat and dirt. One of his eyes is swollen shut, his lip split and bleeding. His wrists are bound, his breathing ragged—but he's alive.

Barely.

Three years.

It's been three fucking years since I've seen those hazel eyes. Since I've heard his voice.

Why did I leave?

Why did I choose duty over him?

Why did I leave *her* behind?

I should have taken Reagan with me.

I should have—

This moment shouldn't exist.

"Kill him."

The words slide from her lips like silk, soft and smooth. *Deadly.*

"Your last tie to that puny village. Cut him loose, and join me."

I stagger back.

"Why did you do this, Ray?" My voice cracks, hoarse, desperate.

She sighs, rolling her eyes like she's tired of explaining something obvious. "Because, Say..." She leans in, her lips curling at the edges. *"Love gets you killed."*

The words slice through me.

"Release the thread connecting you and watch how you will blossom." Reagan spreads her arms, as if revealing some great, magnificent truth. "You will become *powerful. Unstoppable.* All you have to do is *let go.*"

She waves a lazy hand toward Oliver.

He's on his knees now, chest rising and falling in uneven breaths.

Blood stains his skin.

His hazel eyes lock onto mine.

There's no fear in them.

Only *pain*.

Only *regret*.

Only the *silent plea* of a male who knows what comes *next*.

My fingers twitch around the hilt of my blade, the weight of it grounding me as the options circle in my mind—

But I *already* know how this plays out.

I *already* know the ending.

This is the moment I *became* a *monster*.

My own version of a monster.

Not the kind that lurks in the shadows or preys on the weak. No, I became something else entirely—

A female who had to carve out her own power among males.

Three years.

Three years of training.

Three years of being beaten, bruised, broken.

Three years of clawing my way through every rank, only to be used, to be *violated* by the same males I shared a flask of water with.

I destroyed them all.

And when I had nothing left to take—when I had given up my rank, my pride, everything—

I came home.

To her.

To *this* fucking *monster*.

"Ray," I swallow back the lump in my throat, forcing my voice to remain steady. "I'm not hurting Oliver. And I am not going to hurt you. Let him go—just let him go, and we'll leave."

I plead, but I know it's pointless.

I remember how much I just wanted this moment to be *over*—how I just wanted to take Oliver and run.

To escape.

Maybe we could have found some quiet corner of the Underworld—a cottage by a lake, far from all of this... far from the blood, the violence, the hunger for power that has poisoned my sister's soul.

But there's no *running* from this.

Not now.

Not ever.

Reagan's lips curl into a snarl. "Not going to happen."

She flicks her fingers.

The guards descend.

A swarm of bodies, of claws and fangs and snapping teeth.

I hear Oliver scream.

A sound I *never* should have heard.

I fight.

I fight with everything I have—my lone blade cutting through flesh, slicing through armor. But there are too many.

Too fucking many.

Oliver's screams turn ragged. *Agonized.*

Then... they turn wet.

And then—

Nothing.

I can't stop myself from looking.

By the gods, I fucking try.

But the memory version of me won't let that happen.

I see everything.

I see his intestines, glistening and spilling onto the stone floor.

I see his *eyes,* torn from their sockets, drowning in bloody filth.

I see muscles, bones, pieces of the male I once loved scattered like scraps of discarded meat.

My throat tears open with a scream.

Reagan watches, unfazed, standing amidst the carnage like a goddess admiring her kingdom.

"Let it go, sister!" she calls over the chaos. "Free yourself of the burden!"

I turn on her, vision tunneling, rage turning my veins into molten fire.

"Why did you do this to me?!"

Her expression doesn't falter.

No *guilt*. No *remorse*.

Nothing.

Just a quiet, eerie sort of certainty.

"I did what you could never do." She tilts her head, pink hair shifting with the motion. "I overcame who I was designed to be so I could do more than just *survive*."

In that moment, she wasn't my sister.

She was a traitor.

A butcher.

A monster *wearing* my sister's face.

A snarl rips from my throat as I bare my teeth, rage consuming every nerve in my body. I lunge—

Faster than I've ever moved before.

But Reagan doesn't flinch.

She barely flicks her wrist—barely moves—

And yet I'm sent flying.

My body slams into the stone wall with a sickening crack, the impact rattling through my bones. My vision blurs.

Pain.

Fucking *pain*.

A growl burns its way up my throat as I stagger back to my feet, fingers tightening around the hilt of my blade.

I run.

Not at her—

At her guards.

I rip through them, blade carving paths of blood and bone. One after another, I realive them, forcing their reanimated bodies to turn on her.

Her control is slipping.

She flicks them away—two at a time—but I see it now.

She's *struggling*.

Her energy is limited.

And I'm *relentless*.

I keep coming, keep weaving between the chaos, until—

My blade meets her throat.

I see the flicker of *panic* in her eyes.

Her breath catches.

She looks so *small* now.

So afraid.

Tears burn my vision, blurring the sharp edges of my fury. My grip trembles. My whole body shakes with the force of everything she's taken from me.

Everything she's destroyed.

"*Fuck you!*" I scream.

The air erupts. A violent surge of energy explodes from me, shattering the world in a burst of light—

And then— Darkness.

I drown in it.

Only to wake up—

Walking.

Again.

Walking toward her throne.

Again.

Again.

I can't stop. I can't *change* it.

This is my fucking *loop.* And I am fucking trapped.

CHAPTER THIRTY-THREE

Azrael

ANIMAL I HAVE BECOME - THREE DAYS GRACE

"Where the *fuck* is it?" I roar at Quinn, my voice booming through the twisted ruins of this godforsaken place. My chest tightens, every muscle tense as I look around. The place reeks of rot and ancient, forgotten horrors—nothing more than a hellhole that's had far too many centuries to fester in the dark. I can't help but feel that every inch of stone and rubble is mocking me.

The others are collapsed around us, their bodies crumpled like rag dolls, but at least they're still breathing—barely. That's the only thing keeping me from completely losing my shit. I could deal with the monsters, the endless pits of despair, the creeping cold of the Underworld... but watching them—my friends—like this? It's not something I can stomach. Not now, *not ever*.

"Here!" Quinn shouts, his voice cutting through the tension like a knife.

I snap my head around, my eyes immediately locking onto him. He's standing there, facing off with some god-awful, birdlike creature perched in a jagged crack along the wall. The thing looks like it crawled straight out of a nightmare—its hollow, glowing eyes radiating an unnatural light. Thick, black ink drops from its feathers, splattering against the floor. The stench of decay clings to it like a disease.

The damn thing doesn't blink. It just watches us.

Fucking fantastic.

Quinn doesn't wait for an invitation. He steps forward like he's done this a thousand times before. He reaches out with both hands and grabs the creature by its thin, brittle neck, twisting it with a violent jerk. The sound that follows is pure nightmare material—*squish, pop,* like wet parchment being torn in half. Ink splatters across his arms, dripping down his hands, but he doesn't flinch.

The creature convulses once, letting out a final, high-pitched screech before finally falling limp.

The humming—the maddening noise that had been reverberating in the air, pulling my friends under—stops.

For a moment, I hold my breath, waiting. The silence feels too heavy—to final.

I whirl around to check on Luca, Ashton, and Vassago. They should've snapped out of it by now—hell, the second that thing's dead, they should've sprung back to life, right? But they don't. They stay motionless, like they've been carved from stone. The faint rise and fall of their chest is the only indication that they're not completely gone.

A cold stone of dread settles in my gut.

"What the hell?" I demand, my voice rough with frustration. "That was the thing, right? The *thing* we needed to destroy?"

Quinn glances over at me, his expression annoyingly unfazed. "Sternum rubs," he says flatly, already kneeling next to Saygin, who is still unconscious.

Without missing a beat, he presses his palm firmly to her chest, rubbing in slow, deliberate circles. I open my mouth to ask him what the hell a sternum rub is, but before I can even get the question out, Saygin gasps awake. Her body jerks upright like she had just been pulled out of a nightmare. She chokes on the air, her eyes wide and wild, before glaring at Quinn like she's about to throw him into the next dimension.

"I thought I was dead!" she wheezes, her voice hoarse.

Quinn just deadpans, completely unbothered. "You're welcome."

I roll my eyes. But the tension in my chest is still there. Quinn's words, though they sound casual, weigh heavy. The others are still out.

I don't waste another second. I drop beside Luca, pressing my palm firmly against his sternum, moving in slow circles. My mind is fucking racing. My stomach churns as I stare down at him— he doesn't belong here. He shouldn't be lying motionless in a place like this. He should be with Sadie right now, irritating the hell out of her with his incessant teasing, forcing her to admit that deep down, she actually cares about him.

But that's not his reality right now.

Luca jolts awake with a guttural gasp, and my relief is short-lived. Panic hits me almost instantly as his body begins to convulse beneath my hands. The golden glow of his eyes flashes too brightly...too dangerously. His hands grip my arms, his fingers like vices, and his muscles twitch. They are rigid with tension. It only takes a split second before he is thrashing in my grip, growling like an animal in distress.

"*Shit*—Luca, it's me!" I grunt, trying to tighten my hold on him, but he's stronger than I could expect. Stronger than I remember. My arms are starting to strain under the pressure.

The growl that rips from his throat is primal, low, and ferocious, and before I can fully react—his body begins to change. His skin starts to melt, his features shifting, fur sprouting from beneath his skin. His jaw elongates, his teeth morphing into sharp, deadly fangs. He's becoming too slippery for me to hold.

Fuck.

"*Quinn!*" I bark, trying to contain Luca's wild thrashing. "Any suggestions before he mauls me?"

Quinn, still wiping ink off his hands, doesn't even look up from his task. "Yeah. Don't let go."

I roll my eyes. "Wow! So helpful." I mutter.

Luca's thrashing intensifies, his growls turning vicious. I feel the heat radiating off him as his transformation presses on, each second making my grip weaker.

His claws sink into my arms, and I curse under my breath as I struggle to maintain control. The slick, melting texture of his shifting form makes it harder to hold on. My grip is slipping, my bones burning with the effort.

"The worlf needs to calm down!" Saygin calls out from across the room, still working on waking Ashton.

"I'm *trying!*" I snap, the strain making my voice sharper than I intend. "Luca! It's me, *Azrael!*"

"Whatever it was he saw must have really set him off," Orcus hums, his voice strangely amused. "Maybe it was his reflection."

"Not. Helping!" I bark, tightening my arms around Luca as he continues to thrash, his growls becoming more guttural, more feral. His wild frantic energy pulses beneath my hands, and I can feel his transformation trying to force its way through.

And then, as if the universe finally decided I had suffered enough, Ashton stumbles to my side, still groggy from the chaos but functional enough to fish through his pouch and sprinkle whatever magical sand shit he keeps in there over Luca's face.

"*Relax*, my friend," Ashton murmurs, his voice low and oddly calming—eerily hypnotic. I'm almost convinced he could make a storm fall asleep with that tone.

Luca stiffens, his glowing eyes flickering as Ashton's magic starts to settle over him. The brown fur retreats, his skin reforming as his breathing slows. His head tilts slightly, the transformation receding as his pupils adjust, as if he's just waking from a heavy sleep. He blinks sluggishly, his eyes moving from me to Ashton, then back to me with a confused expression.

"...What's going on, guys?" he mutters, rubbing his face like he's trying to shake off the remnants of a nightmare.

I can't help it. I burst out laughing, the sound escaping before I can stop it. The tension that's been building inside me suddenly melts away, replaced by something light—something almost fucking absurd.

"You ever shift before, Luca?" I ask between laughs, still catching my breath from the struggle.

Luca hesitates, clearly embarrassed. "Once. Maybe twice?" His voice is sheepish, and it only makes it worse.

Saygin crouches down beside him, eyeing him like a scientist observing a rare specimen. "Not a typical wolf, are you?"

Luca sighs, dragging a hand over his face in frustration. "Didn't exactly choose to be a freak, you know?"

Quinn, never one to miss an opportunity, flashes Luca a grin. "You're not a freak—*you're beautiful.*"

Luca groans in disgust, dropping his head into his hands. "Please. Let me die."

I chuckle, shaking my head. "Good luck with that, my friend. You're stuck with us."

Ashton stands up slowly, dusting his hands off like he's just completed some menial tasks. "Next time, try not to go full wolf mode on our watch, yeah?"

Luca glances up at him, a tired smile tugging at his lips. "I'll make a note of it."

Ashton and I help Luca to his feet, though his weight is heavy, his legs unsteady. He sways between us, his face still pale, but there's a fire in his eyes now—his survival instinct kicking in. The wolf's transformation is slowly fading, leaving him just human enough to be useful. Just barely.

"We need to keep moving," Vassago says, wiping the sweat from his brow. His voice calm, but there's a tightness to it that sends a warning through me. He's not saying it for our benefit. He's saying it for his own peace of mind. Whatever's coming next, if it comes, it's going to hit us hard.

We exchange silent glances, each of us understanding the urgency, the stakes. The bird-thing was just the beginning. If there's one thing I am learning about this place, it's that it doesn't deal in small portions. Everything here is lethal.

I reach out through the bond, my pulse pounding in my ears like war drums. *Layla?*

Her reply comes swiftly, but there's an undercurrent of panic to it. *Yes?*

That panic tightens my chest. I don't like it. *Stay where you are,* I command, my words are sharp, and I am trying to control them even though I am anything but calm. *We're coming, but if you keep moving, it's going to take longer to get to you.*

Her voice trembles through the bond, a distant whisper of distress. *Azrael, I can't. Drepane is dying!*

I feel the tremble of her words deep in my gut, like a physical blow. Her fear bleeds through, too raw, too fucking sharp. *Layla, I need you to listen to me. Stay put. I'm not going to let anything happen to you.*

She doesn't hesitate. *Azrael, I can't. I need to save him. He—he needs Cronos! If he dies, everything falls apart. Flo will die; I will die!* Her voice breaks, but she presses on. *I'm going to Cronos. He will save Drepane!*

A growl rumbles from deep within me, a visceral reaction to her words. *No!* The command in my voice is hard and biting, the threat of it is unmistakable. *You are my mate. You will do as I say. Stay. Put.*

I can feel her hesitation in the bond, her defiance—she doesn't want to listen. But I can't give her a choice. Her next words strike like a whip: *If this were you and Orcus in this situation, you know I wouldn't question you at all.*

There's a brief, heavy silence before her voice softens, but her words are just as firm. *I would never make you choose between Orcus and me so please don't make me choose between you and Drepane.*

The silence between us thickens, and I clench Orcus, the weight of the scythe grounding me, but it doesn't steady my racing mind. She's right. I know she is. But goddamn it, I'm selfish. I need to see her. I need to make sure she's okay. The thought of losing her—of losing either of them—tears at me.

Layla. Her name is a whisper on my mental lips, full of frustration—full of love.

I don't respond, can't respond. My mind is slit—torn between her plea, her desperation, and the need to act. My chest aches with the weight of it all.

Finally, after what feels like eternity, I break the silence. My voice is quiet and raw, "Where is Cronos' cell?"

Quinn halts mid-step, his boots scraping against the stone as he spins to face me. His eyes narrow with suspicion. "Why?"

I don't hesitate. "Because that's where Layla is going. Drepane is weak—he needs Cronos to replenish him."

A flicker of realization crosses Quinn's face, followed quickly by exasperation. "Ah! Of course she's going straight to the most dangerous place possible." He mutters something under his breath, rolling his eyes, but it's not enough to mask his frustration. "This way. *This way!*"

Without a second's hesitation, Quinn takes a sharp right turn down one of the dark, winding tunnels, his pace quickening as he leads us deeper into the bowels of this damned place. The rest of us scramble to follow. Luca is still leaning on Ashton, his steps faltering, but determined to keep going. The tension is thick, suffocating, but there's no room for anything else right now.

Chapter Thirty-Four

Ashton

I wanna Be Yours - Arctic Monkeys

"What did you see?" Azrael's voice is low but sharp, the weight of the question hanging between us.

I can feel the tension in the air, the others still catching their breath from the chaos. We've barely survived the Mawkin's trap, and it's clear Azrael's trying to get a grip on whatever the hell just happened. The bond with Layla and the urgency of the situation has him more on edge than usual, but this question—it cuts through the air like a damn knife.

I pause, looking down at my hands. I'm still feeling the residual tremors from the memory the Mawkin dredged up, the cold sweat that never seems to leave me. My throat tightens, and for a moment, I almost say something, but I bite it back. There are things that are better left unsaid, and this is one of them.

"You really wanna know?" I ask, voice rough, a small smirk tugging at my lips, though it's anything but amusing.

Azrael's eyes narrow, but he doesn't move any closer. "You've never been one for sugarcoating things. Just spit it out."

"Me *fucking* your mother." I smile, trying not to remember what the Mawkin showed me.

Azrael's eyes narrow, but it's not the playful response I was hoping for. His jaw clenches, and I can feel the tension in the air shift, as if the words hit a little too close to home. For a moment, the space between us feels cold, even colder than the chaos we just escaped.

I force the smirk to stay, but it feels like ash on my tongue. I can hear the quiet hum of Orcus in Azrael's grip, and I know it's not helping. I try to look unaffected, but the truth is, I'm anything but.

Azrael doesn't flinch. He just stares at me, his expression unreadable. There's a flicker in his eyes, the kind that's hard to place—anger? Disgust? Or maybe something else, something darker.

Whatever it is, it sends a chill down my spine.

"Not funny, Ashton," he says, his voice low, but the weight of it presses against my chest like a stone.

I tilt my head, trying to hide the discomfort that crawls up my throat. "Relax, Az. I'm just trying to lighten the mood."

But it's not working. Not with him. And definitely not with me.

He takes a step forward, his gaze never leaving mine, and for a moment, I feel like I'm standing on the edge of something—something dangerous. I can't read him, and that's what makes it worse.

"Forget the jokes, Ashton," Azrael continues, his tone hardening. "What happened in there?"

I swallow, the weight of his words sinking in. He's right, but damn it, I'm not ready to talk about it. Not now. Not ever. There are things that should stay buried, locked away in the dark.

I open my mouth to respond, but the words stick, thick and heavy. Instead, I look over at the others—Luca, Vassago, Saygin—none of them speaking, all of them waiting, waiting for me to crack.

"It showed me Isolde," I finally say, the words slipping out in a hushed rasp. My throat feels tight, like the air's been sucked out of the room. "Reminding me that I couldn't keep her safe."

Azrael doesn't say anything, but I can feel the weight of his understanding. His eyes soften, just barely, but the tension is still there, thick in the air between us.

"You don't have to talk about it," he mutters, almost to himself.

I nod, but I don't look at him. The memory—the Mawkin's image—it's still too raw. It's always going to be raw. I wish I could bury it. Forget it. But I can't. Not yet. Maybe not ever.

Instead, I force my gaze back on the others. They're all just as affected, just as shaken. The silence hangs thick between us like smoke. It's not the kind of silence that brings relief. No, this one's heavy with what's unsaid.

"We need to keep moving," I say, breaking the silence, my voice almost mechanical. "Before whatever the hell else is out there finds us."

Azrael nods sharply, his eyes still fixed on me for a moment longer than necessary, but then he turns, leading the group forward behind Quinn without another word.

And as we move, I can't shake the feeling that something's still *waiting* for me. Something I'm not ready to face.

Saygin steps forward, her gaze flickering briefly to Luca as he trudges along, still not quite himself. She hesitates for a moment, then leans in, her nose twitching as if she's trying to catch a specific scent.

Luca, still a little groggy, notices her approach, but doesn't move away. He furrows his brow, clearly confused, as she leans closer, inhaling deeply near his shoulder.

"Uh... something wrong, Saygin?" Luca asks, shifting uncomfortably under her intense gaze.

She pulls back slightly, her lips curling into a small, sly grin. "Mmm. You smell different. Like... *danger*. And something else. Familiar."

Luca looks even more bewildered. "Danger? I smell like danger?"

"Not exactly," she replies, her voice soft but tinged with amusement. "More like... I don't know. Something about you has changed."

The group slows for a moment, and even Azrael casts a sharp glance over his shoulder, watching the exchange with narrowed eyes.

Luca rubs the back of his neck, uncomfortable under Saygin's scrutiny. "I didn't think I was *that* interesting."

Saygin shrugs, smirking. "I wouldn't be so sure. I've smelled worse." Her eyes flicker to Vassago for a brief moment, and he raises an eyebrow but stays silent.

"Yeah, well," Luca says, his tone a bit defensive, "I'm just trying to keep it together, okay?"

"Of course you are," Saygin responds, her grin widening. "But don't think I didn't notice. There's something off about you, Luca. Just don't go biting anyone, yeah?"

Luca's face flushes slightly at the jab, but he lets out a nervous laugh. "Not planning on it, I promise."

Luca stumbles slightly, caught off guard by the sudden shift in Saygin's tone and her intent staring. His face flushes a deep red, eyes wide as he blinks at her. "What?!" he stammers, completely thrown off balance by her blank stares.

Saygin's smirk deepens as she watches his reaction, clearly enjoying the discomfort she's causing. "I mean," she says, tilting her head to the side, "if you're really in the mood to bite someone, I might as well *volunteer*."

Luca coughs awkwardly, his hand rubbing the back of his neck. "Uh, that's... not exactly what I had in mind when I said I wasn't planning on biting anyone, Saygin."

"Oh, come on," she teases, her voice a playful drawl. "A little bit of danger never hurt anyone. Besides, you smell like it—might as well embrace it, right?"

The tension in the air shifts, becoming lighter, though Luca is still clearly uncomfortable with the direction of the conversation. He glances over at Azrael, who is walking just ahead, his expression unreadable.

"Look, I don't think..." Luca starts, trying to steer the conversation back to safer territory, but Saygin interrupts him with a soft, teasing laugh.

"You think too much, Luca," she says, tapping him lightly on the shoulder. "It's just a joke."

Quinn's laugh rings out, cutting through the light banter, and for a moment, it catches everyone off guard. His expression is mischievous, a glint in his eyes that's hard to ignore.

"It's not a joke," he says, still chuckling, but his tone shifts to something more serious beneath the humor. "Trust me, Wolf, you have no idea what you're missing."

Luca freezes, his face drains of color—if that is even possible with how pale he already looks—as he looks from Quinn to Saygin, unsure whether to be more horrified or confused.

Luca, still processing, gives him a wary look. "I think I'll pass on whatever wisdom you're offering, thanks."

Quinn simply shrugs again, his smile stretching wider. "Fair enough. But it's there, if you ever change your mind."

Azrael, who's been silently walking ahead, suddenly mutters without turning around, "By the fucking gods, Quinn, can you not? We're trying to keep this group from falling apart, not falling *into* each other."

Quinn grins wider, clearly unbothered. "Hey, who says you can't have a little fun along the way?"

Luca just sighs, shaking his head as he continues to walk, but the confusion on his face hasn't completely faded. Saygin, however, is grinning from ear to ear, clearly enjoying the chaos she's stirred up.

Luca's question hangs in the air for a moment, his curiosity getting the better of him. "How did you two meet?" he asks, looking between Saygin and Quinn, a slightly amused, yet cautious expression on his face.

Saygin's grin falters for a split second, but she quickly recovers, leaning against the stone wall with an exaggerated sigh, as if the tale is something she's forced to recount far too often. "Oh, you know. Love at first *fight*," she says, her voice dripping with sarcasm. "Quinn here had a thing for barging into my personal space."

Quinn raises an eyebrow, a sly smirk forming on his lips as he looks over at her. "Personal space? I believe I was doing you a favor, actually. Saving you from getting your ass kicked by someone a lot more dangerous than me."

"*Please*," Saygin retorts, rolling her eyes. "You were just looking for a fight. You practically *begged* me to punch you."

Quinn laughs, the sound rich and unbothered. "And you did, which is why I fell in love with you."

Luca raises an eyebrow, clearly not buying into their banter. "That's it? You two just started fighting, and now you're bound together?"

Saygin's expression softens for a brief moment, an edge of something unreadable in her gaze. "It wasn't *just* a fight," she says, her voice quieter. "It was a lot of things, but yeah, a good punch to the face helped seal the deal."

Quinn shrugs, as if it's the simplest thing in the world. "She's the stubborn one. I couldn't leave her alone."

Luca chuckles, shaking his head. "Well, that's one way to start a relationship, I guess."

Saygin shoots him a sly grin. "I don't recommend it as a *plan* for anyone else, though."

I lean against the cool stone wall, the echo of the chaos still ringing in my ears. I can feel the tremors in my hands, the lingering effects of the Mawkin's cruel torture. The memories it dredged up aren't something I can shake off easily. I try to steady myself, pushing the images back into the dark corners of my mind where they belong.

Then, like a soft breeze against my mind, I feel Sadie's presence. Her voice brushes against me through the bond, and it's like a lifeline I didn't realize I needed.

Ashton... are you okay? she asks, the worry in her tone more familiar than anything else in this godforsaken place. It hits me harder than I expect.

I hesitate, just for a moment, because I know she can feel everything. I don't want to burden her with this—what the Mawkin forced me to relive, the pieces of me I don't want her to see.

Yeah, I answer, my voice quiet, but sincere. *I'm alright... just... I'm okay, little Nightmare.*

There's a pause on the other end of the bond, a heavy silence before I feel her again, as if she's reaching out further, trying to wrap herself around my pain.

I saw it, Ashton. *I was screaming for you before you were screaming through the bond.* She says softly. *Isolde was beautiful... and she gave you the silver streaks in your hair?*

Yes. I look up, hoping the back of my head absorbs the tears. *It was her way of telling me she will always be with me. I'm sorry, Sadie. I didn't mean for you to see that.*

I think I needed to for me to understand your pain. She hums softly, caressing my life thread.

Her words settle into me like a balm, soothing the jagged edges of memories that I can't fully escape, but this... This is better than hiding. It's better than keeping the wounds locked in the dark. I don't feel like I'm carrying this burden alone anymore. Sadie gets it.

Thank you, I whisper through the bond, the weight of my gratitude folding between us. *I know I don't say it enough... but thank you.*

Her presence wraps around me, gentle and warm, the bond humming softly with her quiet understanding. *You never have to say it. I just need you to heal, Ashton. You deserve it, because I might have... I'm safe! But, I'm heading out with E xu.*

I close my eyes, letting her words wash over me. I don't know if I'll ever be whole again, but with her here, I think maybe I can start to piece myself together.

Then my eyes shoot open, *Where the fuck are you guys going? I told you to stay home.*

I won the auction for my dad! I'm headed to go pick him up now.

I'm so over this fucking bullshit.

CHAPTER THIRTY-FIVE

Layla

I WON'T GIVE UP - JASON MRAZ

"I'm sorry, Layla," Drepane hums weakly, his voice strained as he flickers in my grip.

"Nothing to be sorry for, Drepane." I try to steady my breath, but it's harder than I'd like to admit. His energy is fading, sputtering like a candle fighting against the wind.

"Everything to be sorry for," he flickers again, his presence waning, flickering as if he's a candle burning out. "You wouldn't be in this mess if it wasn't for me."

I tighten my grip around him, my fingers brushing over the surface of his form, the energy still so raw and potent beneath the cool touch of his fading presence. "You wouldn't be in this mess if it wasn't for me, and you know that. Don't give up just yet. We have a bargain, remember?"

He hums softly, a sound like wind through a hollow shell, and I can feel his life force dimming. His life thread becoming quieter. "We are in a predicament, young one."

"There has to be a way..." My mind races, desperation clawing at my chest. "Can't you take energy from Flo or me? Just enough to hold on a little longer? Orcus gave you energy. He can do it again!"

"I need *Ancient* energy," he murmurs, and I can hear the weariness, the defeat. "You two... you aren't the kind I can bond with in that way, little one. But I believe in you. Or I wouldn't have agreed to our bond. Orcus isn't Ancient enough to loan me more energy. I could drain him completely and then Azrael and Orcus would be in the same situation as us."

"Drepane," I force the words out between ragged breaths, struggling to walk and talk at the same time. My legs are shaking with the effort, but there's no time for weakness. Not now. Not while he's slipping away from me. "Why did you pick me?"

A long silence stretches between us, like a thread pulled thin over the void. Then his voice comes—calm, certain.

"Because you have the desire to live. You fight to live. And that alone is worth standing behind, young reaper."

His words hit me like a heartbeat that isn't mine, a pulse of fire spreading through my veins. I freeze, the weight of them crashing into me all at once. I understand now. I *feel* it.

This bond—this thing between us—isn't just power, isn't just fate. It's us. I feel it in my soul now, more than I ever have before. It's a force that lingers in the background of my every thought, every breath, every heartbeat.

I finally understand what Azrael has with Orcus. That unbreakable, unforgiving bond—so strong that, at one point, I thought there was no room for me. I thought there would never be a place in that kind of love... with that kind of connection.

But there was room. He *made* room.

Because my bond with Drepane is just as consuming. Just as otherworldly. There is no separation between us now. I am Drepane. And Drepane is *me*.

A rush of warmth blooms in my chest, the force of it so sudden that it almost knocks me off my feet. I feel something deep inside me stir, something that tells me if I just trust this—if I lean into it—I can make it work. I can save him.

But what if it's not enough? What if this bond isn't enough to keep him from slipping away?

I swallow hard, shaking my head. No. I won't let that happen. Not after everything we've been through, not when I'm starting to understand the true depth of what we are.

I clutch him tighter, my resolve strengthening with every heartbeat.

"I won't let you go," I whisper fiercely. "We're in this together, Drepane. We've always been in this together."

His energy flickers, stronger for a moment, like he's heard me. Like he's *with* me in this, despite everything. And for the first time, I feel like I'm not alone in this fight.

I can save him. *We can save each other.*

"His cell is right up there, Layla!" Flo chirps, her paws bouncing with excitement as she trots beside me, the large furball's enthusiasm is terribly infectious. I can feel her urgency even without the bond. She knows what's at stake.

I pick up the pace, my legs moving faster now, the anticipation of Cronos' cell just ahead pulling me forward. It's the only thing on my mind—the only thing that matters in this moment. *I'm so close...*

"Not so fast!" The voice rings out, eerie and cold, like a wind before a storm, cutting through the air with a chill that sinks deep into my bones.

My heart hammers in my chest as I spin around, every muscle tensed for action. The sight of her stops me in my tracks.

Memetim.

Her pale skin seems to glow in the dim light of the dungeon, her blood-red eyes fixed on me with a smirk that sends a ripple of ice through my veins. Her lips match the color of her gaze, a red so deep it almost seems to pulse. Her silky black hair shimmers like liquid ink, cascading around her like something out of a nightmare. And for some reason, I find myself irritated by it.

"I don't have time for your shit, Memetim," I snap, the words leaving my mouth with a bite I can't hide. My fingers tighten around Drepane's handle, but it feels heavy now, the weight of the situation pressing down on me.

This isn't just another fight. This is something else.

She laughs, the sound grating on my nerves, like nails scraping across stone. It's cruel, mocking, and it sends a shiver down my spine. "Doesn't seem like you have a choice, *bitch*."

Her words are like poison, each syllable dripping with venom, and her gaze locks onto mine with a challenge I can't ignore. A dare.

I want to snap at her. I want to scream at her, but the words don't come. Instead, I step back, putting space between us, my eyes scanning her movements, waiting for her to make the first move. I can feel the electricity in the air—the crackling tension between us, waiting to erupt.

Flo, get Cronos... and hurry! I order, my voice filled with urgency. My heart pounds in my chest as I watch Flo nod once, her huge frame darting off toward Cronos' cell, faster than I can track. My giant ally moves like a blur.

I turn back to face Memetim, trying to steady my breathing, my mind racing. I know what's at stake. I know this could be our last chance. I need to keep it together.

I take a deep breath, planting my feet wide apart, preparing for whatever nightmare Memetim is about to throw at me. My grip on Drepane tightens, the metal cool beneath my fingers, but it's nothing compared to the heat that pulses through me. Drepane hums softly in my mind, a low vibration that I can feel through my grip, his presence there like a tether, reminding me that I'm not alone.

If this is our last battle together, I think to him, *it has been an honor... and I am beyond appreciative for you seeing the potential in me.*

Drepane pulses in response, a surge of purple aura swirling around us, thickening the air like a protective barrier. His energy is a tangible force now, swirling in the space between us, and I can feel it like a heartbeat against my own.

Memetim's eyes flash with something darker, something more dangerous. But I don't back down.

I can't.

This ends now.

"Let's finish this," I mutter to myself, though I'm sure she hears me.

Drepane hums again, steady and powerful, and I feel the surge of strength rush through me. I'm not alone in this fight—not in body, not in spirit.

Memetim raises her hands, and with a slow, deliberate wave of her fingers, the shadows around us grow thicker, darker, as if the very air is being smothered by a heavy, suffocating blanket. The hairs on the back of my neck stand up as I feel the temperature drop, the pressure building around us. Dark crows begin to emerge from the gloom, their wings beating against the air, and their eyes glow with a sickly, malevolent light. They gather in a swirling mass, flapping their wings in unison, croaking in sinister harmony, their cries sending a chill down my spine.

I turn to the bond, hoping, praying to hear Azrael's voice again.

Azrael, I whisper, my voice barely more than a broken breath, but I need him—just once more. The words feel fragile, like glass in my throat, and for a moment, I almost wish I hadn't spoken at all.

Layla. His voice rings through the bond, calm but filled with urgency. It's a lifeline. *What's going on?*

Memetim found me. The words taste bitter on my tongue, a confession I can't take back. I almost choke on them, the weight of them crushing me. In my head, it sounds so broken, so hollow.

I'm almost there! I will be there any second now! His voice is full of frantic hope, but even as I hear the words, I feel it. A deep, aching certainty—he won't make it in time.

Azrael, I repeat, louder this time, my heart pounding against my chest like a war drum. Desperation thickens my voice. Please. Please, hurry.

Yes? His voice sharpens, sensing the shift in my emotions, the fear that's starting to cloud the bond.

I love you. The words spill from my mind like a dam breaking, a tidal wave of raw, desperate need. I pour everything I feel into the bond thread—love, fear, hope. My heart aches with the intensity of it. I need him to understand, to know that even in this moment, I'm still holding on to the truth of us.

Layla, say it to my face. I am fucking coming! His voice cracks with a rush of urgency, a promise. His words may be filled with hope, but the weight of the truth is unbearable. He's not going to make it in time. I *know* it.

A sharp, painful lump forms in my throat as I swallow, trying to fight against the rising tide of panic and hopelessness. The truth hits me hard—the pain of knowing I might never hear him say it back to me stings my eyes, swells in my throat. His words, as desperate and loving as they are, may not be enough to save me.

Before I can fully process that devastating truth, Memetim moves.

With a flick of her wrist, she sends the crows hurtling toward me. The air fills with a deafening shadow of wings and shrill cries as the dark mass of crows dives at me with horrifying precision, their sharp talons like knives aimed for my throat. The weight of the shadow pressing against me intensifies, like the world is closing in, suffocating me.

I scream, the sound ragged and raw, and in a blur of movement, I throw Drepane side to side. The sickle swings through the air in a wide arc, cutting at anything that dares come near. The blade slices through the crows like a hot knife through butter. But there are too many. Too many of them.

The claws rake against my skin, tearing through my clothes, and pain explodes across my body. I swipe frantically, my heart racing as I try to fend them off, but the numbers are overwhelming. It's too much.

"Not like this," I whisper to myself, clinging to the flickering remnants of my will to survive. "Not today."

I have to survive. I have to fight. I won't go down like this. Not to Memetim. Not to these damn crows. *Not today.*

With every ounce of strength I can muster, I push through the pain, slashing at the crows that keep coming, the overwhelming fear threatening to drown me. But in that moment, with the bond still buzzing faintly in my mind, I remember Drepane's words: *Because you have the desire to live. You fight to live.*

And I will. I will keep fighting, even if it *kills* me.

I won't let Memetim win. I won't let this be the end.

The crows are relentless, but I am not giving up. Not without a fight.

Memetim launches herself at me, her stiletto nails clinking against Drepane's blade. Each strike sends an echo through the tunnels, sharp and metallic, like a death knell reverberating off the walls. Her presence is like ice. It's cold and biting and sends an involuntary shiver down my spine. But I force myself to stay focused, my grip tightening around Drepane. I push her off with every ounce of strength I have, my leg shooting out to kick her square in the stomach. The force sends her crashing back, the sickening thud of her body hitting the floor almost satisfying in the chaos of this fight.

I take a few quick steps back, trying to catch my breath, my heart hammering in my chest, threatening to break free. The blood rushing in my ears is deafening.

"You don't even realize how much of a vessel you truly could be!" Her voice rings out, high-pitched and mocking, the words like poison falling from her lips.

I shake my head, forcing the growing unease down, swallowing the lump in my throat. "I don't even know what that means, Memetim!" I shout back, using the skills Exu drilled into me—fast, controlled, precise. Drepane slices through the air with sharp accuracy, but Memetim is already moving, her movements as fluid as a shadow, too fast for me to catch.

Her eyes glow with a manic intensity that makes my pulse spike. "You are an Eclyptian," she snarls, her voice dripping with venom. "You were born to destroy the Empty and link the Underworld permanently to the mortal realm."

Her words slap me across the face, hitting deeper than I want to admit, but I don't let her see it. I'm not going to let her have the satisfaction of breaking me. I run at her again, my blade cutting through the air with more force, my desperation fueling every swing. "I'm just *Layla Simmons*!" I yell, the words like an anchor, trying to ground myself, trying to block out the growing horror gnawing at the back of my mind. I can't let myself believe her.

"You wish, girl!" Memetim laughs bitterly, her voice full of disdain and mocking superiority. She parries my attacks effortlessly, her speed almost inhuman, but each deflection makes me more determined, more furious. Her words twist in my mind, but I won't let them take root.

"I don't even need you alive to do it either," she taunts, her eyes flashing with something dark. She's trying to wear me down, trying to break my resolve before I can reach Cronos. To destroy everything I've fought for. To stop me from reaching the only chance we have.

I hear Drepane hum softly, the vibrations flowing through my hand, steadying me, reminding me why I'm here. She's trying to keep us from getting to Cronos. She's trying to wear us down.

I won't let her win.

Flo? I call through the bond, my voice strained with urgency. *Flo, where are you?*

I found the cell, she responds, her voice laced with frustration. *Just trying to get it open so I can wake him up. But Layla, do we know a Grim Reaper with a scythe?*

I don't have time to process the question before Drepane hums again, a low, steady vibration, and answers for me. *Our mate.*

Before I can react, Memetim takes advantage of my distraction, lunging at me with renewed fury. But I'm quicker. I slide just out of reach, letting her momentum carry her forward. As she stumbles, I use the moment to trip her, sending her sprawling to the floor with a frustrated growl.

Azrael's voice crackles through the bond, urgent and sharp. *How do I open the cell?*

I barely have time to respond before Memetim is back on her feet, charging at me again, but this time, I'm ready. I strike, forcing her back with a swift swipe of Drepane.

Use Orcus. He can open Cronos' cell. He'll wake up and come find me. Drepane's voice sounds so exhausted... He's barely hanging on.

Drepane pulses in my hand, a wave of heat spreading through me, his energy infusing me with strength. *Hope is just around the corner, Layla. Keep fighting.*

I glance back toward the cell, my heart pounding, knowing that everything hinges on this moment. This is our last chance, our one shot at survival.

I won't let Memetim stop me. Not now. I fucking can't!

With everything I have, I push forward, swinging Drepane again. This fight isn't over. Not by a long shot.

Chapter Thirty-Six

Layla

The Kill - Thirty Seconds To Mars

I try to keep my focus on Memetim, but the exhaustion is creeping in like a slow tide, threatening to drown me. Drepane feels weaker in my grip, flickering with every movement, like he's fading. I don't think he could handle another sneak attack from her right now, so every fiber of my being is on edge, watching her every move.

She's too damn graceful. Memetim moves like she was born to dance—smooth, fluid, calculating—while I'm over here trying not to trip over my own feet. And her nails... god, those fucking nails. They scrape along Drepane's blade with a sound that makes my teeth grind. Every clink echoes through the tunnels, sending shivers down my spine. I swear, the only thing that's going to make me stop is the fear that I might actually snap.

She doesn't even break a sweat, doesn't even grunt. It's like she's just toying with me, using me for practice.

"Is that the best you've got, Layla?" she taunts, a wicked smile curling on her lips as she steps back.

I take a deep breath, trying to ground myself, to steady the shaking in my hands.

But she stops, tilting her head slightly as if she senses something.

She looks down the tunnel—toward where Flo went to retrieve Cronos—and her smile widens.

"No... no, you don't get to do that!" I shout, launching myself toward her, ready for the next round.

But then she vanishes. Just like that, in a puff of smoke, leaving me in the damn dark, catching my breath.

A low, rumbling vibration rolls through the Empty, shaking the very ground beneath my feet.

Azrael. He did it!

I sag against the wall, letting my body slump down to the ground, finally allowing myself to breathe for a moment.

"Damn it, she just *disappears* whenever she wants!" I mutter under my breath, feeling my frustration rise. "I swear she's got some kind of teleportation spell. And I'm stuck here like a sitting duck—"

Don't talk to Cronos, little one. Let me handle it.

Drepane's voice hums softly in my mind, and I can't help but smile at the thought of him, even though he feels so far away. His energy is weakening, but there's still a fire in him—one that burns just as brightly as mine.

I nod, sitting down on the cold, damp floor of the tunnel to catch my breath. I wipe the sweat off my brow and try to keep the frustration from spilling over.

You've got this, Drepane, I say, more to myself than him.

"You'd think a goddess like Memetim would at least stick around for a decent fight," I mutter aloud, shaking my head. "But nope, she's too fancy for that."

Drepane rumbles in amusement. *I'm glad you're keeping your humor, even in the face of her... whatever she is.*

I can't help but laugh. "At this point, I'm just trying to stay sane. Though it's hard when we're dealing with a psycho goddess who disappears like she's got somewhere better to be."

A pause, then a low hum from Orcus in the background, his voice strong and clear. *She's a headache. We'll finish her off soon enough.*

I shoot that down to Azrael, my thoughts shifting to him. *I hope you're right. Because if I'm going to make it through this, I need her gone... like, yesterday.*

Don't worry, Layla. Azrael's voice hums in my mind, softer than usual, yet still full of his fierce determination. *We'll get her. I'm coming for you, just hold on.*

I squeeze Drepane tighter, the weight of the world still hanging on my shoulders, but somehow, hearing Azrael's voice feels like a lifeline in the chaos. He's coming for me.

And that's the one thing that keeps me going.

The weight of everything that has happened crashes down on me all at once. I haven't seen Azrael or Orcus in what feels like a lifetime, and my nerves start to tremble violently. My body shakes as if I've run a marathon, and before I know it, tears are streaming down my face.

I fucking did it.

I survived the Empty.

I *saved* Drepane.

I'm going home with Azrael and Orcus, back to the place where I *belong.*

I don't know how much danger is still looming over us, but at this moment, none of that matters. I'm going to see Azrael again, and maybe, just maybe, we can have our honeymoon phase—the one that was stolen from us, ripped away by fate and circumstances beyond our control.

I inhale shakily, my chest tight with the relief that finally begins to wash over me.

But then, I hear it—the sound of heavy, dark footsteps reverberating through the tunnel. I look over my shoulder, my heart stuttering in my chest as Cronos' towering form comes into view, moving slowly and purposefully through the darkness. His golden eyes—those hateful, piercing eyes—lock onto mine, and I swear I can feel them burrowing into my soul.

"Well, I'll be damned." Cronos' voice is low and mocking, and I can almost feel the disdain dripping from every word. "Drepane was desperate enough to settle for you? And you were nearly the death of him. Imagine that"

I grit my teeth, not bothering to answer him. My body feels frozen in place, my hands instinctively clutching Drepane's hilt tighter, preparing for whatever he's about to throw at me next.

But Drepane's voice cuts through the tension, louder and more commanding than I've ever heard it. "Enough!"

The force in his tone makes me flinch. This isn't the kind, patient Drepane I know. This is something darker, more powerful. More than I can comprehend.

"She is far more worthy than someone who cared only about power. I require your services *one last time*, Cronos."

There's a long pause, an almost uncomfortable silence hanging in the air as Cronos' eyes flicker between Drepane and me. He's visibly repulsed, his lips curling into a disgusted sneer.

"What do you want from me, Drepane?" Cronos asks, his voice dripping with venom and disdain, like he's being asked to do something beneath him.

Drepane's response is nothing short of a roar. "Replenish me, *you cow*!"

I wince at his words. I've never heard him like this—so cruel, so commanding. It's almost like he's taken on a different form, one that's barely recognizable. But I *know* it's him.

Cronos stares at Drepane for what feels like an eternity, his gaze flickering between Drepane and me. I can sense his reluctance, his distaste for whatever has brought him to this moment.

Finally, with an exaggerated sigh, Cronos closes his eyes, his expression still one of absolute distaste. A golden-red aura begins to pulse from him, floating toward Drepane with an ethereal glow. It swirls around Drepane like a twisting serpent, filling him with energy that he desperately needs.

I hold my breath, watching as the aura moves between them. The air feels heavy with power, with history, with grudges and regrets. But Drepane doesn't waver, and neither do I. We've made it this far, and now we just need to get through this last hurdle.

The air shifts the moment Azrael steps into the tunnel. His presence fills the space in a way that makes everything else feel insignificant, even Cronos. Flo follows close behind him, her huge frame a stark contrast to Azrael's towering, ethereal form. I can feel the electricity crackling in the air, the connection between us stronger than it's ever been. It's almost overwhelming, but I fight to keep myself grounded.

My heart skips a beat at the sight of him in his true form. The one I've longed to see for what feels like forever. I was just so fucking desperate to see him! But I remind myself—*not the place, not the time.* We've come so far. I can't let myself fall into the comfort of his presence just yet. I have to keep my focus on the task at hand.

Azrael's voice breaks through the tension. "I request something as well." His tone is commanding, not leaving room for argument.

Cronos turns around, his golden eyes narrowing. "What?" He asks, exasperation heavy in his voice.

Azrael doesn't falter. "We need more time."

"For what?" Cronos scoffs, already bored by the conversation.

"We only have limited time left before the fabric Quinn and Saygin opened for us closes—but we need to get to Persephone and have Memetim terminated before we can even think about going home." Azrael's stance is resolute, as though he's already thinking three steps ahead. "We need you to slow down time temporarily."

"What do you want with Persephone?" Cronos asks, his skepticism clear.

Azrael's eyes don't waver. "Memetim said something about using Layla to destroy the fabric between the Empty, the Underworld, and the Mortal Realms. As you know, we all are officers for the Underworld and we cannot allow this to happen." His words are final, leaving no room for negotiation.

Cronos chuckles, a dark and hollow sound that echoes through the tunnels. "Persephone would never allow that to happen."

Azrael's eyes narrow, his patience thinning. "What role does she play here?"

"She's the Queen of the Empty. She keeps us all here."

Azrael pauses, his mind working through the implications of that. The silence stretches for a moment before he turns toward Ashton. "Memetim locked Fate down here. How do we know Memetim isn't controlling her the same?"

Ashton's voice is calm, yet serious. *"We don't."*

The weight of that uncertainty hangs in the air, thick and heavy. But it doesn't deter Azrael. His jaw tightens as he faces Cronos again.

Cronos stares at Azrael for a long moment, before he scratches his head with a tired sigh. "You don't—but Persephone is not too fond of me—or any other male for that matter. She might listen to the offspring of Hades, but there's still no guarantee."

For the first time, he looks almost... human. It's a brief glimpse, but enough to show that even gods have their vulnerabilities.

Azrael doesn't hesitate. "We have to try." He turns to Cronos, his gaze unyielding. "Lead the way, Cronos."

Cronos lets out a grunt of annoyance but gives a reluctant nod. Without another word, he turns down a tunnel, and every single one of us falls in line behind him.

The journey through the winding labyrinth feels endless, but there's no time to waste. My mind races. I'm so close to finally being with Azrael, to ending this madness, to putting everything behind us. But in the back of my mind, there's still the gnawing uncertainty about Persephone, about Memetim, about the fate of all three realms hanging in the balance.

As we move deeper into the tunnels, I glance at Azrael. He doesn't look back at me, but I feel his presence like a steady flame beside me, guiding me through the darkness.

My fingers tremble as they reach for Azrael's robe. The fabric is cool beneath my touch. He turns to me, and I catch the warmth of his gaze, the embers in his eye sockets softening just for me. The tension in the air melts away with the simple motion.

"I want to kiss you so bad," he mumbles, his voice low, rough with emotion. His hand finds mine, wrapping around it with a tenderness that surprises me, considering the nature of the male he is. "I'm so thankful you're fucking safe."

His bones, cold like death itself, feel warm against my flesh, a stark reminder of the paradox of who he truly is. The pull between us, the weight of our bond, hums in the air.

I smile, letting the moment stretch between us, knowing that we've made it through hell together. The danger is far from over, but for now, I'm *alive*, I'm *whole*, and I'm standing with the one who holds the fate of the worlds in his hands.

"I own death," I say softly, more to myself than to him. The words are a claim, a declaration that no matter what happens next, I've *accepted* my fate.

Azrael's lips quirk, a brief flash of a smile crossing his face, though there's something darker behind his eyes. "You always have."

And for a moment, the world fades around us. The tunnel, the weight of the war, the chaos of the realms—it all fades away. In this space, it's just him and me, and I know, deep down, that we'll face whatever comes next together.

Layla

JOKES ON YOU - CHARLOTTE LAWRENCE

Cronos leads us out of the tunnels and into an open field bathed in the eerie glow of red stars twinkling in the distance. Their light barely pierces the thick, swirling mist clinging to the ground like a living thing.

"She's... unorthodox," Cronos warns, his gravelly voice cutting through the silence. "She has male slaves who are supposed to pleasure her endlessly. You never know what you'll walk into."

Luca blinks, his brow furrowing in confusion. "Pleasure her *endlessly*?" He pauses, then shakes his head. "What does that even mean?"

Cronos coughs, suddenly uncomfortable. "Just what I said. Unorthodox."

The strange pointy eared female traveling with us snorts. "My kind of woman."

I glance at Cronos, intrigued. "What do you *mean* 'endlessly pleasure'?"

Cronos mutters something unintelligible, his voice low. "She doesn't have a throne room," he deflects quickly.

Luca throws his hands up in frustration. "What does that mean?! I swear, you supernatural types just love being vague! It's like explaining things properly would physically *pain* you. Stop telling just the tip and give us fucking information!"

"I'll touch your tip," the female says smoothly, not missing a beat.

I burst out laughing. "Who the hell are you?" I wipe away a tear of amusement as she turns to face me.

Her white hair cascades down her back in perfect waves, her sharp features almost glowing in the misty light. A cat-like grin spreads across her lips, fangs peeking out, and her emerald eyes gleam with unspoken mischief. She extends a clawed hand—claws that could put Memetim's stilettos to shame.

"I'm Saygin," she says, her voice silky smooth but carrying an unmistakable edge of danger. "You're the mortal mutt we've been risking our lives to save?"

I take her hand, her grip firm, almost testing. "Pleasure to meet you," I reply, matching her grin.

Luca groans, rolling his eyes. "Is that even the correct term to use in a situation like this?"

I chuckle. "I missed you, Luca." I reach out, and he brushes his fingers against mine, his touch warm and reassuring.

Luca sighs dramatically. "Azrael was going to volunteer me to be sounded to save you."

I blink, confused. "What's sounding?"

Silence.

The males freeze as if I've just uttered the forbidden words of some ancient curse.

Vassago, ever the composed one, exhales heavily. "Let's not go there." He starts walking again, determined to ignore whatever nightmare has just been conjured in their minds.

Luca leans in, his voice dropping to a whisper. "It's when Saygin takes objects and—" he clears his throat—"shoves them down a man's pee-hole." His voice is barely audible as he shudders. "She's terrifying."

I process the information. My lips curl into a slow grin.

"That's... horrifying."

"Right?" Luca whispers, still visibly rattled. "I told you."

For a moment, I don't know what to say. I want to sympathize with them, really, I do. But then I remember that supernatural males literally wield magical weapons and seem perfectly fine using said weapons in ways that would make a romance novelist blush. These are the same males who enjoy dark romances full of dubious consent, kidnapping, and all kinds of power play.

But *this*? The mere *thought* of being objectified the way women are *daily* sends them spiraling?

I lose it.

I burst out laughing, doubling over. "You're all ridiculous," I manage between breaths. "If Azrael wasn't my mate—the only male I'd trust with my life and my *sexual innocence*—I'd choose Luca."

Luca straightens, placing a hand over his heart. "I am honored." He bows dramatically. "I humbly accept this responsibility."

Azrael groans, pinching the bridge of his nose. "You've been back for *five minutes*, and you're already stirring up unnecessary arguments."

I cross my arms, shooting him a playful look. "Azrael, you literally *fingered me against my will* before I even knew you existed. So, tell me, who's the real asshole here?"

The group comes to a *screeching* halt.

Vassago turns his full attention to Azrael, and if Azrael wasn't in his true form, I swear he'd be sweating bullets.

"*Azrael!*" Vassago barks, his voice laced with both concern and disbelief. "What the *fuck* is wrong with you?!"

Orcus, ever the instigator, chuckles from the back. "Predator and prey," he muses, his tone rich with amusement.

"Fuck off, Orcus," Azrael mutters, scowling at his scythe.

I watch the whole exchange with a satisfied smirk. This is *pure* entertainment. Supernatural drama is so absurdly over-the-top, it feels like an entirely different world.

And the best part?

I *love* that I'm part of it.

Vassago is still staring at Azrael like he just admitted to sacrificing kittens for fun. Azrael looks *thoroughly* unamused.

"You're going to tell me you never forced some kind of supernatural courtship ritual on anyone?" Azrael challenges, his tone dry.

Vassago lifts his hands. "I have *never* fingered someone *against* their will."

"That's your *defense*?" Saygin snickers, crossing her arms. "*That's* the hill you're dying on?"

Azrael glares at her. "Don't you have a village or someone to terrorize?"

She grins, flashing her fangs. "I'm currently terrorizing *you*, and I must say—" she flicks her claws, inspecting them as if bored, "—it's *delightful*."

Luca sighs dramatically, rubbing his temples. "If I had a dollar for every time we stopped mid-life-or-death during this mission to have an impromptu trauma-sharing session, I could afford to bribe my way *out* of this nightmare."

Orcus lets out a raspy chuckle. "You think there's enough money in the world for that?"

Cronos, who has *clearly* had enough, lets out a long-suffering sigh. "If you're all quite finished reliving your respective war crimes, we need to *move*."

"No, no, let's stay here a little longer," I say, waving a hand. "I want to hear Azrael's full *criminal record* while we're at it."

Azrael shoots me a look, his red embers glowing ominously. "You know, *technically*, you're still in danger. I don't *have* to rescue you."

"Uh-huh." I gesture to the field of swirling mist ahead of us. "Go ahead, leave me here. I'm sure I'll be fine wandering through the spooky death fog alone."

Saygin smirks. "I'd give her *maybe* six minutes before she gets devoured by some kind of soul-sucking nightmare creature."

"Six?" Luca scoffs. "You're being *optimistic*."

"Alright, *rude*—"

"There *are* soul-sucking nightmare creatures," Cronos interrupts, rubbing his temples. "So maybe let's all shut up and *walk* before something decides we're a buffet."

"Agreed," Vassago mutters. He gestures for us to keep moving.

But just as we start forward, Saygin leans in, her emerald eyes glinting with mischief. "So, Azrael, since you're already on trial for *questionable* moral choices, tell me—" she grins wide, "—is the finger thing a *habit*, or was Layla just *special*?"

Azrael groans.

Luca, without hesitation, claps him on the shoulder. "This is your life now."

"Kill me," Azrael mutters.

Orcus, ever helpful, chimes in, "Oh, we *could*! It'd be so easy."

"Do it," Azrael grits out. "Put me out of my misery."

"Sorry," I say, patting his arm. "I *need* you alive, or I'm stuck with these degenerates."

Luca gasps in mock offense. "Excuse me, I am *at worst* a morally flexible businessman."

"Right," I deadpan. "And Saygin's a *humanitarian*."

Saygin tilts her head. "I mean, technically, if you count '*eating* humans'—"

"Oh my *god*—" I manage to squeeze out.

"I *like* her," Orcus comments.

"Of course you do," Azrael grumbles.

Cronos, who by now looks two seconds from abandoning us all, mutters something about Fate punishing him.

But before we take another step, the mist ahead *shifts*.

A low, distorted growl rumbles through the air.

We freeze.

Luca sighs. "Oh, great. More things that want to kill us." He throws his arms up. "Because the *first* five death traps weren't enough!"

The growl grows louder, and glowing red eyes pierce through the fog.

I take a deep breath. "Alright. Who wants to die first?"

Saygin grins, cracking her knuckles. "Oh, *finally*. I was getting *bored*."

CHAPTER THIRTY-EIGHT

Layla

The growling starts as a low rumble, slithering through the mist like some horror movie revving up for its grand entrance. It vibrates through my bones, heavy and ominous, the kind of sound that makes you instinctively reconsider your life choices.

Luca lets out a long, exaggerated sigh, already exasperated. "Oh, *fantastic.* More cryptid bullshit." He throws up his hands, gesturing wildly at the void around us. "Honestly, why *wouldn't* there be some monstrous, nightmarish entity lurking in the fog? That's just *so* on-brand for this trip. Should we expect a ghost choir next? Maybe some *friendly* demonic possession?"

"Would you like some cheese with that *whine*?" Saygin asks, cracking her knuckles, her emerald eyes flashing with amusement, the male beside her laughs darkly. If she's Saygin, he must be Quinn

Before Luca can snap back with whatever scathing rebuttal is loading in his brain, the mist shifts violently, swirling like a storm caught in slow motion. Shadows stretch unnaturally, warping into shapes that make my stomach twist in ways it definitely shouldn't.

Then, *it* emerges.

The thing is about the size of a puppy. Its skin ripples, like something underneath is desperately trying to claw its way out. Too many eyes flicker in and out of existence, glowing like embers, sliding around its shifting face as if it hasn't quite decided where they belong. Its mouth—or *what should be* a mouth—is a gaping hole in the center of its torso, jagged, uneven teeth stretching impossibly wide.

Luca stares at it for exactly three seconds before announcing, "Nope."

He spins on his heel and starts walking the other way. "Absolutely not. I quit. Good luck with—whatever *that* is."

"Shut up, Luca," Azrael mutters, stepping forward like the brave little reaper he can be.

Luca whirls on him, expression incredulous. "Oh, I'm *sorry,* did you see the same hellspawn I just did? Because that—" he wildly gestures at the abomination—"isn't something you just handle like a minor inconvenience!"

Quinn, entirely unbothered, studies the creature with mild curiosity, like it's a mildly interesting zoo exhibit. "It's a Mawkin."

"Oh, *great,*" Saygin deadpans. "Because we just *loved* the last Mawkin we met."

Luca groans. "Wait—*another* Mawkin?"

The creature lets out an inhuman screech, the sound reverberating through my ribs like a gong of existential dread. Suddenly, the mist thickens, pressing in like a weighted blanket filled with nightmares. The ground shifts. The air warps. My stomach lurches as reality bends in a way it absolutely *should not.*

Azrael's jaw tightens. "It's trying to pull you guys into a fear loop again."

"Oh, *absolutely the fuck not,*" Luca snaps.

All I can think about is that moment of fear when Dash stabbed me, when I was laying there begging for the universe to send help. When I was gasping for air...

When I was bleeding out...

I do not think I mentally can relive that.

Luca immediately grips my arm like an overprotective chihuahua with separation anxiety. "You *better* not get lost in there, Layla. I *swear*—if we have to play *Find the Human* one more time, I *will* start charging for retrieval services."

Saygin claps her hands together like a kid about to open birthday presents. "I am going to *love* this part."

"Of course, you will," Vassago mutters.

The air warps again. The world tilts.

And then—

...Nothing.

Everything stills.

We're all standing exactly where we were. Completely unaffected.

The Mawkin stares at us. We stare at it.

A long beat of silence.

Then, the creature makes a confused, wet-sounding gurgle, its many eyes blinking in what I *swear* is uncertainty.

Luca blinks. "Did it... *did it just fail?*"

Azrael smirks, crossing his arms. "Seems so."

The Mawkin shifts uncomfortably, its grotesque form pulsing like it's trying to figure out what *went wrong*.

Saygin grins, stepping forward. "Ohhh, I *like* this. What's wrong, little guy? Are our psyches just too fucked up for you?"

I watch as the Mawkin seems to *hesitate*.

Vassago tilts his head, thoughtful. "Honestly, this makes sense. We've all been through so much trauma that there's probably nothing left to exploit."

"I mean, *I* have plenty of unresolved trauma," Luca says, raising a hand. "But I think at this point, it's just a *chronic condition*."

The Mawkin lets out another weird noise, this one almost... *frustrated*.

Orcus, of all beings, snickers. "This is embarrassing for you, buddy."

The Mawkin makes a horrifying, distorted choking sound.

Then it just... *turns around and leaves.*

We all watch in stunned silence as the *literal nightmare creature* shuffles back into the mist, looking like it deeply regrets every decision that led it to this moment.

I blink. "Wait. Did we just—?"

"Did that thing just *give up?*" Luca asks incredulously.

Saygin lets out an *unhinged* laugh. "Oh, that is *amazing.*"

Azrael exhales, shaking his head. "Honestly? I respect it. I too would not want to deal with this group."

Luca places a hand on his chest, shaking his head in mock devastation. "I just—I cannot believe we were too *mentally broken* for a goddamn *fear demon.*"

I shrug. "Silver lining: we saved ourselves some trouble."

Quinn mumbles. "That was just a baby."

Cronos rubs his temples, looking like he *deeply* regrets coming along. "Can we *please* keep moving before something worse decides to test our luck?"

"Worse than the living embodiment of psychological torment?" Luca asks. "What else could possibly—"

"*Don't,*" Vassago cuts in immediately. "Do not finish that sentence."

Luca shuts his mouth.

Saygin smirks. "Oh, come on. Don't you want to see what else the universe can throw at us?"

"No," Azrael and Vassago say in unison.

Saygin pouts but keeps walking.

And with that, we continue through the mist, knowing full well that something *even dumber* is probably waiting for us.

Quinn shakes his head, stuffing his hands in his pockets. "You know," he muses, "I've seen some weird shit in my time, but watching a Mawkin just *peace out?* That's new."

Ashton, who has been largely silent, finally lets out a slow, thoughtful hum. "Maybe it took one look at us and realized we're already beyond repair."

Luca groans, rubbing his temples. "I *knew* my therapy bill was going to be ungodly, but I didn't think it'd be *supernaturally validated.*"

Saygin slings an arm around him, grinning. "That just means you're *extra special* fucked up."

"Gee, thanks," Luca mutters, deadpanning.

Quinn side-eyes Ashton. "I assume you *could've* just put it to sleep instead of making us endure its existential crisis? That Mawkin was just a baby."

Ashton shrugs. "Didn't feel like it."

Luca throws up his hands. "Oh, *fantastic!* Sandman's *selective* about when to be useful!"

"See, here's the thing," Ashton says, completely unbothered. "If I solved all your problems, you'd never learn."

"Learn *what*?" Luca demands.

"That life is meant to be painful," Ashton replies serenely.

I clap a hand over my mouth to stifle a laugh.

Quinn just shakes his head. "You all need fucking help."

Ashton grins. "I *am* help."

Azrael rubs his face like he's seriously reconsidering *every* decision that brought him to this point. "I don't know what's worse—Saygin's obsession with violence or Ashton's absolute refusal to care."

Saygin flips her hair. "Oh, you *love* it."

"I barely *tolerate* it," Azrael corrects.

Cronos checks the horizon. "We're getting closer."

Saygin raises an eyebrow. "You're acting like we're walking into a brothel of nightmares."

Cronos gives him a flat look. "We *are*."

Silence.

Ashton whistles low. "This just got interesting."

Luca groans. "No, it didn't. This got *concerning.*"

I sigh. "Great. More trauma for the pile."

And with that, we keep moving—because, at this point, *what's the worst that could happen?*

CHAPTER THIRTY-NINE

Layla

SWEET DREAMS (ARE MADE OF THIS) - EURYTHMICS

We silently walk down the narrow path until it opens up, revealing brick stepping stones. The closer we get, the more the air feels heavy, as if something is just waiting to pounce again. The pathway narrows until we are forced to walk in a single-file line, and the atmosphere feels thick with expectation.

At the end of the path, a throne appears—high-backed, regal, and somehow wrong in this setting. A naked female lounges in it, her skin a rich, almost fiery red, her eyes glowing yellow like a warning sign. Horns curl from her forehead, and her posture, splayed across the throne, exudes power and entitlement. But what strikes me the most are the three males below her, positioned in a way that makes my stomach churn. Their heads bob up and down between her legs which are spread wide open, resting on her throne's armrests.

Her voice is a slow, almost lazy purr. "Suck it right there. Right there. *Fuck*, that feels so good." She leans back, letting out a deep moan, her pleasure spilling into the air like poison.

I glance at Azrael, expecting him to be unfazed, but there's a flicker of something in his hollow eyes—maybe surprise, maybe disgust, maybe even a little discomfort. It's hard to tell. His usual composed demeanor is cracked, and I can't help but feel a twisted satisfaction at the sight.

The woman notices us, her gaze cutting through the room like a blade. She doesn't move from her throne, her legs still spread wide and still resting on the armrests of the throne, her attention flickering lazily over us.

"Who are you?" Her voice is sharp, demanding, though laced with a sickening sweetness that only enhances the unsettling atmosphere.

Ashton shifts uncomfortably, repositioning his pants, and clearing his throat. "This is the weirdest fucking mission I've ever been on."

Luca, looking like he's trying to avoid eye contact with the chaotic scene, adds, "This one popped my mission virginity, and I'm not okay."

I bite my lip, trying to keep my face neutral, but I can't help the chuckle that escapes. "You might get used to it, eventually. I think"

Vassago and Quinn, beside him, remain unphased, like they've seen this all before. But Azrael—Azrael looks like someone just slapped him across the face. His usual confidence is cracked, like he's unsure of how to navigate the madness in front of him.

For a second, everything feels frozen, caught between the strange intensity of the female in front of us and the uncertainty of our mission. But I can't help the thought that crosses my mind: this is what we've been fighting for, and yet, it feels so *wrong*.

I push past the others, stepping forward with purpose. "I am Layla Simmons, mate of Azrael and the Queen of the Underworld."

The female bursts into laughter, a sound laced with mockery and disbelief. "Another female in power? One tied to the Hades bloodline? I bet he *hates* that."

She reaches down to one of the males between her legs, gripping his hair and yanking him away with a casual strength. "You're released. Go to your cell," she orders, and the male scurries off, looking relieved.

"I haven't had the pleasure—uh, I mean, time—to ask him," I quip, staring at her with a mixture of awe and a slight tinge of jealousy. She's everything I thought I'd never want to be—yet somehow, I want to *be her*. This power, this control, it's *intoxicating*.

She tilts her head and regards me with a dark smile. "How can I help you, Layla?" she purrs, her voice a deep, sensual drawl. Then, without missing a beat, she throws her head back in pleasure, another moan slipping from her lips.

I swallow hard, forcing my attention back to the task at hand. "Memetim," I begin, my voice low but steady.

Her head snaps forward, and the shift in her expression is immediate—cold, calculating. She pushes the males away from her with a single wave of her hand. "Leave. Now. Back to your cells," she commands, and they scurry away, leaving her alone with us.

She crosses her legs slowly, eyes locked on mine, her gaze challenging something deeper within me—my *sexuality*, my strength, my right to be here. "What about that *cunt*?" she asks, her voice dripping with disdain.

I take a deep breath, my heart racing as the weight of the situation settles over me. "She's trying to use me to tear the fabric of the Empty."

Persephone's eyes glisten with an unsettling gleam as she surveys Luca, a slow smirk stretching across her lips. "You're something I haven't seen in a while," she muses, her voice smooth as velvet.

Luca shifts uncomfortably, running a hand through his hair. "Why are all these supernatural women attracted to me?" he grumbles, casting an exasperated look at the group.

Persephone tilts her head, amused by his discomfort. "You're the last of your kind," she says, her voice almost a purr. "We thought your kind was extinct."

Luca, ever the realist, raises an eyebrow. "Werewolves are everywhere. Especially in Mississippi and Texas."

She chuckles darkly, stepping closer to him. The sway of her hips draws everyone's attention, and her breasts bounce slightly with each step. "Oh, sweetie," she croons, placing a hand on his chest. "You're no *werewolf*. You're *not* a mortal's nightmare. You're the *Underworld's nightmare*."

Luca, a bit taken aback, frowns. "What does that even mean?" he asks, clearly puzzled.

Persephone leans in, her breath warm against his ear. "You're a *Lycan*," she whispers. "Supernatural females are enamored by you because you mix Lycan blood with any other species... and you can single-handedly *destroy* the Underworld and Hierarchy."

The group falls silent, the gravity of her words sinking in. Luca's eyes widen, his mind racing as he processes the implications.

"They were banished by Hades eons ago," Persephone continues, a mischievous smile playing at the corners of her mouth. "Left to mix with mortals and wolves. Once the wolves learned about the Lycan lineage, they hunted and killed them all—mortals and immortals alike."

She presses a finger to his lips as if sensing his disbelief. "But you're *different*. You're the *last* of them, sweetheart. And now... now you can have *whoever* you want. *Whatever* you want."

Before Luca can respond, Persephone steps closer, her body a mere inch from his. She reaches down, guiding his hand toward her groin with a boldness that leaves the other males in stunned silence.

Luca, momentarily frozen, looks around at the group, his expression torn between shock and disgust. Then, without a word, he cups her intimately, slipping a finger inside her with practiced ease.

Persephone gasps, her back arching as she moans in pure pleasure. "Ahh! Yes... right there," she murmurs, her voice thick with desire. Her legs instinctively wrap around his waist, pulling him closer, deepening the connection.

The air crackles with tension as the rest of the group stands in stunned silence, their faces a mix of disbelief, discomfort, and curiosity.

She laughs softly, her fingers trailing down his chest. "Why bother with games when I can have what I *want, when* I want it?"

Is this really happening in front of us all? I glance around at the group, and the only one who seems unfazed is Saygin. But her gaze is sharpened with a mix of *jealousy* and *rage* as Luca steps closer to Persephone.

I never expected him to reveal such a powerful presence. He releases his cock from his pants and I am taken back from the view.

I would have never imagined someone like Luca, so soft spoken and shy, to be so... so fucking *huge*...

Persephone leans into him, her breath catching as she wraps both of her legs around his waist, and Luca forces his cock inside of her. The intensity of the moment is heightening the atmosphere. Luca's grip tightens on her hips, his energy pulsing with a force that matches his newfound strength. It's almost like he's a different being—his eyes glowing faintly as he moves with an intensity I haven't seen from him before. He is thrusting with such power; I am *afraid* he might break her! He is intently staring at her while fangs grow from inside his mouth.

He starts to thrust with more force until Persephone screams, and Luca releases a howl.

Persephone slowly places her feet on the ground, her legs trembling slightly. "By gods, I haven't been *fucked* like that in ages," she says, her voice teasing, but there's a sharpness in her smile. "Wolf boy, would you perhaps stay and become my pet?"

Luca snaps out of his daze, quickly grabbing his pants and pulling them up, flustered. "Uh... oh... um... sorry, I... I can't."

I look at Azrael, and we exchange a brief, bewildered glance.

What just happened?

Persephone lets out a low laugh and waves a hand dismissively. "I'll help your little crew take care of Memetim. But after that, you'd best be on your way to the Underworld before I change my mind about keeping the wolf."

"How do we lure Memetim, is the question," Azrael says, clearly trying to refocus.

"Lure?" Persephone smirks, looking at us like we're all amateurs. "Sweetie, this is *my* realm. All I have to do is snap my fingers, and she'll be here."

We exchange looks, unsure of what to make of this. "It's that easy?" Ashton asks, raising an eyebrow.

"It's. That. *Easy*," she giggles, clearly enjoying the reaction she's getting. "The quickest death anyone could ever ask for."

"I was hoping for something more... drawn out," Orcus hums, clearly not satisfied with the simplicity of it all.

"I've got better things to do. The quicker, the better," she replies, leaning back on her throne. "I have a life of my own. Your drama doesn't bother me, but I will protect the *balance* of my realm."

"Then do it!" Vassago commands, his patience wearing thin.

"When?" Persephone teases, not in a hurry.

"Right *now*!" he barks.

"Ugh," she groans, rolling her eyes. "*Fine.*"

Chapter Forty

Layla

Glory and Gore - Lorde

Persephone snaps her fingers with an air of indifference, then blows on her nails as though she's just finished a manicure. The world shifts around us in an instant, and Memetim appears between our group and Persephone. She stands there, looking bewildered, like a cat suddenly dropped into a room full of dogs.

"Well, well, well," Persephone muses, smirking as she leans back. "Must be an experience to realize you're nothing more than a *pest* in my realm. I could squash you like a bug whenever I please, you know."

Memetim hisses in response, unfazed. "Ah, your majesty," she sneers. "How can I assist you?"

Persephone arches an eyebrow. "Cut the small talk, darling. What's your reason for being here in my realm?"

Memetim stands tall, her eyes glinting with cold purpose as she glances around but never fully acknowledges the rest of us. "I want to destroy the Underworld and the mortal realm. I intend to expand the Empty, bringing the

313

dead back to feast on those living," she states as though she's discussing the weather. Nonchalant. Detached.

I almost gag at how casually she speaks of such destruction.

Orcus lets out a low whistle. "Bold move. Also incredibly dumb."

"Agreed," Saygin adds, cracking her knuckles. "But please, do go on. I love hearing delusional villain speeches."

Memetim ignores them.

Persephone's sharp laugh echoes, cutting through the air. "And what do you plan to do with *her*?" She flicks a finger in my direction, a smile creeping across her face.

Memetim doesn't even flinch at the gesture. "She's the key to the three realms."

Persephone's expression turns interested. "How so?" Her voice is like silk—smooth, enticing, and dangerous.

Memetim stands silent, her lips sealed tight. It's as if she's considering whether she should give us the answer at all.

Persephone sighs dramatically, her eyes narrowing. "Aht, Aht," she warns, wagging a finger in the air. "You will speak, and you will speak *now*."

Memetim glares at her, but her defiance crumbles. With a sharp inhale, she gives in. "She's an *Ecliptian*."

"A what?" Persephone laughs, clearly intrigued but still not fully understanding the gravity of what that means.

"*An Ecliptian*," Memetim repeats, her voice colder than before.

Luca raises a hand like a student in a classroom. "Yeah, I second that question. The hell's an Ecliptian?"

Memetim turns her head slowly, her cold eyes locking onto mine. The weight of her gaze sends an involuntary shiver down my spine. I try to hold my ground, but there's something about her presence that makes my heart race in a way I can't explain.

She tilts her head, as though considering me more closely now, before answering. "An Ecliptian is a being who exists between the living and the dead. Someone who has the power to cross between the realms, to merge them and twist them to their will."

A sickening thought hits me like a freight train. "You mean... I'm the one who could tear everything apart?" My voice shakes, but I force myself to stay calm, to stand tall.

Vassago lets out a low breath. "That sounds... horrifyingly dangerous."

Persephone's eyes glitter with dark amusement. "Oh, honey, you're not just the key. You're the fuse. And I'm guessing you have no idea how big the explosion will be when it goes off."

I swallow hard. "So, if I'm the fuse... how do we stop it?"

"Simple," Persephone says with a grin that could cut glass. "*You don't.*"

Azrael crosses his arms, his expression unreadable. "You're enjoying this far too much."

"Of course I am," Persephone replies, feigning innocence. "It's *entertaining*."

Memetim glares at her. "You think this is a joke?"

"No," Persephone says, her voice suddenly laced with steel. "I think you're an insect. And I don't tolerate insects in my home." She giggles.

I glance at Azrael, who looks like he's chewing on something sharp and unpleasant, his expression unreadable. He's been quiet for too long, and I can't tell if he's processing what's happening or if he's just waiting for someone else to act.

Luca shifts uncomfortably, his eyes darting between the three of us. "So, what? We're just supposed to sit back and let her take control?" he asks, his voice laced with disbelief.

"Why fight it?" Persephone shrugs, eyes flashing with a predatory glint. "Maybe you'll learn to enjoy the ride." She winks at him, but it's clear she's enjoying the chaos she's stirring.

"Not the point," Vassago mutters, shaking his head. "We need to know how to stop her."

"So why destroy the balance?" Persephone asks, her voice dripping with curiosity, though there's an underlying amusement in it.

Memetim's eyes flare with cold fury. "She took what was mine, and I want them to suffer."

Persephone chuckles, shaking her head in disbelief. "A scorned female," she muses. "You do realize you're trying to wipe my son from existence, right?"

Everyone looks to Azrael. His presence suddenly feels heavier, darker, the atmosphere shifting around him. She's talking about him, right? —or Vassago. I look towards him, but he's staring at Azrael.

"My mother is Charon," Azrael says, his voice low, the weight of his words settling over the group like a dark cloud.

Persephone lets out a loud laugh. "Sweetheart, Charon is incapable of bearing a *Reaper*. Her grandfather," she gestures toward me with a wicked grin, "had me murdered. He tried to prevent *your* birth. With my last breath, I cursed his bloodline to be tied to mine." She cackles, the sound shrill and sharp. "Charon was my lifelong friend. She *raised* you for me."

The room falls into an eerie silence, everyone stunned into disbelief.

My mind spins with the implications of what she just said.

"So... you're saying Charon was not my—" Azrael begins, but the words die in his throat.

Persephone's eyes snap to Memetim, her smile twisting into something far darker. "Yes, darling, that's exactly what I'm saying. Isn't it delicious?"

Orcus' voice echoes through the bond. *Dude, you were just eye fucking your mom.* He bursts into raucous laughter, shaking the very air around us with his amusement.

Azrael's embers flicker dangerously, his anger radiating off of him in waves. The air around him grows hot and oppressive. I glance at him, my heart pounding, wondering how much longer he'll hold it together before he explodes.

My eyes flick to Memetim, and for the first time, I see her truly stunned. Her mouth opens, but no words come out.

Persephone leans back in her throne, tapping her fingers on the armrest, clearly enjoying the chaos she's caused. "Don't you just hate Fate? How they can be bullied into giving you answers, but always leave out the most *trivial* details."

She sighs dramatically, shaking her head. "Memetim, I've had enough of this nonsense."

Memetim lunges toward her, a last-ditch effort fueled by rage and desperation. But Persephone barely blinks. She lifts a hand, snaps her fingers, and the air around Memetim distorts. Her body locks up, her limbs spasming violently as she begins to convulse. A sickening crunch echoes through the atmosphere as her bones snap out of place, one by one.

The scent of burning flesh fills the air. Her skin bubbles, boils, then splits open as an unseen force peels it away in strips. She tries to scream, but her throat collapses inward, choking the sound before it can escape.

Luca turns away, gagging. Quinn swears under his breath.

Memetim's body crumbles, piece by piece, like an overripe fruit being torn apart by unseen hands. Her ribs burst outward with a wet pop, her insides spilling onto the floor in a grotesque display. A puddle of viscera pools beneath her twitching remains, steam rising from the carnage.

Persephone yawns. "*Boring.*"

I stare at what's left of Memetim, bile rising in my throat. It's over. Just like that.

"Well," Persephone says, stretching languidly, "now that that's handled, what's next?"

Lucas claps his hands together. "I vote we never talk about what just happened."

Vassago shudders. "Agreed."

"Well," Persephone says casually, as if she just flicked a fly off her shoulder, "I prefer females supporting each other. I can't stand catfights."

Her gaze sweeps over us, amused as always.

I'm still trying to process what just happened. I nearly *died* fighting for this—fighting for an answer—and Persephone just *snapped her fingers*, taking care of everything. It's almost too surreal.

Azrael stands still, his expression a perfect mask of fury, but there's a cold calculation in his eyes. I can feel the heat of his anger radiating from him, but he doesn't speak.

He doesn't need to.

I glance at Luca, and even he looks shaken by the sudden violence. But it's clear: this is Persephone's world, and we're all just living in it.

"*Well then*," Persephone continues, standing from her throne, her laughter ringing through the air, "what's next, darling? It's all so *boring* now."

The tension in the room hasn't disappeared, not by a long shot. If anything, it's grown, like a storm ready to burst. But Persephone doesn't seem to care. She's already moved on to the next game, the next challenge.

And all I can think is: *what the hell are we supposed to do now?*

"Okay... so, we're done here?" Saygin asked, her voice still laced with disbelief as she glanced around, trying to make sense of the chaos.

Persephone nods, her fingers snapping again in a fluid motion. "Azrael?" she adds with a playful wink.

Azrael, still simmering with the fury of the moment, turns toward her. "Yeah?" he responds, his voice low but sharp.

"Bring your father to me, won't ya?" she teases, leaning back in her throne, looking almost too pleased with herself.

Azrael smirks, his ember-like eyes flickering with a dangerous promise. "Sooner than you realize."

He turns to leave, his steps deliberate, but before anyone can follow, Saygin's voice rings out as she begins chanting under her breath. The air around us shifts, and a door opens before us—black, swirling with ethereal light.

"*Wait!*" I yell, my voice cutting through the moment, and everyone halts in place, eyes turning toward me.

I swallow hard, the weight of what I'm about to ask sitting heavy on my chest. "Persephone. I need a favor."

She arches an eyebrow, amused but not unkind. "Sure. What is it that I can do for ya?" Her tone is casual, but I know better than to mistake it for indifference.

"My best friend's Guardian Angel," I start, my throat tightening. "Song! She was killed by Memetim. I want her back."

Persephone's gaze sharpens. She studies me for a long moment, and I can feel the weight of her scrutiny. Every inch of my spine feels like it's being pressed under a thousand-pound weight, but I hold my ground, trying to meet her gaze.

She says nothing at first, and I'm not sure if she'll grant my request or turn me away. It feels like an eternity.

Finally, she smiles, a predatory grin stretching across her face. "Done." She snaps her fingers once, and before I can even react, Song materializes before us.

Her silver hair cascades over her shoulders, glistening like strands of moonlight. She's small—delicate, even—but there's an undeniable strength in the way she carries herself. Her wings fold neatly behind her, feathers soft but powerful.

She looks first at Persephone, then at me, but her gaze soon finds Vassago. Without hesitation, she runs to him, her tiny frame colliding into his arms, as if she's been dying to be held again.

I can't help the surge of emotion that fills me—relief, gratitude, but most of all, a deep, unspoken thank you. I nod toward her, a silent acknowledgment of the gift Persephone has given us. It's *everything*.

Vassago tightens his hold on her, whispering something I can't catch, his eyes filled with something rare—softness, something that hasn't been there in a long time.

"Thank you," I whisper under my breath, hoping the words reach Persephone, even if she doesn't need to hear them.

She doesn't look at me, but the wicked smile on her face tells me that she's enjoying the moment just as much as I am.

"Well," she says, clapping her hands together with fake enthusiasm, "now that we're all feeling warm and fuzzy, what's next?" She laughs.

I breathe in deeply, my body still humming with tension, but for the first time today, I feel like there might be hope.

CHAPTER FORTY-ONE

Ashton

THE ONE - THE CHAINSMOKERS

The familiar weight of exhaustion pressed into my bones as I stepped inside my house. The Empty had drained all of us, and now, my home felt like a sanctuary more than ever. Layla was curled up in one of the chairs, her eyes half-lidded with weariness. Vassago was talking in low tones with Azrael near the fireplace. Saygin paced, restless as always, and Luca sat stiffly at the table, like he wasn't sure how to relax. Quinn is passed out on the couch, like he isn't even phased by what we just went through.

But my mind wasn't on any of them. It was on Sadie.

She should be back soon. I hadn't heard from her since she left with Exu to pick up her father, and I needed to know she was safe. I hadn't reached out to her through the bond since... since the incident with the Mawkin. I don't know if it was shame or embarrassment that she saw what I went through and what I did for Isolde. Probably both. That wasn't the kind of thing you just put on display for someone, even your mate. And yet, she had seen it—felt it.

And she hadn't run.

That scared me more than anything.

You alive? I finally worked up the courage to reach out, caressing her life thread. It was like exhaling a breath I hadn't realized I'd been holding. Just that small connection, that brief touch, eased something tight in my chest. I had reached my limit of not seeing my mate. I needed her now.

Her response came almost instantly. *Unfortunately.*

I huffed a quiet laugh, shaking my head. Unfortunately, my ass. If she wasn't enjoying herself, she'd be raising hell about it.

When are you getting back?

There was a pause. Then she flicked my thread. *That depends. You miss me that much?*

Yes. I didn't say it, though. That was the problem. There were so many things I wanted to say to her, but getting them out felt like trying to squeeze blood from a stone. Instead, I leaned against the counter, tapping my fingers on the surface before responding.

Maybe I just want to make sure you didn't get sold back to the black market.

Please. They couldn't afford me. She responded.

That made me smile. A genuine, deep-in-my-chest kind of smile. I could hear it in her voice, the way she says it with that exaggerated confidence, like she was daring the world to test her.

So? ETA? I asked.

Soon. Just gotta make sure Exu doesn't traumatize some poor mortal on the way.

That wasn't reassuring. *How bad?*

Let's just say I've had to talk him out of five different crimes, and I think he might have stolen a cat.

I pinched the bridge of my nose, exhaling slowly. *Do I even want to know?*

Probably not. Just be happy if I make it back without a felony charge in the Underworld. If those even exist here.

I chuckled under my breath, but the lightness in my chest faded almost as quickly as it had come. I missed her. The house didn't feel right without her voice filling the space, without her chaotic energy keeping me on my toes.

I missed the way she would touch my chest like she had every right to.

How she would eye-fuck me and tease me in the middle of our fucked-up little family, knowing damn well I couldn't do anything about it until later.

How she could strip me down to nothing with just a look—and somehow, I didn't mind.

I rubbed the back of my neck, debating my next words. So many things I could say. So many things I *wanted* to say.

Be safe.

There was a longer pause this time. Then she responded. ...*You too.*

Something in my chest unclenched. I stared at the wall for a moment before turning around to everyone else in my house. Time to acknowledge that we survived one of the most fucked-up missions we could have ever gone on.

Sadie would be home soon. I just had to be patient.

Easier said than done.

The house fell into a quiet rhythm, the crackling of the fireplace and the soft murmurs of Vassago and Azrael blending together into background noise. Layla shifted in her chair, her tired eyes meeting mine for a brief moment, but I didn't have the energy to offer more than a small nod.

Saygin, ever the restless spirit, continued pacing, her boots tapping against the floor. I envied her. The way she moved with purpose, like she always knew what to do, always had somewhere to be, even if it was just circling the room in frustration. I didn't know what that felt like anymore. My purpose had always been wrapped up in keeping things from falling apart, but with the Mawkin behind us, I felt... adrift. Like I was waiting for something, but I didn't know what.

Luca sat at the table, his shoulders tense as if he were still bracing for some invisible threat. I could almost hear the gears turning in his head, his mind undoubtedly racing through scenarios and strategies even now, trying to find a way to regain control of whatever had slipped from his grasp.

It was hard to focus on anyone else, though. My thoughts kept drifting back to Sadie. To the space she had occupied in my life—one I hadn't realized how desperately I needed until she was gone. Her presence had always been a chaotic kind of grounding, something I never wanted to lose.

I stared down at my hands, the scarred palms still a reminder of the past, and sighed heavily. I wasn't sure if I was ready to face whatever was brewing between us, but I didn't have much of a choice. The longer I stayed quiet, the harder it would become to tell her what I needed to say.

I couldn't wait forever.

The door creaked open just then, cutting through my thoughts, and I whipped my head toward it, every muscle in my body tensing. For a split second, my heart stopped in my chest.

But it wasn't Sadie. It was Exu.

The caramel-complexioned male stepped inside with an almost imperceptible nod, his locs falling in controlled waves around his face. His expression was neutral, as always, and in his arms... he cradled a small, fluffy cat—its fur a vibrant contrast against his skin.

"I brought her back," Exu said in his usual low tone, his face unreadable as he handed the cat off like it was no big deal.

I raised an eyebrow. "You... actually stole a cat?"

Exu didn't respond, not with words anyway. Just a shrug.

Sadie's voice rang out from the hallway. "Exu, if you don't bring that fucking cat back—"

And then there she was, stepping through the door with that familiar swagger, her wild, black curls bouncing with every step.

My heart skipped a beat, and the tension in my chest loosened a little.

"Didn't steal it," Exu muttered, completely unfazed. He shot me a glance, and without another word, he turned to leave.

Sadie's eyes met mine instantly, and in that moment, everything fell away. All the silence, all the fear, it didn't matter anymore.

She was here. She was safe.

"Good to see you too," I said softly, my voice almost hesitant, as if I didn't know how to say what I was thinking.

Sadie raised an eyebrow, a smirk tugging at the corner of her lips. "What, no 'I missed you' or 'I was worried sick'?"

I could feel the weight of my silence between us. The words were there, but they never came out, and I hated that.

"I was worried sick," I said finally, though it wasn't nearly enough.

Her gaze softened, the playful edge fading just a little as she stepped closer. "You don't have to say it, Ashton. I can fucking *feel* it. You've always been able to keep me at arm's length, but I know."

My chest tightened, my hands instinctively reaching for her. "I'm scared, Sadie."

She didn't need to ask why. She already knew.

"You don't have to be," she said, her voice soft, understanding. "I'm not going anywhere."

But I wasn't sure if that was a promise she could keep, and that scared me more than anything. The thought of losing her, of something happening to her the way it happened to Isolde... It was a burden I wasn't sure I could bear. No matter how many times I keep telling myself that Sadie is safe and that she will be okay, it is in the back of my mind that I have enemies that wouldn't think twice about taking her from me.

Killing her.

I pulled her into me then, my hands on her back, holding her like if I let go, she might slip away. "I don't know what I'd do if I lost you."

Sadie didn't pull away. She didn't even flinch. She just rested her head on my chest, letting the moment stretch between us. And for the first time in what felt like forever, I allowed myself to believe her when she said she wasn't going anywhere.

"I'm here," she whispered. "And I'm not going anywhere. I don't like this pathetic, sad version of you. I need my sand boy back." She shoots me a half smile. "Now where the *fuck* is my best friend?"

CHAPTER FORTY-TWO

Layla

BAD ROMANCE - LADY GAGA

"I so can't wait to tell Exu how you were googly-eyed over your own mother fucking the wolf," Orcus laughs. "Can we revisit the 'team werewolf' shirts? You know, just to commemorate the event?"

Luca scratches the back of his head, looking genuinely embarrassed. "I'm sorry about that, guys. I don't know what came over me. It's like... I wasn't even myself."

"Came over you? You came *all* over Azrael's mother!" Orcus bursts into laughter, practically shaking the room with his amusement.

Luca's face turns an even deeper shade of red, and he raises his hands in surrender. "Okay, okay, I get it! Please stop!"

"Enough. Enough," Azrael mutters, his voice dripping with annoyance. He's already had enough of this, but Orcus isn't letting it go. I couldn't help but notice how calm he has been since returning "home".

"Imagine it. Just imagine... someone so shy and soft-spoken becoming your step-daddy. If only I had hands to give Luca a high five. You're not so bad after all, wolf," Orcus says, and I can hear the teasing in his tone.

I burst out laughing, unable to hold it back any longer. It's too good, too ridiculous. I crawl into Azrael's lap now that his anger isn't a hindrance to his mortal form. His cheeks are flushed from embarrassment, and I can feel his discomfort radiating off of him.

I lean in close to his ear and whisper, my voice low and teasing, "You can call me mommy anytime you want if you're into that kind of thing."

Azrael's eyes widen, and he immediately pushes me away, a look of pure disgust on his face. "Don't make me puke."

I laugh even harder, leaning back into his lap, completely enjoying the show. "You're no fun," I tease.

"I swear, I'll *throw* you off my lap," he grumbles, trying to keep his cool. But his hand instinctively goes to the back of my head, like he's both annoyed and reluctant to push me away. It's endearing, really.

"Let's be real here," Orcus adds, clearly loving every moment of Azrael's discomfort. "Luca might be shy and soft-spoken, but in bed... I think the wolf's got some *bite*."

Luca groans, burying his face in his hands. "I swear, I'm never going to live this down."

"I mean, can you blame him?" Orcus continues, ignoring Luca's mortified expression. "Azrael's mom's got that... *allure*, you know? And the wolf? Looks like he got caught up in the moment."

Azrael shoots him a death glare. "One more word, Orcus," he warns, his voice dark with the promise of violence.

I lean back against Azrael's chest and grin, whispering to him, "You know, if you ever get tired of being the terrifying Grim Reaper, I can always introduce you to the world of humiliating public ridicule. It's *very* effective for keeping your enemies on edge."

"Stop," Azrael mutters again, but there's a hint of amusement behind his irritation.

"Can we *please* get back to something important?" Luca interrupts, desperately trying to change the subject. "Like, I don't know, maybe saving the realms or something? Can we focus on that, perhaps?"

Orcus snickers. "Right, right, 'saving the realms.' But first, Luca has to deal with his new identity as 'step-daddy.' Maybe we should start a support group."

"Alright, *enough*," Azrael says again, his voice no longer annoyed but... resigned. "Layla, no more embarrassing comments about my mother. And Orcus, *stop* making this worse."

I chuckle, rolling off Azrael's lap and sitting up, giving him a wink. "You really are too easy, Azrael. You know that?"

Azrael sighs heavily. "I should have known I'd regret letting you sit on my lap."

"Too late now," I reply with a grin, as Orcus' laughter rings through the room again.

"They call those milfs." Vassago adds, darkly chuckling. "Honestly though, I am sorry you were glamoured into fucking Persephone, Luca," he continues, trying—and failing—to hold back laughter.

"That's like... rape, right?" Luca looks around, genuinely uncomfortable, his face scrunched up in confusion and discomfort.

"Don't know, you seemed to enjoy it." Orcus hums nonchalantly, clearly amused by the situation.

Drepane, however, is having none of it. His presence slicing the tension like a hot knife through butter. "Double standard thinking males cannot be raped. Luca was not able to give consent. You were so willing to defend Layla against Azrael but want to make jokes about what happened to Luca. You are *insufferable.*"

"So I've been told." Orcus chimes in, unfazed, clearly enjoying every second of this.

The room falls silent for a moment, and then Azrael mumbles under his breath, "Why is no one apologizing to me? That was fucking traumatic."

Drepane doesn't miss a beat. "No amount of apologizing can erase the dumbassery you cause yourself," he hums. "Grow up. *All of you.*"

I burst out laughing, stroking Drepane's handle. "Lighten up some! We all nearly died in the Empty. Some cope with dark humor. Nothing wrong with that."Drepane growls in response, clearly not impressed, but I'm enjoying the banter too much to even care.

"Can we *never* talk about this again?" Luca asks, looking like he's about to combust from the awkwardness. "Please?"

Just then, Vassago walks closer to Luca with an all-knowing smile on his face. "Until we hear that Azrael has a little brother," he adds, clearly enjoying the chaos.

Luca groans, and at the exact same moment, Azrael yells, "Not funny!"

Vassago chuckles as he flops down on the couch, staring at us all like we're some kind of comedy show.

"Any dark and gloomy news to bring in?" Ashton asks while walking into the room, clearly expecting the usual Vassago response.

"No." Vassago fucking smiles, his teeth flashing like a shark.

"How's Song?" I ask, genuinely curious, remembering how drained she looked when we walked through the portal door.

"Well, considering she was dead and one of the few in the Empty who gets everlasting sleep, then all of a sudden gets woken up and brought back to life? She's great, ya know given the circumstances," Vassago says, his tone a bit softer now.

I raise an eyebrow. "Are you two, like, a *thing*?" I can't help myself; they've got that "*will-they-won't-they*" vibe.

Vassago's features flush, and he stammers a bit, clearly caught off guard. "No? I don't think so. I am just her *mentor.*"

"That's a romance novel trope, Vassago," I laugh, enjoying his discomfort far more than I should.

Vassago glares at me, but there's a small smile tugging at the corner of his lips. "You read too much."

"Not possible," I say, grinning ear to ear. "Now, about that little brother of Azrael's..."

Azrael groans, burying his face in his hands, probably trying to pretend we're not all discussing his non-existent younger sibling.

"Just... stop." He mutters.

I grin, loving every moment of his discomfort, but I know I can't keep this up forever. It's too fun watching him squirm, but I can't let him drown in it alone. After all, the room's energy is so heavy with teasing that it would be a crime to not add to the chaos.

I glance over at Luca, still visibly mortified, and give him a wink. "Don't worry, Luca," I say, making sure my voice is light. "This too shall pass. But remember: next time, work on your self-control some, will ya?"

Luca looks at me, half in gratitude, half in disbelief. "Yeah, sure," he mumbles, clearly still a little shaken by everything that happened.

I lean back, stretching out on the couch, my eyes scanning the room. Orcus and Vassago are still clearly in their element, both enjoying the tension they've created. Azrael's irritation is palpable, but I can tell it's more about the discomfort than the actual embarrassment at this point. He's just tired of us poking fun at his personal life.

The group falls into a somewhat awkward silence after Drepane's blunt reminder of what's not funny, and I take the opportunity to break the stillness with a little more lightheartedness.

"Okay, okay. Maybe we've hit the limit on '*Azrael's Family Drama*,'" I say, holding my hands up in mock surrender. "But, uh, Luca? If you ever need someone to make sure you're not slipping into another glamour trance... just give me a shout. We can get you a support group for '*Formerly Glamoured Wolves Anonymous.*'"

Luca actually manages a nervous laugh, which, considering how much he's been squirming all night, is progress. It's enough to ease the tension, at least for now. "I think I'm good," Luca says, giving me a wry smile. "But thanks. I'll pass on the support group for now."

I nod, content with that for now. But then my gaze shifts to Vassago, who's still lounging on the couch, a glint of mischief in his eyes. "So, Vassago," I start, turning the attention back to him. "You and Song, huh? You're not fooling anyone. Come on, spill. What's going on there?"

Vassago's flushed expression is the only answer I need. I'm honestly enjoying this far more than I should, and I can tell Azrael feels the same way, even if he's trying his hardest to pretend like he doesn't.

"I'm serious," I press, my grin widening. "She's clearly got you wrapped around her finger, and you're not fooling anyone."

Vassago rolls his eyes but doesn't deny it. "It's not like that," he mutters again, though his tone lacks the conviction it had before.

"Uh-huh, sure," I tease, my voice dripping with mock innocence. "You keep saying that. But I think you might want to start writing your love letters now, 'cause I see the way you two look at each other."

Azrael groans, finally lifting his head from his hands to shoot me a tired, exasperated look. "Can we focus on something other than my family's drama?" he pleads, but even he knows it's a lost cause.

"Yeah, yeah, Az," I say, still grinning. "We'll get back to the 'saving the realms' thing. But first, we need to confirm whether or not Vassago and Song are the next big power couple of the Underworld."

The room bursts into laughter again, and this time, even Azrael cracks a smile despite himself. He leans back into his seat, resigning himself to the inevitable chaos that seems to follow us everywhere.

And honestly? I wouldn't have it any other way.

Chapter Forty-Three

Layla

Just a Girl - No Doubt

I hear the door creak open, and just like that, the room shifts—turning from chaotic laughter to something... softer, more grounded. I know that sound. Sadie's back.

She steps in first, a little out of breath but smiling, her curly hair bouncing with every movement. Ashton stands up from the couch, his usual calm presence a stark contrast to her infectious energy. Exu follows behind Sadie, looking as unbothered as ever, his dark eyes scanning the room briefly before settling back on Sadie. But it's the last figure that catches my attention, the one I wasn't expecting: Sadie's father.

My eyebrows shoot up, and I exchange a quick glance with Azrael, whose face hardens just slightly. Ashton didn't mention her father had made the trip back from the Underworld's black market—let alone that he was part of this strange deal Sadie had made.

Sadie's father... well, that's a whole different story.

"Layla, you won't believe what I had to go through to get him here." Sadie's voice is light, almost teasing, but I can hear the edge of something darker beneath it. I'm sure her father is a complicated subject, and it's clear she's been navigating some deep waters to pull him out of whatever life he's been living on the other side of the Underworld.

"I can only imagine," I reply, standing up from the couch. I walk toward them, my gaze flicking over Sadie's father, trying to place him. His eyes are tired, older than I remember, but his posture tells me he's never truly lost that sense of authority, even in a place like this.

"Yea, don't mind me..." Sadie waves a hand dramatically, her face the perfect picture of indifference. "Just purchasing my own father off the Underworld black market as a house slave. You know, just the norm for me now, I guess."

I blink, trying to process her words. "Wait, *what*?"

She grins widely, her eyes sparkling with mischief. "Oh yeah. I placed a bid for his ass at the Underworld auction. It was either him or a pack of hellhounds, and frankly, I figured I could use a little more sass in my life."

Her father just chuckles softly, clearly used to Sadie's wild ways. "She's kidding," he says with an exaggerated sigh. "Mostly."

Ashton snorts. "Mostly? That's the understatement of the century."

Sadie flips him off, completely unbothered. "Whatever, sand boy. Don't pretend like you wouldn't auction yourself off if the price was right. I've seen the way you look at those 'mortal treasures' in the marketplace."

"So, this is... your father?" I ask carefully, not quite sure how to word it. It's been a long time since I've seen him, and he's never been a regular part of Sadie's life because he died. The fact that she bought him back from the black market is both shocking and somehow fitting for the way Sadie handles the chaotic world she's in.

Sadie gives me a grin, but there's a flicker of something complicated in her expression. "Yeah. The one and only. Meet the man who's apparently worth more alive than dead." She laughs lightly, but it's a little too forced.

Her father doesn't speak right away, just eyes the room with a careful wariness. He's tall, with a strong jawline that carries the marks of years of hard living. There's a certain hardness to him, but also something fragile beneath it—a weariness that feels like he's been running from something for far too long.

"Well," he says, his voice rough, "it's good to be here, I guess."

I can't help the laugh that escapes me at the awkwardness of it all. "Welcome to the madness, then," I say with a wink. "You've just walked into the most dysfunctional family reunion in the Underworld."

Exu makes a noise that sounds like an attempt at suppressing a chuckle, though it doesn't quite work.

Ashton steps forward, a little more tactful, his cool demeanor a contrast to the rest of the room. "It's good to have you here," he says simply, nodding to Sadie's father. His tone is neutral but warm, just enough to smooth over the awkwardness.

Sadie glances at me, her lips curling into a playful smile. "Yeah, well, I hope you all can handle one more unpredictable character in the mix. I certainly didn't bring him here for a family photo."

The room pauses for a moment, the atmosphere thickening, as we all take in Sadie's unexpected—and somewhat unsettling—move. But despite the weight of the situation, I can't help but admire her confidence, the way she stands there, unflinching and unbothered by the chaos she's brought into the room.

"Let's just say I've got a few more cards to play," she adds with a wink, her usual sassy edge cutting through the tension.

I smile at her, the only thing grounding me right now in this bizarre moment. "As always, Sadie. As always."

Sadie's voice rings out, sharp and full of disbelief as she rushes toward me.

"I didn't think these idiots would pull it off! You're really home and safe!" she screeches, her arms immediately pulling me into a tight hug before I can even respond.

I let out a surprised laugh, a mix of relief and exhaustion flooding my chest. She's always been so strong, so sure of herself, but this... this moment cracks her tough exterior wide open, and I can feel the weight of her relief in her embrace. I return the hug, holding her tightly, my face buried in her wild curls for a moment.

"I'm fine, Sadie," I say, pulling back slightly to look at her. "A little worse for wear, but I'm fine."

Her gaze softens, but only for a second. Then she's back to her usual self, grinning and teasing. "You sure? I mean, you look like you've been through hell and back—oh, wait. *You have!*"

I snort, half-laughing, half-sighing. "It feels like it too."

Sadie looks me over again, her expression turning serious for just a beat. "But you're home. You're safe. And that's what matters." Her voice cracks, and I can see the fight to keep her composure.

Sadie's excitement bubbles over, her hands still shaking as she pulls away from her father. Her wide grin is contagious, and I can't help but laugh as she bounces on her feet, practically vibrating with happiness.

"I can't believe you're really back, Layla!" she exclaims, giving me a playful shove as she steps back. "It's like the family reunion no one knew they needed."

"I swear, you're like a walking ray of sunshine," I joke, shaking my head with a grin. Sadie's energy always fills the room, making everything feel lighter. She runs down the hall quickly.

Before I can catch my breath, Saygin and Quinn, who had been quietly watching the scene unfold, stand up, clearly preparing to leave. Saygin strides over to Luca, a mischievous glint in her emerald eyes. Quinn is right behind her, his calm demeanor betraying a small, smirking smile.

Luca, who's still sitting at the table, looks up, eyes wary as he feels their presence looming over him. He opens his mouth to say something, but Saygin speaks first.

"Luca," she purrs, voice dripping with mischief. "I think you owe me a little...
apology, don't you?"

Luca's face goes a shade of red I didn't know was possible as he stutters,
"W-what? I don't—"

"Don't worry, Luca," Quinn adds, his voice dry but amused. "It's nothing
personal, right? Just making sure you remember who's really in charge here."

Saygin's cat-like grin spreads wider as she leans down, practically hovering
over Luca's shoulder. "I mean, you did get a little... distracted with Azrael's
mother." She pauses, letting the words linger in the air, heavy with playful
menace. "Careful, or I might start believing you like *older* females."

Luca's face falls into his hands in utter mortification. "I didn't ask for this!"
he groans, desperately trying to hide from their teasing.

Quinn pats him on the back, chuckling low in his throat. "Sure you didn't,
wolf. Sure you didn't."

Saygin gives him a wink. "Enjoy it while it lasts, Luca. It'll make for some
great stories down the line."

As they turn to leave, Luca looks up at me, his embarrassment still palpable.
"Please tell me this nightmare's over."

I smirk, crossing my arms. "For now, maybe. But I'm not making any promises."

Saygin and Quinn share one last glance, their laughter echoing as they head
out the door, leaving behind an utterly mortified Luca. I can't help but laugh at
the entire scene, watching Luca struggle to regain some dignity.

"I swear, I'm going to need a drink after that," Luca mutters, still red in the
face. He looks at me, desperate for some sympathy. "Tell me you're not going to
bring that up in front of Sadie, Layla."

I shake my head, biting back my grin. "Oh, no. I think I'll save that for later.
Maybe after a few more rounds of teasing."

Luca sighs, defeated. "I'm never living this down, am I?"

"Nope," I say, relishing the moment a little too much. "Not a chance."

Sadie's voice rings out, filled with innocent curiosity as she steps closer, her eyes darting between Luca and me.

"Never bring up what?" she repeats, a mischievous grin starting to form on her lips.

Luca's face goes pale, and he quickly scrambles to his feet, his hands up in defense. "Nothing, Sadie. Don't worry about it!" he says, almost too quickly, his attempt to steer the conversation away falling flat.

I can't help it; the urge to tease him is too strong. I lean in, grinning wide. "Oh, just Luca's latest... adventure with Azrael's mother," I say, my tone sugary sweet, making sure to emphasize the *adventure* part.

Sadie's eyes widen for a split second, then she bursts into laughter, her whole body shaking with it. "No way," she says, practically choking on her own amusement. "Luca? You didn't!"

Luca looks like he's about to combust. "I did not—well, technically, I didn't—uh..."

I shake my head, unable to contain the laugh bubbling up inside me. "Oh, he totally *did*," I tease, stepping away, letting him stew in his own embarrassment. "It's a whole thing, really. But I'll let him tell you the details."

Sadie's laughter rings through the room, her eyes bright with amusement as she claps Luca on the shoulder. "You know, Luca, I always thought you were the quiet, shy type. But this? This is next-level."

Luca groans, putting his face in his hands again. "I didn't ask for this. Please just—"

"Don't worry," I tease, my grin never fading. "We'll all be here to *support* you through it. Maybe you should write a book. *'Luca's Adventures in the Underworld.'* Might be a bestseller."

Sadie practically doubles over with laughter, and I can't help but join in, my own chuckles mixing with hers as Luca struggles to maintain some semblance of dignity.

"Please. I'm begging you," Luca mutters, voice muffled by his hands. "Can we just move on from this?"

Azrael lets out a long, pained groan from behind me, clearly trying to tune out the chaos. He's sitting off to the side, his hand pressed against his forehead as though he's trying to block out the madness in the room.

"Can we not?" he mutters, his voice laced with discomfort, like he's one awkward conversation away from losing his sanity. "I already regret being part of this conversation. Please, let's just pretend none of this ever happened."

Sadie, still laughing, takes a dramatic step back, raising her hands in mock surrender. "Alright, alright, I'll ease up. But you know... we're never letting Luca live this one down."

Luca glares at her, but it's more out of exasperation than anything else. "I swear, you guys are the worst."

Azrael leans back on the couch, looking like he might just melt into the furniture if he tries hard enough. "I'm about two seconds away from going back to the Empty, just to get away from all this," he mutters under his breath.

I glance over at him, trying to keep my grin in check as I take a seat beside him. "You know," I say, voice light and teasing, "I think I'll remind you of this moment every time you try to give me a hard time."

Azrael shoots me a look, eyes filled with mock annoyance. "Yeah, well, just make sure you don't remind me when we're in public," he warns, but there's a glimmer of amusement behind his words.

Luca, still trying to salvage his dignity, shifts awkwardly in his seat. "This is never happening again, right?"

"Not a chance," I say, my grin widening. "I think we're just getting started."

CHAPTER FORTY-FOUR

Layla

NOTHING ELSE MATTERS - METALLICA

I look around at the dysfunctional family we've somehow managed to piece together, brick by chaotic brick. Saygin and Quinn reluctantly take their leave, but not before Quinn shoots Luca a playful, but affectionate, look. It's clear that while they're connected in some strange way, it's not enough to keep them from wandering their separate paths. Luca remains, a quiet anchor in the madness of it all. I breathe out a long sigh of relief, finally feeling like I'm home again.

Home. It still feels surreal, after everything that's happened, that this is where I'm supposed to be. I lean toward Azrael, resting my head against his broad shoulder. I breathe him in, grounding myself with his calm presence. It wraps around me like a blanket, and the tension in my chest starts to ease, even as my heart continues to hammer like a war drum.

He looks down at me, his deep ice blue eyes softening with affection, and his lips curl into a smile that does more than make my heart flutter—it settles it. He leans in, brushing his lips across mine, slow and deliberate, as if he's swallowing every ounce of fear I have left, devouring it entirely.

"I'm safe," I whisper against his lips. "I'm safe, Azrael."

He doesn't answer with words, just with a quiet, knowing kiss that reassures me in ways words never could.

"You're safe," he murmurs against my skin, his breath warm against the coolness of my neck.

And in that moment, I know he means it.

Across the room, Sadie is being Sadie. Teasing Ashton, playfully tugging at his belt buckle as if she were on some sort of mischievous mission. Ashton, ever the calm one, slaps her hand away, but not in the way a lover would—more like a parent scolding their child before dessert. I can't help but chuckle softly, my breath hitching with the sound.

"Sadie, you really know how to keep it classy, huh?" I call out, still chuckling.

She flashes me a grin. "Classy's overrated."

Flo, the enormous feline that has become an unlikely companion in our little family, sprawls lazily in front of the fireplace. Her large form takes up nearly half the room, and she's soaking in the warmth, her purring vibrating through the space. Exu had mentioned that she might learn to shrink into a smaller form, but right now, she's basking in the one thing the Empty never gave her—warmth. I watch her, a soft smile tugging at my lips.

I shiver, the memory of the Empty still fresh in my mind. It was cold. It was unforgiving. But none of that matters now. Not when I have this—these imperfect, messy, drama-filled, supernatural beings, who somehow ran into the Empty without hesitation, without fear, to drag me out.

"Forgot something," I mumble to myself, then turn toward Sadie, who is still locked in her little playful tug-of-war with Ashton.

Sadie doesn't even look up from her antics. "Mm-hmm. What's up?"

I clear my throat. "I got Song."

Sadie pauses mid-swipe at Ashton's belt. She looks up, her eyes widening. "Song?"

"Yeah, I—" I blink back sudden tears, my chest tightening with emotion. "I brought her back."

Her mouth falls open, and for a moment, I think she might faint. Her eyes glisten with unshed tears. "How? How did you—"

"She's resting," Vassago interrupts, his voice smooth but soft. "She needs time to adjust."

Sadie's eyes dart between us, her pulse quickening. "She's really here? She's really alive?" Her voice cracks, a mix of disbelief and joy.

"Yes." I nod, feeling the weight of what I've done settling over me. It wasn't easy, but Persephone... well, I owe her.

Sadie stands up, her hands still grasping Ashton's in a death grip as if she might be afraid to let go of him. She looks at me, her voice a little frantic, a little wild. "How the hell did you pull that off? What—"

"I asked Persephone," I answer quietly, knowing full well it will raise eyebrows.

Sadie stares at me. "You asked... *Persephone?*"

The room goes silent, and Orcus, who had been lounging casually, bursts out laughing. "After Persephone fucked Luca, no less!" he adds, making sure everyone knows.

Azrael lets out an audible groan, rubbing his forehead. "Please don't start," he mutters, clearly exhausted by the circus we've become. "Not right now."

I shoot a pointed look at Orcus. "Could you be a little less... *obnoxious?*"

Luca, who has been standing by, looking almost unbothered by the entire conversation, arches an eyebrow. He's becoming number to the subject.

Sadie, still beaming, wraps her arms around me in a tight hug, nearly knocking me over. "You're a fucking miracle worker, Layla. I swear to the stars, I *love* you."

"I'm just glad she's back," I whisper, fighting back more tears. But for the first time in a long time, they're happy tears.

Ashton leans back in his chair, his long legs stretched out in front of him, looking as relaxed as ever despite the chaos unfolding around him. He casts a sidelong glance at Luca, a playful smirk tugging at the corner of his mouth.

"So," Ashton begins, his voice casual but with an underlying hint of mischief. "Remember that promise you made? About the feast? You know, the one where you said you'd cook for all of us when we made it back?"

Luca looks up, a faint eyebrow raise in amusement. "Ah, I remember," he says slowly, a smirk forming on his own lips. "But I'm not sure how much of a feast you actually want. I mean, we've got a rather… interesting mix of appetites here." He gestures vaguely around the room, his eyes flicking to everyone, including the still lounging Flo by the fire and the half-exasperated, half-amused Sadie.

"Oh, I'm not picky," Ashton says, leaning forward slightly, his tone now a touch more serious, though it's still laced with humor. "Just something hearty. Something that'll make us forget about *all* the drama we've just survived." He winks at Sadie, who, with a dramatic eye roll, throws her hands up in defeat.

Sadie, never one to miss an opportunity for humor, chimes in, "Yeah, Luca. You owe us big time. *Big time.* You don't just get to run around being all mysterious and fucking everyone's mother without cooking us something at least somewhat edible."

Luca chuckles, shaking his head. "I'm far from mysterious. You sure you're up for it? I've got *skills*, but you're talking about feeding an entire room of… well, *you all*." He gestures to the group, then glances at the ceiling like he's about to pray for divine intervention.

Azrael, who had been silently observing the back-and-forth, leans in with a knowing smile. "Don't worry, Luca," he says smoothly. "We're not asking for a five-star restaurant experience. Just… don't burn anything."

Luca, stretches his arms as he shakes his head, a laugh escaping him. "I'll make sure to keep it *alive* this time."

Flo, lying by the fire, lets out a soft, curious meow as if agreeing with the idea of a feast, which only adds to the tension of anticipation.

Sadie, eyes gleaming, smirks. "Well, you heard him, everyone. Prepare for a feast... and a *spectacle*."

Luca shrugs, unbothered. "Just wait. You'll all be *begging* for seconds."

I smile to myself, feeling a warmth grow within me that isn't from the fire. For all the chaos, all the dangers, there's something undeniably comforting about this moment—the people around me, their humor, their resilience, and their ability to pull together when it matters.

"All right then, Luca. We're counting on you," I say, my voice soft but filled with a quiet optimism.

Luca grins at me, a flash of something almost fond in his eyes. "You've got it, Layla."

As he heads toward the kitchen, the weight of the past feels lighter, and for the first time in what feels like forever, I let myself hope that things might just be okay.

CHAPTER FORTY-FIVE

Luca

CHASING CARS - SNOW PATROL

I watch everyone eat, the sounds of laughter and conversation filling the air as I poke at a stray piece of green bean on my plate, pushing it around aimlessly. The tension in my chest doesn't ease; it's been there all night, a weight I can't seem to shake. As much as I try to engage in the moment, the laughter, the jokes—nothing seems to drown out the roar of my memories. They're like the noise in the background of a song you can't turn off, a constant hum in my head that I can't escape.

It wasn't really Saygin or Persephone that had been bothering me. Sure, their presence was jarring, but what really haunted me—the thing that keeps gnawing at my insides—was the Mawkin. The terror loop, the nightmare it dragged me through, forcing me to relive a memory I buried so damn deep in my mind that I nearly forgot it ever existed.

My mother.

I was just a boy when I lost her. Too young to understand what was happening, too naive to know that I wouldn't mentally survive it. I can still feel the cold of that night—how I slaughtered our entire pack, how I sat beside her lifeless body, waiting for help that never came. Days passed before my aunt finally found me, starving, thirsty—completely alone. I remember the stench, the rot that filled the air, but more than that, I remember the silence. That awful, suffocating silence. The kind that clings to your skin, settles in your bones, and doesn't leave.

I think of my aunt—how she held me when I couldn't hold myself together, how she gave me the little bit of pity that carried me through. Her love was the only thing that made sense in that hellhole of a time.

The inheritance my mother left for me was significant, enough to make sure I had a foundation to build on, a future that could start fresh. My aunt never touched a penny of it, though. Stubborn as hell, that woman. It was her pride, her way of showing that I wasn't just her responsibility. I was her family.

I glance across the table at Azrael, studying him for a moment. How the hell did he know my father? Or my father's front? There's so much I don't understand, so much about the Underworld that seems to be linked in ways I can't even begin to comprehend. One thing is for sure though—every male at this table has daddy issues. Me, Azrael, Vassago, even Ashton... we all carry that weight in some form or another.

I let out a silent sigh, exhaling a breath I didn't even realize I was holding.

I take a sip of my sweet tea, the taste is a small comfort, though it's not enough to soothe the ache that runs through me. Sweet tea is something I never expected to find in the Underworld, let alone teaching the others how to make it. Ashton had to trek all the way to the mortal realm to get me tea bags and all the other things I requested. I can't help but chuckle at how ridiculous it all is. Goblin's ass, learning how to cook that like a rump roast? Nah, that's not for me. It's the little things that have started to matter—the simple comforts I've learned to crave. Tea, coffee, a clean plate to eat off of... Things I used to take for granted.

My memories start to take hold of me again, this time drifting back to my mother, to her cafe. *Celeste's Cafe*—her dream, her *legacy*. I smile softly, the memory of her face, her kind smile, washing over me.

The way my aunt used to stand by the register, arranging flowers, picking ivy from the plants that wrapped around it. I remember how proud she was when I told her I'd use every penny of my inheritance to open that coffee shop, to make it something my mother would've loved. I was going to make her proud.

It was everything she wanted it to be—bright, full of life, flowers and greenery everywhere. I took care of every little thing. The ivy at the register? I babied it like it was my own child. But the pain that followed when my aunt died... that was another thing. It felt like I lost the last piece of my mother. I was completely alone, but even then, I wasn't. I had the cafe. I had the customers who became my family. The vampires who came in for their morning fix, the sirens who would occasionally trot through—each of them gave me something to hold on to. But then Azrael came into my life and brought the kind of danger that shattered everything.

I can still see it, the wreckage. My shop, destroyed, the walls splintered like they were made of paper. I tried to save them, my customers, the only thing that remained of my mother's dream. But I was too weak. Too powerless. And now, I'm stuck here in this group of misfits, who treat me like I'm incapable of defending myself. Like I'm still that frightened little boy from the past.

Maybe they're right. Maybe I can't protect them—or myself—but damn it, I should've been able to protect *Celeste's Cafe*. That was the last piece of my mother I had left. And now... it's gone.

I feel a small tear gather in the corner of my eye, but I quickly wipe it away, trying to mask it with the same walls I've learned to build up over the years.

"Wolfy boy, you good?" Sadie's voice cuts through the fog of my thoughts, snapping me back into the moment.

I glance up at her, giving her a half-smile. She's messing with me again, her usual front in place, always teasing, always making light of everything. I can see through it, though. We're both masters of pretending. We're both out of place here. We don't belong in this Underworld—none of us do.

"Yeah," I mutter, my voice tight. "Just... thinking."

Sadie gives me a knowing look, but she doesn't press. She knows as well as I do that sometimes, it's better to leave things unsaid. Still, I can't shake the feeling that I'm more than just a werewolf. I'm not just some Lycan, some creature of the night. There's a part of me that still belongs on the earth, where my mother's feet once touched. That's where my true mark lies—unfinished, waiting for me to return.

I've been thinking about Saygin's offer more and more. That bargain. It tempts me in ways I can't even explain. The chance to undo the past, to fix things, to return to what was lost—maybe I'm an idiot for not taking it. It's everything I've ever wanted. But... at what cost?

I shake my head, pushing the thoughts away, even though the temptation claws at me relentlessly.

I should, shouldn't I?

The thought lingers in my mind like a shadow I can't shake. I can't help but feel like I'm no better than the help Ashton owns. There's a part of me that's tired of being weak, of feeling like I'm nothing more than a lost cause in this place. Everyone else has their purpose—Azrael with his death and his fate, Sadie with her fierce loyalty, even Vassago. And then there's me... a wolf who couldn't even protect his own business, a Lycan who can't seem to figure out where the hell he belongs.

What's stopping me from taking the bargain, from finally being something more than the leftover parts of what everyone else left behind?

I look at Ashton across the table, his usual carefree expression at odds with the way I feel. He's been through hell too, I know that. But the difference is, he has this calm, this sense of purpose even when things go to shit. His past doesn't haunt him the way mine does. He doesn't carry the weight of so much failure.

I guess that's why he's so damn easy to like—because he's not burdened with the same feeling of worthlessness I carry around like a badge of honor. He's not stuck in a loop of wondering if he should've done something different, made a different choice.

And here I am, debating whether I should throw myself into something that could change it all.

The more I think about it, the more it feels like it's my only shot at making something of myself, at finally feeling like I'm worth more than the pain of my past. Maybe taking Saygin's bargain *is* the answer. Maybe that's *how* I stop being the guy who's just along for the ride.

I clench my fist, my nails digging into my palm, the self-doubt making me feel like a fool. Because deep down, I know the truth. I'm terrified of what it means, terrified of what kind of person I'll become if I take that leap.

But... can I really keep going like this? Can I live with the weight of my past, always looking over my shoulder, wondering if I'll ever be enough? Or do I take the bargain, take control, and carve out a future that's *mine*—one where I'm no longer just a reminder of the things I couldn't save?

I look around the room again, the faces of my friends, of my *family*, all staring back at me. And for once, I wonder... maybe it's time I finally stop running and actually *do* something.

I take a deep breath, the decision weighing on me. Maybe, just maybe, I need to stop pretending like I don't deserve something better.

Chapter Forty-Six

Sadie

Heavy - Linkin Park

I can't help but notice Luca. I swear, this kid's always battling himself, but today it's like he's got a war raging inside. His face is locked in that familiar grimace—the one where you know he's trying to fight off something he'd rather not face. And it's not like I'm the only one who sees it. But sure as hell, no one else at the table gives a damn. Everyone's too busy enjoying their little reunion to care that Luca is practically drowning in his own head.

You know, sometimes I feel like that's all we do here. We fight our own heads, trapped in this fucked-up Underworld drama, and nobody ever asks how we're doing. How we really are. Layla's got Azrael and the Queen of the Underworld vibes. Vassago's her loyal lapdog. Exu trains everyone but me—because Ashton said so, of course. But I'm starting to wonder if he just wants to keep me locked up, all safe and sound like I'm some kind of porcelain doll. I mean, sure, I get it. *I do.* But come on, *fuck him.*

I'm not Isolde. I'm not her. I'm not some broken picture-perfect soul from his past.

I mean, let's be real. Ashton killed his father, and all that drama... what more could possibly be out there for him? I don't understand why someone would hate Ashton so much they'd isolate him, but then again... wait. No. Azrael is *annoying*. I can totally get why Layla would be a target.

But then there's me. I'm sitting here, simmering in this petty jealousy that threatens to boil over every time I see Layla. She's got everything. She got Dash. She got help. She had a beautiful home, both parents who actually cared about her... when my dad died, I had *no one*. I was taken in like some stray dog, an orphan for the Simmons to take on as their "good deed."

And hey, I'm not ungrateful. I get that I should be thankful they took me in. But let's not kid ourselves. I'm not a fucking charity case, am I? It's like... I'm living in her shadow, the perfect golden child, and I'm stuck in the background trying not to become the person everyone points to as "the fuck-up." I worked so damn hard to pull myself out of that hole. And still... I can't shake this sense of never being *enough*.

I can't even lie and pretend it doesn't sting, especially when I realize that I've been keeping something from everyone. A little thing that's *mine*—but only for now. Because, realistically—I want to blurt it out.

Here's the kicker. I'm fucking *pregnant*.

Yeah, that little nugget of a secret is just swirling around in my head, a secret I can't keep much longer. I want to scream it from the rooftops, tell everyone at this damn table—let them know that I'm more than just the snarky little sidekick. I'm a fucking miracle in the making. But I can't. Not yet. And if I'm being honest, it's making the whole "I hate Layla" thing a lot more complicated. Not because I *actually* hate her—hell, I don't. I know she deserves her happiness. But this? This envy is a bit... hormone-driven. Yeah, sure, maybe it's my mood swings talking. But goddamn, I can't ignore the pangs of jealousy every time I see her, knowing she's got the world handed to her while I'm here, sitting in this mess, trying not to ruin everything.

God, just saying it in my head feels like I'm about to explode. The guilt, the jealousy, the twisted pleasure in knowing that maybe—just maybe—I excelled in training faster than Layla did. It's a sick little pleasure that I've learned to keep tucked away behind a smile. I can mask emotions better than anyone else here. I've perfected the art of compartmentalizing my feelings, even hiding them from Ashton. He's the last person to know what's really going on in my head. He doesn't have a fucking clue. But I can't keep *this* secret forever. Not when it eats away at me like this.

I want to scream it out. I want to tell them all.

I want them to *accept* me. I want them to be happy for me.

I look over at Luca again. Poor guy's holding it together by a thread. He's fighting tears, and yet, everyone else at this table is just... oblivious. Or they don't care. But hey, at least Layla's home, right? At least she's safe and back with Azrael. That's something. Maybe Luca's pain is just one of those things we don't talk about. I wonder if that's what we all do now.

We pretend like the hard stuff never happened, never even fucking mattered.

"Wolfy boy, you good?" I ask, my voice soft, even though I'm itching to rip into someone. It's my way of letting him know that someone sees him, even if everyone else is busy ignoring him. He looks at me, slowly, like he's not sure if he wants to acknowledge me at all.

"Yeah," he mutters. "Just... thinking."

I sit back, crossing my arms and observing. I want to say something to make him feel better, but I don't know how to put into words that I get it. I get that feeling of drowning in your own thoughts, wishing someone would just notice you long enough to care. And yet, here I am, stuck in this mess of emotions that don't seem to fit.

But the truth is, I can't be mad at Layla. I don't hate her. In fact, we both got our happy endings, right? She's with Azrael, and I'm with Ashton, and in some way, we're both happy. But... God, sometimes I just wonder if it's enough.

I mean, I'm carrying a freaking baby here, and all I want is for someone to acknowledge that.

I look over at Ashton, my handsome protector, trying to tune out the chaos around us. He's laughing with the guys. Maybe he just doesn't realize that I need him right now, that I need him to *see* me. See what this is doing to me.

But then again, he's Ashton, and he's been dealing with enough shit of his own.

I focus on the feeling I get when he looks at me. It's real. I know it's real. But that doesn't mean I have to like everything about being here.

When will they all go home? I don't even bother looking at Ashton when I ask him. He's joking with the guys, not even paying attention to me.

He doesn't even look at me, but the answer comes anyway. *Azrael has one last thing he needs to take care of before we can all go our separate ways. I promise, soon.*

I repeat it in my head, over and over. *Soon.*

And then, without thinking, I blurt it out through the bond. *I'm pregnant, Ashton.*

Ashton chokes on a bite of steak, his eyes widening in shock.

"You okay over there?" Azrael asks, concerned, but Ashton just looks like he's seen a ghost.

Luca jumps up, panic flashing across his face, while Vassago slaps Ashton on the back, trying to help him breathe.

I can't help but smirk. Well, that went better than I expected.

He regains his character, that cool, calm, and collected demeanor that somehow always manages to melt my insides. The way he stays composed, despite everything, it gets me every time. There's something about having a loud mouth woman with a guy like him—a quiet, steady presence—that just works. It's picture-perfect in its own odd way, like a contrast that somehow makes sense. He's my steady rock in a world full of chaos, and right now, I can feel every ounce of his focus on me.

Ashton turns to me completely, his body shifting to face mine, and his hand reaches out, warm and strong, to take mine. "Really?" he asks, his voice low and laced with disbelief. He's not mocking me, though; it's more like he's trying to process what I just said, as if he's waiting for me to confirm that this isn't just some weird joke I'd throw out for attention.

Suddenly, all eyes are on me. *Fuck.* I wasn't ready for this. Not this much attention. I feel the sweat building up on the back of my neck, pooling down my spine. I can feel my face heating up, my mouth dry, my brain on overload. The words I want to say are stuck, buried beneath a mountain of anxiety I can't shake off. I can't make a sound, can't push the words out fast enough.

I just nod.

It's all I can do.

Ashton doesn't miss a beat. He jumps up from the table with that effortless grace of his, pulling me up with him. Before I can even process what's happening, my feet are lifted off the ground, and he twirls us both into the kitchen, spinning me around with the kind of joy that can only come from an unexpected moment.

The entire room goes silent, eyes wide, watching us as if we've just done something ridiculous. I feel the stares digging into me, the weight of the moment setting in.

"Whoa, Ashton!" I laugh, my voice full of tease. I can't give him full satisfaction, I still have to fuck with him and give him a hard time.

I can hear Luca chuckle softly from across the room, but it's Vassago who says, "You're really doing this now?"

"I'm going to be a dad!" Ashton yells, his voice booming as he sets me back down on my feet. He's practically glowing, and there's a kind of joy in his expression that's so pure, I swear the whole room can feel it.

"I'm going to be a dad!" he repeats, louder this time, like he's announcing it to the entire Underworld. And I'm standing there, blinking, my eyes welling up with tears that I didn't even know were coming. *God, I am not this fucking weak,*

I think to myself, but the damn hormones are everywhere. I can't control this mess, and it's driving me crazy. One minute I'm laughing, the next I'm tearing up over everything.

These fucking hormones.

I glance up at Layla, and she looks at me with such softness in her eyes, it makes my heart clench. It's a look that tells me everything. She's truly happy for me. I know that. But then the jealousy hits me like a sucker punch. *Why the fuck are my hormones so focused on hating her right now?* I love her, with everything I've got, and it's not even her fault that I'm losing my damn mind.

"You're pregnant, Sadie?" Layla asks, her voice gentle, full of the kind of warmth that makes my insides twist. I feel it all—the love, the happiness, the care—and it makes everything inside of me break apart. She's so happy for me, and the fact that I'm over here feeling like I want to claw her eyes out for existing in her perfect little world makes me want to vomit.

She's my best friend. No, more than that—she's my *sister*. I've fought for her, and she's fought for me. *I love her.* So why do my hormones keep dragging me into this headspace where I feel like everything she does is a fucking personal attack on my inadequacy? What the hell is wrong with me?

Tears spill down my face, hot and angry, and I wipe them away quickly, hoping no one notices. I can't even look at Layla right now.

But she sees me, of course. She always sees me.

"I'm sorry, I didn't mean to make you feel bad." Her voice is soft, regretful. God, that only makes it worse. It's not her fault. It's just... *me.*

I feel a flare of irritation, then guilt, and all of it crashes into a jumbled mess of feelings that I'm not used to dealing with.

For a second, I fucking hate being a Leo. I hate how my emotions feel like they're on a fucking rollercoaster that I didn't even sign up for. I just want to feel normal again. To not want to strangle my best friend and to not hate myself for feeling jealous when I know she's been through her own shit, just like me.

But damn it, right now all I can do is smile through the tears, even if it feels like my heart is being ripped in two. "Yeah," I croak, swallowing hard. "Yeah, I'm pregnant."

Layla's smile brightens, and it breaks me all over again. "I'm so *happy* for you, Sadie. Really. This is *amazing*."

And despite everything, despite the mess inside my head, I can't help but smile back. Because Layla's right. It *is* amazing. And I love her too much to let these damn hormones tear us apart.

"I can already imagine it. That little human, crying in the middle of the night. You and Ashton arguing about who's more tired, while I just sit here, silently judging both of you. How entertaining." Orcus' blade glints with a knowing gleam.

"When did you find out?" Ashton asks, ignoring Orcus, his tone still filled with awe and excitement. His eyes are so focused on me, like he's hanging on every word, waiting for the moment it all sinks in.

I grin, feeling a little more at ease now that I've got the spotlight off me for just a second. "It's why Exu and I were gone so long," I say, my voice playful. "He took me to one of your fancy medicine women to confirm." I smile wider, knowing the image of Exu—who's usually so calm and serious—having to go with me to some magical healer is probably hilarious to everyone who knows him.

Ashton's eyebrows shoot up, clearly not expecting that. "Exu?" he asks, chuckling. "You made Exu go with you to a healer?"

I nod, biting my lip to keep from laughing. "Yeah, poor guy looked like he was about to choke the healer with his bare hands when she asked if the baby was his."

Ashton lets out a low whistle, trying to hold back a laugh. "Oh, I can just imagine that. Exu's not exactly the 'talk about feelings' type."

"That's Exu for you," Azrael says, his voice dripping with amusement. "Doesn't help that the healer probably caught him off guard with that question. He's a man of action, not... *discussion.*"

I roll my eyes, smirking at them both. "Oh, you have no idea. He nearly had a stroke when she asked if he wanted to be there for the birth." I glance at Ashton, who's barely holding back a full-on belly laugh. "You know how he is—too cool for everything. But there he was, looking like he might break someone's neck over a simple question."

The whole group laughs, and I can't help but join in. It feels good to have a moment of lightness in all this chaos.

Azrael raises an eyebrow at me, still chuckling. "I'm surprised he didn't try to strangle her for even suggesting he'd be involved in the *birth* part."

"Oh, so the healer thought Exu was the father? Well, that's adorable. Clearly, she hasn't met a male who knows how to avoid commitment as well as he does. Must've been the brooding aura that gave him away." Orcus chuckles darkly, his voice dripping with sarcasm.

I shrug, feeling a sense of relief spreading through me. "He kept it together, but just barely. I think he needed a stiff drink afterward."

Ashton finally stops laughing, looking at me with a soft expression. "I'm glad you had someone with you, Sadie. Even if it was Exu."

"I can't imagine Exu getting into the spirit of parenting. He'd probably throw a tantrum if the kid asked for a bedtime story instead of a battle plan." Orcus' voice sharpens... But I am trying my best to ignore him. My hormones are already blaring. The last thing I need is a back and forth argument and fight with a fucking talking blade.

I smile, squeezing his hand. "Yeah, me too. He may be gruff, but he's got a heart underneath it all."

"I'm sorry I wasn't able to be there." Ashton mumbles.

Orcus' voice hums with amusement, sharp and biting as always. "Oh, right. You couldn't be there when she found out she was pregnant, because you were too busy playing the hero in the Empty, saving Layla. How noble. Meanwhile, Sadie's over here dealing with 'big life changes,' and you were off fighting creatures from the hell itself. Sounds like a great trade-off." He chuckles, the sound dark and mocking. "But hey, don't worry, Ashton. You were probably too busy being all brooding and tragic to notice you were missing out on one of life's more interesting announcements. At least you got a nice hero moment out of it, right?"

And fuck ... here comes the rush of hateful hormones that are lashing at Layla.

Chapter Forty-Seven

Layla

Wanted - Hunter Hayes

I roll over to Azrael, instinctively reaching for him before I'm even fully awake. He never sleeps—I should have known he'd still be lying there, but after everything, part of me half expects to wake up alone, for all of this to dissolve like mist in the morning light. The days—maybe even a week?—I spent trapped in the Empty made me feel like freedom was just a dream, a cruel mirage my mind conjured up to keep me from breaking.

But he's here. He's *real.*

My fingers find his face, tracing the sharp angles and curves, the familiar features I thought I might never see again. His skin is cool under my touch, his expression unreadable until his eyes—those piercing, ice-cold blue eyes I've grown to love so damn much—lock onto mine.

Without a word, he pulls me closer, wrapping me in the warmth of his body. He holds me like he's afraid to let go, like if he loosens his grip, I might slip away again. And maybe I would. Maybe I'm still half-stuck in that endless void, teetering on the edge of reality, waiting for something to drag me back.

The Azrael I left behind is not the Azrael I returned to.

Something about him is different. Not just the exhaustion lining his features, not just the shadows in his gaze. He *reeks* of something I can't quite place—something dark, something heavy, something that clings to him like an invisible shroud. It's in the way he looks at me, the way he breathes me in, the way his hands tighten ever so slightly around my waist, as if trying to convince himself I'm truly here.

He leans in and kisses me, slow and deliberate, like he's searching for an answer in the way our lips meet. When he finally pulls away, his voice is a husky murmur against my lips.

"Good morning, tiny mouse."

A warmth spreads through me, deep and consuming, as if his words have settled into my very bones. It's ridiculous how easily he affects me, how just the sound of his voice, low and rough, makes my heart stutter in my chest.

I swallow hard, forcing myself to focus. "Morning," I whisper, letting my forehead rest against his.

I don't want to move. I don't want to leave this bed at this moment. Because once we do, reality will come crashing back in. The war. The deals. The bargains. The ghosts of what we've lost and the uncertainty of what's still to come.

But right now, in this fleeting moment, it's just us.

Azrael exhales sharply, rubbing a hand over his face as if he's already exhausted just thinking about it. "So. Sadie's pregnant." His voice is flat, unimpressed, like someone just informed him that a category five hurricane was on its way, and he had approximately zero time to prepare. He grimaces. "Seems we'll have another one of *her* running around in a couple of months."

I snort, burying my face against his chest to stifle my laugh. "Oh, come on," I tease. "You *love* Sadie."

Azrael makes a low, disgruntled sound in the back of his throat. "Love is a strong word, Layla. *Tolerate*? Barely. *Survive*? So far." He shifts, staring up at the ceiling like it personally offended him. "And now there's going to be *two* of them?" He turns his head toward me, eyes narrowed. "How did Ashton let this happen?"

I blink at him. "You *do* know how babies are made, right?"

He glares. "Obviously. But you'd think he'd have some self-preservation instincts. Sadie is *already* a menace. Now she's going to be a menace with offspring."

I bite my lip, trying to suppress another laugh. "You're being *dramatic*."

Azrael groans and throws an arm over his eyes. "Mark my words, tiny mouse. That child is going to be *chaos incarnate*."

"Why are you this way towards her?" I ask, tilting my head as I study his expression.

Azrael sighs, dragging a hand down his face before looking at me. "Because she's *Sadie*," he says as if that explains everything.

I arch a brow. "And?"

"And that means she's loud, reckless, infuriatingly stubborn, and has no sense of self-preservation." He pauses. "She also insults me every chance she gets."

I smirk. "You insult her *right back*. Honestly, you two are just different sides of the same coin."

Azrael scowls. "I *resent* that."

"You *are* that," I tease, poking him in the chest. "Besides, I think you secretly like her."

He makes a noise of pure offense. "Absolutely not."

"You do," I insist, grinning. "You'd never admit it, but you care about her. In your own grumpy, brooding way."

Azrael grumbles something under his breath before exhaling heavily. "Fine," he mutters. "Maybe I *tolerate* her. But if that child comes out with even half her attitude, Ashton is on his own."

I laugh, curling into him. "Sure, sure. Whatever helps you sleep at night."

"Nothing helps me rest," he grumbles. "Especially not the thought of a baby Sadie running around."

Azrael goes still. His grip on me tightens, just a fraction, but I feel it. His silence speaks louder than words, the weight of what I just said settling between us like a thick fog.

I press on gently. "You know, Ashton might have *wanted* this. I heard about Isolde and his son."

His jaw tightens. "Who told you that?"

I hesitate. "Vassago."

Azrael exhales sharply, shaking his head. "Of course he did."

I watch him carefully, searching his face for some hint of what's going on in that guarded mind of his. "Why does it bother you?"

"It doesn't," he says too quickly.

I arch a brow. "*Liar.*"

Azrael looks away, staring at the ceiling as if it holds the answers he refuses to say out loud. Finally, after a long pause, he mutters, "Because he never talks about it. Not even to me."

I frown. "But you're his best friend."

"*Exactly.*" His voice is flat, but there's something raw underneath it. "And he *never* once told me."

That surprises me. Ashton and Azrael are closer than anyone I know. If Ashton had buried that part of his past so deeply that even *Azrael* wasn't aware of it... that meant something.

"Maybe it was too painful," I say softly.

Azrael's fingers trace absent patterns along my arm, his mind clearly elsewhere. "Maybe," he says, but I can tell he's not convinced.

I hesitate before asking, "Do you think that's why he's been so hesitant with Sadie? Because of what happened with Isolde?"

Azrael exhales through his nose. "Wouldn't you be?"

I think about it. About what it would feel like to lose a mate. A child. To have something that precious ripped away and then be expected to move forward like it never happened.

I shudder. "Yeah. I would."

Azrael finally looks at me, something unreadable in his eyes. "That's why I worry about him. He acts like nothing gets to him, like he's untouchable, but..." He trails off, shaking his head. "*This*? This is different."

I nod, pressing closer to him. "Then maybe Sadie's the best thing for him."

Azrael huffs a dry, humorless laugh. "Or the worst. That woman is chaos incarnate."

I smile. "And yet, Ashton *loves* her."

Azrael doesn't argue. He just holds me a little tighter.

Azrael stays quiet for a long moment, lost in thought. I can tell he's still trying to make sense of it all—of Ashton's silence, of Sadie's impact, of the past creeping into the present when no one wanted it to.

I reach up, brushing my fingers over his cheek. "Do you think he's scared?"

Azrael scoffs, but it's not unkind. "Of course he is. Ashton doesn't do scared, but this? This is different." His voice is softer now, more thoughtful. "He's already lost one family. And now he's got another. That's a risk he's never going to take again."

I think about Sadie, how fiercely she loves, how she fights for the people she cares about. She's not the kind to let fear dictate her life, but Ashton? He buries things. He hides from the wounds that don't heal.

"He won't lose her," I say firmly. "He won't lose the baby, either."

Azrael looks down at me, something heavy in his gaze. "You don't know that."

I open my mouth to argue, but the words don't come. Because he's right. I *don't* know. The world we live in isn't kind, and fate doesn't care about love.

But I *believe* in Sadie. I *believe* in Ashton.

"I know she'll fight for him," I say instead. "For their family. Even if he's too scared to do it himself."

Azrael exhales, running a hand through his hair. "Yeah. That sounds like her."

A comfortable silence settles between us, but I can tell Azrael isn't done thinking about it. He never stops thinking—about the people he cares about, about the ones he's lost, about the ones he might still lose.

I rest my head against his chest, listening to the steady rhythm of his heart-beat. "You'll look out for him, won't you?"

Azrael scoffs again, but his arms tighten around me. "Of course I will."

I smile against his skin. "Good."

Because if there's one thing I've learned, it's that family—whether by blood, bond, or sheer stubbornness—means never letting each other face the dark alone.

"Why are we talking about them when we could be doing dirty... *dirty things*, little mouse?" Azrael shoots me a wicked grin

I laugh, swatting at his chest, but he catches my wrist with ease, pulling me even closer. His grin deepens, that dangerous, wicked thing that always sends a thrill straight through me.

"You're insufferable," I mumble, though the way my body melts against his completely betrays me.

Azrael hums in amusement, brushing his lips along my jaw, his breath warm against my skin. "And yet, you *love* me."

"Debatable," I tease, though the soft sigh that escapes me when his teeth graze my pulse says otherwise.

He pulls back just enough to look me in the eyes, his gaze dark and full of intent. "You keep saying things like that, tiny mouse, and I might just have to remind you exactly how much you do."

Butterflies erupt in my stomach, and a flush creeps up my neck, but I meet his gaze with a smirk of my own. "Oh? And how exactly do you plan on doing that?"

Azrael's grin turns predatory, and in one swift movement, he flips me beneath him, caging me in with his body.

"Let me show you."

I gasp as his weight presses me into the mattress, his hands sliding down my sides, slow and deliberate. His touch is possessive, like he's trying to etch himself into my skin, reminding me that I'm *his*.

"Still debating it?" he murmurs, his lips brushing against my ear.

I shiver, tilting my head back to meet his gaze. "Maybe," I whisper, just to push him a little further.

Azrael's eyes darken, his smirk turning razor-sharp. "Brave little mouse," he mutters before claiming my lips with a searing kiss.

His grip tightens on my hips, dragging me beneath him as his kiss deepens, his tongue parting my lips with a slow, teasing stroke that has me arching into him. He takes his time, savoring me, like he has all the time in the world to unravel me piece by piece.

And by the gods, he *does*.

I lose myself in him, in the heat of his mouth, the weight of his body, the way his hands move like he's memorizing every inch of me. He tastes like fire and something darker, something intoxicating that leaves me dizzy.

When he finally pulls away, I'm breathless, my heart hammering against my ribs.

"Still think it's debatable?" he asks, cocking his head, that smug, wicked smirk playing on his lips.

I glare at him half-heartedly, still dazed from his kiss. "You're impossible."

He chuckles, brushing a stray strand of hair from my face. "And you, little mouse, are completely and utterly *mine*."

I should argue, should say something snarky, but as I look up at him, taking in the way he's staring at me like I'm the only thing in existence, I realize...

I don't want to.

Because he's right.

Azrael watches me like a predator that just caught its prey, but there's something softer beneath it, something unspoken. His fingers brush along my jaw, tracing the curve of my cheek, his thumb brushing over my bottom lip like he's considering devouring me all over again.

"You're staring," I murmur, my voice a little breathless.

His smirk deepens. "Can't help it, little mouse. You're my favorite thing to look at."

My heart does a stupid little flip, and I hate how easily he affects me. "You're *ridiculous*," I mutter, but I don't pull away.

He leans in again, kissing the corner of my mouth before trailing lower, his lips grazing the sensitive skin of my neck. "And you love it," he whispers against my skin, his breath sending shivers down my spine.

I do. I really, really do. But he doesn't need to hear me say it right now.

Instead, I tangle my fingers in his hair and tug him back up to kiss me again, pouring everything I feel into it—the relief of being back, the lingering fear of the Empty, the way I need him more than I want to admit. He groans against my lips, his grip tightening on my hips.

"Fuck, Layla," he breathes, pressing his forehead against mine.

For a moment, neither of us speaks. We just stay like that, tangled together, lost in each other. The weight of everything that's happened lingers in the air between us, but right now, it doesn't matter.

Right now, I just want this.

I want him.

But, of course, reality doesn't let us stay in this perfect little moment for long.

There's a sharp knock at the door, followed by Vassago's voice. "Azrael, I swear to every god that exists, if you don't get up and come deal with this shit, I'm dragging you out by your hair."

Azrael groans, dropping his head onto my shoulder. "I hate him."

I laugh, running my fingers through his hair. "No, you don't."

"I do right now."

Another knock, more impatient this time. "Don't make me come in there," Vassago warns.

Azrael sighs, pressing one last kiss to my lips before reluctantly pulling away. "This better be fucking important," he grumbles, throwing on a shirt and stalking toward the door.

I sit up, watching as he yanks it open. Vassago is standing there, arms crossed, looking thoroughly unimpressed.

"Oh good, you're alive," Vassago says dryly. "Now get your ass downstairs. We have a problem."

CHAPTER FORTY-EIGHT

Azrael

TAINTED LOVE - MILKY CHANCE

The dining room feels heavy, suffocating almost, like the air itself is resisting every breath. What used to be a place of warmth and laughter now feels like a battlefield—like the calm before a storm. Ashton stands in the doorway, his posture tense, face drawn tight. The easygoing demeanor he used to wear like a second skin is gone, replaced with something darker, more urgent.

"We have a problem," he says, and the weight of his words hangs in the air, thick and suffocating.

I tense, my hand unconsciously curling into a fist. "What kind of problem?" My voice comes out sharper than I intend, the calm that used to settle over us all now a distant memory.

"The kind of problem that followed us from the Empty." Ashton's voice is grave, the words hanging between us like a dark omen.

"What do you mean?" I ask, my stomach twisting in unease.

Ashton lowers himself into a chair, raking a hand through his hair. There's no sign of Sadie, and for a moment, the empty seat beside me feels like a void. "Layla," he says, his eyes locking onto hers. "Do you feel... different?"

"Ashton, if you're asking if I'm pregnant, I'm not," Layla responds flatly, her voice tight with frustration. She looks back at Ashton, clearly annoyed.

I glance back at Ashton, my own unease growing. "No. Not that," he says quickly, his words stumbling. "You absorbed something from the Empty."

"Absorbed?" Layla and I say in unison, confusion thick in our voices.

Drepane's low hum cuts through the silence. "I thought I felt it, but I wasn't entirely sure. The bond feels chaotic since we added Flo."

Flo hisses in the background. I turn toward her, feeling a surge of impatience. "What do you mean? What does it feel like? Should we be worried?"

Drepane falls quiet for a moment, like he's trying to organize his thoughts. Then, finally, he speaks. "It's just a lot of power. It didn't come all at once, which is why I didn't notice it right away, I guess. But now that Ashton's said something, I do feel it. It's like a rush of water, or drowning in a waterfall—more than normal power. A lot more."

A sick feeling churns in my stomach. "What do we do?"

Ashton looks from me to Layla, his gaze sharp and unwavering. "She has to learn to control it. This isn't just energy. This is *power*. It's affecting her and her aura."

"Okay, but what is it?" I can't keep the edge from creeping into my voice. I need answers—*real* answers.

"Erebus," Orcus hums, his voice calm, but there's an underlying note of caution. The room feels colder as the name falls from his voice, like we've just crossed some kind of line into unfamiliar territory.

The air feels heavier at the mention of Erebus. It's like the room collectively holds its breath, waiting for something we don't understand to make itself known.

"Erebus?" I echo, my voice trembling slightly. "What the hell is that?"

Ashton looks at me, his expression unreadable. "It's an ancient force. A power that exists in the shadows—something that's been trapped for centuries. It's not exactly a being, but it's... *alive*. It feeds off of darkness, and it can be incredibly dangerous if it isn't controlled."

"Wait," Layla says, her voice soft but steady. "So, you're saying this is... inside me now?"

Ashton nods slowly. "It doesn't just *attach* to someone. It merges. And once it merges, it can be hard to tell where the power of Erebus ends and where the being begins. That's why you're feeling off."

I watch Layla's face as she processes this. There's a flicker of something in her eyes, something I can't quite read. She's scared, but it's buried beneath layers of anger and frustration. She's always been strong like that.

"So, what now?" I ask, my voice a little too sharp. I can feel the tension coiling tighter in my chest, my thoughts racing. "How do we fix this? Or *control* it, like you said?"

"Erebus isn't something you fix," Orcus says, his voice oddly distant. "It has to be understood, carefully navigated. It will *take* if it's not kept in check. Layla's got a lot of power running through her right now, and if it goes unchecked—"

"It could consume her," Drepane finishes, his tone low.

I glance at Layla. Her face is pale, but she's doing her best to mask the panic creeping up on her. I can see it in the way her fingers twitch. It's like she's ready to fight this with everything she has.

"How do we stop it from consuming me?" Layla asks, her voice calm but tight with uncertainty.

"You'll need to learn how to control it," Ashton answers, his voice gentle but firm. "The more you give in to it, the stronger it gets. It's not about fighting it, it's about *coexisting* with it. You have to learn to control your connection with Erebus, or it will start controlling you."

There's silence for a long moment, broken only by the sound of Flo's soft hiss, as if she, too, understands the gravity of the situation.

Finally, Layla speaks again. "And how the hell am I supposed to do that? I've never even heard of Erebus before today."

My nerves are wrecked as I watch Layla, her face a mask of resolve that hides the fear buried deep inside her. The room feels colder still, the tension thick enough to cut through, but there's no time for comfort. No time for reassurance.

I take a step closer to her, the weight of the situation pressing down on my shoulders. "We'll figure it out," I say, though even to my own ears, the words sound hollow, like a promise I can't be sure I can keep. My voice cracks under the strain. "We've faced worse than this."

I reach out, my hand brushing against hers, offering what little warmth I can. There's a flicker of something in her eyes—trust, maybe—but also a hesitation. She pulls back almost imperceptibly, but it's enough for me to feel the distance growing between us. Maybe I am just imagining it.

Why does this keep happening to me? She shoots down the bonding thread.

I sigh, *We will figure this out.*

A letter from Orcus:

Well, well, well. You've made it to the end, huh? Surprised? I bet you thought you had it all figured out, but life—*and death*—isn't that simple. You've been on a journey with Layla, Azrael, and the rest of the crew. It wasn't a smooth ride, was it? Full of chaos, power struggles, and a lot of things you probably didn't see coming.

But you made it through. Good for you.

You might think this is the end of the story, but I've got news for you: in our world, it *never* really ends. There's always more lurking in the shadows, waiting to stir up trouble. What happened here? It's just the beginning. Layla's not done facing challenges, and Azrael's definitely not finished with his throne-worthy struggles.

You'll find yourself wondering what's next, how much worse things can get, and if *they'll* ever get a break. But hey, don't hold your breath. The real game is just getting started.

So, as you close this book, remember one thing: Death may be inevitable, but the future? That's anyone's guess. Don't get *too* comfortable.

And don't forget about me. I'll be waiting—patiently, of course.

— *Orcus*

About the author

Peggy is a passionate author who thrives on crafting stories that delve into romance and thrillers, weaving tales that keep readers hooked until the very last page. Born on August 8, 1995, Peggy finds inspiration in life's twists and turns, as well as the works of literary icons like Penelope Douglas and Brynne Weaver. As a mother to four biological children and a loving mentor to many "adopted" kids, Peggy believes in the power of family and connection, themes that often resonate through her stories. When not writing, she enjoys exploring new creative avenues and diving into the thrill of a good book.

Pegngremlin.com